9 50

Praise for

"Cutter comb[...]
a fascinating l[...]

"[An] exciting look at Hungarian mythology."
— Harriet Klausner

And her debut novel, *Paper Mage*

"I don't believe that there are enough superlatives to describe this book. Splendid comes to mind, as does magnificent, wonderful, excellent, and superb. Leah's writing is at one and the same time both powerful and delicate. . . . This is an exceptional tale by an exceptional writer; this is writing at its finest. It doesn't get any better than this."
—Dennis L. McKiernan, author of
Once Upon a Summer Day

"Leah Cutter has written an enchanting novel, skillfully rooted in Chinese history and myth. . . . I wholeheartedly recommend *Paper Mage* to all lovers of fine fantasy. It's a strong debut, and I look forward to reading more of Cutter's work in the years ahead."
—Terri Windling, coeditor of
The Year's Best Fantasy and Horror

"Magic, myth, and adventure unfold in this intriguing tale by Leah Cutter, of a young mage who must prove herself in a time and place where traditional roles are the rule. *Paper Mage* is a terrific first novel."
—Kristen Britain, author of *Green Rider*

"Leah Cutter has created a magical world as solid and believable as our own, meticulously researched and drawn with loving attention to detail."
—Cecilia Dart-Thornton, author of
the *Bitterbynde* trilogy

continued . . .

THE JAGUAR
AND THE
WOLF

LEAH R. CUTTER

A ROC BOOK

ROC
Published by New American Library, a division of
Penguin Group (USA) Inc., 375 Hudson Street,
New York, New York 10014, USA
Penguin Group (Canada), 10 Alcorn Avenue, Toronto,
Ontario M4V 3B2, Canada (a division of Pearson Penguin Canada Inc.)
Penguin Books Ltd., 80 Strand, London WC2R 0RL, England
Penguin Ireland, 25 St. Stephen's Green, Dublin 2,
Ireland (a division of Penguin Books Ltd.)
Penguin Group (Australia), 250 Camberwell Road, Camberwell, Victoria 3124,
Australia (a division of Pearson Australia Group Pty. Ltd.)
Penguin Books India Pvt. Ltd., 11 Community Centre, Panchsheel Park,
New Delhi - 110 017, India
Penguin Group (NZ), cnr Airborne and Rosedale Roads, Albany,
Auckland 1310, New Zealand (a division of Pearson New Zealand Ltd.)
Penguin Books (South Africa) (Pty.) Ltd., 24 Sturdee Avenue,
Rosebank, Johannesburg 2196, South Africa

Penguin Books Ltd., Registered Offices:
80 Strand, London WC2R 0RL, England

First published by Roc, an imprint of New American Library,
a division of Penguin Group (USA) Inc.

First Printing, May 2005
10 9 8 7 6 5 4 3 2 1

For every loss, there is a gain—
this is for those who have lost something.

Character Names

Iselander (Viking) Humans

Character Name	Description	Pronunciation
Tyrthbrand	The leader of the Vikings.	TEERTH-brin
Einar	Second in command on the Golden Tree.	EYE-nar
Thorolf Mosturbeard	Large blond, full of life.	THOR-ohlf
Snorri	A blacksmith.	SNORE-ree
Illugi	Smartest of the Iselanders.	EE-loog-ee
Ketil	A priest of Tyr.	KEH-til
Vigfus	Son of Ottar, a great trader.	VEEG-foos

Itza (Mayan) Humans

Character Name	Description	Pronunciation
Lady Two Bird	Former high priestess of Ix Chebel in the City of Wells (Chichen Itza), special duties included making feathered cloaks.	
Lord Smoke Moon	The spiritual leader of the City of Wells, follower of Itzanam, brother-in-law to Lady Two Bird, married to Lady Star Storm.	
Evening Star	New high priestess of Ix Chebel on the goddess' island of Tzul.	
Eighteen Rabbit	Lady Two Bird's childhood friend, the former high priestess of Tzul.	
Lord Six Sky	Friend of Lady Two Bird, leader who goes out to meet the Iselanders, worships Ekchuah.	
Jeweled Skull	One of the Red Hand warrior twins.	

Character	Description	Pronunciation
Waterlily Jaguar	One of the Red Hand warrior twins.	
Cauac Sky	Spiritual leader of the Red Hands.	KAH-ouck
Lord Kan Boar	Military leader in the City of Wells.	KAHN

Iselander (Viking) Gods

Name	Description	Pronunciation
Tyr	God of justice, war, the sword, lightning.	TEER
Loki	The trickster, wife is Sigyn.	LOH-kee
Odin	Current head of the gods.	OH-din
Freyja	Goddess of fertility and the home.	FRA-yah
Idun	Goddess with the golden apples.	EE-doon
Liðami	Snake goddess from southern Sweden, associated with death and the afterlife.	LEE-thah-mee
Hel	Goddess of the underworld (Niflheim), half-black and half the color of flesh.	HEL
Aegir	God of the sea, also known as Hlér and Gymir, whose wife is Ran and whose nine giant daughters are waves.	A-geer
Ran	Goddess of the sea. She captures those who drown in her net and carries them to her hall where she takes care of them.	RAN
Skrymir	A giant who tricked Thor into thinking that his glove was a grand hall, his drinking cup filled with water from the ocean (and so couldn't be emptied), and so on.	SKRII-meer

Name	Description	Pronunciation
Thor	Fertility god. Wife is Sif.	THOR
Gullveig	Seeress who foretold of Ragnarok.	GOOL-veg

Itza (Mayan) Gods

Name	Description	Pronunciation
Ix Chebel	Goddess of madmen and suicides, weaver of rainbows, comforts women during childbirth.	Eesh Che-bell
Itzanam	Old Iguana god, founder of the Mayan culture.	EETZ-ah-nahm
Bacab (singular), Bacabnob (plural)	Four protective deities, giants who hold up the sky at the cardinal points: Cauac, Ix, Kan, and Muluk.	BAH-kahb, BAH- kahb-noob, KAH-ouck, IISH, KAHN, MOO-look
Ekchuah	Merchant god, always portrayed carrying a sack of merchandise on his back. The owl is his messenger.	EHK-choo-ah
Feathered Serpent	God of war and sacrifice, newer deity, brought by Puuc invaders.	
Hero Twins, Hun Ahaw (day aspect) and Yax Balam (night aspect)	Twin gods who tricked the lords of the underworld into accepting incense as sacrifice, not always taking blood, and who enabled the creation of mankind and the start of daylight.	HOON AH-how, YAHSH BAH-lahm

Prologue

"What are you doing?" Two Bird whispered as she came up behind her elder sister. It had taken what had seemed like a long time to find Star Storm in the dark, sweating halls of the temple. She hadn't asked any of the adults for help, though, particularly not any of the priests who towered over her; they scared her a bit with their black facial tattoos, wildly painted torsos, and staring eyes.

"Shh," Star Storm replied. She glanced behind her and made a "get down" motion with her hand before she faced forward again and started her awkward, bent-kneed, crablike crawl down the ill-lit hallway.

Two Bird grinned as she crouched down and mimicked her sister. She loved it when they played together and wondered what prize—imagined or real—they were stalking today.

"Where are we going?" Two Bird asked after they'd crawled for a while.

"This way," Star Storm answered. Of course. She never told Two Bird anything.

Mama had sent them to tell Papa about Grandma being sick. But Papa was busy with a ceremony and he'd left the girls on their own, waiting in a tiny side room until he was finished. They were supposed to stay there, but Star Storm had left when Two Bird wasn't looking, and after a bit, Two Bird had gone after her.

Two Bird shuddered as they passed by a carved and

painted image of Itzanam, the iguana god of mystery whom their father served. He was the terrible shape shifter, Sister Jaguar, Father Iguana, bringer of life. Though it was the Hero Twins who had tricked the Lords of the Underworld into being sacrificed, the old man god was trickier still. All the gods and goddesses changed aspects according to the season, the day, or the moon, but Itzanam's faces truly frightened her. She was glad that she'd been dedicated to Ix Chebel, who was his wife. Chebel was the goddess who comforted women in childbirth, wove the rainbows after a storm, and loved the madmen of the world.

"Back," came a sudden fierce whisper. Two Bird scrambled backwards, away from the hallway that crossed theirs. She paused, silent fear setting her heart pounding as voices approached, then departed.

"Where are we going?" Two Bird asked again after straining her ears for long moments, listening for the next danger.

"Just follow me," was the only response she got.

It wasn't fair. She was always the one following. She stayed as quiet as a shadow, following close behind her sister as she flitted across the hallway and through the blanketed door opposite them.

Candles filled the small room with a honeyed scent and a golden glow. Sacrificial pots with brightly painted faces leered at them from shelves lining the walls. Man-sized statues of the Hero Twins stood in one of the corners, their blowpipes raised, as if sighting their prey. Precise circles and lines crossed the floor—drawings of the flights of the stars, Two Bird realized.

"Over here," Star Storm said, beckoning Two Bird over to the side of the room.

For a moment, Two Bird hesitated. This was one of the preparation rooms that the priests used just before they conducted a sacrifice. They weren't supposed to be there—no one but the priests were supposed to come in here. She stayed well away from the grinning pots as she approached Star Storm, unsure of what magic they might hold, worried that they actually saw her and were going to tell Papa.

A small statue held Star Storm's attention. It stood on a low shelf, maybe half the size of a child. Its features were crudely carved, and whatever paint it had once worn had long ago flaked off.

"What is it?" Two Bird hated to ask, hated not knowing, but she had to rely on her sister sometimes.

"Papa said they'd found a buried statue."

Two Bird shuddered. Only old gods were buried, and there were strict laws about disturbing their slumber. Why? Why would their father dig it out, bring into the open, and maybe cast bad luck on himself and their family?

Star Storm spoke before Two Bird could open her mouth to ask. "He was curious about it."

Papa *was* always curious, always asking questions. He would match her question for question sometimes. He said it was part of his training to be a priest.

Two Bird looked more closely at the statue. How could this be an old god? It looked like a representation of Itzanam. It took the girl a while to figure out that it wasn't quite right.

"Why is Itzanam holding Feathered Serpent's war staff? And why is he standing on the Platform of Skulls? I thought only Feathered Serpent was allowed to stand there."

"Papa said that an old uncle told him that his grandfather had told *him* that before the Puuc came there was only one god. That two stand now where there had only been one."

Two Bird nodded sagely, as if she'd already known this, though she hadn't. But it made her wonder. The buildings on the south side of the city looked different than the buildings on the north side, and they were sometimes called the "Puuc houses," even the temples. There had been great battles when the invaders had first come, but then peace had been arranged between the Itza and the Puuc. Two Bird had learned about it with the history of the great kings of the City of Wells.

"Come on," Star Storm said, already turning toward the door.

"Where are we going?" Two Bird asked, not caring that she sounded as whiny as their little two-year-old cousin.

Star Storm just passed through the door and didn't answer.

Anger flared through Two Bird. It wasn't fair. Star Storm never actually included her in her plans and only let her join in when she stumbled across them. And then she *always* had to follow.

Sometime, *she* would be the one leading. Someday, her sister would have to follow *her*.

With that vow, Two Bird snuck after her sister, unwilling to be left behind.

Lady Two Bird stood at the top of the temple stairs, full of pride, watching the progression slowly rising toward her. Lady Star Storm, her eldest sister, had just married into one of the ruling families from the City of Wells. A feathered cloak stitched together by Lady Two Bird's hands adorned Lord Smoke Moon, the groom. Now, as part of the wedding ceremony, Lady Two Bird, in her position as Ix Chebel's high priestess, was about to greet them on behalf of her goddess, blessing their marriage and praying for many children.

Raising her hands in benediction, she chanted as her sister and new husband climbed, invoking the goddess in all her aspects, asking her to keep away the face that encouraged madness, to instead bring forth the crone who soothed those in childbirth. She repeated words of praise for the goddess, bringer of life,

easer of suffering, she who wove rainbows at the end
of a storm.

When the wedding party reached the top of the
stairs, Lady Two Bird welcomed them into the presence of the goddess, reminding them that they were
still her children and should seek her guidance
through all their days.

The other priestesses stepped forward, and all of
them now recounted their beginnings, telling how,
with a single word, the gods drained the dark waters
that surrounded them at the start of all things. Land
formed from the mists, the mountains rose, and the
jungles spread. The newly drained earth was empty of
life, though, and darkness enshrouded it.

The gods tried creating men but they kept failing.
They swept their useless experiments away in flood
and fire.

Finally, the gods were successful. They created men
who understood their place in the universe, that is, to
feed the gods as the gods fed them. By giving blood
and making sacrifices, men kept the gods healthy and
alive. In return, the gods brought the rains in the right
season, encouraged the crops to grow, gentled the
storms, and made them victorious in war. There was
always reciprocation, if not in this lifetime, then in the
next. The paths of gods and men were closely
intertwined.

As were now the lives of the two who stood before
them. They were tightly woven with the City of Wells,
with their people, with their gods and goddesses.

After the final blessing, when everyone had descended from the top of the temple and settled in for
the feast, Lady Two Bird stayed on the side for a
while, watching, listening, seeing what new gossip she
could learn. As the high priestess of Ix Chebel, she
knew so much already about the inner workings of
the City of Wells and its three leaders. Now, with her

sister marrying into the line of one of those leaders . . .
maybe she could become his right hand. Her goddess
would be worshipped by all, and her temple would
become rich.

Slowly Lady Two Bird made her way to her sister's
side. The women all clustered around Lady Star
Storm, congratulating her on her special day. One of
the old aunts came up, claiming that she should eat
more guavas to give her strength for her wedding
night. Everyone laughed; then another aunt spoke up
and said that she should eat more of the special cake
instead if she wanted her first night with her husband
to be special.

"Which should I take?" Lady Star Storm asked,
turning toward her sister.

"The cake," Lady Two Bird replied decisively. It
had been made from corn, which always died in the
fall, only to be reborn in the spring. It represented
fertility much more than the fruit did.

She laughed with the others when her sister reached
for the whole plate.

There was more ribald joking, but Lady Two Bird
no longer paid attention. It suddenly occurred to her
what had happened.

It had taken almost twenty long years—a full
k'atun—but now, finally, her sister was following her,
looking to her for knowledge and approval.

Life could only get better.

Chapter 1

Another wall of water crashed onto the deck of the *Golden Tree*. Tyrthbrand fought the steering oar, trying to guide the ship between the black furrows of water. Wind whipped rain through the leather pants and vest Tyrthbrand wore, leaving his teeth chattering and his legs chapped. Clouds blinded the moon, spreading murky blackness across the sea. Tyrthbrand clenched his jaw, still refusing to call upon his god, Tyr, either to curse or beseech him.

Einar, Tyrthbrand's second in command, crawled from the group of men huddled on the deck up to Tyrthbrand. Einar had to put his mouth directly to his leader's ear and shout as if on a battlefield to make himself heard over the monstrous wind.

"Nothing," was the only word Tyrthbrand made out. Nothing to see. Nothing lived beyond the boat but the land of whales and rain—no earth, no stars, no shoals. It would be impossible to divert around an obstacle even if they did see one.

Normally, Tyrthbrand would have run for land at the start of such bad weather. But the tempest had sprung up without warning and raged against them with cunning, as if aware of its quarry, forcing them away from the shore.

Another wave slapped the rear of the boat, rocking them sideways. The steering oar swung the other way. Tyrthbrand's shoulders popped, as if the guiding branch warred against him, trying to rip his arms out of their sockets. Not that it would matter if he let go of the oar. The storm had them in its maw, directing their course in its unnatural anger. The men at the sides, bailing water, helped their situation more than Tyrthbrand did. However, they expected to see their leader standing at the rear of the boat, struggling against the useless guiding beam. So he fought, silently, alone.

The rain stung Tyrthbrand's neck, like the tiny darts the Vinland natives—or the *skraelings* as Leif Eriksson had called them—had shot at them three days before. Two of his men had died after being pierced by the seemingly harmless bolts. Rage still boiled in Tyrthbrand's blood at the thought. No one wanted to believe that such a small wound had caused the death of a huge oak like Ankel the healer. Ketil the priest had reminded them of the insignificant mistletoe that had felled the god Baldur, while Vigfus had declared the darts poisonous.

Tyrthbrand had risked the righteous wrath of his men by refusing to turn back, insisting they could get their revenge later, on their return trip back up the coast to Leif's camp. They'd just rounded the southern tip of Vinland and he hadn't wanted to stop, not with the promise of empty vistas ahead. Reluctantly, the men had agreed.

With a soaked hand, Tyrthbrand wiped the water from his eyes and peered into the inky night. He couldn't see anything but rain and waves, couldn't hear anything but the challenging roar of the wind, couldn't taste anything but salt thrown up by Aegir's wrath. He tried to shield his eyes from the rain with his arm, bringing the brand around his right wrist, Tyr's mark, into contact with his forehead. A chill that had nothing to do with the rain descended on him.

Tyrthbrand had long refused to call on his god, Tyr the one-handed, the feeder of Fenris the wolf, though he'd battled the waves for hours. Tyrthbrand wanted to be a true gold giver to his men. How could he show his mettle if he always relied on his god to save him? He didn't regret calling on Tyr in the past, but was determined not to do it in the future, if possible. His god would favor him or not, without his asking. He wouldn't be seen as a begging woman, as some at Leif's camp had called him.

A scream pierced the snarling wind as the sea steed bucked. Tyrthbrand could just make out a huddled group of men at the side. The boat slapped down against the water, threatening to loosen the hold of the man clinging for life on the wrong side of the boat's edge.

"Come on, you whore!" Tyrthbrand brawled. "Turn!" He yanked at the oar, trying to drive the boat to the side. He would *not* lose another man.

The boat pitched again, slamming the steering oar into Tyrthbrand's belly. He wrapped both arms around the oar and pulled. Either his efforts or luck casue the boat to rock the right way, and the man scrambled back inside.

The wind shifted, and now the cruel rain struck Tyrthbrand in his face. He clenched his jaw and anger flooded his sight. This storm knew too much. It wasn't natural. He couldn't fight it and win—no man could.

He took a deep breath, then let it out with a sigh, sagging as he deflated. He had no other choice. Tyrthbrand stomped down on his pride, raised his right fist—his brand held high—and beseeched his god.

"With my mind full of fire
And the salty land full of mirth
Bear my words as witness.

Over sea depths I ride
Burning thirst for new land brims in me
Places for gods and men, I will find.

Strength I ask not for
Nor easy passage, nor gold nor rings
Only an eagle's perch to weather the storm.

I pledge my life for a small branch
And a bargain it shall be
In exchange for new sights and country bones."

Rolling thunder followed Tyrthbrand's declaration. The brand around his wrist flashed in the sudden lightning. Warmth coursed down Tyrthbrand's arm.

To the east, behind them, the clouds lessened. The wind still roared, but with a note of defeat woven through its snarling. Dawn approached.

The gods had favored them, but only after he'd begged again.

"The procession should not end underground," Lady Two Bird repeated. She felt the walls of the temple hall closing in on her, but she refused to show her anger or her fear. She forced herself to remain calm, kneeling, her head bowed, showing her deference to Evening Star, Ix Chebel's newest high priestess on the island of Tzul.

"We all return to Xibalba," Evening Star replied.

Lady Two Bird blanched at the mention of the underground hell. She refused to panic. "Eighteen Rabbit—"

"Died of old age, not in childbirth or war. She won't automatically ascend to the stars to be born again. She must begin her journey underground, among the roots of the World Tree. She has to outwit the Lords of the Underworld before she can climb the branches to the highest levels of Heaven and await rebirth."

Lady Two Bird allowed herself to look up at Evening Star, in part so that she wouldn't see the darkness that stretched to either side of her, where only a few torches brightened the damp stone and illuminated the brilliantly colored murals. Attendants sat on pillow-covered stone benches situated between the lights, doing handwork as part of their duty to the goddess, stitching feathers into cloaks and headpieces, using drop spindles to spin thread and yarn, repairing the clothes of the chosen of the goddess—the madmen the temple looked after. Lady Two Bird knew better than to glance all the way up, toward the sloped ceiling. She always feared that the center flat stone in the precariously balanced, squared-off arch would come crashing down on her.

Evening Star continued. "I don't understand your objections, Lady Two Bird. You claim Eighteen Rabbit was your dearest friend. Don't you want her to have incense, food, and jade, which she can use to bargain with the Lords of the Underworld? Why would you make her journey longer by forcing her to start aboveground? She still must visit the roots of the World Tree before she can travel to heaven."

"But she loved the light," Lady Two Bird said. She could not admit that it was *she* who needed the open air and sunshine.

"As do we all," Evening Star said. "I have made my decision though. The funeral procession will go as planned."

"My lady, I do not think—"

The high priestess cut Lady Two Bird off sharply. "You might be related to Smoke Moon, who shares the Jaguar Throne in the City of Wells and oversees the city soul, but here, *I* am the one in charge."

"I know, my lady," Lady Two Bird said, the bitterness welling up in her mouth. At one time, her brother-in-law had been the least of the pillars on which she rested her power. However, age had forced her out of her position as high priestess in the City of Wells, and her fingers could no longer weave the feather cloaks she'd once been famous for. Now her connection to royalty seemed to be the only piece of power she had left.

Evening Star smiled coldly. "Good. I may not be royalty, but you will treat me with the proper respect. The priestesses have designated *me* as the next high priestess, not you."

Lady Two Bird sat, barely blinking, surprised. Was Evening Star so insecure that she believed Lady Two Bird would try to take her place?

"Ix Chebel herself has welcomed me into her temple," Evening Star continued. "She wove a rainbow for me this morning. I have listened to your counsel. Now I must pray and prepare myself for the funeral. I suggest you do the same."

Evening Star rose from her bench without another word and left her audience hall.

The priestesses sitting on the benches on either side of the hall continued their quiet work. Lady Two Bird knew it was a sham. The fight she and Evening Star had just had would be the only topic of conversation among the temple initiates for days.

Lady Two Bird made herself stand and walk out of the hall without deigning to look at anyone. Instant relief filled her when she stepped out into the open. She unclenched her hands. New bruises from where she'd dug her nails into her palms throbbed. She stopped and took in the fresh air, feeling as though she could finally fill her belly. She knew there was nothing wrong with the halls, the temples, or even her room. But she couldn't convince herself that there was ever enough air for her to breathe in an enclosed space.

Giggling erupted from the hall behind her. Lady Two Bird's back stiffened. She held her head high and began walking across the courtyard. She could hear the mocking tones of the initiates now, discussing her strange request, speculating as to why she had made it.

No one knew of her increasing fear, which seemed to have grown in proportion to her loss of power, the slow grinding down of her days. First she'd noticed that she felt anxious underground, then she'd found herself panting as if there were no air in closed-in places, until now she could barely stand the thought of leaving the open air.

Lady Two Bird had been taught all her life to listen to her elders, told that she could benefit from their wisdom. Wisdom. Ha! Young Evening Star certainly hadn't taken Lady Two Bird's words as wisdom. The new priestess didn't know her predecessor as Lady Two Bird had.

Lady Two Bird still grieved for the loss of her friend, her "Little Rabbit." They'd met for the first time when they'd both been girls, chosen virgins for the goddess Ix Chebel, both on their first pilgrimage to Tzul, the island of the goddess. Lady Two Bird had come from the City of Wells, in the northern part of their land, the city located almost in the center of the peninsula. It had been her first time away from her home, and the journey to the coast had lasted almost two weeks. Little Rabbit had come from the far south and had traveled up the coast with her family. They hadn't understood each other's dialect initially, but that hadn't stood in the way of their friendship. As they'd both gained responsibilities, Lady Two Bird in the City of Wells, Eighteen Rabbit on the goddess' island of Tzul, they'd seen each other less often— usually only once a year, during the holy days at the start of the growing season when every woman who was able to made a pilgrimage to the island. However, every time they'd met, it had been as if they'd never parted.

Lady Two Bird hoped that their friendship would endure when they met again in their next life.

"My lady?" came a quiet voice.

It was Seven Waterlily, Lady Two Bird's oldest attendant. Lady Two Bird realized with a start that she'd stopped walking and was standing on the path with her eyes closed.

Not only had she lost all her ability to persuade, she was losing her mind. Ix Chebel would still welcome her if dementia took hold, though Lady Two Bird didn't relish the prospect.

It would make it easier for her to leave her goddess' service, though. She hated the honorary position she had, her opinion politely listened to but rarely heeded. It was time for her to retire completely, maybe even leave the City of Wells.

"We must hurry," Lady Two Bird said, taking another deep breath. She walked quickly across the courtyard, her attendant in her wake. Lady Two Bird needed to get to her room and compose herself before the funeral. Her room had a window that faced the sea, and she could pretend she was outside when she was there.

Lady Two Bird would not shame Little Rabbit by showing fear during her funeral. Her friend had loved all the rituals, incense, and prayers. She'd once said that during processions, the priestesses looked like clouds of flowers as they descended the temple stairs. It was only Lady Two Bird who could no longer face the gloomy underground.

The funeral started at daybreak. Evening Star wore the headdress Lady Two Bird had presented to her. Lady Two Bird suspected that Evening Star had wanted to refuse, had not wanted to accept anything from Lady Two Bird after their continued disagreements about Little Rabbit's funeral, but she couldn't— it was too beautiful. The feathers on the headdress flowed down Evening Star's back and almost brushed the floor. Lady Two Bird had used the last of the long-tailed jay feathers she had designing it. Her attendants had done the actual weaving. Lady Two Bird had had to trade both cacao beans as well as jade for the brilliant plumes, but they'd been worth it. She wished she could have used quetzal feathers as well, but only men were allowed to wear those.

Lady Two Bird made herself concentrate on the flowing feathers, on the way they bobbed slightly as Evening Star promenaded toward the altar. Lady Two Bird pretended that the feathers moved in a soft breeze, as if there were plenty of air in the cramped cavern. She forced herself to breathe normally and not in short gasps. A mountain's worth of stone crouched above her, pressing down on her. Flickering torches illuminated faces in the rocks: the Lords of the Underworld come to take her. The masks that the other priestesses wore turned grotesque, nightmarish. The edges of Lady Two Bird's vision grew dim.

Two more deep breaths. She would *not* panic. She would not disgrace her friend.

Evening Star called upon the goddess they all served, Ix Chebel, protector of women and madmen, she who brought floods and wove rainbows. Evening Star invoked the different aspects of the goddess, her nightly moon body, her daily sea face. Acolytes repeated her gestures, each emphasizing the characteristic of the goddess to which they had been assigned, including the five unnamed, unlucky days when the goddess' influence could be great enough to drive men insane.

Lady Two Bird shifted from one foot to the other, trying to relish the familiar words and gestures, fighting off her terror. She loved her goddess' rituals, the flow of the litany, the enacting of her phases, the naming of days. Only the tiniest of alterations had been allowed in her ceremonies since Lady Two Bird had been a novice. Local variations occasionally crept in; however, they were viewed with great suspicion and inevitably led to bad luck.

Lady Two Bird found she couldn't lose herself in

the service, or wallow in her grief. The walls squeezed all the breath from her. She dug her nails into her palms, hoping the pain would distract her from how dizzy she felt. She even tried counting the days—*Imix*, the waterlily, *Ik'*, the wind, *Ak'bal*, the night—but nothing worked. She'd had nothing to eat but a little *atole* that morning, a gruel made from honey and cornmeal, before dawn, but it threatened to erupt from her stomach.

After all the elements of Ix Chebel had been brought into their sacred space for protection and the four Bacabnob giants who held up the corners of the sky had been appeased, Evening Star stepped into the center to open the heart of the altar as a gateway to the other worlds. This was the most dangerous part of the ceremony, when a priestess could lose herself or be tricked. Lady Two Bird added her own prayers to the ones chanted by the other priestesses.

Shadows flickered around the room. Lady Two Bird refused to look at them, name them, or give them strength. Snake-thin ropes of blackness swam through the air and approached the acolytes acting as guardians. Or was it just smoke from the copal incense? Lady Two Bird held herself back from screaming like a three-year-old. She closed her eyes and prayed to the goddess, beseeching her protection as a woman, not as a lunatic.

The cave grew quiet. Lady Two Bird opened her eyes in time to see Evening Star close the heart and step back. Lady Two Bird forced herself to swallow, trying to reduce the raw taste of fright that filled her mouth. The worst was over. She could breathe again.

Her relief was short-lived however. Two initiates now came forward, one carrying a vertical turning stick, the other, a squat piece of wood with five burned patches in it, as well as tufts of dried moss, called maiden's hair. Lady Two Bird stiffened and her throat dried. Evening Star had decided to do the creation ceremony in addition to the burial. Lady Two Bird wondered bitterly if the high priestess had chosen this ritual to punish her.

The two young women knelt at the heart of the altar while Evening Star began the story of the beginnings of the world, of the Maker, the bearer, the begetter, and the modelers. Lady Two Bird flinched as the acolytes put out their torches, one by one. She wanted to crouch down, to touch the earth, to make sure she was still real, but she couldn't. She swayed, almost crying out. Sweat dampened her neck and back.

Evening Star chanted of the darkness that had filled the world, of the blackness that all the people lived in until the Hero Twins stole light from the Lords of the Underworld. With that, the rasping sound of the turning stick filled the background, behind the priestess' words. Lady Two Bird found herself panting. Her fervent prayers for light, for air, for escape, grew. Finally, the initiates answered her entreaties and succeeded in making the virgin fire for rebirth. As the attendants relit the torches, Lady Two Bird felt the tight bands around her chest loosening.

Finally, the ceremony ended. Lady Two Bird trembled as the procession passed her, awaiting her turn to leave. She swayed as she walked, touching the rocks of the tunnel as she reached the open air. They felt warm under her clammy hand, and for a moment, she thought they vibrated. She had a brief image of a huge stone mountain shuddering to wakefulness, stretching itself as if after a long slumber.

Lady Two Bird paused and spread her fingers out, sliding her palm across the sweating stone, but nothing else came to her. She shook her head, then dismissed it. She must have imagined it, or she was more tired than she'd thought. Rocks talked to people sometimes— everyone knew the stories—but she couldn't imagine any reason why the gods would want to communicate

with her. She had no power here, as she'd been reminded again and again. Also, the brief image she'd
seen had been nothing like the tales she'd heard: the
rocks hadn't chanted words of foretelling or echoed
with warnings of great danger.

The sunlight blinded Lady Two Bird as she left the
darkness behind. She blinked her eyes hard to clear
them of tears. She glanced fearfully back toward the
black opening that lurked on the side of the hill, waiting to suck up her soul. She vowed never to go back
to such a place, never to leave the surface of the
earth again.

Of course, that meant she'd have to leave the service of her Lady, as many of her ceremonies were
performed underground.

Lady Two Bird was so lost in thought she didn't see
the dip in the path, and she stumbled. She let Seven
Waterlily lead her to a stone bench to one side, letting
the rest of the funeral procession pass. Lady Two Bird
stared at them unseeing. She knew what she had to
do. The way seemed clear. She didn't know what she
could do instead of serve Ix Chebel, but she would do
anything before facing the black unlit places of the
Underworld—at least until her death.

There were other ceremonies that the priestesses
had to perform that day: scattering leaves and petals
along the shore for Little Rabbit to find her way; sanc-
tifying the paint that Evening Star would use to color
the temple to show the start of her days as high priestess; then blessing the solid food that everyone would
share that evening for dinner, breaking the liquid fast
most of the initiates on the island had begun when
their head priestess had died. Lady Two Bird had been
looking forward to them, as they would all be outside.
Now she just needed to rest, and to spend some time
firming her resolve to leave her lady.

With a hurried excuse to the other priestesses and
a sharp command to Seven Waterlily to stay where

she was, Lady Two Bird made her way to the Garden
of Statues. As she walked, it occurred to her that her
eldest sister's children were of an age to be inducted
into the mysteries of the goddess and learn the riddles
of the *Chilam Balam*. It wouldn't be following in Lady
Star Storm's footsteps again—Lady Two Bird would
be leading, teaching her sister's children, giving them
knowledge that Lady Star Storm didn't have. Also, as
a tutor, she could always foist the ceremonies that had
to be held underground off on another, probably one
of the younger priestesses, even if it did mean giving
up more of what little power she still held.

Bitterness filled her mouth, and her gut burned
with shame.

Finally she reached the Garden of Statues. The
bright colors and soft, sweet scents made her pause
and lightened her dark outlook. Walls hemmed in the
small plot of land on all sides. The priestesses would
have reclaimed the ground, used it for housing or
growing food, if they hadn't found old gods buried
there. Lady Two Bird smiled a bit as she recalled Little Rabbit's story of the frightened workers digging up
a snake figure, and the bad luck that had followed. It
had happened before either of them had been born,
but the tale had lost none of its potency.

The goddess Ix Chebel now ruled here. Pink aza-
leas, orange lilies, brilliant white orchids, and fragrant
purple spikes bloomed in profusion. Birds—the living
colors of the world—sang prophecies that only the
trained could understand. A small *sak beh*, made of
the same white stones of the roads that connected the
cities, wound through the garden, visiting blessed
spots, as well as sacred ceiba and nance trees, before
making its way to the main figure in the garden, the
carved statue of Ix Chebel.

Lady Two Bird approached the goddess slowly. This
was her favorite representation of her lady, even
though it showed her as a youth, her face both

haughty and kind, with a sly smile lurking in the edges of her eyes. The figure towered over its supplicants, one foot in front of the other, in the walking aspect of the goddess, representing the calm she brought after storms. She also held a drop spindle in one hand and a colorful flowing cloth in the other, representing the rainbows she wove. The dazzling paint covering the statue's gown outshone the flowers growing around it.

Wishing stones littered the feet of the statue. When someone wanted something, she took a small rock, held it in both palms, wished and prayed, then placed it at the foot of the goddess. Ix Chebel had been known to grant wishes, as well as talk through stones.

Lady Two Bird remembered the way the rocks had jittered under her fingers as she'd left the dark cave. She assured herself that it had been nothing, or maybe just a remnant of the hurricane that had passed through the evening before. The storm hadn't done much damage to the island or its structures, though the winds had howled like angry beasts.

A glittering rock resting on the path caught Lady Two Bird's eye and she picked it up. The sun had warmed it. If she were foolish enough to make a wish, what would she wish for?

Change.

The word came unbidden to her thoughts. The goddess moved from one aspect to another, but always in a prescribed circuit, like one wall ran into its adjoining one. Lady Two Bird saw the march of her days to her death, one not the same as the next, but the procession never varied. The vision suffocated her, as if she'd descended below the earth again.

All those days, and to what end? If she could change her past, she would. She'd never known a man, and now, would never have children. She'd had hopes as a young priestess, dreams of leading her people, but her time had passed. Her name would never be written on the temple stairs. Nothing would remain of her after her death. She'd be pressed into the earth, no light to guide her out of the blackness. Despair swallowed her, encased her in its gullet. She saw no way out.

A raucous screeching brought her back to the sunny day. Out of the corner of her eye, she caught a glimpse of red. A brilliant macaw had come into the garden and now sat in the ceiba tree next to Ix Chebel, scolding her.

The macaw was a trickster—before the Hero Twins brought the light into the world, Seven Macaw had puffed himself up and pretended to be the sun. Its feathers were beautiful, though. When she turned to look at it, it nodded to her, then flew to a flowering okota, just a few steps along the path. It turned back to her and bobbed, as if asking her to follow.

Was it trying to trick her? As she had been tricked out of her entire life? Promised a position of power that had faded before her eyes?

Lady Two Bird laughed quietly. Even she could hear the resentment threaded through the sound. She hadn't been tricked, not exactly. Being the high priestess for Ix Chebel had been rewarding in its own way.

But nothing remained now. And there was nothing she could do about it.

Angrily, she placed the wishing stone among the others at the foot of the goddess.

Change. Something had to change, or she would end her days alone and in sorrow. Turning her back on her lady, she walked up the path toward the brilliant bird. The macaw jumped off the branch it rested on and landed again, like a child leaping for joy, before it flew to the next bush. Then, as Lady Two Bird approached the colorful messenger, it took off like a stone flung by a warrior's leather strap, flying over the wall, and gone in an instant.

Just as her life had disappeared before her eyes.

"Land!"
Tyrthbrand forced himself out of the semitrance into

which the slightly rocking boat, the far horizon, the heat, and the lack of sleep had lulled him.

Vigfus, the son of Ottar the merchant, called again. "Land! Portside!"

The steering oar turned sluggishly. Clouds still lay collected at the far edge of the water, even after the storm had blown over. Tyrthbrand imagined them like great cats, biding their time, waiting until their master's back was turned so that they could pounce again, this time to worry their prey to death.

The *Golden Tree* needed repairs before it could survive another such storm. Some of the wood on the side of the boat had sprung loose and the mast listed. Tyrthbrand didn't know for certain, but he feared the keel might have cracked while bounding over some of the larger waves.

Wind blew from behind them, puffing out the sail like a proud bird's chest. Long tracks of dead foam spread like ribbons across the top of the water. The ship slid through layers of colored water, from blue-black to green to sky colored. Seagulls and other birds broke through the constant whooshing sound of the wind. When the storm had disappeared, stifling air had encased them again. As they'd sailed south, they'd come into summer weather, sticky and oppressive. The wind they sailed with blew hot and brought only partial relief. The men braided their hair and beards tightly in an effort to keep cool.

Tyrthbrand stood at the rear of the boat as he had during the storm, gripping the steering oar, fighting despair. He'd called on Tyr during the storm and his god had saved them. Tyrthbrand should be content, but he wasn't. *He* hadn't saved his men. Tyr had. What would happen when Tyr no longer favored him? Would Tyrthbrand have the strength to save himself? He wanted to vow never to call on Tyr again, but feared the consequences of such an oath. His god gave him strength, but he wanted to be known for his own courage as well.

A great red hill began to make its shape known to those on the boat.

"Look at the color!" Snorri the smith exclaimed as he walked up the deck to where Tyrthbrand stood. "Do you think it's made of ore?"

Illugi followed the short dark smith like a blond mountain. "I doubt it. The color isn't orange enough."

"Maybe that's because it's out in the air, and some of the deposits have washed away," Snorri said.

Illugi kept staring at the rock. "There's something wrong with that hill."

"What do you mean?" Tyrthbrand asked. Though the merchant sailor was wider than an oak and always wore a huge, easy grin, Tyrthbrand knew the mind that worked behind that mien was sharper than icy winds in midwinter.

"The land—and I think it's an island—lays on the horizon like the giant Skrymir's glove. The mountain doesn't stick up like a thumb though. See the edges? They're too straight."

"That could just be because of the angle we're approaching from," Snorri countered.

Illugi shrugged. "Possibly."

Tyrthbrand squinted, trying to get a better look at their destination. It lay southwest across the glittering whale road. However, unnatural or not, there was no question about whether or not they would stop. They had to make landfall. Tyrthbrand needed to check his boat and make repairs, and they had to replenish their drinking water.

Ah—new land. What riches lay there? The dark strips around the mountain might be trees, possibly with exotic properties that would fetch whole herds of cows. Or maybe vines grew there, like they had near Leif Eriksson's property up north, so they could get rich selling wine back in Iseland, as he had.

Thinking about Leif and what had happened at his camp made Tyrthbrand frown. A bullying braggart named Hrolf had teased and insulted Tyrthbrand without mercy from the first day he'd set foot in Vinland. Hrolf had been Odin's man, dedicated to the god since birth. But he'd also found this new Christ, and wore a cross above Odin's ring. Tyrthbrand had started life as a farmer's son, and had worked hard to escape his situation—his *wyrd*—to be a warrior and a merchant instead. Hrolf wouldn't let it pass, though, and was always throwing digs at Tyrthbrand about his fighting abilities.

Eventually, he'd challenged Tyrthbrand to a *glima*. The long days of work, with no women for diversion, made all the men in camp eager for any kind of entertainment, especially a wrestling match. The area where the fight was to be held had been marked out and many bets had been made. However, Hrolf had made an unlucky fall, and Tyrthbrand had accidentally killed him.

Only Tyrthbrand's oath to Leif of finding a new land, with new resources for the Iselanders to exploit, had saved him from being banished from Iseland or dancing in Odin's playground with a rope stretching his neck.

To himself, Tyrthbrand had vowed to find an unpopulated area that he and his men could possess without interference, a place with no natives, no *skraeling* to constantly defend against. Land and farms he could deed to his brothers' children, if not his own, after he went back to Iseland and found a wife.

Maybe this island was such a place.

And if not here, then somewhere else. Vinland was so huge, the coast stretching longer than Odin's beard.

A wave smacked the boat, the spray flying into Tyrthbrand's eyes. It stung as he wiped it away. He realized where the troll wives' winds had taken him. Tyr didn't appreciate his followers referring to Odin. Tyrthbrand tried to change his metaphor to compare the shore to an attribute of Tyr, instead of Odin. He thought for a moment, then it occurred to him that the coast ran as long as Tyr's honor was solid.

Tyrthbrand shook his head. He was being ridiculous. Tyr didn't listen to his thoughts. He'd just been on his feet too long, on watch and on edge. His god wasn't a jealous god—or at least not insanely jealous—not like that new one the followers of Christ proclaimed as *konungur*.

They drew inevitably closer to the island. The reddish cast of the mountain turned pinker as they approached. Tyrthbrand smelled land on the wind, baked and warm. He dreaded leaving the sea. While they were on the water, they had some relief from the heat. Away from any breeze, the land would be like the inside of a forge.

The unusually flat top of the mountain started to show itself. Had the writhing of the Midgard Serpent, the snake who circled the world with its tail in its mouth, thrown the hill up in such a condition? Or had men leveled it off? Tyrthbrand had never seen a hill so symmetrical.

A gusting wind shoved them forward. They drew closer, traveling faster now.

"That's not a mountain," someone said, startling Tyrthbrand from his musings. He looked up. Illugi stood at the prow of the ship, calling back his warnings.

"That was made by man." A hush fell over the crew. "There are no other hills nearby. Its sides are too even to be natural. It must be man-made." Tyrthbrand recalled travelers' tales he'd heard of a land in the desert with mounds this high.

"Or it was raised by giants," Ketil the priest said. He looked back at Tyrthbrand, challenge and defiance blazing in his face.

There was no reply that Tyrthbrand could give. Ketil, being a priest as well as a learned man, was the most religious of the group. He also resented Tyrthbrand's connection to their shared god. As Tyr's priest,

Ketil felt that the men should have been following him, and that he should have been put in charge of their expedition set by Leif. However, Tyr had never answered his call, at least not as the exaggerated stories about Tyrthbrand and his first battle now claimed. Tyrthbrand would gladly give the burden to Ketil, but none of the others would follow the swarthy, diminutive man.

Tyrthbrand avoided confronting the priest when he could. Ketil's sword, Wolf Feeder, had separated more than one head from its body. Ketil angered quickly and fought with ferocity. Wolf Feeder had been passed down at least two generations. Its strength lay in the twists of iron and steel that the original forger had used in perfect combination. It was a thing of deadly beauty.

The long shore of the island was clear now. A stretch of sand called to them. Dark trees ran to the water on either side of it. Shoals protected the beach from the direct onslaught of the waves. Tyrthbrand thought he saw a path through the rocks.

"Boats!" came the warning call.

Tyrthbrand saw them now—stick figures shoving small crafts into the water, paddling like mad to reach his boat.

"Prepare to come about," Tyrthbrand called. Shouts and exclamations rose from his crew. The *Golden Tree* needed to stay in the open sea so she could maneuver. They'd never be able to ship the oars if they allowed themselves to be hemmed in.

"Hold!" shouted Thorolf Mosturbeard.

While everyone's attention had been focused forward, a swarm of the little boats had approached from the side and from behind. They were surrounded. If the *Golden Tree* turned heedlessly, she would ram the smaller boats.

Tyrthbrand hesitated. He'd run over the natives if he had to. But only if he had to.

Einar ran up to Tyrthbrand. "Keep us steady," Tyrthbrand said to his second in command as he surrendered control of the steering oar. "Half-mast!" Tyrthbrand called out to his crew. Men rushed to the halyard. By lowering the sail halfway, they would slow their speed, but the wind would still be able to aid them.

"Oars!" he shouted. Men scurried to follow his orders.

Tyrthbrand rushed to the side of the *Golden Tree* to get a better look at their opponents. The little boats reminded him of the ones the damn priests from Eire used—coracles—just hollowed-out trees, not properly timbered ships. The natives knew how to use them, though, as they dashed across the water.

One of the oars shot out of the side of the *Golden Tree* seeking the water. The closest coracle drove straight for it, one of the men in the boat reaching up to grab the oak stick.

"Pull the oars back!" Tyrthbrand called. There were too many opponents. He had a vision of the natives scrambling up the oars, using them as bridges to board his ship.

"Orm, Brand," Tyrthbrand yelled. The brothers came running, bows already strung. "Keep them back. Don't kill them unless you have to. We don't want to fight. We need to convince them to trade. We must get water."

The brothers nodded as one, then each raced to a side of the boat. They would keep the *Golden Tree* safe, for a while. After a few warning shots, the little boats pulled back, not out of arrow range, but no longer swarming within easy reach of the merchant vessel either.

The *Golden Tree* slowed. Tyrthbrand took a long look at the natives themselves.

They didn't appear to be human.

Their skulls were misshapen, elongated, and flattened, giving them a snakelike appearance. They had high, prominent cheekbones, aquiline noses, and black hair pulled back and tied into neat queues. Their skin was copper colored, as if they'd been dipped in Thor's ale cauldron. Their ears hung long and low, close to their shoulders.

However, these were no *skraeling*. Their chins were clean-shaven. They only wore breastplates. Their arms were bare. Crimson, azure, and black paint swirled over their exposed skin.

Tyrthbrand peered carefully at their weapons. He didn't see anything that looked like a bow. He recognized spears, and many held leather thongs, loaded with rocks.

How to communicate with them? To show them his peaceful intentions?

Vigfus called Tyrthbrand to the opposite side of the boat. In the water sat the largest of the native coracles. One of the natives stood in the center of it. He wore an elaborate headdress, with green and black beads hanging from it and feathers streaming down his back. Complicated purple designs swirled across his ribs and raced up and down his arms. Large round, verdant pieces of stone were plugged through his earlobes. A bloodred and white chest plate protected him. He held a spear in one hand, a leather strap and rocks in the other.

He wasn't attacking the boat. He seemed to be waiting for something.

Tyrthbrand got an idea. He held out his hand to Vigfus, who handed his leader his spear.

Tyrthbrand hefted it. He didn't want to throw it into the water. That would put him in debt to Vigfus. Plus, the other *skraelings* they'd met had no iron. He didn't see iron tips on the natives' spears, though at this distance he couldn't be certain; losing a spear when they had no ready replacements could be disastrous later on. He already regretted the loss of the brothers' arrows.

He had no choice. He threw the spear straight down. It sank deeply into the water and quickly disappeared. Then he held his hands up, open and empty. He'd done this before when trading with foreigners. Show your weapons, then put them down and approach with empty hands held out to show that you meant no harm, though you could protect yourself.

The native with the headdress handed his spear to one of the other men in his boat, then put a rock into his leather strap and swung it over his head.

Had Tyrthbrand misjudged? Did these natives not understand?

The rock flew short of the boat.

The native yelled and waved the unloaded leather strip over his head three times. Then he handed it to the other man in the boat, straightened back up, and held his hands out, open and empty.

Tyrthbrand had never seen a *skraeling* who had understood this pantomime. It implied that these natives regularly traded with people far from their home, who didn't speak the same language. It also suggested the possibility of wealth for Tyrthbrand and his men, without constantly having to defend against attack.

Maybe they had found their new land.

The man standing in the boat gestured for the *Golden Tree* to follow them, then sat down and shouted commands. His companions turned his coracle around. The other natives followed suit.

Tyrthbrand wondered at the man's actions. Was it bravery that enabled him to turn his back? The men on the *Golden Tree* had a clear shot at him. Was it confidence? Or was it the sacred nature of trade?

With a few shouted orders, the men of the merchant ship lowered the sail all the way and sprang to the oars. Tyrthbrand let Einar remain at the steering beam.

Two ridges of shoals lay before the island. Little coracles sat on either side of the holes between the reefs, their bows pointing the way for the larger boat. Orm, Brand, and Illugi found landmarks, shouting out descriptions for Einar and Tyrthbrand, so the *Golden Tree* could leave without the natives' assistance if necessary.

Once through the protective rock barrier, Tyrthbrand called Illugi to his side.

"Use your hawk eyes to tell me as soon as possible when we can drop anchor," he told the blond man. Tyrthbrand didn't want to take the *Golden Tree* too close to the shore, where it would be difficult for them to turn and flee if necessary.

The blue-green water grew shallow quickly. The wind stayed constant, but heated up. Yellow, emerald, ruby, and sapphire fish danced under the waves. The shadow of the ship cut across the white sands like an ice giant's arrow. Soon, Illugi called out for them to drop the stopping stone.

Tyrthbrand counted the crew. He selected seven men—one-third of those who remained—to wade with him to the land. The natives seemed to ignore the boat now. All of the coracles had been pulled up onto the shore. They'd lured the Iselanders into their harbor and seemed content with that. Tyrthbrand didn't trust them. He set the rest of his crew to turn the boat around as soon as he and the men got out, so it would face the shoals and they could leave in a hurry, if necessary. The men also agreed to constant watches. Tyrthbrand didn't want the natives to swarm up, surprise his men, and take his ship. He didn't know if his preparations were necessary. He hoped they weren't, but he wasn't going to take any chances, no matter what the fates decried.

Surprisingly warm water came up past Tyrthbrand's waist as he slipped over the side. He tasted it. It held more salt than the northern waters did. As soon as the other men had breached the water, he led them to the shore. Their heavy wool pants and leather boots weighed them down. However, the men walked as if they wore as little as the natives did. Their pride allowed nothing less.

When the men reached the shore, the natives lost none of their reticence. As Tyrthbrand had suspected, he and his men, even Ketil the priest, towered over these people.

The one with the elaborate headdress slowly approached the group. Up close, the ugliness of the natives amazed Tyrthbrand again. Their long sloped foreheads reminded him of his cousin's slow child, the one who should have been left on the mountain, but instead had been taken care of, even though he'd never learned to speak properly. The native before him was slightly cross-eyed, adding to the general impression of stupidity. A picture of a black sword puckered up by his eye and coasted down his cheek. Tyrthbrand wasn't certain if it had been painted on the native's skin or if it was a tattoo. His people never marked the skin of their faces with designs, only their arms and sometimes, their torsos.

Then the native smiled. Tyrthbrand forced himself to stay still and not jump back. Sharp pointed teeth—like a dog's—filled the man's mouth. Bits of green and red were embedded in his teeth. Tyrthbrand didn't always believe Ketil's tales of giants and Hel-inspired creatures, but he wondered briefly if the being standing in front of him was human.

A flowing string of sounds floated from the native, followed with gestures. Tyrthbrand assumed that he was being welcomed. He smiled back, carefully showing his very human, unadorned teeth. Now came the hard work of learning to understand each other. Regardless if this being was a man or not, they could still communicate.

And trade.

After the macaw disappeared over the walls of the garden, shouts flew on the wind to Lady Two Bird's ears. She paused, wondering if she should go see what had happened. However, she wasn't in charge of or responsible for this place, as Evening Star had made abundantly clear. Anger filled her. The temple stones did not speak for her.

Stones. With a start, Lady Two Bird made her way back to the statue of the goddess. The wishing rock she'd placed there nestled comfortably between Ix Chebel's feet.

What had she been thinking? The goddess granted wishes, but in her own time and place. By asking for something so large, so unfocused, who knew what Ix Chebel might give her? Why couldn't she have asked for something more solid, more useful, like a good growing season, or more healthy children for her sister? Lady Two Bird reached out to remove her wish.

The stone vibrated when she touched it.

The priestess snatched her hand away instantly, then, slowly put it back, lightly resting her fingers on the rock.

The pebble didn't start with the formal words of prophecy, "It is the *k'atun* of . . ." It didn't give her words at all, like she'd heard in tales. An image rose in her mind of sharp, strange-looking rocks. Rocks born in pain and fire, shaped with hammers into long knives. Knives that cut through jungle and men's flesh with the same ease, knives that battled dust storms and land. A land that was both altered and the same, different, but recognizable, like a meandering stream as it travels down the mountainside.

When the sensations ended, Lady Two Bird brought her hand to her lips without picking up the stone. The priestess didn't know why her goddess had chosen her, now, during her twilight years. She didn't doubt, though, that the pebble had talked to her. It was not the right time for her to leave her lady. She still had things she must do. Maybe her life could have meaning.

The message hadn't been clear—it came through the smoke of god talk—however, Lady Two Bird thought she understood.

Change was coming, in the guise of something new. Change so great it would alter the face of the land. Change that was the will of the gods.

Lady Two Bird put aside her plans of quitting her lady's service. This was more important than her petty fears. If her goddess asked it of her, she would go under the ground again, though the thought of it turned her spine to granite and made her as immobile as the statue in front of her.

The shouts grew louder. She heard people running beyond the garden's walls. She hurried to the archway leading back to the complex. Seven Waterlily came rushing up to her.

"There's a ship out on the water, a foreigner's ship. It's coming from the red lands to the east. Lord Six Sky went to meet it."

"Foreigners? Who are they? What do they want?"

"No one knows. No one's seen anything like it before. It's a huge ship, as big as the traveling barges that come from the black lands to the west. It has a great colored tapestry in the center of it, and many men."

Change. As inevitable as the seasons, the aspects of the gods, the phases of the moon. She'd asked for it, her anger guiding her instead of her intellect. Now, with trepidation, she went to see what the goddess had blessed her with.

"Are they human?" Seven Waterlily whispered, staring hard at the strange foreigners who now stood dripping on the beach.

Lady Two Bird wrinkled her nose. "They smell like animals. Animals who have been at sea for many weeks and need to use the baths."

"Ugly white-handed barbarians," Evening Star said. She turned to her right and spat, barely missing Seven Waterlily's foot.

A pang of worry assailed Lady Two Bird. The island of Tzul lay on the major water trade route around the peninsula. Boats from as far away as Janni stopped there on their way down the coast with their hulls full of beautiful figurines. What would happen if the high priestess didn't welcome foreigners, and so fewer tradesmen prayed to Ix Chebel, asking for her to smooth the storms? In the City of Wells, Lady Two Bird had had to navigate through tricky political webs, negotiating and balancing between the three kings, keeping the general people's favor of her goddess high. Without the expensive offerings that foreign tradesmen left at Her temples, the priestess' power, as well as Ix Chebel's, would diminish.

Lady Two Bird peered at Lord Six Sky, who was struggling to communicate with these very strange beings. She wondered if they were even human. Might they just be cleverly trained animals? They certainly looked like beasts, with all the hair they wore on their faces, even if they did wear it forked, beaded, and braided.

How could they stand to wear such heavy leather clothing in the heat? She shook her head at their chest plates and strange shoes. Their upper garments were cut from a light-colored cloth, and covered their arms to their wrists. The sun had reddened their necks and any other skin not protected.

She glanced at their belts, the strange bags tied to their waists, the obvious weapons. They would have many interesting things to trade. She hoped that Evening Star would overcome her prejudice and see that. Unique items from these creatures would be sure to please the goddess and give the temple much more prestige.

The two groups seemed to be introducing each other. These new beings had an interesting custom of greeting, of clasping forearms, instead of holding their hands up and bowing. She gasped when she saw the lead foreigner's hand wrap around Lord Six Sky's arm. The foreigners were as big as giants. Lord Six Sky almost looked like a child standing next to them.

After Lord Six Sky had introduced himself to all the foreigners, he looked behind him, then beckoned for Lady Two Bird and Evening Star to come forward.

Lady Two Bird stayed one step behind Evening Star. She knew that Lord Six Sky should introduce her first—she *was* related to royalty—but she wanted to flatter Evening Star, to make up for their earlier fight.

The foreigners didn't try to greet the women the same way they'd greeted the men. They bowed their heads with their hands behind their backs, like prisoners.

They used short names—nicknames, Lady Two Bird assumed. Everyone knew the power of your true name, it seemed, even these barbarians. They smelled even worse closer up.

She noticed that the gaze of the leader—Tyrthbrand, as he called himself—lingered on the black quetzal tattooed on her face. She turned her head so that he might have a better look. The delicate bird's head floated on her elongated forehead, its neck stretched down past her temple, its round body filled her cheek, and its long tail feathers lined her jaw. She knew from smoky reflections in pyrite mirrors that she'd gazed into how skillfully the bird had been rendered.

Normally, only men were allowed to wear quetzal feathers. She'd been granted permission to have the bird tattooed on her face when priests from Cobá captured and killed Smoke Moon's older brothers, and so her brother-in-law had been raised to the level of high priest. She'd thought it appropriate at the time, as the feathered cloaks she'd made for his ascension had received the most praise.

. Now it represented the one thing she would never lose: her royalty.

She glanced over all the foreigners. Not one of them had their faces tattooed. Nor did they wear any paint. It made them appear more like beasts.

Lord Six Sky and the foreigners stared at each other for a moment after the introductions were made. Each seemed to be waiting for the other's lead. The sound of quiet waves slapping the shore was audible.

Lady Two Bird didn't know what prompted her. Maybe it was the memory of the stone vibrating under her fingers, the feeling of water reaching its destination. Maybe it was because she was old and didn't care anymore. Maybe it was because this was her one chance to have her name written on the temple stairs. Or maybe she was just tired of standing, impatient.

She took a step forward. All eyes flew to her, like darts from a blowpipe. She took the woven fan that Seven Waterlily had been using to shade her from the fierce sunshine and scratched a line in the sand with the end of it.

"*Huntul*," she said. One. She drew a second line. "*Katul*." She drew five lines, naming each, then went back and started at one again. Animals couldn't count. But perhaps these strange creatures were more human than beast.

The big foreigner nodded. "*Einn*," he said. He named every line, then repeated the words using his fingers, to show that he was counting and that they exchanged numbers.

Lady Two Bird smiled at him to show that he was correct, that they understood each other. He smiled back, but his expression looked strained. Lady Two Bird couldn't understand why. Even Evening Star had commented on how beautiful the jade embedded in her teeth looked.

They were barbarians. But hopefully, they could be of value, and she could use them to restore her diminished power.

Chapter 2

A sword of lightning streaked through the darkened hall, sizzling and crackling, expanding as it discharged without hitting anything. No thunder pressed in after the blue illumination died. "By Yggdrisil's roots, I should have let that human drown!" the god Tyr swore. Dancing electric flames swirled around his arms and crisscrossed his chest as he paced. Wall tapestries depicting battles and victories fluttered in his wake, disturbed by the strong current of air. The stone floor didn't mark his passing; the coiling crimson and gold inlaid serpents continued their twisting unabated, endlessly looping, sounding like softly sifting snow.

The electric tide gathered strength again. Tyr's fine blond hair lifted from his head, as if he faced a breeze from the sea. The little lights that covered the god's body multiplied and wove together like a coat of blazing rings. They danced on the stump that marked the end of his right arm, then extended to a ghostly outline of his missing hand. "Blast it!" Tyr roared. Lightning surged from him again, arching under the tall ceiling timbers and dissipating, again without finding a target. The fire in the center of the hall reached up to lick at the passing bolt.

Light laughter filled the room as the hissing died down. Tyr whirled and bore down on the intruder. "Damn you, Loki—what are you doing here?" Tyr asked.

"Idun told me you were doing a poor imitation of

Thor the Thunderer. Thought I'd come and see the show myself." The slight man lazed in Tyr's high seat, his legs swinging over one of the arms of the chair. A haze seemed to flow from the figure and settle on the fire, leaching its warm ruddy glow and transmuting it into something darker, more primal, and eager. Suddenly, shadows grew, hiding the face of the man on the chair. Cold wind whisked through the hall, tugging at the tapestries.

"Stop your cursed tricks, Loki," Tyr said. He put his left hand out, then pulled it back toward himself, sucking the darkness and the wind into it. As he completed the motion, the blue streaks outlining his body faded. Sunlight crept back into the hall.

"What's wrong, O straightforward one?" Loki asked, his head lolling to one side as he looked up at the other god. "Air not suit you here?"

Tyr bristled. He opened his mouth to tell the half god that it was none of his damn business, but found himself telling the truth instead, as usual. "I don't know what disturbs me. Tyrthbrand used a kenning with Odin's name, compared that damned coast to him instead of me. That never used to distress me. My followers should be able to use whatever language they want. But I find that it does."

Loki nodded and got out of Tyr's high seat without being asked. He invited Tyr to sit in it, using a courtly gesture, with both his hands and his head bowed.

Flustered, Tyr sat. He didn't feel like sitting. He wanted to continue striding through his hall, dark and terrible, the coppery taste of power in his mouth. He wondered if dampening the fire and getting him to sit in the high seat were tricks of Loki's, designed to encourage Tyr to calm down.

"So what are you going to do, O mighty *dæma*?" Loki asked.

Tyr looked at the other man sharply. Was Loki mocking Tyr in his own hall? The scars crossing Loki's face made it difficult to discern his intentions, though a smile tugged at the edges of his mouth, as always.

"I don't know what I'm going to do. I am—this place—confuses me. I am more myself, more powerful, more judging. Yet I used not to be so single-minded. I am not a mercurial god. But I seem to recall myself as less focused, more changeable, more balanced, less extreme."

Loki said nothing, just nodded and smiled, so Tyr continued. "Have you seen those damn vines out there? Twining through the trees in this land we've joined?"

"Kind of hard to miss."

Tyr glared at Loki, but continued. "I feel like that now, like I'm more *connected* to the things around me, to my human followers, as well as to this land. It's as if all my reserve were melting. And the wind— it's so warm."

Loki smirked, raising one eyebrow. "Location is everything."

Tyr didn't understand. Then again, he usually didn't comprehend half of what Loki said. Or what he did. For example, Tyr didn't know why, in this sliver of Ásgard, Loki manifested with scars spoiling his face: the marks came from poison that dripped from the snake that the other gods had bound above Loki's head after Baldur's death. Loki didn't have to look like a child's nightmare all the time—he could appear as blond and fair as any of the gods. Tyr had wondered if Loki's appearance wasn't his choice, if the land or an evil *wyrd* had forced it on him. Tyr gestured for Loki to continue.

"You're *not* yourself," Loki said. "I'm surprised that you're sensitive enough to discern it. Didn't imagine a great lug like you would have been able to."

"Is that all you have to say? Insults?"

Loki chuckled. "Of course, you don't know why, do you?"

Tyr pressed his lips together hard and shook his head, determined to get something useful out of the other god, even if he ended up strangling him later. Fortunately for him, Loki loved the sound of his own voice.

"That's the truly interesting part. You've never traveled this far away from the original incarnation of Ásgard, have you?"

"I have traveled beyond the veil, in the world of men. I have. I raised this sliver of land, these mountains and fjords and valleys, forged this reflection of the original Ásgard through myth and magic, so that we might journey with our followers, keep their faith alive in their hearts."

"But this land, as well as its gods, reflects the beliefs of men."

Tyr shifted uncomfortably in his chair.

The lands of Norway, Jutland, even Iseland, all carried their own slices of Ásgard, each with its own manifestation of the gods. The men who lived there didn't have identical faiths; however, they bore enough resemblance to each other that the slight deviations didn't matter. The gods who lived in those lands didn't truly differ from land to land, only men's perceptions of them differed. Tyr still felt a part of himself tied to those lands, sitting in judgment in halls that stood there, the cold encasing him.

"In Vinland we didn't feel this different," Tyr said, aware of the petulance in his voice.

"In Vinland we didn't encounter as many other men, with such different beliefs."

"What do you mean?"

"Here, the people, and the gods, are more firmly tied to land. Interwoven. Like the vines. It directs their actions, like their followers."

"So Tyrthbrand—" Tyr began, fearful of Loki's answer.

"Isn't your only influence, or problem."

"Damn tree-infested place," Tyr snarled as he pushed himself out of his high seat and strode across the floor. No single land tied his men down—they were warriors and merchants, always traveling, nowhere and everywhere being their home.

"It isn't just the land, though," Loki warned. "It's also the great number of people here. Too many of them, too few of us."

With an angry growl, Tyr poured himself a flagon of mead and drained it. His human followers were supposed to find an *empty* land, free of *skraelings* so they could gather goods without battle, grow powerful and rich.

But a land empty of people also meant a land without gods, making it easy for this manifestation of Tyr to remain the head of the gods in their sliver of Ásgard. He still remembered a time when he had been the chief god, before the followers of Odin had come to the northern lands, before they'd reworked legend and he'd lost his place, as well as his sword hand. It was another reason why he'd set his men on this path. If his followers multiplied, maybe when they journeyed back to their lands up north, Tyr could inspire new myths and take back the place that Odin had usurped.

Anger and pride forced away Tyr's doubts. He felt stronger now than when he'd been in Odin's lands. He didn't care where that strength came from, or what shapes it forced him into. He was more vigorous than when he'd been the leader of the gods and had thousands of men to call his own. Mightier even than when he'd had two hands, before his oath and unbending nature had made him lose one to bind Fenris the wolf. He'd never thrown lightning before, never had such strength.

Yet, at the same time, he'd never felt so . . . dependent on Tyrthbrand and his other men, needing their beliefs and prayers to feed him.

Gods and men had their own paths that only sometimes converged. Partly this was because it took a lot of the god's power to bridge the worlds and reach across into the land of men, but partly it was because when the gods interfered in the lives of men, disaster usually followed. Tyr had been lucky in his interactions with Tyrthbrand so far. Now that they'd reached this new place, he'd planned on letting Tyrthbrand find his own way.

Tyr wondered if this new land would let him, or if it, like the vines, had already started to weave the pair of them more tightly together.

"Look," Loki said, suddenly serious. "You're changing here, and quickly, faster than a rainbow. It's due to both the people and the land. As the days of the week are the same, yet different, so are the faces of the gods here. Don't make any oaths, not to any of the gods here, no matter how sweet the prize. It will cost you more than your hand."

Tyr nodded in reply, still focused on the other things Loki had said, how the land was now tied to him, how the men here could affect him.

"Promise me. Promise me instead of them."

"I prom—" Tyr stopped himself. Loki was such a trickster. Tyr refused to swear an oath to someone so unreliable.

Loki looked down at his boots and shook his head. His sigh was audible through the hall. "I tried," he said, his voice holding a note of sorrow that Tyr had never heard before. Then the half god pointed accusingly at Tyr and said, "Never again lecture me on how a man's *wyrd* can always be shaped by the choices he makes. Sometimes the Norns, those cruel sisters of fate, win." Then he threw back his head and laughed, loudly, before he disappeared.

Tyr was confused for a moment, but then anger surged through him. How dare Loki try to trick him into a promise? Tyr never broke his oaths, as all the gods—especially that usurper Odin—well knew. The lightning gathered quickly and charged through the hall. After a moment, a punch of thunder finally followed. "Poor imitation of Thor indeed," Tyr said into the emptiness. Though no actual sound greeted his ears, he still heard Loki's mocking laughter following him out the great carved doors.

Two monkeys chattered at each other, their long tails holding on to the tree branches tightly. They pointed at the distance, first one, then the other, and talked with each other some more. They wore identical headgear: white cloth wrapped over their ears, then twisted around many times, creating a kind of crown. They stored their quills and pens in their headpieces. Embroidered crimson and cyan loincloths covered their groins. They each carried a small shoulder bag, with edges of fan-folded books poking out the top.

"See the way the paths merge?"

"See the way they unwind?"

"See that one grow—"

"—and that one die?"

With simian grace, they leaped from their perch to the next tree. The land changed unexpectedly as they followed the trails into the new place. The twin monkey scribes knew all the plants that flourished in their jungle, but they couldn't name the greenery growing in this new place, this strange land now joined to theirs, brought by the foreign gods. They'd never traveled along such massive trunks, with rough bark and leaves as large as their palms, or seen the funny little berry-covered bushes that grew between the massive wooden steles.

They stayed close to each other, the odd forest before them making them nervous. Where were the vines? Where were the birds, the jewels of the trees? Where was the comforting warm air? What were these cold winds that told of colder places and not of storms?

Then they reached an impossible place—the end of the trees.

Before them lay a large, flat space, an ocean made of earth. As far as they could see, the land held no trees: no branches to hide in, no fruit for food, no place to go for comfort when they grew scared, nowhere to sleep but the bare earth. Azure streams cut through the jade-colored rocks. Mountains hunched in the distance. A few large, strange white birds circled above the plane, their raucous calls echoing through the emptiness.

Without another word, the monkey scribes fled. They had to tell Itzanam, the old iguana god, of this horrible new country they'd seen.

Itzanam looked out from the forest onto the open terrain. It was as chilled and nude as places man created, yet gods—albeit foreign gods—lived there. The two lands still worked their way into each other, blending and meshing. Trees reached toward one another to both his left and his right, while the bushes between them spread closer and closer, their branches now almost touching. Vines from his jungle couldn't cross the breach; the very air on the other side shunned them. Birds didn't venture out either, though he recognized hawks on both sides. The winds seemed to be fighting for dominance; first, they blew hot from behind him, then icy fingers slapped his front, carrying the smell of snow.

Itzanam had seen the land of the gods that the foreign men dragged with them, like a strange bird tethered to their boat, floating above and behind them, a reflection of their hearts. He'd sent the Bacabnob— the four giants who held up the corners of the sky— to create a hurricane to drown the boat, drive the new humans away, and destroy this sliver of land.

The strange men's gods had saved them, but he'd decided at the time that it didn't matter; there weren't enough men on the single ship to threaten his people.

Now, privately, he questioned the wisdom of his patience. He'd been certain of his superiority. But had that really been his motive? Had it been cowardice instead, an unwillingness to face these new beings and possibly lose? He'd been split, gone from one god to two, so recently. Had he been afraid that his time had come, that it was his turn to die and not be reborn?

As his anger kindled, Itzanam's face began to shift. His teeth grew thorn sharp, his nose pushed out like a snout, and folds of skin gathered behind his ears and along his neck. Cold-blooded rage filled the iguana god. He vowed to tear down this new land, cover it with proper jungle, melt its ice and warm its streams. Whoever these upstart gods were, they wouldn't rule here. Itzanam refused to die as the old gods had. His people would not forget him, bury his statues, cover his temples and cocoon them with holy places dedicated to others.

With a snarl, he turned his back on the foreign land. The gods of that place didn't have roots as deep as his; he could smell their youth. They would be easily blown over, like immature trees in a hurricane.

The Bacabnob still argued with each other in Itzanam's stone hall.

"These new men aren't the White Hand invaders foretold by prophecy," Cauac declared, his red face blazing. His crimson and blue tattoos formed an interlocking geometric pattern and stood up from his body, raised like bands of armor.

Painted murals depicting victory and sacrifice surrounded them. Smoke from burning copal, the *itz* of the trees, floated through the air. A diffuse orange light that came from nowhere and everywhere illuminated the four giant siblings.

"And what would you know of it, brother?" countered Kan. "Will they come through your realm? Are you the one who must constantly be on guard for them?" The yellow circular tattoos swirling across the giant's torso glowed like the rising sun.

"You are *not* the only one who has to watch. Vision through the spirals of time is rarely clear, and the glimpses the gods catch of these foreigners are more muddled than most," Ix said, as flamboyant in his words as his gestures. "The White Hands are supposed to come not just from your province in the east, but from mine in the west, as well." Black tattoos making a pattern of jaguar spots covered his skin.

Pale Muluk stood silent, his face turned to the north, as always.

"We must conjure another hurricane. Blow these new humans, and their gods, away from our land," Kan said, thrusting his hands out to illustrate his words.

Ix nodded. "In that, brother, I agree with you. Just say the word. The Chaob and their winds are still gathered in my realm, boiling and ready."

"But what if they *aren't* the White Hands? What if these men are, as they claim, merchants? Would you risk angering Ekchuah?" Cauac asked.

The other Bacab fell silent. The merchant god with his bag of goods and glowing cigar had grown powerful. His leathery visage could be seen in many temples these days. More smoke and sacrifices blew his way than ever before.

"You'll imperil our people, bringing them poverty," Cauac continued. "If men don't have money, they don't burn sweet incense or let honeyed blood flow."

Kan shook his head. "If good men have bad luck, they sacrifice more, not less. I say we let the winds loose."

"And if that doesn't work?" Cauac asked. His tattoos raised a bit more, as if getting ready to leap off his body and attack his brothers.

"We could always trick Kabrakan. Challenge him to a contest. Or flatter him. Whatever it takes to make him pound the mountains," Ix replied. His black tattoos widened, like holes in his skin, ready to pour out midnight-tinted air.

Muluk pivoted to face his brothers. "You would bring earthquakes to our people?" The words hissed out like falling rain. "Yes, Kabrakan would take the souls of these foreign men into an underworld from which they'd never escape. They would never be reborn. At the same time, he'd take many of our own people's souls as well." Muluk glowered at them, as ashen as the stars in the celestial monster. A tattoo of the beast covered the Bacab's face; a twisted openmouthed head on either cheek, connected by a black body flowing over the bridge of Muluk's nose.

Only Kan, his yellow radiance still glaring, dared to meet his eldest brother's stare.

Into the prolonged silence, Muluk added quietly, "There is another you have forgotten about. Another who might solve this problem."

Ix dismissed his brother's statement with a wave of his giant black hand. "Feathered Serpent is not the answer. He only knows one thing—sacrifice. He's Itzanam's newest shadow, not Itzanam himself."

Cauac agreed. "Feathered Serpent would kill these men, but their spirits would stay here, as would their gods."

"Brothers," Kan said, his hand raised. The other three looked up at him expectantly. "And what if Feathered Serpent did take them? As well as their gods? All for himself?"

The others rocked back from Kan, their faces caught in an identical, horrified expression. The blood and lives men sacrificed fed the gods and the land,

made them all stronger. How powerful would Feathered Serpent grow if he sacrificed these men's gods?
If he took their power from them and didn't share it
with the land?

Muluk, the eldest, recovered first, finding his individuality again, his wan face breaking free of the mien
that held them all. "Has anyone told Feathered Serpent of the arrival of these men?"

Now all the brothers looked ashamed. Until the arrival of Feathered Serpent, the Bacabnob had been
servants of Itzanam. Through myth, contests, and legend restrung, the newcomer had won their services.
As a result, their duty should have been clear. They
should have told Feathered Serpent of the new men
and their gods. Instead, when Kan had seen them approach, he'd gathered his brothers and gone straight
to Itzanam, who had ordered the failed hurricane.

"I suppose we should do our duty and inform
Feathered Serpent," Ix said slowly, in an exaggerat-
edly careless tone.

"In a while," Kan said. He gestured at the mural
to his right. "I think we should do something to
strengthen the land first. It may need renewing in the
coming days."

The painting took up the entire wall. The brilliant
colors seemed more vibrant than those found in real
life. The picture depicted the land of men in a band
across the middle. Representatives of all types of humans were shown there: peasants who hunted, farmed,
and occasionally, went to war; artisans who carved and
painted history on the temple walls and stairs; warriors
with shields, spears, blowpipes, and throwing straps;
noblemen and women with feathered headdresses that
floated to the ground behind them, while slaves tended
and fanned them; and scribes writing in their folded
books.

In the very center of the wall, two priests, covered
only in sacrificial blue paint, held a naked man down

on an altar. A third priest had his hand inside the sacrificed man's chest. A rich fountain of blood swirled out from the man and encircled the priests, the red transmuting into the life-giving jade green of a magical ceiba—the World Tree—that stretched up from the dying man toward the stars, as well as grew down, under the world of men.

The Lords of the Underworld lurked between the roots, catching stray drops of blood, mostly having to satisfy themselves with smoke. The gods of heaven sat along the branches of the World Tree, sheltered by it, given substance from it, fed by the sacrifice, and, in turn, feeding men and their world. From their positions on the tree, the gods sprinkled rain, held back deadly winds, made the earth fertile, brought the almighty corn to fruition, scattered animals that men might hunt, comforted those in childbirth and pain, and guided souls through the labyrinth of roots in the underworld so they could be reborn.

The Bacabnob understood what their brother asked of them. By going through the pain of sacrifice, Kan would bolster the land. His blood would water the ground, feed it, like rain never could. In return, the land would continue to support all of them and comfort them, let them draw their strength from it.

Kan placed his right hand over his heart and held his left hand out, as was his duty. The foreigners had come from his realm, the east. The giant stepped forward, toward the mural, shrinking as he did so. His canary-yellow tattoos swirled faster until they buzzed around his body like a swarm of bees. When he took another step, the horde of color started slipping away, down his legs, into the floor. In another two steps, Kan was as naked as the sacrificed man in the mural. The only difference between them was a crude black tattoo in the shape of the sun that marked Kan's right cheek.

Kan took one more step and walked into the picture.

The three other Bacabnob took on human proportions as well as they walked forward. They wore the blue ceremonial paint of priests intermixed with their tattoos. They joined their brother in the mural, the heat of the world beating on them, the smell of baked earth and sweat sweeter than incense. The orange porcupine fingers of dawn streaked across the sky. Drums echoed in the distance. Jungle sounds—keening insects, screaming monkeys, playful birds—filled in the spaces between the beats.

Kan led the procession up the temple stairs, followed by his brothers and other representations of men. He lay down on the altar and stretched out, preparing himself. Muluk held Kan's hands over his head, while Cauac took his feet. Ix took his place as the sacrificing priest at their side.

As the sun rose, bringing light and life back to the earth, Ix released Kan's heart from his body, feeding the land that fed them—blood for blood—strengthening the ties between the brothers, their world, human myths, and their gods.

"Plague take it!" Freyja said. She straightened up from where she'd been bent over planting and began adjusting herself. The keys at her waist jingled as she shook, the noise carried away on the curious warm winds that slid around her every time she left her hall.

"What is it?" Idun asked, coming up from behind, holding her heavy basket with both her hands. Their words sounded hushed in the open field. They couldn't see the new border from where they stood: their own solid oaks and pines blocked their view.

"Do you see this ridiculous armor?" Freyja asked, turning. She tugged at the leather piece bound across her chest and pushed one breast, then the other, down farther inside it. "I keep feeling as if I'm about to fall out of this stupid thing."

Idun nodded sympathetically. "I understand. I feel it too. Do you see how big my hips have grown? I feel as roomy inside as if I could give birth to an ox."

Freyja pushed on herself one more time. "It's those damn men. I feel so lusty all the time. We need some women followers. They would tone down our curves, give us tenderness, children, and sorrow."

"Men can give you sorrow too," Idun replied quietly.

"Ah, child, you are right." Both goddesses were silent for a moment, listening to the strange wind. "Come, rest with me a while," Freyja said. She sat down, then patted the ground next to her.

"For a short time," Idun said. "Then I really must get back to the hall and prepare the apples for dinner."

The two goddesses sat together, listening to the quiet. Then Freyja pushed with her hands, clearing away the grass around them. She took cut roses and lilies from her basket and began sticking them in the ground. Each flower rapidly multiplied until the women sat in the middle of a flower garden. Bees came quickly, gathering up their golden bounty. Butterflies followed, then birds arrived to brighten the air with their songs and to eat their fill of the insects.

"Did you hear Tyr this morning?" Idun asked.

Freyja snorted. "Who didn't?" she asked. "Roaring like a drunkard. All that lightning."

Idun chuckled. "No thunder, though."

"Couldn't make it rain."

"All talk, no action."

"Typical man."

The two goddesses giggled.

"Are we through traveling? Do you think we'll stay here?" Idun asked.

Freyja bit her lip. "I don't know, young one. The land seems to believe we will."

"Really? Did you tell Tyr?"

"Do you think he'd come ask me?" Freyja tsked with a mocking tone. "These men think they control their own destiny, that they act on will alone. They won't acknowledge that their strength also comes from the earth."

"The land is . . . changing," Idun said.

"Speak your fears, child," Freyja commanded. She felt her smile fade and her face grow stern. Shrinking armor or not, she was still the head of the household.

"This place—beyond the trees—it's so warm."

"And?" Freyja prompted.

"My apples. They need cold to ripen."

"And we need the fruit of your labor to stay young. Without your efforts, we age and die," Freyja said.

"It's no great thing—"

Freyja interrupted her. "Do not try to fool me. The men may be blind to your efforts. I'm not. You must give birth to those trees to renew them."

Idun hung her head.

"Child, it's no shame. You create such a marvelous gift for us every evening. Why do you think you must do it without effort?"

"What's that?" Idun asked, looking beyond Freyja's shoulder.

"Don't try to dis—" Freyja whipped her head around when the earth under her vibrated slightly. "Get behind me," she said, standing and pulling out her sword. It felt as though it was made of solid rock and weighed her arm down. "Damn these men for only praying for soft women! Don't they understand a woman has to be strong enough to be able to defend herself?"

The ground undulated, like a cat stretching, spilling the recently grown flowers. Great clawlike hands emerged from the raw dirt a stone's throw in front of Freyja and Idun. Each hand clutched the head of a snake. The soil rolled off the figure's arms in waves, leaving them alabaster white. A woman's head soon

issued forth, with long wavy black hair. Her bulging
eyes were turned up in the sockets, so only the whites
showed. Blood flowed from her arched nose. Her face
held no expression—not fear, terror, or ecstasy. Even
statues conveyed more emotion.

The figure continued to rise. The great snakes she
held curled their bodies around her outstretched arms,
their tails flickering. They seemed more alive than the
woman did. Now her bare breasts had crested the
earth, the nipples hard and colorless.

"Who is she?" Idun asked. "What is she?"

"She is Liðami. She lived in the south," Freyja said
over her shoulder, never taking her eyes off the rising
goddess. "She had powers over death, and aided those
in the afterlife. I haven't seen her for many years."

Freyja held her sword steady between them. The
killing twig had grown lighter the longer she'd held it,
and she'd felt her womanly proportions shrinking in
response. It was as if the longer she held the sword,
the more transformed she became, until one aspect
no longer resembled the other. The realization both
frightened and elated her.

"What is she doing, buried in our field?"

"This land carries echoes of all lands, even those
south of ours, not just those of Iseland, Norway, and
Jutland," Freyja answered. "When the last of her followers passed away, she sank below the earth." Liðami's flaccid belly broke free. The exposed part of
her body elongated. Her pale skin grew more ashen
as she stretched. It was as if some giant had grabbed
hold of her and pulled her unwillingly from the earth.

Strands of her dark hair began to wiggle, simulating
snakes. Colors coalesced in each spike. The pieces
grew stiffer, until she appeared to have a crown of
bright feathers.

Freyja didn't know what force took Liðami, but it
wasn't kind. Power crackled around her, and the

meadow filled with a sizzling sound, similar to spitting meat cooking over a fire. The goddess jerked. Her pelvis surfaced, her legs pressed tightly together, minimizing her sex. She'd never been a fertility goddess. But whatever was wrenching her from the ground was remolding her as she emerged from the dirt, emphasizing her breasts, rounding her hips, enlarging the serpents until they wrapped not only around her arms but her waist. Her legs were split apart, and the snakes found their way down her thighs.

Suddenly, her relentless progress from the earth slowed. Freyja thought that Liðami struggled, awakened at last to her fate. The colors in her hair darkened, and the original black streaked through it again. Her nose stopped bleeding. Her snakes twisted, bulging, covering her arms like bands of armor.

Freyja took a step back. She didn't know what protection she could offer Idun should the focal point explode, if her sword would take the power, or if she could direct the energy into the land. She longed for a shield instead of a basket of flowers. She planted her feet firmly in the earth, ready to call on the land for help if necessary.

The battle continued. Liðami inched farther from the earth. Her feet came out slowly, first her heels, then the arches, then one toe at a time. She hung suspended for a moment after her soles left the ground. Brilliant threads of rainbow colors coated her hair, overcoming the black. Each acted as if it had a life of its own, and began to crawl toward her face. Feathers now streamed down her back, like a headdress. Her hands grew into paws, the white skin taking on a molted, patched appearance.

Yet the serpents now seemed to move under her command. They expanded, wrapping around her like a twisting shroud. The colors couldn't touch the skin the snakes covered. Chilling winds suddenly gusted through the field. The smell of graveyards—limestone and ash—pulsed through the air. The colors slowed their progress.

Freyja felt a momentary hope. Maybe Liðami wouldn't be taken.

A brilliant blue tendril of Liðami's hair wriggled its way into her mouth. Once it had gained entrance, the wind died and the snakes shrank. Feathers sprang up between the coils. The goddess bent back, curved like a Saracen's sword, glowing and multihued. Then she streaked toward the sky like a bird-snake, a serpent that had grown feathers.

Freyja watched Liðami's progress for a moment, the trails of her flight leaving clouds in the pure sky. Then she looked down and put out her hand, intending to heal the hole in the earth from where the snake goddess had been plucked. The dirt Liðami had pulled out with her was darker than the earth of the field and very rich. Freyja put her sword away and reached out with both her hands now. She felt something else pushing its way out of the ground—not another goddess—a plant, something that had roots and branches. She encouraged it, glad of any living thing to come, to mark the passage of Liðami.

Too late, Freyja realized the foreign nature of the tree that sprang up. It matured in moments under her encouragement. Before she could stop it, the tree towered above the clearing. She'd never seen anything like it before. Squared-off roots, like planks, dipped their fingers into the earth, the tops taller than a man. The size of the tree astounded her. The gray, cracked trunk grew straight, not deigning to bow toward either light or shadow. Massive branches stretched from the top of the tree, sprouting waxy, dark green leaves. Shadows of vines appeared, but they stayed insubstantial, as though fearful of the cold air.

When one of the beamlike roots tried creeping beyond the black dirt of the hole, Freyja turned the surrounding soil into sand. She would not allow this tree to grow beyond the borders she'd set.

Part of Freyja wanted to destroy this foreign tree, deny it life in her realm. She didn't want foreign plants creeping across the border into her land, even though plants native to Ásgard would do the same—they would migrate, seeking new earth. However, part of her accepted its right to exist, as well as the symbol it represented, of the mixing she knew would have to come for them to survive here.

The damage had been done. She dreaded telling Tyr of Liðami, but knew she must. Freyja turned around to inquire after her young companion.

Idun knelt, gathering up her apples. Her basket had spilled over. Freyja reached down to help her. She picked up the apples carefully, brushing off the dirt, smoothing over any bruises she saw.

"Why?" Idun asked without looking up from her task.

"Why was Liðami chosen? I believe it was because she was an old god, long since put to rest."

Idun sat back and glared at Freyja. "Will something like this happen to all of us, as our followers die? Will we all be taken, ripped out of our homes like weeds, by strange new powers?"

Freyja stood up, sword in her hand again, chin set in stone. "Not if we can help it. We will fight."

Idun looked beyond Freyja to the strange tree. She didn't say anything, but her response echoed through the clearing, as clear as the cry of a hawk.

They would fight. And lose.

Ix Chebel made her slow progress up the temple stairs toward the platform at the top. Pale skinny trunks of the *chuhuk* tree had forced their way between the steps, causing her to swerve now and again. Her sloping back had refused to straighten that morning, and her old knees popped and cracked as she ascended. She didn't want to stop and rest, though she felt the age of the world in her joints.

Men counted and named the days, using their figures to keep track of seasons and the phases of the stars. Today was known as Four *Kimi*, Ten *Muwan*. The aspect of the goddess that day reflected this count: a death head overlay her own face and owl feathers—the bird of silent killing—made up her headdress. In this guise, she brought swift death to those who were unwary, or to those whom she chose. It was an unlucky day for women to go into labor, a quiet day for madmen who usually howled, and a good day for those who chose to commit suicide.

Ekchuah came over from where he stood at the corner of the platform to greet the goddess as she crested the edge. A wreath of smoke swirled around his head. His eyes glowed as bright and amber as the tip of his cigar. He didn't manifest the aspect of the day in his face; it held its usual leathery appearance, with long lines and broken nose. She wondered if he instead carried death in the bulging sack he wore strapped to his back.

"Mother of all, welcome to our humble gathering," Ekchuah said, holding out his hand to help her take the last step up.

Ix Chebel smiled at him and touched his cheek with her free hand. "And what favors are you seeking from me?" she asked.

Ekchuah leaned back with one hand to his chest, his eyes wide open. "You wound me, assuming that my kindness has motives other than a desire to help you."

Ix Chebel clicked her tongue at him, tucked her hand into his arm, and pulled him closer. "Why would I assume you would behave in a way other than that dictated by your nature?" she asked. "What have you heard?"

She knew she placed herself in his debt by asking

the question, but not by too much. Ekchuah loved
to gossip.

"There's a new land joined to ours," he said, leaning over and speaking softly, as if sharing some
great secret.

"Tell me more," Ix Chebel purred. She glanced at the
other gods and goddesses who had already gathered on
the top of the platform, drawn together by the strange
vibration in the land. She had a momentary regret that
she hadn't arrived earlier so she could have listened to
their talk. Then she pulled on Ekchuah's arm, keeping
at the edge of the platform, away from the others. He
would know more useful information than all of them
put together, anyway.

"It was brought here by foreign men. Traders. They
carry goods, and gods, with them."

"Hmm," Ix Chebel replied, barely paying attention,
waiting for Ekchuah to say something interesting. Instead, she studied the other gods, noting who stood
next to whom, wondering what new alliances were
being formed, what new danger she would have to
guard her husband against.

"You already knew!" Ekchuah accused her.

"Of course I already knew," she said, smiling up at
him. She felt the death mask overtaking her grin, turning it skeletal and crazed. "The men landed on the
island of Tzul, near my main temple."

Ekchuah didn't pull away from the goddess, but his
arm stiffened. Ix Chebel averted her gaze. Only Ekchuah had had the courage to tell her how her eyes
spun when she talked of her insane followers. "Can't
bargain with a madwoman," he'd said, as an explanation of his distaste. So Ix Chebel tried not to use her
mad aspect to disconcert the merchant god.

"Strange they should come now," he said.

"What do you mean?"

"So many temples were lost in the last cycle. So
many people gone in the great famine. Why are the

foreigners here now, after we've regained our
strength? While we are at peace? Why not earlier,
when we were weaker?"

"Others *did* come when we were weaker," Ix
Chebel said. What was the merchant god getting at?
The Puuc had come, and Itzanam had been forced
to divide himself in order to subsume their bloody
feathered god.

Ekchuah didn't respond. Ix Chebel looked up at
him. His eyes were focused on the distance, and he
nodded his head. "Shall we?" he asked, indicating
with his hands that they should promenade around the
edge of the platform.

Ix Chebel felt the extreme age creep away from her
joints as they traversed the square, her back straightening. She was still old, but no longer crippled. A
great calm descended on her. The walk was making
her shift aspects, away from the old woman who
tended childbirths and foretold futures, to the version
of her that people prayed to while on the road, the
one who quieted storms and made journeys safer.

Ekchuah had changed during their walk as well.
He'd grown younger, his bag seemed to bulge more,
and a walking stick had manifested in his free hand.
They paused at the first corner.

"Thank you," the goddess said. She never remembered how walking with the merchant god made her
change aspects, causing her to match his, until they
both wore a younger, traveling guise. Though she resented Ekchuah for manipulating her into a different
form, she was grateful as well. She needed her wits,
not her insanity, for the coming confrontation.

"So why did he do it?" Ekchuah asked as they began
their journey along the second side of the platform.

Ah. This was why Ekchuah had helped her, the real
heart of his ploy. He assumed that she, as Itzanam's
wife, would know her husband's mind.

Ix Chebel picked her words carefully. Though she

and Ekchuah joked about position and power, the battles for influence between the merchant god and the iguana god were fierce. "He chose to let the foreigners come," she said. She assumed she spoke the truth, though she didn't know for certain. "They aren't the dreaded White Hands, those horrible foreigners that Feathered Serpent keeps predicting," she added. She wanted to give Ekchuah something extra for his kindnesses.

Ekchuah chuckled. "Other gods have predicted the coming of the White Hands. No one but Feathered Serpent, however, has assigned them the bloody task of destroying us and all our people." Ekchuah paused, then patted her arm. "Thank you," he said. He knew when he'd spent his coin. They finished the second side of their walk around the square platform and rounded the corner, starting their third, in silence.

About midway down the stretch, Ekchuah said, "Why do you think—"

A flurry of wings interrupted him. The scent of burned blood—rich and dark—swirled around them. A rainbow streaked above the trees and coalesced in the center of the platform.

"One of yours, my dear?" Ekchuah asked, leaning over and whispering in Ix Chebel's ear.

She bit her lip to stop herself from smiling, and instead, nudged him sharply in the ribs. She merely wove the rainbows that came after the storms. She wasn't responsible for the idiots who snatched them from the sky, turned them into cloaks, then paraded about in them.

Feathered Serpent glowered at the other gods and goddesses on the platform as he manifested.

"Why wasn't I told of this new land?" he demanded before giving any greeting. He did not welcome them to this holy place, address the five directional points to guard their speech, or even bless the sacrifices along the path.

Ix Chebel told herself not to be offended. When madmen held her aspect, she'd done far worse things.

She did have an excuse—she couldn't control herself. Feathered Serpent should have been able to.

"I wonder if he'll ever mature?" Ekchuah whispered.

On another day, Ix Chebel would have laughed. Now, though, she felt the death mask creep back across her countenance. Feathered Serpent might drive all of them into extinction. Gods of war demanded much. Continual battles drained everything: jungle, crops, and lives.

He was a new god, proud of his individuality, unwilling to share. The City of Wells had three leaders now, all kings in their own right: one was dedicated to spiritual matters and Itzanam; one was in charge of trade, a follower of Ekchuah; and the third plied the art of war, a discipline of Feathered Serpent. The humans saw the importance of dividing power, so if one of their kings died or was captured, their city-state would not be lost. Ix Chebel wondered if Feathered Serpent saw the wisdom of the human's newest style of government, or if he scorned it and longed for a return to a single, godlike king, dedicated to his worship alone.

She remembered the time when Itzanam and Feathered Serpent had been one, and wore Itzanam's face. If they merged now, whose aspect would prevail?

"Where are the Bacabnob?" Feathered Serpent asked.

Ix Chebel didn't look around her as the others did. She closed her eyes to feel them. The earth tugged at her. A wet heat enveloped her skin. Drums beat in time with the jungle's heart. She breathed deeply, tasting the musky baked earth of the Bacabnob temple on the back of her tongue. They'd gone to strengthen the land, to feed it against the unknown threat, as the other gods should have done when the newcomers had arrived.

She let the giddiness of Kan's perfect, willing sacrifice float to the top of her head, bringing the madness of suicide to her eyes as she opened them. Then she walked forward. She tried not to use this aspect on Ekchuah; Feathered Serpent, however, was another matter.

"I know where they've gone," she said in a singsong voice. The sane part of her resented how the other gods and goddesses cleared a path for her instantly, as if afraid her insanity was contagious. Then she grinned her skeletal grin. Maybe it was.

Ix Chebel turned in a tight circle. The air swirled around her, caressing her cheeks as it passed, stripping away the veils that even the gods wore, blinding their sight. All the gods claimed to know why they were sometimes blessed with foresight. None of them would admit that they didn't really understand it, though.

For the goddess, being able to see through the spirals of time was just another phase of her being, as unpredictable as a spring shower, as welcome, as forgettable, and as brief. She began chanting:

"Now is the k'atun of famine.
Two lands have become one.
The earth vies with the gods,
Stealing prayers meant for them.
The ground sings of its hunger, its longing for blood.
The blood stone isn't enough.
Gods' lives aren't enough.
Nothing will sustain it through the evil white tides
That bring nothing but dust to the jungle."

"What do you see?" commanded Feathered Serpent.

Ix Chebel laughed. He could not order her sight. She stood beyond him, outside them all, beyond even the White Hands, their skeletal fingers reaching for her lands, looking for new places to dig in. The earth cried out to her, its jungles and its oceans soon to be under siege from the coming catastrophe that nothing— not even all the blood of all the gods—could prevent. A foreign name whisked around her, here, then gone, a name that soon would cause even the great kings to tremble.

Cortéz.

He would come, him and his followers, with their gloved white hands, black beards, and loud, talking sticks.

She would not speak that cursed name out loud.

Turning her gaze away, she found that she could see into a different spiral of time, an alternate future, one where the White Hands still came, but they didn't bring so much death with them—the blood stone survived, as did her people. The fear dropped from her, falling away like a withered leaf, quickly forgotten, along with what she'd seen. Youth sprang into her limbs as she dove through the next circle of time, the slim possibilities of what could be now filling her eyes.

"Then there is the twisting k'atun
The bringing together
Blood stone and stone.
Hearts given, hearts lost, two hearts beating as one.
O king, will you give as much?
Or as little?"

She twirled and leaped as she sang, the owl portion of the day freed by her acceptance of the death mask, giving her feet wings.

"What do you see?" Feathered Serpent demanded again.

Someone else answered for her. "She sees what I see."

Ix Chebel cackled loudly through the sudden silence. The real king, the true heart of the world, her only love, Itzanam, had arrived. Even in her madness, she knew the others wouldn't listen to him any more than they would her. Still, his presence drove her toward ecstasy. The glory of all creation bore down on her, breaking the thread of reason that tied her to her other aspects. Chaos crowded in, the mad multiplying of beasts and birds, gods and stars. She continued to caper around the platform.

"Two may become one with the arrival of these foreigners," Itzanam proclaimed.

The words Itzanam spoke stroked the flame in Ix Chebel's quicksilver core. She was both fire and water, burning calm and storming rainbows. She wove between the gods and goddesses standing there, binding them into her private vision of the universe, bright stars against her midnight canvas.

No one else moved or spoke.

"Why do you not ask what I see?" Itzanam said.

"You speak in riddles and threats. I would learn more directly," Feathered Serpent answered.

Ix Chebel marveled at how Itzanam's face changed as she moved across the platform. Her sight was influenced by whatever god or goddess she stood near: Nacon saw a weak man with a lined face and sharp teeth; to Tohil, Itzanam appeared almost as a whirlwind, sucking in all light and sacrifices; and to Votan, the iguana aspect was strongest. It didn't matter to her what Feathered Serpent saw—she didn't have enough rationality to wonder.

"I see a time when gods who are scattered like raindrops gather together to form a single stream. Instead of being blown by the wind, directionless, we force our way through the world of men, flooding souls as we have need."

Ix Chebel allowed her dance to become more graceful and flowing, swaying as she surged between the others, still weaving them into a single unit. She could see the river her husband spoke of—it was part of the alternate time, where her people survived. The waters were mighty and deep. Streams sprang off the river as well as fed it. The gods wouldn't lose all their individuality, just some of it—there would still be private cults, here and elsewhere. However, they wouldn't lose themselves completely either, be forgotten and dismissed, overtaken, as they would with the coming of Feathered Serpent's White Hands. The jungles wouldn't turn to dust.

Her husband didn't see the blood stone. She wasn't aware enough to ask him why.

"Bah—your visions are driven by your desires. You would suck everything into yourself, deny the rest of us our share," Feathered Serpent said.

The image before Ix Chebel shattered, its pieces scattering like a flock of startled parrots. She saw again the darkness falling over the land with the coming of the White Hands, dropping all the gods into ignominy and ignorance.

Feathered Serpent continued. "You do not fool me. I name you trickster, veiler of truth."

How prettily the sun shone through the trees. It would always shine, whether she was there to see it or not. And if Feathered Serpent continued to fight with Itzanam and did not aid him or help him reach his future of joining, she would not see it. Her temples would fall; the jungle would cover all the roads and cities. No one would remember her holy days.

"Though we call him father—" Hun Ahaw, the day aspect of the Hero Twins said, stepping forward.

"He is not as cunning as we are," Yax Balam said, finishing his twin's sentence.

"We can always find," Hun Ahaw continued.

"The founding deceit of a plan," Yax Balam added.

"And we do not see any trick here," they ended in unison.

Ix Chebel stopped suddenly. The proclamation of

the twins surprised her, bringing her a touch of sanity with their words. Would they stand beside her husband? Or was it just some power ploy of their own?

"You say that only because of some hold he has over you," Feathered Serpent accused.

"Did he rescue us from the Lords of the Underworld?" Hun Ahaw asked, puffing out his chest.

"Or did we rescue him?" Yax Balam said.

After a moment, Ekchuah added quietly, "I say Itzanam's price is fair."

Ix Chebel whirled. The merchant god never showed his hand in anything. He *always* stayed mute. What bargain did he hope to drive now, by speaking? The madness drained out of her, into the jungle air. Calm pervaded her skin, soaking her like a sudden rain. She spun slowly, as though her mad aspect continued to hold her. She wanted to see how the other gods and goddesses reacted, who else believed in the joining vision of her husband.

Too few.

"I have no need to listen to these lies," Feathered Serpent said. "These foreigners bring nothing but new blood for my line."

"And what of their gods?" Ekchuah asked.

"Them too," Feathered Serpent replied decisively. In one quick motion, he wrapped his feathered cloak across his chest and streaked into the sky.

"Ohhhh," whispered Itzanam.

Ix Chebel turned to her husband. He wasn't impressed by that youngster's flashy exit, was he? Then she saw that the *geis* of foresight had entrapped him. He stood as still as a stone, his back arched, his face toward the sky, and his eyes rolled back until only the whites shone. He appeared in the aspect of a vessel to her, with the *itz* of the world pouring into him.

The death mask came back over her mien. The rictus grin couldn't be denied. She approached her husband and asked, "What do you see?"

At her touch, Itzanam's rigid body loosened. He covered her cold hand with one of his warm ones and stroked her cheek with his other. For a moment, no one else existed. The wonder of his vision filled her. He smiled. The iguana nature of his being disappeared. Youth suffused his face.

For the first time since she'd known him, Ix Chebel saw hope in her husband's face.

It fled so quickly she wondered if she'd been mistaken. Then he started to speak, and she knew she hadn't been.

"I've seen an ageless time. When we no longer die like our ancestors. Killed in battle or for sacrifice, yes. Our bodies are still lowered into the earth, and we must make our way out of the nine layers of Xibalba. But we rise, young still. Eternal, we rule."

The day began to change. The death head receded in Ix Chebel, while the hand—the doing, making, and weaving aspects—began to rise.

"It will be a good time," Itzanam proclaimed.

Ix Chebel turned away so her husband couldn't see her face. Owl feathers twirled in her stomach. It would be a good time, if it ever came.

However, her changing self denied endlessness. She couldn't imagine . . . consistency. Day changed to night; rain followed the dry seasons.

Her husband's vision was more fleeting than rainbows, but she wouldn't deny him the only hope he'd ever had.

The new humans and their gods and their blood stone would have to live. She would have to see to it. No matter what other sacrifices it might take.

"I will blast him from here to Muspell!" Tyr swore, the words echoing through his hall. Lightning flickered across his chest and he heard the crackling of thunder in the background. How dare Tyrthbrand make a wish to a foreign goddess? Tyr would send wolves after him, let ravens feast on his entrails, burn his family and cast their ashes to the winds.

And yet . . . Tyr forced himself away from the end of his hall and approached his high seat. Why did it matter so much? It shouldn't. It was a single indiscretion. Back in Iseland, or even in Vinland, Tyr probably wouldn't have known what Tyrthbrand had done, unless he'd happened to be looking at the time.

Though here, when the human had placed his damn stone between that foreign whore's feet, a shadow of it had slipped between the veils that shielded the worlds of gods from the worlds of men and had hit Tyr's boot, something else that had never happened before.

Maybe it was because they had so few followers here.

Or maybe it was because of what Loki had been trying to tell him, that the covenant between men and gods was different here, that it wouldn't take so much power, or planning, for them to interact, and maybe the results wouldn't end in ruin. Loki kept talking of litanies, of call and response. He'd said that the men here were more tied to the gods, and that the gods were more tied to the land.

Slowly Tyr sank into his seat, a sense of calm stealing over him. Tyrthbrand had chosen a different path than the one Tyr had set for him, first by landing here, in a land already full of gods, and now, by letting himself be seduced by them.

Fine. If that was the way Tyrthbrand wanted it, Tyr wouldn't answer his next call. Just because Loki thought they were more dependent didn't mean anything. Tyr would survive the death of Tyrthbrand. He wasn't the only follower of Tyr who had come on the *Golden Tree*. Besides, Ketil could be fervent. He'd convert every native he met if he could.

Tyr would survive if Tyrthbrand turned from him. Wouldn't he?

*   *   *

Early afternoon found Tyr still sitting in his hall on his high seat, anger and fear tumbling through him. Sunbeams searched for chinks in the tapestries covering the windows, slipping into the room and brightening the unlit hearth. The slithering snakes in the floor reflected the god's unease by twisting faster, their passage sounding like the rushing of a rain-filled creek. Tyr had sent his meal back untouched, though his stomach had alternately grumbled with hunger and unease when the faint odors of roast pig floated up from the back.

He didn't understand what had happened to Liðami, why she'd been ripped from the earth. Had Tyrthbrand's wish caused this? None could advise him. No one had ever seen such a thing. Even Loki had seemed surprised. Such a thing was not part of their creation or destruction myths. Tyr couldn't recall the last time something truly new had happened. Stories changed, but slowly. Not like this.

Maybe a seeress could breach the spirals of time and tell him the future. He wondered if he should try to raise an aspect of Gullveig, the witch who had foretold the final twilight of the gods—the Ragnarok— to Odin.

A timid voice interrupted his thoughts. "My Lord."

Tyr beckoned the man in. It was one of his humanlike guards, a raised soul. He wouldn't have dared disrupt his god's thoughts unless it was important.

"There are two . . . two who have come. Are here to see you. They asked to see the one-handed god."

"Bring them forward," Tyr commanded.

Light filled the hall as Tyr, with a mere thought, shoved the thick tapestries away from the windows and caused the fire in the center of the hall to blossom. Cold sunshine glared and fractured when it struck the pounded gold on Tyr's high seat. The crimson snakes inlaid in the floor slowed their constant twisting. Wooden pillars covered with carved vines slimmed and extended, raising the roof of the hall, enlarging Tyr's domain.

Two creatures came through the great doors. They stood shorter than the men Tyr had standing guard. They wore embroidered loincloths and sheets wrapped around their heads, and carried bags.

As they drew closer, Tyr saw that they were not men. Perhaps at one point they had been, but they'd been corrupted. Or cursed. Wonder shivered through him.

Thick brown hair covered their skin, tails dragged between their legs, and their faces were pushed forward into muzzles. Long thin arms and legs stretched out from their squat torsos. Elongated palms and fingers stretched at the ends of their arms, while squared-off feet marked the ends of their legs. They walked with a hunched-over, rolling gait, knuckles below their knees, as if they didn't usually travel upright.

Without preamble, they bowed as one to Tyr, then began to speak. He heard their words in the language of the his people, the Æsir, but he also heard the echoes of their native tongue. They'd been given the gift of language, so Tyr might understand them. Had the god who had sent them done this as a courtesy? Or had he assumed that Tyr couldn't have bestowed this gift himself?

"We bid you greeting," started one.

"Welcome you to this limb of the World Tree," said the other.

"We rejoice in your arrival—"

"—your place, your being."

Did they only have one brain between the pair of them?

"We ask your presence—"

"—you, yourself—"

"To meet, to parlay, to talk and dance."

"Will you come?"

One messenger sat down on the floor while the other stayed standing. The one seated pulled something out of his bag. The cover of it was made of wood. In the center was something brightly colored and folded, like stiff cloth. He placed it on the floor in front of him, pulled a stick out of his headdress, then sat poised, one hand over the cloth, holding the stick.

It took Tyr a moment to realize that this was a scribe, like those damn monks from Eire, and he was about to record Tyr's answer. Though these two were probably the least of the followers of the god who had sent them, they could read and write, which gave them power.

"Who shall I meet?" Tyr asked, using the most formal forms of the words that he knew.

"Father Iguana," said the one standing. He paused. The seated twin didn't speak. The standing messenger continued alone. "The risen sun, the white bird of spirit, the old creator."

The other finally spoke. "Itzanam, as named by men."

"He comes alone?" Tyr asked. Their summons had made it clear that they wanted him to come by himself. He had to go. He'd been invited, and his own sense of hospitality and honor demanded it. However, he didn't need to walk unwittingly into an ambush.

The two looked at each other. Their inhuman faces were impossible to read. Did they smile?

"As alone as any god ever is," the one standing finally responded.

"Then I shall meet him," Tyr said. He didn't understand what they meant. Did they imply that the gods who lived here were never alone?

"When the sun rests two fingers above the western trees," the standing one instructed Tyr.

He nodded grimly. "Where?"

"At the border, near the empty place."

The shudder that ran through one, then the other, piqued Tyr's curiosity. Why did an open field scare them so? Were they the only ones scared? Or did all their gods share this fear? How could he use this knowledge to his advantage?

The seated one finished his writing. He picked up the thing he wrote on, blew on it, then folded it up carefully and placed it in his bag. He stuck his writing stick back into the white cloth wrapped around his head and stood in a fluid motion.

The two messengers bowed as one.

"Thank you, great one—" started one.

"—for both your forbearance—" continued the other.

"—and your acquiescence."

"Until our trails bring us close again."

They bowed again and made their slow way out of the hall. Tyr waited until they had left, then walked to the door to watch them.

They walked without speed for a ways; then, as if they couldn't stand it any longer, they leaped forward. No longer upright, they moved swiftly on hands and feet, loping like misshaped dogs, their bags and tails floating behind them.

Their leap into the trees startled Tyr. He quickly lost sight of them once they'd reached what he realized was their natural habitat.

Tyr knew better than to think that all the gods would be as such, living in trees instead of on solid earth. They were gods of men. He'd seen the temples their followers had built.

Yet he still had hope that he could use their obvious differences to his advantage.

Tyr waited on the edge of the clearing alone, facing the bright sunshine. The wind blew warm this close to the other land. Some of the other gods—Loki, Freyja, Thor, Frey, Idun, Heimdal—stood inside the ring of trees behind him, in the shadows and out of reach of the light. They were gathered too far away to help Tyr if this Itzanam attacked him, but they would be able to avenge him, if necessary.

A man-shaped creature broached the opposite side of the open field, stepping through the impossible shadows the trees cast. His appearance changed in the dappled sunshine, as if he were both man and beast. He looked from one side to the other as he walked, talking as if he argued with others.

Was this what the two messengers had hinted at? That this Itzanam always traveled with unseen advisers? Whatever Itzanam's hidden companions said, Tyr saw it was useless. The god stopped arguing and walked forward, out of the shade and into the sunlit clearing, moving more surely than death.

The jungle crept up behind the old man. Tyr felt the bristling presence of trees closer to his back as well, though he refused to turn around to see. Then the forest pulled back. Its shifting appearance matched the ancient god, whose face took a different mien with every step.

Tyr realized suddenly that change was the essential nature of things in this place. In the northlands, little ever changed. Season flowed into season, year into year. He wasn't used to such rapid change—none of the Iselanders were. This pace of change would alter their lives, their relationships—even their souls would be different. Too different. Fear skewered his core. His missing hand ached.

Consciously, Tyr brought his pride forward. What did it matter to him how these other gods lived? They would keep their own high holidays and unchanging nature, keep themselves pure and apart. He kept his gaze forward and flexed his left hand. If they couldn't negotiate how to live with words, his sword would ensure his bargain.

As the elderly man drew closer, the shifting slowed.

His face settled into a single expression, ancient and leathery, sketched with lines of grieving. His left eye appeared and disappeared, the empty socket darker than any cave. White hair covered an unusually long, sloping forehead. Tyr wondered at the deformity, if the shape, was natural, or if during some myth or contest the god's head had been pressed too tightly. A large headdress full of colorful curling feathers sat poised at the peak of Itzanam's skull and flowed down his back. The great face of a bird made up the front of the headdress. Itzanam leaned heavily on a walking stick, his left leg missing. Occasionally a ghost of it appeared—sometimes as smoke, other times, as a serpent.

"Greetings, Itzanam, Father Iguana," Tyr said when the other stopped in front of him, recalling the first title the messengers had given their god. Though Tyr didn't know what an iguana was, he hoped that using the familial aspect of the other god's name would be the safest.

When the old man smiled at the greeting, his sharp pointed teeth shone.

Tyr wondered if male iguanas ate their young.

"Greetings, Tyr, one-handed judge," Itzanam replied. "You are much as my vision of you indicated you would be."

Tyr heard the echoes of Itzanam's actual phrase under the words he understood. "Vision" could have been translated as "smoke-cleared trail," "serpent's path," or "blood-won sight." Poetry filled this god's native language. Tyr longed to hear their myths.

"What did your dream tell you?" Tyr asked, his words sounding harsh after the fluid syllables of the elder god.

"Wealth I saw, guided by your judgments. A joining of your strength with ours, the many against the one, followed by a time of merging, when five hearts beat together."

The old man's eyebrows grew bushy, and the stick he leaned on elongated and sprouted carvings. Tyr didn't step back, even though he recognized the face now in front of him. This Itzanam was similar to Odin. They shared the same essential characteristics: a gray god, cunning and magical.

Tyr didn't understand all of what he saw, why this god now manifested with a face like Odin's, what Itzanam was trying to show Tyr of his visions. What Tyr did see was clear enough though.

If they followed the course of Itzanam's vision, Odin would come, possibly brought by other groups of Iseland humans. Tyr would not regain his dominance over the Æsir. The usurper would rule here as well.

"No," Tyr replied, refusing Itzanam's mien. Tyr had not traveled this distance, followed his believers across the whale's path, just to be lost again.

"Other trails lead from this meeting," Itzanam said, shrinking back into his former self. Light blazed from his one eye. "Some are much worse," he warned.

Tyr smirked. "For you, old man? Or for me?"

Itzanam merely shrugged.

Like Odin, Itzanam's shifting nature hid a trickster's heart. Tyr felt his own features grow stern.

"We will remain within the fjords and open fields of Ásgard for a while, mingling not." Tyr thought he perceived a fleeting expression of distaste in Itzanam at the mention of the empty places that Tyr loved. "Let us see which trails remain clear, and which close, from this talk."

Itzanam nodded. "There is wisdom in what you say. Are the others bound by your oath?"

"You would have me swear to this course?" Tyr asked. Ghosts of tingling pain flashed across his missing hand, memories of other promises, misgotten oaths.

He also remembered Loki asking him not to make

any promises. Briefly, Tyr wished he'd fallen for the half god's ploy, that he'd bound himself to the trickster, so that his word wouldn't cause him so much pain again. Though he didn't trust Loki and his poisoned face, Tyr trusted this Itzanam less.

"No, no, your say-so is good enough," Itzanam replied.

Echoes of Itzanam's native language reverberated under the words Tyr heard. The word for "oath" had actually been related to something with blood, while "say-so" was a word without weight, a thing that was spoken without being written down or bled over. The persistent references to blood concerned Tyr. He wondered briefly how his human followers fared.

Before Tyr could ask about conduct for his men, Itzanam continued. "I agree that we should not move as hastily as our lands have joined. Yet I would learn of your beginnings, as well as show you ours."

Tyr nodded. The world of the Æsir had to be remade from time to time. The gods walked the paths of creation, back to the time before time, to when the great cow Audhumla had licked off the ice to uncover the first giant, so the earth and the stars could be formed from his bones. This renewed the land, as well as strengthened the bonds between men and gods. Tyr assumed that the same must be true in this foreign place.

"Let us start sharing myths not from the very first day, but from later, near the end of the first days," Itzanam proposed.

Tyr nodded. It was a safe place from which to begin, when there was still creation magic in the world, but not as much. They would learn a little about each other.

"I suggest one of your people come watch the Hero Twins, Hun Ahaw and Yax Balam, trick the Lords of the Underworld into allowing the coming of day."

Now it was Tyr's turn to smile. "Loki shall accompany them," he said. Let these twins match wits with the scarred one. Tyr would bet on Loki any day.

"Until our paths cross again," Itzanam said, bowing his head.

"Until then," Tyr replied.

The old man made his way back across the clearing, shifting in the setting light. Tyr wondered what wisdom the old man had gained by the loss of his eye and his leg, and if that wisdom had done him any good.

Tyr drew an uneasy breath as he turned around and walked toward the familiar, comforting trees of his homeland. What sacrifice would Itzanam demand of Tyr if he made a rash promise to the old god?

Somehow, Tyr knew that Itzanam would ask for more than just his hand.

Chapter 3

Tyrthbrand and Lady Two Bird spent the morning in a strange garden, full of bright flowers and half-buried statues of grotesque, inhuman gods. Using colors, they taught each other their words for true and false, then using the statues, wishes and prayers. Lady Two Bird laughed more freely that morning, surprising Tyrthbrand. She almost looked pretty as well, or maybe, in the three days since they'd arrived, he'd just grown accustomed her flattened skull and the strange bird tattoo that covered one side of her face. Even her pointed teeth didn't bother him as much when she smiled.

Then Lady Two Bird tried to explain the collection of small stones scattered in between the striding feet of Ix Chebel, the protector of the island. She wanted him to add a stone to it as well. Eventually, Tyrthbrand understood that Lady Two Bird didn't expect him to pray to the goddess, but to make a wish. She found a brown pebble shot through with quartz for him to use.

The light in her black eyes when she looked up from the ground seemed otherworldly. The skin across his shoulders twitched in response. He regretted not listening to Ketil that morning and so wore only a simple blessed pouch around his neck for protection. Did she have some kind of magic in her blood?

Tyrthbrand didn't want to make a wish, and told her that he didn't want anything as well as he could;

he was on solid ground, and the crew was making repairs to the ship. Life was good. Making a wish now felt too much like tempting the gods, throwing raw meat in front of a rabid wolf.

But her face fell, and Tyrthbrand reprimanded himself for his inflexibility and acquiesced.

He closed his hand around the stone while he thought. If he was truthful with himself, he did have a wish, one he always carried with him now, as Thor bore his hammer.

Tyrthbrand wanted to be his own man, to make his own mark, change his own *wyrd*. He didn't want to always be seen relying on his god. When they'd been at Leif's camp, Illugi had told him time and again not to listen to Hrolf's insults and insinuations, but they still worried at him. A man's reputation was as important as his word, and he wanted to be known for his deeds.

With trepidation, he did as Lady Two Bird instructed: he cradled the pebble in his palms and considered his wish, letting it fill his mind. It struck him as funny to ask a foreign goddess to release him from his own gods, but he knew of no way to rid himself of the brand around his wrist.

After another moment he carefully placed the warm pebble beside the others—one wish among many— and comforted himself with the belief that it wouldn't be heard, that the goddess would pay attention to her own people first, and since he hadn't called upon Tyr, his own gods would ignore him.

Lady Two Bird shivered when she saw the Iselanders pull out their long knives and engage in a mock battle. She didn't pay much heed to the men or their technique, beyond noticing that they fought together like a pack of wild dogs—they had no finesse, no strategy, unlike the Itza warriors.

Their weapons however, captured her attention.

More than once, they saved the Iselanders. They were incredibly strong—she'd seen a tall blond man catch a blow with his blade that would have shattered even the toughest obsidian. While some of the success of the Iselanders had to be because of their greater height and reach, their weapons were magically powerful. They glinted in the afternoon sunlight, shiny like a reflecting pool. The brilliance nearly blinded her.

When the battle was over, she walked up to Tyrthbrand. "May I see it?" she asked, pointing to the sword.

He obviously didn't understand what she asked for, so she pointed to the sword, then to her eye. He nodded and held the sword out for her inspection.

She ran her fingers gently across it, not knowing how to ask about the strange angular markings carved close to the hafts, so unlike her people's own glyphs, or the long channel cut along its length. It wasn't as pretty as her own people's jade weapons, but it still held its own kind of deadly beauty.

Tyrthbrand then handed her the sheath that the long knife lived in. She marveled at the soft fur that filled it. A strange orange color stained it and marked her fingers when she touched it. It smelled like water sometimes did when it came from a well deep in the earth.

"What is this?" she asked, pointing to the discoloration, showing him her fingers.

Tyrthbrand replied with something unintelligible. Lady Two Bird asked him again. He pointed to the sword, then to the sheath, then to the sword again. Lady Two Bird shook her head no, to show that she didn't understand.

Finally, Tyrthbrand picked up a water jug. He poured a little onto the sword, caught one of the drops with his finger, then used it to dampen the fur-lined sheath.

A touch of orange color appeared, as if he'd wiped away a drop of blood.

Lady Two Bird reached out to touch the strange long knife again. A tingling through her palm told her everything she really needed to know.

The blade was important. It was what she'd seen in her vision. She marveled at how such a small thing as a knife could change the world.

Or was it the material—the blood stone—from which it had been made? Her people only knew stone.

She let the men talk while she looked again at the Iselanders. Other parts of their outfits appeared to be made of the same substance, like the pin and loop that held the knife sheath. It seemed as big a part of their culture as stone was to hers.

She spent the rest of the afternoon trying to get the Iselanders to talk about the strange material of their weapons, this "Ja-ron." They wouldn't trade outrageous amounts of food and supplies for even a single spear tip. The only knowledge she gained was that it wasn't a single rock found only in their faraway mountains. Instead, they had made the blood stone from a collection of different rocks melted together.

Like from her vision, stones born in fire.

Her people must have that recipe.

Lord Six Sky approached Lady Two Bird after the Iselanders had gone to their camp on the beach. They walked for a while in silence down one of the paths between the temple buildings, their respective attendants following at a discreet distance.

"Ugly, aren't they?" he finally said, using the most casual form of the words.

Lady Two Bird couldn't help her smile. She'd known Lord Six Sky since childhood. He never treated her with formality. They'd played together as children, and he'd complained more than once that it was difficult for him to call her a lady when he still remembered her with mud in her hair. Though he was dedicated to Ekchuah, he'd accompanied her on her annual pilgrimages to Tzul for many years, his guards providing her extra protection. He justified it as a trading venture, and though he always brought back magnificent goods, everyone knew the true purpose of his journey.

"The foreigners? Or their weapons?" she replied, still thinking about the blood stone.

Lord Six Sky grunted and looked thoughtful for a moment. "Why so interested in weapons all of a sudden?" he asked.

"Why—what—I don't—"

He shushed her, chuckling. "You should keep your thoughts to yourself."

"I don't understand," Lady Two Bird said. Of course, she hadn't told Evening Star that Ix Chebel had spoken to her. She was certain Evening Star wouldn't believe her, even though it was the high priestess' duty to investigate all prophecies. Besides, Evening Star seemed to hate the foreigners, and would have automatically decried Lady Two Bird's seeing as false because it involved them.

Lady Two Bird had decided to tell Lord Smoke Moon when they arrived at the City of Wells. Her brother-in-law would believe her. She didn't look forward to the tests he would put her through to prove the truth of her prophecy, but she would rather do it there, in the city of her birth, where she had the protection of her temple, than here.

"So when would you like to return to the city, my lady?" Lord Six Sky asked, teasing.

"Don't try to distract me," Lady Two Bird said. "I want to know what you meant."

"I think we should leave in three or four days," Lord Six Sky continued, seeming to blithely ignore her hard stare. "It will take us about two weeks to get back, so we would be back in time for the Celebration of the First Baptism."

Lady Two Bird sighed loudly, then shared a smile with her old friend.

Still teasing, Lord Six Sky said in a pompous, lecturing voice, "There are many miles between here and the City of Wells. We must be vigilant." He dropped back into his normal tone. "I've heard—never mind," he interrupted himself as one of Evening Star's attendants came up.

"It is time to gather together for prayer and sustenance," she said haughtily.

Lord Six Sky laughed. "In other words, it's time for dinner."

He shared one last smile with Lady Two Bird as they followed the girl. Lady Two Bird wanted to ask him what he'd meant, what he'd wanted to say to her, but she knew better than to do it in front of one of Evening Star's women. Had he heard some rumors about them being attacked on the road?

Just before they got to the hall where everyone had gathered, he took her arm again and said quietly, "Just be careful, all right?"

Lady Two Bird nodded. She hoped that she'd be able to speak to Lord Six Sky after the evening meal, but Evening Star had asked for more guards around the Iselanders, and Lord Six Sky had had to go see to his men, and so they didn't have a chance.

That was the last time she saw Lord Six Sky alive.

Later that evening, Tyrthbrand stared into the fire on the beach and thought of his wish, as well as the things he would do as his own man. No longer beholden, he could take pride in all that he accomplished. He envisioned farms and fields back in Iseland listed in the books of the province under his name, which he knew without a doubt that he had earned. He could hire his own skald, who would sit in his hall during the cold winter months and weave songs and stories of Tyrthbrand's mighty deeds. He saw herds of cattle, acres of fine cloth, horses, and barrels of fish all bearing his family's mark. Mead the color of Freyja's fine hair overflowed his cup.

The thunk of a rock landing in the sand next to his knee only drew Tyrthbrand halfway out of his dreams. He peered at the stone dully, thinking at first that it was the same pebble he'd used for making his wish—that the goddess had rejected his plea and had hurled the rock back at him. It took him a long moment to recognize the small whirling sound, the whisper of flight, the muffled fall of a large body.

"To arms!" Tyrthbrand yelled as he stood. He turned from the fire and peered into the dark trees beyond the sandy shore, cursing his lack of night vision. He grabbed handfuls of sand and threw them at the fire, cutting the light, making his men harder targets to find. The Iselanders could rely on their ears and noses in battle, like any good hunter.

Tyrthbrand scrambled away from the fire, then rolled and ran a few paces before he paused to listen. The Itza had given Tyrthbrand and his men a demonstration of their skill using their leather thongs to hurl rocks at targets. Another rock missile thudded into the sand to Tyrthbrand's left. He felt the smile of the wolf overtake his features. The Itza and their leather throwing strips didn't have the distance Orm and Brand had with their bows, but they did have a deadly accuracy.

That is, if they could see their targets.

Shouts broke through the dark night. Tyrthbrand pulled his battle fire from its home. The oiled lamb's wool that filled the sheath made the drawing silent, while at the same time, kept rust from eating at the sword's metal. He and his men had had problems with blood tears collecting on their blades from the extreme wetness in the air on the island. Even while at sea, they hadn't had so much rust.

Tyrthbrand ran into the trees, off the beach, out of

the open. The Itza wouldn't be able to use their distance weapons in the heavy brush. Grunts to his left indicated men fighting. To his right he heard more people engaged, a proper sword storm, so he went that way, his blood already pounding.

In the next clearing, just beyond the trees, the torches had not been extinguished. Two battles raged. The Iselanders fought off one group of Itza, while Lord Six Sky's men engaged another.

Tyrthbrand stayed on the sidelines for a moment, watching the fight, looking for other traps, determining the best place to join in. Iseland swords and spears met Itza spears and daggers, with cursing and yelling from both sides, as well as the occasional joyful shout of laughter from the Iselanders. Blood dripped across both leather armor and war paint. The hollow sound of wood on wood, from where spear met spear or shield, underlay the battle like drums.

Tyrthbrand didn't understand everything he saw in the battle, but one thing did become clear: his men were losing. Their iron swords gave them a huge advantage over the Itza stone knives, splitting shields and spears like they were kindling. However, it wasn't enough. Each one of his men defended themselves well, but the Itza didn't fight as individuals. Both the Itza and the Iselanders had been reticent to demonstrate too many of their weapons or fighting techniques, so Tyrthbrand hadn't seen how the Itza fought in an actual skirmish. They had obviously trained as a unit, harrying his men from all sides, pressing every advantage. Plus, there were too many of them. If their weapons had been equal, his men would have all been captured by now.

A good leader led his men into as well as out of battle—he gave them a safe return from strife. If his men died here, there would be no proper burial. Tyrthbrand didn't want to have to kill his men a second time when they returned to haunt him as angry ghosts, clamoring for the lifetimes they'd lost.

More Itza poured from the trees into the clearing. Lord Six Sky and his men were falling under the waves of the attackers. Tyrthbrand whistled four times—one long tone, followed by three short yips— a piercing sound carrying through the growling of the men and the ringing iron storm. The signal meant retreat.

He whistled again, then a third time, trying to slice through the bloodlust that had overtaken his men. He knew they didn't want to pull back once they had engaged in battle. Yet need left him with scant choice.

Finally, Illugi added his voice to Tyrthbrand's signal, shouting out, "Hod's darts are on us! Pull back!" He took a step away from the melee.

The men seemed to recognize their peril. Even a wolf pack retreats when it's overwhelmed. The men turned, back to back, and as a revolving circle, moved toward Tyrthbrand. He whistled yet once again, directing their path, before he joined in the slaying. The Itza before him, though they had heard his calls, seemed surprised to be caught between two forces. Excitement thrilled through his bones. His sword might not be as sharp as the black blades of his opponents, but his arm was strong, and his battle fire burned bright.

Tyrthbrand fought his way to his men, then together they made their way through the trees and to the beach. The skeleton crew he'd left on the *Golden Tree* shouted encouragements, jeered at their attackers, and laughed at everyone's antics. The Iselanders on the boat knew better than to join in the fray—they needed to protect their only means of escape. Arrows slammed into the attackers on the beach, now that Orm and Brand had clear shots.

The assault of the Itza doubled once the Iselanders

reached the water. Obviously, they didn't want their prey running off. However, it was equally obvious that they'd never fought in waves. Though the heavy leathers of the Iselanders made them awkward, they knew how to judge the swells, and used the water to float up, as well as push their attackers down.

"Raise the sails!" came Einar's clear command over the water. A surge of power flowed through Tyrthbrand's arm as he hacked down another opponent. They must be near the boat. He didn't know how many men he'd lost. He'd left enough on the ship to ensure being able to sail her away even if every man on shore died. He didn't understand why the Itza hadn't attacked her first. Had they been so sure of their victory?

A harsh barking laugh came from the shore. Tyrthbrand wiped the water from his face and looked back. He could barely make out the dark forms, but he recognized the voice as well as its tone. Thorolf Mosturbeard had killed another man with his ax. A hissing curse, calling a man's human ancestry into question, reached Tyrthbrand. It made him smile. Only Snorri the smith could fling so many insults—enough to make the battle a *flighting* contest—while overwhelmed with battle.

Tyrthbrand could see his men now, their height distinguishing them from their opponents. Without a doubt, they would soon fall under the swell of Itza coming from the trees.

A stone thudded into the wooden ship at Tyrthbrand's side. He looked up at the boat next to him, then back to shore. Einar's voice called out again. Hands pulled at Tyrthbrand, trying to draw him aboard. After a moment, he pulled away from them.

The echoing sound of the stone hitting the wood had reminded him of his wish. To do battle on his own, to make a name for himself. He saw the path clearly, though the eye of the night was less than half open. He didn't have to call on Tyr, beg his god for more favors. This was his chance. He could save them, his men. If he moved to the left here, then swung his sword that way, then pushed with his shield . . . Without thinking of the dance he performed, Tyrthbrand found the solid ground of the shore beneath his feet, the waves retreating from his legs.

In another moment, he'd joined the skirmish. Laughing now, the battle rain fell from his sword and swirled up his arm. "To me!" he cried, drawing his men out. He could do this. They would come to him and then to the ship and then . . .

. . . The ominous whirl of leather slipped over the sound of Tyrthbrand's harsh panting. His right leg buckled under the impact of the stone hitting his thigh and he fell to one knee. Illugi tripped over him and hit the ground with an ominous crack. Thorolf's laughter stopped abruptly. Another sharp rock slammed into Tyrthbrand's arm, making him drop his sword.

Joy disappeared as the tide turned. No choice now, no chance for escape. The Iselanders faced their deaths. The men that still stood fought on, snarls and growls instead of laughter intermixed with the Iselanders' cursing now. Tyrthbrand struggled to his feet, determined to stop at least one or two more of their attackers with his bare hands, regardless of the throbbing and weakness in his injured arm. Sharp pain cut across his left bicep. Tyrthbrand struck the spear of his attacker out of the way with his forearm, reaching for the Itza with his other hand. He pulled the man forward, his raised knee crushing the other man's vulnerable groin.

The singing sound of a blade through the air forced Tyrthbrand to step back. He turned as he did so, angling his body so when he stepped forward he was under the man's guard.

The other man swung out with his shield. Tyrthbrand easily sidestepped it. He reached for his opponent's wrist. Burning pain exploded across his shoulder, then the back of his skull, from an opponent he hadn't seen.

Tyrthbrand fell to his knees. He prepared himself to surge up again, as relentless as the sea, when a shield hit his chin, knocking him onto his back.

For a dazed moment, everything went black. Tyrthbrand shook his head, trying to clear it. He sank his elbows into the sand to push himself back up when a long spear nicked his throat. Tyrthbrand reached for it, but the warrior above him stepped on his arm, pinning it to the ground. Tyrthbrand found his other arm also trapped. He tried to raise his torso, but he couldn't move.

Silence rang in his ears. The clash of swords and the cursing of men had fallen off. The battle was over.

He tensed, waiting for the spear at his neck to bear down, to remove his head from his neck. Hands wrenched his arms out, then together, over his chest. Rough twine bound his wrists together.

Tyrthbrand continued to struggle even after another blow to his head made the edges of his vision darken. Capture was ten thousand times worse than dying during battle. He didn't have any choice, though. He'd misread the signs of the stones. He'd refused to call on Tyr, wanting to save his men on his own. Now they all would pay the price of his pride.

A hoarse shout woke Lady Two Bird from her tangled dreams. Another followed quickly, along with the sounds of fighting.

They were being attacked. By whom? Was this what Lord Six Sky had been trying to warn her of? Or had the Iselanders turned on their hosts?

Seven Waterlily came in with a lit torch and looked at her lady with wide, scared eyes.

"What's happening?" she asked.

"Shh," Lady Two Bird replied, going to the window and sticking her head out, into the darkness. She strained to hear any sound that might explain their situation. She made out the rumbling laughter of the Iselanders, as well as the terse calls of the Itza soldiers, ordering formations and units.

She also heard counter orders from other Itza guards.

"Quick," she said, turning from the window. "Help me dress."

Seven Waterlily looked at Lady Two Bird as if she were too much under the influence of Ix Chebel, and had gone mad.

Lady Two Bird hurriedly explained as she crossed to the chest holding her dresses.

"I think that our fellow city-state, Cobá, has decided to flex her muscles. I must be ready."

Seven Waterlily nodded slowly. If, indeed, the attackers were from Cobá, the largest city-state rival to the City of Wells, it meant only one thing for Lady Two Bird: death through sacrifice. Royalty flowed through her blood, making it precious. They would hold her prisoner, torture and bleed her for weeks, possibly months, until the auspicious day for her sacrifice made itself known to the priests. Cobá wouldn't try to ransom her: she was a sister-in-law, not sister, to Lord Smoke Moon; she had no children or husband of her own in court to demand her return; and she was dedicated to a goddess, still a virgin—which made her blood doubly sweet, almost like a second royalty.

Lady Two Bird covered her plain dress with a stole dyed royal purple, with green, yellow, and scarlet feathers woven into the skirt. The jade earplugs she wore in her earlobes had patterns of butterflies carved in them, a symbol for warriors as well as for rebirth. She completed her outfit with a necklace of rounded turquoise beads, each one the size of a baby's fist. She was properly dressed for a ceremony—or a sacrifice.

They waited, tense, straining to hear any sound that the night carried to them. The deep laughter of the

Iselanders still underlay the muffled screams and harsh *thunks* that told of the fight. Lady Two Bird knew that the foreigners wouldn't last long. They might have formidable weapons and be fierce fighters who obviously found joy in battle, but they were just a few.

Slowly, the sounds of the confrontation died. Lady Two Bird found herself holding her breath, struggling to catch a word or voice that might tell her what had happened, or, more important, who had won. Shouted orders carried over the false peace, but too dimly for her to understand.

Echoes of sandals on stone approached the blanket covering the entrance to her chambers; then, without pause, three guards carrying torches pushed their way in.

Lady Two Bird felt her marrow freeze. These were not Lord Six Sky's men. However, they didn't look like men from Cobá either. Their skin had the weathered look of soldiers who spent all their time in the jungle, between cities. Though their chins had been depilated, the hair on their heads was wild and stood in spikes around their faces. After another look, Lady Two Bird realized it was deliberate, as if to make their heads bigger. They wore simple loincloths and high-backed sandals, and carried their shields in one hand, spears in the other. Each bore a painted red hand on his chest, overlaying the swirling colorful designs of his war paint.

Before the guards could approach her, Lady Two Bird stood. She would go to her fate with dignity, under her own power, looking her best.

Two of the men came forward, as if to take her arms. Lady Two Bird glared at them and said, "Your assistance isn't necessary."

Startled, they stopped short.

"Don't we need to go?" Lady Two Bird asked, trying to keep them off balance. Without waiting for an answer, she started for the door.

One of the men stepped around her quickly so as to be in front of her, while two stayed behind her. Without another word the group swept out the door. Lady Two Bird didn't have to turn around to know that Seven Waterlily followed. It wouldn't be proper for her to be without any attendants, even if she was walking to her death.

The group walked through the silent temple complex. Unfamiliar guards, also with red hands painted on their chests, stood at the entrances to all the buildings, along the walks, as well as at the intersections. They watched with cold, hard eyes. Lady Two Bird kept her chin up, not certain who she was trying to impress with her steady pace, but still determined not to let her fear show. Only one or two dark patches stained the white stones that made up the walkways. Lady Two Bird presumed this meant most of the fighting had occurred outside the main area, not that only a few people had been killed.

A multitude of torches covered the great pyramid that hulked at the northernmost part of the complex. The priests and priestesses used it only for sacrifices on the most holy days. The guards led Lady Two Bird that direction. That the attackers had set their "court" on it was arrogant as well as within their right—a symbol that they had won the battle.

More than one crumpled body lay at the foot of the great pyramid, dark pools of blood watering the ground. Lady Two Bird could only afford a quick look at the bodies. It appeared that the attackers had sacrificed at least two of the Iselanders, a few of Lord Six Sky's guards, and Lord Six Sky himself.

Lady Two Bird composed her features, willing them to be set in stone as she continued forward. She would mourn for her friend later. At least he would have a chance at rebirth, having been sacrificed on the temple stairs.

But why had the attackers killed him so quickly?

She could understand the murders of the guards and the Iselanders. They were warriors. The attackers needed to demonstrate their power, their victory, by making a sacrifice of at least a few of their opponents immediately. However, Lord Six Sky's death made no sense. He actually had royal blood on his mother's side—he hadn't married into royalty as she had. They should have saved him, savored him. She pushed the fear of her own sacrifice to the back of her mind. She had to think clearly, not let herself get mired in the dark, stifling ground that awaited her.

Just because her goddess had spoken to her of change didn't mean that she would live to see it.

On either side of the grand stairs stood a row of guards holding torches. Lady Two Bird walked up alone, proud that her body was still youthful enough to step gracefully up each steep stair. Two men, strangers, sat on benches on the first platform located halfway up the stairs. They still wore the body paint of battle and had the same red hands and strange hair of the guards.

Lady Two Bird paused several steps below them. She bowed deeply, then rose to her full height and walked the rest of the way up to the gathering on the platform. She wasn't some foreigner or peasant. Though she had no power in this situation, they had better treat her well, particularly if they meant to kill her that night.

Evening Star stood behind the two men in a place of honor, not bound. A scribe sat at the two men's feet, ready to record every word, as if this were a real court.

Maybe six or seven Iselanders lay bound in ropes on one side, naked, but alive. A priest covered in the blue paint of sacrifice stood behind them. Lady Two Bird's feelings of dread multiplied. She had to save the rest of the foreigners, to delay their deaths some-how. She couldn't save their lives—nor did she want

to—they'd given those to the gods the moment they'd
set foot on the island, whether they'd realized it or
not. But there were useful, as well as useless, sacrifices. Killing all of them now would be stupid. Not
when the Itza had so much to learn from Iselanders.

If nothing else, they needed to learn the secrets of
the blood stone. Lady Two Bird was certain it was
what she'd seen cutting through the jungle. She had
to obey her goddess' wishes and delay their deaths, if
only for a little while, even if it meant her own.

A crier stepped from behind the pair on the thrones
and made the introductions. Lady Two Bird didn't
recognize their claimed heritage. They didn't come
from any of the important families in the City of
Wells, though the crier tried to imply that they did.
The formality both calmed her and worried her. On
one hand, it was a ritual with which she was familiar.
But on the other, if they were going to sacrifice her
they would follow the entire procedure, complete with
tearing out her fingernails, scoring her back, and drawing her blood out of her tongue before they killed her.

Waterlily Jaguar sat on the left, in the weaker position, symbolizing night. A splotchy birthmark on his
left cheek resembled a paw print, a powerful sign from
the gods. On his right cheek was a similarly shaped
tattoo. His face bore a dark and hidden expression.
Like the guards, he had a red hand painted on his
chest. Lady Two Bird didn't allow herself to react
when his eyes swept over her. He held himself with a
military readiness, and his entire being shouted power.

No natural mark of the gods distinguished Jeweled
Skull, even though he sat on the right, in the stronger
position of the day. He didn't need it—Lady Two Bird
realized with a start that the pair of them were twins.
Jeweled Skull had probably been born first, which was
why he sat in the more influential seat. He looked at
Lady Two Bird with undisguised contempt.

"You are familiar with the foreigners' language,

yes?" Jeweled Skull demanded as soon as the crier stepped back, before Lady Two Bird could make her greetings. The rudeness surprised her.

"Yes, I am," Lady Two Bird said. She stood proudly before them, ignoring the glare Evening Star shot at her.

"Have they spoken of the White Hands?" Jeweled Skull inquired.

"Lord, they are—" Evening Star stopped herself when Jeweled Skull raised his hand to silence her. Then he gestured for Lady Two Bird to continue.

"Sir, we learned each other's words for colors only this afternoon." In the garden. When she'd convinced Tyrthbrand to make a wish. Had he inadvertently called this attack upon them through that simple action? Could it have been only a few hours ago?

"What do you know of their gods?"

"A little. They follow a god named Tyr, a one-handed god, and Freyja, a goddess who fights with one of their long knives, and—"

"Why did they come here?" interrupted Jeweled Skull. He twitched on his seat, like a young boy impatient with his lessons.

"Trade. They follow Ekchuah in their hearts." Lady Two Bird knew she took a risk by declaring them for one of the Itza's own gods, but she needed to do something. She had to delay their sacrifice.

"Hmm," said Waterlily Jaguar, speaking for the first time. "I would have thought they followed the Bacabnob."

Lady Two Bird barely controlled her shiver of fear. Waterlily Jaguar's tone was mild and sophisticated, and more deadly because of it. He was like a poisonous snake hidden among flowers.

"Why the Bacabnob?" Evening Star asked.

Even Lady Two Bird wanted to roll her eyes. She'd known the new high priestess was not as well trained as she should have been, but Lady Two Bird hadn't

considered that it might be because Evening Star
was slow.

"Their size, my dear. They're like giants," came
Waterlily Jaguar's quiet rebuke.

"Have they spoken of the end of the world?" Jeweled Skull asked.

An ominous silence fell over the platform. Regardless, Lady Two Bird felt like laughing. An instant
later, she decided to follow her impulse, and let her
laughter ring out.

"My lords," she said when she finished, using the
honorific form of the address, not the one that implied
they were royalty, "we've learned each other's names,
the names of gods, countries, colors, numbers, and a
few basic words, such as 'ship' and 'now.' Speaking of
the end of the world would be a bit much at this
point, don't you think?" She didn't bother to hide her
mocking smile.

"Lady Two Bird—" started Jeweled Skull heatedly
until a hand on his arm interrupted him. The twins
looked at each other for a moment. With a nod, Jeweled Skull sat back and Waterlily Jaguar began.

"You are, perhaps, correct in your assessment that
it's too early to discern their true purpose. And yet,
because of the dire nature of the prophecy, we need
to make haste."

"Which prophecy?" Lady Two Bird asked. She had
to know, even though admitting ignorance in this audience could prove to be the wind that toppled her
from the temple stairs to her death. Had the stones
spoken to someone else? Had the goddess given a
complete vision of the foreigners to a more worthy
receptacle?

Waterlily Jaguar looked at her sharply for a moment. Lady Two Bird felt like an agouti caught out in
the open, far from her hole. But the hawk passed over
without swooping down on her, and Waterlily Jaguar
began reciting:

"Bloody is the face of this k'atun.
Even hidden jungles bring no relief.
The jaguar and quetzal flee, sacred ponds burn.
The White Hands come,
Bringing plague to those who touch them.
Bound is the mouth of the people,
Until the children forget their native tongue.
No corn will grow, and the fields become dust.
Women try to make bread from tree bark, grass and
  rocks,
And die.
Our temples host foreign gods,
Even the priests lose the counting of days.
Forests march over our cities,
Hiding our shame and the lucky dead."

Lady Two Bird caught her breath at the horrific
picture Waterlily Jaguar painted. She'd never heard a
prophecy like this before. Of course, the world might
stop at the end of the great count, but that was just
part of the natural order of things—like the summer
passing into the rainy season. A new people coming
and destroying everything, though, was beyond her
imagining. These weren't like the Puuc invaders.

"And the Red Hands . . . ?" Lady Two Bird asked,
wanting to be sure she knew the answer.

Waterlily Jaguar nodded, a small smile of approval
touching his lips. "We are dedicated to fighting the
White Hands."

"Lord Smoke Moon doesn't recognize the prophecy," Lady Two Bird said, almost to herself, looking
down. A plan coalesced in her head. "And Lord Kan
Boar, the military ruler of the City of Wells, doesn't
acknowledge your troop, does he?" she said louder,
looking up, not challenging Waterlily Jaguar, but Jeweled Skull.

Before she could be interrupted, Lady Two Bird
hurried on. "So when you bring the Iselanders to the

City of Wells for sacrifice, they'll be forced to reckon with you, won't they?" If she could talk them into this, she could save the Iselanders for a while, as well as herself. She didn't know for how long, but she felt, in her bones, that every day helped. That she was following her goddess' wishes by keeping them alive.

Jeweled Skull looked startled, as if he hadn't considered the possibility of not sacrificing them immediately. Waterlily Jaguar just looked smug, as if this had been his plan all along, but he hadn't bothered to articulate it.

"They must be sacrificed now," Evening Star said. Everyone ignored her.

"Will you aid us? With an audience? Bring us before the rulers of the City of Wells?" Waterlily Jaguar said. Now his voice was as oily as his look.

This was the real reason why they'd brought her before them—not to talk of prophecies or foreign threats, nor to kill her, but to promote the Red Hands troop and their cause. Waterlily Jaguar might be the younger brother, but he was the real power of the two. And he'd kept his influence hidden by using her.

She took a deep breath in relief before she said, "Yes."

Waterlily Jaguar permitted himself a small smile, while Jeweled Skull grinned fiercely.

Lady Two Bird was very aware what she was giving them—guaranteed free access to the powers of the city-state. She didn't want to ally herself with the Red Hands. However, she had to, if she was to save the foreigners long enough to learn from them. The sacrificial knife was still only a hand width away from her own heart, but it had been stayed for the time being.

Also, if the Red Hands troop did prove to be a force to be reckoned with, aligning herself with them might not be a mistake. She could possibly regain some of the power she'd lost with age, not just be remembered as Smoke Moon's sister-in-law.

After the twins dismissed her, Lady Two Bird walked down the stairs and back to her room, barely cognizant of her surroundings or of Seven Waterlily following her. It wasn't until she was safely ensconced inside, alone, that she let her knees buckle and her gasping fears tear through her lungs.

She'd survived another night, pushed off the long darkness.

But for how long?

Regardless of how her old bones ached, Lady Two Bird made an effort to walk as fast as the others did. She didn't want to admit that this might be the last time that she would be capable of making this trip to the coast and back. It wasn't that long a journey—only two weeks or so. The trip over the water, from Tzul to the mainland, wasn't bad at all, and took only half a day. But the constant walking, for many hours every day, grated on her. Her joints complained every night, and even the pepper medicine that Seven Waterlily worked into her knees and ankles would eventually lose its potency.

Lady Two Bird fanned herself as she walked. Dazzling white stones made up the raised road they followed. The jungle pressed in hard on all sides, dark, ominous, and loud. They'd been traveling for two days, primarily in the mornings and evenings, but they still couldn't avoid the inland heat, every step taking them farther away from the cooler sea winds. Blistering, heavy air bore down on them. The Iselanders, though clothed only in sandals, suffered the most, as much from biting insects as the temperature. Lady Two Bird had tried to ease their suffering, even going so far as bribing one of the guards to bring them more watered-down wine to drink, but there was little she could do.

They looked different without their heavy clothing, their boots, and their weapons. Their skin grew red and blistered in the sun. Strange designs of birds, exotic trees, and unknown animals decorated their arms. Though they still towered over their captors, they all seemed shrunken in on themselves.

Jeweled Skull called a halt at the next small roadside temple. The Red Hands leader had sidled up to Lady Two Bird more than once during their journey, but she found she had little to say to him. She helped them only through necessity. She'd discovered that while they believed in the gods, they didn't understand how their aspects changed. It was all part of the pattern, of the call and response, that they didn't understand. Lady Two Bird felt that change in her marrow now. All she had to do was to look at the drooping blond heads of the Iselanders to know. Her faith was stronger than ever, strong enough to carry her through all the untamed jungle that lay ahead, old bones or not.

It hadn't been difficult to find out what had happened to Lord Six Sky. According to Evening Star, he'd become too influenced by Ix Chebel, caught in the storm and unable to find the rainbow. Lady Two Bird knew that Lord Six Sky hadn't gone insane, but there was nothing she could do about it now. It was her word against the head priestess', and Lady Two Bird knew her place well enough.

She still missed his cheery conversation as they walked, and his protective strength. She hadn't told the twins that he'd been worried about the journey back to the City of Wells—she didn't know if the attack he'd feared had been them.

Lady Two Bird stood to one side while Seven Waterlily and the two attendants Evening Star had insisted Lady Two Bird take with her prepared a bench for her in the shade. She knew that the two were spies, reporting not just to Evening Star but also to the twins, and would make trouble for her once they reached the City of Wells. Lady Two Bird didn't care. She made use of them and treated them like slaves when she had the chance. She'd even made them wait on Seven Waterlily the previous evening when she'd complained of being tired.

Once her attendants had placed cushions and a rug on the bench, Lady Two Bird sank down gratefully. She made the two attendants stand in the sun and fan her, while Seven Waterlily brought her a cup of a honeyed corn drink and stayed in the shade behind her. The drink wasn't cool, but it still refreshed her.

Lady Two Bird felt as though the heat had melted her bones and sapped all the strength from her muscles. Still, her mind darted from one thing to the next, like a greedy hummingbird, making it impossible for her to rest; from stones trembling under her fingers to hulking rock threatening to crush her, Lord Six Sky's unnecessary sacrifice, and her own inevitable death, the fate of the Iselanders and the death of her people. After finishing her cup and refusing more, she nodded at her attendants. They parted so she could stand and walk between them.

"Wait here," she told them. They dropped to their knees, nudging forward a bit so at least their heads were in the shade. Seven Waterlily knelt behind the bench.

Lady Two Bird wandered around the cleared courtyard of the small temple, sticking to the shade as much as she could while she walked, though it brought little relief from the over-bright sun. Exhaustion rolled through her, making her steps sluggish, but her thoughts niggled at her like ants crawling in her blood, forcing her to move.

Statues were scattered in the various nooks: Ekchuah, Itzanam, Feathered Serpent, even Ix Chebel. A World Tree stood in the center. The roots represented Xibalba, the underworld, the crosspiece had a carved mouth on either end symbolizing the celestial monster that blazed across the night sky, and a quetzal perched on the top, a messenger of the gods. Lady Two Bird had noticed the Iselanders looking askance at a World Tree they'd passed by earlier. She'd wondered why, and resolved to ask them why the symbol of the cross made them so anxious.

The statue of Ix Chebel in the clearing stood with her feet together, spindle in hand. Her brightly painted cloak dropped past her knees, though the hem of it on the right side was just stone: many fingers touching it, asking for luck and only mild storms while they traveled, had worn off the paint. Scattered stones covered the platform the statue stood on.

Lady Two Bird checked the ground around the pedestal, intending to pay her respects, but she didn't find any loose rocks there. Strange—the earth almost looked as if priests had raked it clean—though no one actively tended these statues. She walked back up to the road, picked up a tiny white quartz pebble, then returned to Ix Chebel.

Lady Two Bird wasn't planning to make a wish with the rock. She'd made enough wishes for a lifetime. She would never again force another to make a wish either—she still wondered what it had been that Tyrthbrand had asked for.

For a moment, she considered dropping the stone, not placing it carefully, so that she wouldn't receive any more messages from the goddess. A part of her was still scared of what had happened, so many men dead, her own life hanging off a faulty hook, being at the mercy of the Red Hand troop.

With thumb and two fingers, Lady Two Bird rested her rock next to the right foot of the goddess, making sure to brush her hand lightly against the statue as she put the pebble down.

Images of men wearing rags and carrying cruelly gleaming weapons poured over her. They wove their shields together like soldiers even though they were dressed like bandits. She watched in horror as they slaughtered the Red Hands troop. Both of the twins fell quickly.

A cawing macaw drew her attention away from the main battle. In her vision, Lady Two Bird turned and watched the attackers kill the helplessly bound Iselanders. Bright sunlight glinting off a blood stone blade blinded her as Tyrthbrand fell.

Lady Two Bird couldn't help but blink. She drew a hand up to shade her eyes and found herself standing in the jungle again, in front of the statue of her goddess.

The message from the stones was clearer than any she'd ever heard of. Soldiers, probably from Cobá and dressed as robbers to hide their true origins, would attack them that afternoon.

The twins, all the soldiers, as well as the Iselanders would die if Lady Two Bird didn't help them.

Glancing around the temple yard at the resting group, she started to plan.

Morning just meant heat with more light, and Thorolf Mosturbeard was tired of it. Tired of the shame of being a prisoner, tired of looking forward to little but darkness. By the balls of Tanngrisni, he was not going to give in.

So that morning, their second day of traveling the white roads inland, when the guards came to rebind his hands, he held a piece of rope between his fingers and laughed, working hard to make his voice loud and booming.

"Hey, Illugi, you see these ropes?"

The other Iselanders all seemed dazed and didn't look up at the noise. But after a moment, Illugi turned his head and squinted at him.

"A small man's dream," Thorolf said, holding it with one hand while jerking it with his other, much like how a man might pleasure himself.

Illugi choked back his laughter for a moment, then let it ring out. The sound seemed to wake the others.

They blinked and looked around slowly, stupefied in the early-morning haze.

The guards yanked Thorolf's hands together harshly. Illugi stood, letting himself be bound. "You have to wonder who they're actually making safe by tying us up this way," he said in a conversational tone.

"Can't be their women," Snorri the smith replied. "If we're all tied up, how can we defend ourselves against the randy whores?"

Ketil the priest laughed at that. "I'm a religious man, I am. Always ready to wield 'Tyr's sword' if asked."

"Or demanded," Thorolf added.

Vigfus smiled up at him—probably the first time the boy hadn't looked like he was crawling over dead puppies in days. Tyrthbrand didn't join in though, and his mouth still curved down, as if he'd swallowed something bitter.

Nothing for him then. The world could be a sour place, yes, but Thorolf was all for finding what sweetness he could.

Tyrthbrand sat with his men, head bowed, sweating. He didn't know his body could leak so much water and still feel this hot. His swollen fingers felt like stupid sausages attached to his palms. Even though the Itza hadn't given them much to eat during the three days they'd been on the road, the heat stole any hunger he might have felt. His lips distended over slimy teeth. He longed for even a warm breeze against his wet skin—anything to cool him down just a little.

He couldn't join in the others' banter. Not because their guards forbade it, but because his guilt overwhelmed his tongue.

Though his men didn't blame him for the Itza capturing them, Tyrthbrand knew it was his fault. If only he hadn't made that stupid wish with the stone. If only he'd been paying more attention that night, not daydreaming of going back to Iseland with riches that would never come. If only he hadn't insisted on pushing on, leading the *Golden Tree* farther down the coast, chasing fool's gold. If only his pride hadn't drawn him away from his god's favor.

The shuffling of the guards closest to Tyrthbrand alerted him that their rest was over. The midday break had ended and it was time for the evening portion of their journey. He foolishly hoped that the night would bring some coolness with it, though he knew it wouldn't.

A loud feminine giggle drew his attention, as well as the guards'. They all turned toward the young girl who came up to them smiling and holding out a broken fan. Tyrthbrand had seen the girl before—she was a servant of Lady Two Bird—he thought her name was Seven Waterlily.

"Tyrthbrand."

Lady Two Bird had approached the prisoners from the other direction, opposite to where all the guards now looked. He heard a quiet thump next to his feet. "*Taka steinn*," she said in a low voice. Then she clapped her hands and strode forward, her tone scolding. The servant looked appropriately chastised and the women walked away.

Take stone? Tyrthbrand looked down. A chipped black rock now lay at his feet. He shook his head and laughed quietly, bitterly. This god-ridden place and its damned rocks. He blamed no one but himself for their current predicament. He hadn't called on Tyr when he should have during the battle, and now he wouldn't. Never again. His pride would kill him, kill them all, he knew. He'd abandoned his god.

He refused to call on Tyr only to find out for certain that his god had abandoned him in return. He also didn't want to call on his god and find that he couldn't save himself, his men, on his own, either.

Be careful what you wish for. Tyrthbrand knew that now. More than he'd ever wanted to.

What should he do? Should he pick up the abominable stone?

What else could he do? Nothing, just continue his own damnation. He'd escaped the *wyrd* of being a farmer—but left it for what?

Tyrthbrand scooted forward a little, until his legs were over the rock, then reached down with his tied hands and picked up the long black thing. He nearly dropped it as soon as he wrapped his fingers around it. It felt slippery and cold, like chipped ice. It was also sharp enough to slice through flesh. It wasn't just a stone. It was from a volcano, a piece of a black-mountain glass, chipped into a knife.

Illugi bumped into Tyrthbrand's shoulder. Tyrthbrand nodded without looking up, understanding the signal. The blond had seen the stone and had probably also heard what Lady Two Bird had said. The nudge indicated he was ready for whatever Tyrthbrand deemed appropriate.

Tyrthbrand shook his head in disgust. What was he supposed to do? Even if they freed themselves, they were miles from the coast—no water, no clothes, no way of escaping.

But maybe flight hadn't been Lady Two Bird's plan. Maybe she just wanted to grant them a warrior's death, in glorious battle. Maybe she didn't want to see them slain like cattle.

It didn't matter. Tyrthbrand slowly got to his feet when the guards tugged on his ropes, palming the knife, keeping it hidden between his hands and his belly. All his men would be free by the time they stopped that evening, when it grew too dark to travel.

Then it would be time to die.

A muffled roll of drums jerked Tyrthbrand out of daze he'd been walking in. The sun had just dropped behind the trees, bringing no relief from the tyrannical heat that swaddled them all. Illugi caught his eye, then bumped into Thorolf, who then started shouting and cursing. They'd all agreed that as soon as the sun left the sky they were going to break free, or die trying.

Then men poured out of the jungle, charging toward their captors with weapons drawn and shields raised.

Lady Two Bird had moved closer to their group only moments before. She didn't seem surprised by the attack. Tyrthbrand wondered again if she was some sort of seeress. She certainly looked like something not quite human. He'd wondered about her connection to the gods. Could she be marked as he was?

He'd also seen her act haughty with the leaders of the Red Hand group. Had she made some secret deal and planned this raid with another lord, as Evening Star had?

The Iselanders had all had a turn with the knife before the attack, sawing through their ropes enough that a quick tug would break them. Tyrthbrand had never thought he'd be so happy to have his hands free. He shook them a few times, flexing them into claws. Being naked didn't bother him as much as being weaponless. He solved that matter quickly, running into the back of the guard closest to him, knocking the man over, and grabbing his spear. After a brief struggle, he also had the man's shield.

He heard Thorolf laughing behind him, calling out in his deep voice, "Time to go hunting, little brothers!"

"Tyrthbrand!" came a high-pitched shout.

He swung his head around. Lady Two Bird pointed urgently at the ill-dressed attackers and made a gesture like wielding a spear. It was suddenly obvious to Tyrthbrand: she'd freed the Iselanders so they could defend her people, their captors, as well as themselves.

Tyrthbrand shrugged in return. He couldn't guarantee he could hold off the righteous wrath of his men. He would do his best, though, to keep her safe. He owed her that.

"Shameful, bandits attacking a good party like this,"

he said in his loudest voice as he feinted a blow to the head of the closest attacker. The man stupidly raised his shield, and Tyrthbrand skewered his exposed belly.

"Bandits?" Vigfus took up Tyrthbrand's thread, appearing beside him to relieve the downed attacker of his weapons. "They must do a good trade then," he said as he hefted the shield.

Thorolf called out, "And they're well trained."

When two of the bandits joined to assault Tyrthbrand, he understood what his companion had meant. The pair worked in tandem, one harrying their chosen victim while the other attacked, always keeping him off balance.

Being limited to an Itza spear made it more difficult for Tyrthbrand to fight his opponents. The solid metal of his sword would have instantly cut through their shields and their wooden armor. The elements in his favor were his greater reach and his despair: they wouldn't take him again, at least, not while he still breathed.

Ketil came to stand beside Tyrthbrand. The shorter man aimed his blows low, while Tyrthbrand focused on head and arm strikes. Then Ketil and Tyrthbrand separated, forcing the bandits to turn, so they could no longer fight together but back to back. Finally, they were evenly matched, one-on-one.

Tyrthbrand roared a wordless challenge and stepped closer, banging his shield against the other man's. At the same time, he choked up his hold on his borrowed weapon. He used the spear like a sword, getting in under the other man's defenses, slicing his arm, his chest, and finally, his neck. Ketil dispatched his own attacker at the same time, and the two Iselanders found themselves grinning at each other like foolish boys. It felt so good to fight, to be in charge of their destiny, instead of being prisoners, even if they held foreign weapons in their hands.

"Tyrthbrand," called a feminine voice, low and urgent. He swung around. No one threatened Lady Two Bird, but she seemed agitated. She pointed to the side.

The spear shower still raged beyond where the Iselanders had defeated the group that had attacked them. A large troop of the false bandits encircled the remaining Itza. From where Tyrthbrand stood, it was impossible to tell who was winning, though he suspected it wasn't his former captors.

His grin grew wider. His lady . . . *his* lady? Since when had he started thinking possessively about her? He shook his head. It didn't matter. She understood. About dying. Like a man.

He called his men to him with a whistle, then, howling like a wolf, led them into battle.

The attackers didn't have a chance. The Iselanders rolled over them like breakers over rocks. Though there were only six of them, their attack was unexpected, and their ferocity overwhelming. Tyrthbrand and his men fought as if skalds would sing about every stroke for decades to come. Blood flowed over the white stones, and while the laughter of the Iselanders rang out, the bandits cursed.

Though the tide of the battle had turned the moment the Iselanders had joined in, the attackers didn't realize it until it was too late. Three tried to get away as their companions fell. Whirling stones from the Itza dropped two, while the third sank to the ground and onto the spear impaling his chest—thrust all the way through his body from the force with which it had struck his back. Thorolf Mosturbeard quickly picked up another spear from one of the fallen bandits when the Itza turned to stare at him.

Silence descended suddenly. Tyrthbrand whistled again and his men formed a circle, back-to-back, spears outward, facing their captors, determined not to let the Itza capture them again. They were naked and bleeding from minor cuts. The adrenaline of the fight began to drain away, the exhaustion from being denied food, clothes, and respect filling them.

But they were also armed, alive, and desperate.

Lady Two Bird's voice broke through the stifling tension that gathered between the two parties. She spoke with a scolding tone. Waterlily Jaguar replied, his lazy drawl failing to hide his anger and excitement. Tyrthbrand didn't know what they said, but the leader obviously wanted more blood. A group of the soldiers collected the bandits who had been only slightly injured, and not killed, during the attack, binding them in the same white and black ropes that they had used to bind Tyrthbrand and his group. The priest came up, blue paint recently applied, to take them.

One of the few words Tyrthbrand understood came from Jeweled Skull: sacrifice. Probably what they intended both for the Iselanders as well as the few remaining bandits.

Lady Two Bird still argued.

Illugi spoke quietly. "Stay sharp."

Tyrthbrand nodded. His body ached with exhaustion, but the hostility permeating the clearing held him upright. Lady Two Bird pointed to the ones they had captured, numbering them, then to the six Iselanders. Tyrthbrand wondered if she was trying to talk the twins into a different sacrifice, the bandits' lives for theirs.

Lady Two Bird shouted out to Seven Waterlily and the verbal battle descended into icy silence. The girl ran from the group, then returned, clutching one of the Iselander swords with both hands. Lady Two Bird drew it from its sheath and argued some more with Jeweled Skull. Finally, he seemed to acquiesce. Lady Two Bird nodded, clutched the sword in both hands, then walked toward Tyrthbrand.

Pride rippled through Tyrthbrand's chest when Lady Two Bird, with a look that would shrink the gonads of all but the bravest men, forced her way through the ring of Itza surrounding them and made her way to Tyrthbrand. She touched the sword blade with one hand, then looked up.

"Trade. Live. For blood stone."

Lady Two Bird's face had never looked more alien. In the light of the setting sun, the stones in her teeth glittered and her elongated forehead made her eyes black and serpentine.

But carved snakes decorated Tyrthbrand's sheath, the hilt of his dagger, and covered his arms from wrist to shoulder. Snakes could protect as well as kill.

"Snorri?" Tyrthbrand asked.

"You get me the ore, and I can smelt as well as forge you anything you like," boasted the smith.

Tyrthbrand turned and stared. "Don't make me an oath breaker."

The smith's arrogance trebled. "I've gone through the entire process. From rock to sword."

Still, Tyrthbrand waited.

Snorri sighed. "Maybe it *was* only once," he finally acknowledged. "But I wouldn't make you foreswear yourself."

With a nod, Tyrthbrand acknowledged the smith's pledge. "Illugi?" he asked next.

"I know how to look for the areas where we should find ore. As well as the type of charcoal we'd need to make a hot enough fire to smelt it," the blond asserted.

"I could help with that too," Vigfus chimed in. "Ottar, my father, traded in everything at one time or another, so I've learned the difference between grades of ore."

Tyrthbrand smiled at the younger man, encouraging him. Vigfus always stood in the shadow of his legendary merchant father. It was good to see the son finally claiming some of the skill his father had taught him.

"It isn't right," Ketil spoke up.

"What isn't right about it? Live now, pay later, and only if we have to," Thorolf said, staring hard at the smaller man.

"I will *not* be an oath breaker," Tyrthbrand said.

Thorolf nodded. "I'm not asking you to be. But when the next ship comes, maybe we'll renegotiate the bargain. That isn't breaking your word."

Tyrthbrand tightened his lips. Thorolf was right. Changing circumstances, or shifting power, often altered trade deals. But this . . . He had to be true to his word. Lady Two Bird had some kind of sight. She'd proved it at this battle.

He'd turned away from his gods, but he was damned if he'd turn away from his own word.

He laid his left hand—the hand without Tyr's mark—on the blade. He looked up at Lady Two Bird, into human eyes resting in an alien face, and said, "Yes," binding his honor, his pride, even his soul, in the bargain. No matter what the future brought, he was now hers.

Lady Two Bird could barely hold back her crow of triumph. She'd seen the shifty looks Tyrthbrand's men had given her as well as each other. They would only hold to the bargain as long as necessary, and would endeavor to alter it as soon as possible. However, she knew Tyrthbrand hadn't. He'd given his word, and would never break it.

Why had this foreign man bound himself to her? He was exceedingly ugly, a single step removed from a beast, with his hairy face and hulking stature. His tattoos wound around his arms like vines around a tree trunk, marking him as something that lived closer to the jungle than the city.

Maybe it was just his nature to be faithful, like a hunting dog. But the fight she'd just witnessed had proved that he wasn't truly an animal. His spirit had

shown through his ferocity. Even Waterlily Jaguar had
spoken with grudging respect after Lady Two Bird had
pointed out that the foreigners had saved his life.

He wasn't her equal. He never could be, unless he
was adopted into a royal family. Possibly, though, he
could be her friend as well as her charge.

She needed to reward him for his good behavior,
to show him that he'd done the right thing, train him
as she would a child. She ordered washing water for
them, to clear away the white and black stripes across
their torsos that marked them as prisoners. She also
insisted that their clothes be returned, or at the very
least, some kind of covering for their bodies. Not that
they necessarily needed it. The Iselanders seemed to
have grown in height with weapons in their hands, and
stood unashamed of their nakedness.

Lady Two Bird touched the blood stone again. The
rightness of her actions filled her. This was the sharp
stone that destroyed the jungle that Ix Chebel had
shown her in the first vision. It was essential to de-
feating the coming of the White Hands, to prevent the
destruction of her people. When the White Hands
came, they too, would have the blood stone. And only
similar weapons would defeat it.

And *she* would bring the knowledge of it to her
people. It would be *her* name written on the temple
stairs, given over to immortality. Every time she'd
stroked the strange stone, it had brought her relief
from her fear of the dark places. Now she knew why.

Another small temple lay just beyond where the
false robbers had ambushed them. Jeweled Skull declared that they should journey only that far that evening, though the sun hadn't completely set and they
could have gone farther. He asked Lady Two Bird to
attend the sacrifice of the bandits. She graciously
agreed. Waterlily Jaguar had insisted that Tyrthbrand
attend as well. Lady Two Bird didn't know why, but

it didn't matter. She'd delayed the sacrifice of the Iselanders for yet one more day.

Tyrthbrand pretended not to understand what the
guards wanted him to do with the paint and headdress.
He struggled and cursed every time they came close
to him. He continued to ask for Lady Two Bird. Eventually, they fetched her for him.

After greeting her as best he could, Tyrthbrand
asked in his language, keeping the words simple,
"Ocean. Boats. Return there. Yes?" He and his men
had agreed that it would be best to make their way
back to the coast to see if the *Golden Tree* had
come back.

"Maybe," Lady Two Bird replied in the same
language.

"Ah," Tyrthbrand said, as if he finally understood.
He held his arms open and let the guards with the
paint start to put swirling glyphs on his chest.

"We need to return," Tyrthbrand said, putting as
much urgency as he could into his voice. Lady Two
Bird might not grasp the meaning of all his words, but
he knew she'd understand the tone.

Lady Two Bird seemed to be thinking, lightly biting
her lower lip, her eyes far away.

"Maybe," she finally responded, using his language
still. She said something else in her tongue, something
Tyrthbrand didn't understand, but he assumed it
meant she'd try.

That was all Tyrthbrand could ask for.

It made sense to Lady Two Bird to go back to the
coast. More Iselanders meant more knowledge. Plus,
it meant an additional delay before they reached the
City of Wells. She could spend the time learning as
much as possible of the Iselanders and their language.
What little knowledge she'd gained from the Isel-

anders made her greedy for more. Their lives were so different. They weren't tied to the land like her people, and they used the remarkable blood stone as casually as her people used plain stone. They even used it for cooking pots.

Bringing the blood stone to her people would change their lives beyond giving them better weapons. And it was the will of the gods.

She decided to use that angle—more information—when she presented the idea to the twins, after the sacrifice, which had been set to coincide with the final rays of the sun slipping beneath the earth.

Lady Two Bird covertly watched Tyrthbrand as the six bandits had their fingernails torn off, their backs scourged, their tongues removed, and finally, their hearts torn out. He seemed more curious than disgusted, and he didn't try to speak once she'd instructed him to be quiet. She wondered how bloody his own people's sacrifices were. They had much to talk about later. He conducted himself with dignity though, and that pleased Lady Two Bird.

Finally, the priests recited the last prayers, the guards escorted Tyrthbrand back to his men, and Lady Two Bird approached the twins, escorted by Seven Waterlily. They still didn't give the proper greetings, barging instead right into questioning her.

"The Iselanders have brought up an interesting point," she said, stretching the truth of the conversation she'd had with Tyrthbrand. "Their ship should be returning for them soon. They'd like to go back to the coast to greet their men."

Jeweled Skull sputtered. "No—no—we can't. We must get the White Hands to the capital."

Waterlily Jaguar looked thoughtful.

"It would be easier to prove their threat if you had more of them with you," Lady Two Bird said. She paused, seeing how they took her meaning. Though she'd argued for the Iselanders' lives earlier, now she made it clear that she was still willing to sacrifice them. "Besides, foreigners who are here can't go back to their people, then return. With enforcements."

The twins nodded as one. Lady Two Bird knew she walked an unmarked and dangerous path. If a prophecy didn't occur, was it because it had been prevented? Or hadn't it been a true prophecy in the first place? While the twins were desperate for legitimacy, was it worth the welfare of their people, the people they claimed to protect?

"We will think on—" Jeweled Skull said.

"No, we should go back," Waterlily Jaguar interrupted. "I mean, we wouldn't want to upset any other plans you might have, right?"

"Excuse me?" Lady Two Bird asked, terror forming in the pit of her stomach.

"I saw the ropes that had tied the foreigners. They'd been cut. Someone must have given the Iselanders a knife. And the guards said you weren't surprised when the attack came."

Lady Two Bird kept her smile, pretending that Waterlily Jaguar didn't intimidate her. She knew she'd done the right thing in saving not only the Iselanders, but all of them, from the attack. Ix Chebel would be proud. Now Lady Two Bird just needed to keep her heart in her body.

"I have no idea where the Iselanders got the knife from. They're clever and grabby, like monkeys. As for the attack, if your guards had been doing their jobs instead of paying attention to me, maybe we wouldn't have lost so many men."

She let her smirk grow as nasty as Waterlily Jaguar's. "Isn't it easier for the guards to blame the attack on someone else, rather than on their own lack of ability?" She filled her next words with as much sarcasm as she could. "Someone whom the Cobá priests would bleed and torture for months?"

Jeweled Skull sat back, eyes wide. Obviously, he

hadn't considered that possibility. Lady Two Bird
couldn't read Waterlily Jaguar's expression. She continued, using a reasonable tone. "You know how we
treat traitors. We lie to them, get what we need, then
sacrifice them. Why would you expect the Cobá to be
any different?"

Waterlily Jaguar nodded. "It's good that you understand the realities of diplomacy."

Lady Two Bird bowed her head and waited, confident that they would listen to her. She had no fear of
sacrifice from them, at least not for the immediate
future.

The two brothers looked at each other for a moment,
then Jeweled Skull nodded. "We will go back—" he
started.

"My lords!" A guard came running up, breathless.

The twins rose immediately, gripping their weapons.
The guard dropped to his knees and bowed low.
"Cauac Sky approaches."

Lady Two Bird observed the twins carefully at the
announcement. She had no idea who Cauac Sky might
be. Jeweled Sky seemed to be looking forward to
seeing him, while Waterlily Jaguar, less so. She
stepped back and to the side, hoping they would forget
her, wanting to witness this reunion.

A phalanx of guards came marching up. A tall man
walked in the center of them. His bald head reflected
the torchlight. An arrogant nose perched below deep,
hooded eyes. He moved with the strength of a man
used to traveling, with an easy gait, though the wrinkles on his face and the way his skin hung on his
bones proclaimed that he had passed well beyond
youth. Black outlines of red hands covered the scarlet
cloak he wore. Tendrils of a priest's blue paint flowed
up his arms and around his neck. A geometric dia-
mond pattern of dots tattooed his face.

"My sons," he said as way of greeting as the guards
parted and the man approached the twins. They

moved forward and dropped to their knees as one to receive his blessing. He settled his hands a little way above the two heads and chanted a short prayer. The two surged up when he finished. Jeweled Skull took his arm and led him to the bench, fussing over him, making sure the man was comfortable.

"Sir, how are—" started Jeweled Skull.

"What are—" said Waterlily Jaguar at the same time.

"And who do we have here?" the man interrupted, peering at Lady Two Bird. She didn't like the hungry way he looked at her, like a merchant appraising a piece of jade.

Waterlily Jaguar held up his hand when Jeweled Skull would have spoken. The younger twin motioned forward a crier, who performed the formal introductions between Lady Two Bird and Cauac Sky.

Lady Two Bird listened to Cauac Sky's titles with interest. He wasn't royalty, but his father had been a respected trader, one that even she'd heard of, Nine White Sack. It wasn't unusual for a third or fourth son to be dedicated to the gods and become a priest instead of following in trade, particularly for a successful man. She wondered if Cauac Sky been the one who had seen the prophecy.

When the crier finished, Lady Two Bird stepped forward. "I greet you, Cauac Sky," using a neutral form, not to an equal, but not to an inferior either.

"And I welcome you," Cauac Sky returned, using the form of an inferior to royalty. "I am more pleased than I can tell you to find you traveling with my boys." His look had become more calculating as well as hungrier.

"Are these your sons then?" Lady Two Bird asked. She hadn't heard his name mentioned in their titles when she'd first heard them. While her order didn't allow children, other orders did.

He shook his head, looking both embarrassed and

proud. "No, I have no children of the body. But they follow my heart." He smiled fondly at the twins. Jeweled Skull returned the smile. Lady Two Bird noted that Waterlily Jaguar's smile was less sincere.

Cauac Sky looked expectantly at Jeweled Skull, who stumbled over his explanation of Lord Six Sky's growing madness, Evening Star's invitation, and the exciting discovery of the foreigners. When he got to the part of Lady Two Bird's involvement, and possible introductions at court, Cauac Sky's gaze returned to her.

Though his eyes burned bright enough to glow, Lady Two Bird felt icy rain trickling down her spine, freezing her in place.

"You've seen the White Hands. You know what they can do. It must have been preordained for you to be on Tzul when the foreigners arrived. For you to have a complete cycle together."

Lady Two Bird didn't reply. She recognized that her destiny was tied to the Iselanders'. But it was to bring the blood stone to her people, not to be born, live, and die with them, as Cauac Sky's phrasing implied.

"So when we return to the City of Wells—" he started.

"My lord, we were discussing going back to the coast when you arrived," Lady Two Bird interrupted. She forced herself to stay relaxed and smiling when he turned to her, though a part of her wanted to run and hide. His eyes held a ravenous look now, as if he were a priest of Cimi, the Lord of the Underworld who never had enough blood to sate him.

"The roads are far too dangerous," he admonished. "We must make all haste with our precious—cargo. Too easily do precious flowers and exotic birds get spoiled while traveling."

Jeweled Skull started telling the story of their attack by the Cobá bandits while Lady Two Bird and Cauac

Sky continued to stare at each other. She'd heard the threat under the priest's solicitous tone and nodded once, to show that she'd understood that he didn't want her to make any trouble. She was old, and everyone knew that this was possibly the last trip she would be able to make to the coast. Plus, accidents befell travelers on the *sak behs* all the time. No one would think to question her death.

After Jeweled Skull finished his account, Waterlily Jaguar spoke up. "Are you sure we shouldn't return to the coast? These foreigners believe more of their people are coming—"

"Go back? Nonsense," Cauac Sky overrode the warrior. "The threat of the White Hands is upon us. These foreigners have come. Who knows how many more are behind them? We must warn the city. At once."

Waterlily Jaguar looked as if he might say more, then bent his head in acquiescence. Lady Two Bird wondered if he'd spoken up because he agreed with her, or because he was contrary by nature and liked to try to thwart Cauac Sky when he could.

"I shall take my leave, then," Lady Two Bird said. With a quick nod to the men, she turned and walked away.

Lady Two Bird felt as though burning eyes watched her as she made her way past Cauac Sky's guard. It wasn't until they could see the Iselanders' camp that she felt as though she could breathe again.

She'd met madmen like Cauac Sky before, through the service of her lady, men who hungered for blood like a god, though usually they were not as well mannered. He didn't need a reason to kill her—the act of killing her would be reward enough for him. She never regretted the loss of Lord Six Sky more than at that moment. The Iselanders would protect her—if they could.

She hoped that the promise of the introductions at court would be enough to stay Cauac Sky's hand, and vowed to be extra careful in the meanwhile.

Einar fought the great steering oar as he tried to tack again, bring them closer to shore. The winds howled around him, laughing at them as it batted the *Golden Tree* between the waves. Piercing rain drove into his aching legs and waterlogged arms.

After the attack on the beach when they'd lost Tyrthbrand and the others, the *Golden Tree* had slunk along the coast, just out of sight of the land so as to avoid another attack, while they'd tried to make repairs at sea. They planned on going back and rescuing the others once the ship was fixed.

The clear warm waters had let them dive under the keel and check the great planks.

There had been too much damage for them to risk the open whale road. They would have to make landfall to finish their repairs.

They snuck in, closer to shore, and spent a few days looking for another harbor in which to hide.

Just as they rounded the northern edge of the land, the storm struck without warning, as if it had been waiting to ambush them.

As the curtain of water fell around them, Einar made a run for the shore. The wind battled him with cunning and skill. Einar knew their luck had run out, that the gods no longer favored them, but he endured. He cursed the storm, cursed Tyr, and cursed the fate that had brought him to this damned island.

He never saw the rocks the ship dove onto.

With a sickening creak that sounded over the roaring wind, the ship began to list. Einar shouted at the men, telling them to try to swim for shore. A huge wave smacked the boat and the *Golden Tree* turned onto its side abruptly.

Einar struggled to hold on to the steering oar, but

the next wave shook the ship like a dog with a bone. He slid under the water, surprised at how cold it was under the surface. He tried to kick, to make his way back to the air, but the seaweed below him seemed to grow hands. A massive darkness swirled beneath him. It was not the net of Ran, the goddess of storms, come to gather him and take him to her hall, but a place full of tree roots and dying men.

Cursing his fate once more, Einar went under, into the foreign hell that would hold his soul forever, without hope of rebirth.

The storm that rolled through the camp that night would have made Thor proud. It came from the sea, and carried scents of fish and fresh sand. The thunder shook Tyrthbrand's bones, and at one point, the lightning had been so constant that the clearing where they camped had been lit up as bright as day. Trees creaked and toppled from the wind. Rain lashed their skin, froze their limbs. For the first time since landing, they were cold.

The next morning, Tyrthbrand found Illugi examining some of the debris the storm had left just beyond the perimeter of the camp. The ground was littered with branches, some as wide as Tyrthbrand's waist.

"Can you help me test the weight of this?" Illugi asked. "I want to see how strong the winds must have been to blow down such a sturdy tree." With an effort, Tyrthbrand shook off his dark thoughts. The tall blond bent down to pick up one end of a large branch. "Can you get the other side?"

Grunting, Tyrthbrand hoisted his end waist high, keeping his hands away from the sharp end, where the wood was twisted and jagged, as if it had been tortured before being pulled apart.

After a moment, Illugi nodded, and lowered his end. Tyrthbrand followed suit.

"I don't know if even the great hall of Harald Fine-

Hair would have stood up to such winds," Illugi confided to Tyrthbrand as they walked toward the center of camp.

Thorolf's booming voice greeted them as they returned. "Bah—look at that pack. It's ruined." He gave them a huge grin as they came closer. "My wife couldn't have laid waste like this. Not even if she'd discovered me with her sister."

"If the wind had been blowing in the right direction, the *Golden Tree* could have flown home last night," Ketil added.

Silence crashed down on them, more harsh and cold than the rain from the storm. Flying home was a wonderful fantasy. They all knew that the ship couldn't have survived such a storm, not injured as she had been. There really was no point in going back to the coast now.

They all bent their heads and mourned.

Just before they started walking again, Tyrthbrand knelt down next to the road. The *sak beh* gleamed in the morning light. The stones seemed undisturbed. The storm might have rearranged them, switched one with another, but it was impossible to tell. Their path inland would continue unabated.

Tyrthbrand gathered his men, then encouraged them to move closer to Lady Two Bird and her attendants. The new priest scared her. Though she hadn't said as much, she'd tried to teach him the word for "accident"—and he'd assumed that if there was a deadly accident, the priest would be behind it.

Tyrthbrand vowed again to protect his lady, keep her alive, healthy. He didn't want to acknowledge how, besides his men, she was the only thing he had left. That, and his word of honor to try to teach her how to make iron.

Chapter 4

Kan's heart sank slowly into the dirt at the center of the perfect circle. Ix could have used Kan's blood to draw a different symbol to represent the world, but he chose the simplest, strongest, and most direct. The other Bacabnob stood in a line behind Ix on the top platform of the pyramid.

After Ix had taken Kan's heart, he'd led them in the ritual of resurrection, healing his brother's wound, making him whole, bringing him back to life. This didn't bring youth—it simply raised him from the dead. Kan hadn't washed the blood from his torso. Instead, he'd used it as the base design for his streaked canary-yellow tattoos, a reminder of the ritual he'd just gone through. The pain he'd suffered, as well as the blood he'd spilled, would strengthen the land. And the land, in return, would continue to support them and provide them with substance and power.

Movement caught the gods' eyes, and they turned their heads as one. A rainbow streaked through the heavens, heading toward the temple. Ix stepped back to join his brothers. If Feathered Serpent had come to chastise them, they needed to present a solid front. He glanced at his brothers, assessing their mood. They seemed to have the same thought, and had all adopted the same stern mien.

The rainbow hit the platform with a dull *thunk*, touching down inside the circle Ix had drawn, just north of the heart. A familiar scent of incense and sacrificed blood rolled out from the apparition, but the sound of unfurling wings didn't follow its appearance. For long moments, no recognizable god manifested out of the bands of color. The rainbow maintained its shape, long and skinny, stretching toward the cloudless sky.

Then it undulated, each line of color fiercely vibrating, and the image at the center shimmered into clarity.

Two large snakes entwined up her raised arms and down her thighs. Colorful wormlike tendrils made up her hair. Splotchy black spots—like jaguar fur—covered all the skin between the coils of the snakes, and her hands were curved into paws. She was obviously not a fertility goddess: her breasts and pubic area were in human proportions.

"Who is that?" Kan asked.

"I've never seen her before," Cauac replied, his brothers nodding in unison.

"And we won't be seeing her soon," Ix added.

The goddess was rapidly disappearing, like a heavy stone falling through a vat of honey. She'd already sunk into the ground up to her calves. Though her back held an unnatural arch, she still dropped below the earth without breaking the circle.

Silence thundered across the platform. The normal jungle sounds of birds, beasts, and bugs stilled, as if all who lived held their breath. Even the wind stopped its whispering. No audible pop occurred when she disappeared, just a quiet sifting of leaves. The dirt rippled, then smoothed out, removing all traces of her passage. After several heartbeats, a macaw called from the jungle, followed shortly by another, and then the insect chorus started again.

The brothers looked at one another, uncertainty reflected on all their faces. The heart still lay in the circle, brightly illuminated by the morning sunlight, partially absorbed. It continued to sink: the land hadn't rejected their sacrifice, but it hadn't desired it either—or at least not as much as it desired the unknown goddess.

A single question echoed, unspoken, between the brothers: why did the land feel it needed to sustain itself by taking not just a whole body, but a soul as well? They'd all felt the goddess slip completely away as she'd been sucked into the earth—heard the earth breathe out her name one last time—Liðami. No one would ever see her again. She'd never be reborn. She was nameless now, like the old gods the Itza buried, who had no followers left to celebrate their holy days.

As one, the brothers turned and marched toward the back end of the temple, away from the sacrifice. Normally, they'd descend the same way they'd ascended, but it didn't seem right to leave in triumph.

They didn't need to talk with each other to know that they were on their way to see Itzanam. They stepped off the last step of the temple and disappeared onto one of the unknowable paths through the jungle, confident that the paths would lead them where they needed to go, as they always did.

Though Loki had heard Tyr tell Itzanam that the Æsir would keep to their side of the joined lands, he figured that didn't necessarily apply to *him*. He went where he chose. Besides, he wasn't going to the places where the other gods lived. They weren't what interested him, though he wouldn't leave if one of them came up the same path.

Loki felt a great compulsion to explore this new land. He justified it to himself as being part of the aspect he wore here—his itching scars made him do it. He felt so tired all the time, just sitting in his hall, doing nothing. He would probably admit under duress, however, that it was just his nature to be curious. Besides, the more he knew, the more he'd be able to defend himself . . . though he didn't know what would protect him from being taken like Liðami. He didn't like to think about it. He'd figure out a plan, escape, and end up on top, as always.

The jungle seemed a very different place at night, compared to when he'd walked it in the daylight. The trees wore heavy shadows. Vines protected the animals hidden behind them, their eyes glowing like jewels scattered across velvet. Loki had explored the dense forests, filled with malignant oaks and evil pines. The danger here felt different, casual, as if taking his life wouldn't have any meaning beyond the blood spilled.

Loki felt he could spend the rest of his days exploring it.

He admired the large, silent cats while they took down their prey, was amazed at the size of the snakes twisting through the branches, and cheered the owls spearing their kill with delicate claws.

After a bit, the path he followed led him to the ocean. He squatted on the beach in the half-moon light, fascinated with the patterns of light dancing on the waves.

As the true dark of the evening gathered, he decided it was time to return to his hall. But first, he wanted to make one last stop. To see the men—and their followers.

He walked to the border path, three steps windward of where he'd passed before. Not only rainbows and Yggdrisil linked the worlds—a god's will, woven with light from ice and fire, moon and torches, could also bridge the shadows that veiled the worlds from each other.

After only a few more steps, Loki stood on the shore of the men's camp. He waited in the quiet, letting the sweet scent of the smoke waft over him. He was near the human world now, close enough to touch, a single veil cloaking him. Only if he were playing a trick would he reach through.

Tyrthbrand was daydreaming, of course. Why Odin hadn't picked such a one, Loki would never know. Tyr had just gotten lucky, the man's imaginings ripe pluckings for any god. His inner strength glowed almost as brightly as the fire he sat beside.

When the first whirling stone came flying through the air, Loki turned it to the side, away from Tyrthbrand, without thinking.

Then froze in astonishment. The scars across his face stung as if the poison still oozed in them.

He shouldn't have been able to do that. It took work for the gods to affect the mortal world, particularly before a human entreated them. Yet he'd just saved Tyrthbrand, without ritual, prophecy, or curse. Just because he'd stepped closer to the veils.

His only fear now was that he'd just fated Tyr's chosen to a horrible death.

Of course, the only way to ensure that didn't happen, at least not that night, was to keep interfering.

Loki couldn't contain the grin that took over his face, even if it did pull at his scars.

Time to have some fun.

He turned into a small shrew and flew up into the trees, above the battle. He didn't try to direct the players in the marvelous game unfolding beneath him, but he did guard Tyrthbrand from the stinging stones.

He justified his actions to himself, telling himself that Tyr would have wanted him to do that.

And if maybe more shadows jumped into the fray, confusing the enemy, well, he couldn't really be blamed for that, now, could he?

Pride filled Loki's chest as he watched the skill of the Iseland warriors. He hopped excitedly from one foot to the other as they fought. Yes, a few died. Not too many though. This was just thinning the herd, leaving only the strongest alive. The Itza were much more interested in killing each other. Tyrthbrand was gathering his men to him now, retreating to the boat, where they could wait out the insurrection, then come back and deal with a confused, possibly weakened enemy.

After Tyrthbrand was in the water, Loki flew out of the trees and into the rigging of the boat. He turned away one last thrown rock as it sailed toward Tyrthbrand's head, causing it to smack against the bow of the ship with a loud *thunk*.

That last stone, however, though thrown by a human hand, had gained something extra as it flew through the air.

When it struck the boat, it also sliced through the veils between the worlds, like a knife through skin. It struck the shadows Loki balanced on, hard enough to cause them to pitch to the side, throwing him off his perch. He flexed his wings and neatly avoided going into the ocean. It took Loki a few moments to find a stable place to land.

By then it was too late.

Tyrthbrand had gone back to shore and been captured.

It wasn't all his fault, Loki told himself as he flew wearily back to the solid land of the gods, away from the borders. That last stone had fallen with the weight of prophecy. Loki had only been trying to save Tyrthbrand's life.

Tyr was still going to kill him.

"Don't worry," Itzanam repeated to the Bacabnob. "This is all part of my vision. I've foreseen it." He nodded in what he knew appeared to be a wise manner, looking down on them from his two-headed jaguar throne. The lights in his hall glowed warmly, scents of sweet incense swirled through the air, and Itzanam maintained a single face. He talked while stroking the cool carved-stone heads on either side of where he sat. The only hint that something was wrong was the murals—they were all unnaturally still in their reenactments of creation.

Itzanam saw the glances the brothers gave to one

another but he remained silent. He didn't know how else to reassure them. Particularly since, while he wasn't exactly lying to them, he wasn't completely telling the truth either. He'd seen a merging of the two houses in his vision, but it had only involved the gods joining, not a fusing of the gods with the land.

What did this portend? Would the rest of them be absorbed? Had this goddess somehow angered the land? Or had she been taken for a reason?

It was a sign of something, he knew. A memory niggled at him, of a time before his latest vision. Something about a hungry *k'atun*, when even the blood of the gods wasn't enough.

"Can you tell us more of your vision?" Muluk, the eldest and usual spokesman for the four, asked.

"Now is not the time," Itzanam replied, distracted from his thoughts. He'd remember it later. "Feathered Serpent wasn't pleased with your disappearance," Itzanam added, directing attention away from himself.

"We needed to strengthen the land," Cauac said. His reddened face conveyed both belligerence and determination.

"He cannot fault us for that," Kan added, his yellow tattoos swirling in tighter knots, covering more of his body.

Itzanam let sarcasm ooze through his words. "Of course not. He's very understanding about deities other than himself receiving sacrifices."

The brothers flinched in unison.

"You might not want to say anything to him about this foreign goddess being taken," Itzanam added. Who knew what interpretation Feathered Serpent would give to it? That it was acceptable for him to sacrifice all the new gods? To take their gifts into himself? He was strong enough already.

He wouldn't listen to any warnings Itzanam might give him that this was another prophecy—particularly not one that came from Ix Chebel.

After another silent exchange of glances Muluk said, "Agreed."

Ix laughed, his black face showing no delight, and added, "Why put ideas of additional sacrifices into his head?"

Itzanam was surprised at how well the brothers understood him. He only hoped that they wouldn't take it amiss when it came time for him to take the one-handed god himself.

The Bacabnob bowed, said their ritual good-byes, and left. Itzanam didn't know what path they would take through the jungle; however, he suspected it would take them to Feathered Serpent rather than to their individual homes.

Itzanam debated making another sacrifice himself: to strengthen the land, to strengthen his ties to the land, to ensure that if the same sort of thing happened to him, that he'd be absorbed by *his* land, and not that empty alien place that was now intertwined with them, like a barnacle eating into the bottom of a boat.

But he also didn't want to see his sacrifice rejected, or see another's accepted in his stead. So he did nothing.

Loki walked through the jungle along an elevated white road, confident that it would take him where he needed to go, even though he couldn't see beyond the next curve. Birds screamed all around him, and insects droned in the rising heat. Wet air slipped over his skin, hot and stifling, tasting of dirty leather. He rolled it around in his mouth, relishing it. Though he felt tired, cool determination filled him, and he couldn't help smirking. He'd always won, no matter what the game, ignoring those occasions when the cost to himself had been great. Loki pushed down on his weariness and didn't allow himself to feel doubt.

The jungle opened onto a gorge, the rocks pale and sharp in the twilight. Dust caught at the back of Loki's throat. Two figures waited for him by the edge, one dark, the other darker. He approached them slowly, as if he were walking up to partially tame horses, giving them time to study him. He knew that leisurely greetings ensured better impressions.

His scars burned that morning, though they felt cool to his fingers when he touched them. They bled his strength away—he always felt weary and old when they manifested. He didn't know why he had to bear them in this place, these markers from the Midgard serpent's poison. But this land demanded his skin be marred, and Loki accepted his fate. He'd seen the tattoos both the native people and their gods wore across their faces, and wondered if the land associated the two, the tattoos and his scars. They seemed a counterpoint to the whip scores branding his back, painful memories of Tyr's rage at his interference with Tyrthbrand on the beach.

The twins wore loincloths and sandals made of the spotted fur from one of the great cats that ruled the jungles. One of the twins had similar patches tattooed on his cheeks. Black, cyan, and sky blue paint covered their chests, necks, and arms. The headdresses they wore made them appear taller than Loki. He'd never seen such long feathers before, scarlet and emerald colored, iridescent even in the gloomy light.

"We have been summoned," said Hun Ahaw after giving formal greetings to Loki.

"We disturbed the Lords of the Underworld with our ball game and they have challenged us," Yax Balam continued.

"What happens when you win this game?" Loki inquired as the twins turned toward the cliff.

"Daylight will come."

Loki tried not to be impressed. All the gods were required to refresh and re-create the world from time to time. It was one of the ways they renewed the earth and connected to men. Loki had done it in the land of the Æsir. He'd only watched the very beginning of it, though. He'd never partaken in it. He wasn't one of the first gods.

He told himself that it didn't matter as he followed them down the twisting path hewn in the canyon wall. In this jostling for power between the gods, he'd always end up on top.

Loki opened his eyes to a twilight sky. The Hero Twins stood before him, along with a crowd composed of peasants and Lords of the Underworld.

"What happened?" he asked, jumping up off what appeared to be a stone altar. For the first time since they had come to the land of the Itza, he felt amazingly alive. The last thing he remembered after going to Xibalba with the twins was going through a series of trials set by the Lords of the Underworld, surviving the Fire House, the Jaguar House, the House of Whirling Blades. The last one they'd been in had been the House of Bats.

"After the monster bit off your head," Yax Balam replied.

"We raised you back to the living," Hun Ahaw said.

Loki put a worried hand to his neck. The skin was smooth. He couldn't feel a scar. There was no indication that he'd been injured.

"Feel your face," Hun Ahaw directed.

Loki didn't need to run his fingers over his face to know that the poison scars no longer ran deep groves through his cheeks. The relief from the burning left him light-headed.

"Why . . . how?" Loki said.

Yax Balam shrugged. "One of us needed to die so that we could be resurrected, renew the land, and deny the Lords of the Underworld the lives of men."

Loki nodded, upset that he hadn't been included in their plans, but still overwhelmed by their abilities.

Idun's apples only kept the Iseland gods young.

He knew of no way to resurrect someone. Once a god died, he or she was dead for good.

Now, not only was he alive after his head had been cut off, he felt refreshed, renewed, complete in ways that he hadn't known were possible. He felt as giddy as a pony, drunk on fresh spring grass and sunshine. The land beneath his feet almost pushed back as if actively supporting him. He didn't feel younger, but—more whole, complete, as if all his trickery and magic from all his selves across the slivers of Asgard were available to him. He wanted to turn into a crow and soar into the air, across the ice fields and mountains. No one, not even Odin, would have been able to catch him.

Loki stayed with the twins through the remainder of their myth, the tricking of the Lords of the Underworld, killing them but not resurrecting them until they'd extracted promises for men. He saw the dawn, marveled at the porcupine fingers of color across the sky. He laughed, danced, sang, and celebrated, reveling in his newly completed self.

And planned and plotted as well. His people needed this ability to resurrect themselves.

Tyr needed it.

"You're *whole* now?" Tyr asked again. He felt as though semifrozen water filled his limbs and slowed his brain, though he sat in his hall and the fire blazed.

"Yes, whole!" Loki replied, twirling in a tight circle.

"And the land—"

"It's *there*. Like it wasn't before. The Itza said they drew their strength from it. I don't, not yet, but now I understand."

Tyr stayed seated on his high seat while Loki skipped around his hall. He'd seen the trickster unable to sit still before, but it had usually been because Loki had just planned a joke that was sure to make everyone angry, or a jest had gone well. Since they'd come here though, Loki had moved more slowly, as if he still carried chains that held him fast to the side of a boulder.

Maybe that was it though.

"You say they chopped off your head," he said.

"A bat bit it off, actually, but yes. And they brought me back."

Tyr couldn't believe it. He'd never heard of such a thing.

"The Itza are forever losing arms, legs, eyes. Resurrection makes them whole. The Hero Twins told me about this one time with Seven Macaw, the bird who pretended to be the sun, and—"

"Is this some trick, Loki? What new game are you playing?" Tyr asked, letting his voice thunder through the hall.

Only now did Loki pause. "No trick, O mighty *dæma*. I was headless. Now I am not." His arms flickered for a moment, crow feathers darkening his skin.

"Why should I believe you?"

"Why would I trick you?" Loki looked honestly puzzled.

Tyr let loose a bitter laugh. "Because that's what you do?"

"Why would I put you in debt to the foreigners?"

"Where do your allegiances lie?" Tyr asked. "Tell me."

Now Loki glared at Tyr. He crossed his arms over his chest and stood still, though one foot gave away his continued excess energy by wiggling slightly. "I will make no promises that will destroy us. Can you say the same?"

The half god spoke the truth. Tyr shifted uneasily in his seat. Loki had accused him of rash oath making before, had tried to stop him their first day there. Would Tyr make a fool's bargain again, bartering away more than his hand this time? Was that his *wyrd*?

"You said, though, that they didn't bring back the Lords of the Underworld after they killed them."

"Not right away. They extracted promises from them first. Don't worry." Loki's bubbling mood overflowed again, and he capered around the center hearth. "I'm sure we can find something to trade with them. Or maybe trick them. We aren't new to this, you know. We can make you whole again."

Tyr shook his head, dazed by the thought. Whole. He could have his sword hand again.

If his human followers were successful here, he could go back to the other aspects of Ásgard, maybe do battle with Odin the usurper, and regain his place over all the gods. Not just here, but everywhere, in all the different incarnations of the lands of the gods.

Tyr stopped listening to Loki spin his tales of how they could trick the twins, and instead let visions of removing Odin's other eye fill his head.

"More mead!"

The call echoed across the empty cold land and penetrated the joined jungle effortlessly. Itzanam rolled over on his platform once more. He had moved his temple along the roads, closer to the foreigners, not trusting the monkey scribes to keep a good watch, partly because they were easily distracted, but partly because they couldn't conquer their fear of the treeless place.

Itzanam didn't understand why the new gods were celebrating. Their chosen trickster hadn't shown himself very well against the twins—he'd asked their help across the rivers, in the house of fire, and elsewhere. He had helped the twins sometimes, yes, but Itzanam didn't know what the foreigners thought they'd won to make them so loud. This Loki had been the one tricked into being sacrificed.

The horns of the newcomers ran like rakes down Itzanam's spine, causing him to shift, and shift again.

Rhythmic clanging sounds that he didn't recognize kept striking him. It sounded like a mock battle, but with what kind of weapons?

Unable to rest, as well as curious, Itzanam finally left his bed and padded silently through the jungle, across the empty places, to the great hall in the center of the foreign gods' compound. He let his jaguar aspect overtake his features as he slipped through the dark, melting into shadows, eyes reflecting the light.

Humans, or those who had been human at one point, stood guard at the door, a ceremonial post. Itzanam avoided them easily and circled the building, choosing a far window to peer through.

He cursed the monkey scribes silently after his first glance. They'd been too scared to give him an accurate description of Tyr's hall. Itzanam expected the snakes writhing in the floor, the carved pillars, and the huge center fire. He hadn't known about the rich tapestries. The scribes should have studied them closely and reported their illustrations to him, for they told of the foreign gods' myths and battles, and would have revealed much about these people.

With a sigh, he looked around the rest of the hall. Two wide tables had been set up on either side of the fire. The gods sat at them, facing each other. More humans gathered here, serving and entertaining the gods. They fought each other with long thin knives made of some kind of shiny stone that Itzanam had never seen before—the source of the odd clanging that had kept him awake. Large hunting dogs lazed on the edges of the room, tossed the occasional bone and haunch of meat.

Tyr sat on his high seat, overlooking the feast, drinking from a large flagon. Itzanam wondered at the dark liquid, not smelling any trace of honey in it, though he could tell the other gods drank something similar to the mead his people consumed. A female god sat next to the fire on a small stool, playing a sweet-sounding instrument made of wood and string. Horns constructed of bone sounded occasionally from the corners.

The little god who had accompanied the twins sat in the center of one of the tables, laughing and joking with his companions. Itzanam marveled at his appearance. He'd taken the resurrection well. He seemed so solid in comparison to the others.

Then Itzanam took a closer look at the other gods. Though he considered them upstarts, their appearance tonight was different. Wrinkles lined their faces. Golden and red hair held streaks of white and silver. Spots dotted hands and other exposed skin. Was night when their aspects aged? Resurrection renewed his own people after battle, made them whole, but it did not make them young.

One of the horns blew a complicated pattern. Slowly, silence spread through the room. A young, robust woman walked in, carrying a large basket in front of her, its handle wrapped over both her arms. Itzanam winced at the roar that greeted her arrival. She curtsied first to Tyr, then, without much ceremony, drew out a golden sphere and handed it to the first god at the table.

The reverence with which the god handled the gift surprised Itzanam. He watched as the god took a small knife made from the same strange shiny stone as the larger ones and split the sphere into slices.

Itzanam suddenly understood that this was a fruit of some kind. Though the girl continued to circulate around the tables, handing out her prizes, he watched with interest as the first god took a bite. The audible crunch echoed around the room.

No one remarked on the effects of the fruit. Not one of the gods paused for more than a brief moment to thank the girl with the basket. But Itzanam knew he would have fallen to his knees if she'd handed one of the golden spheres to him.

The fruit made the gods grow younger.

Resurrection renewed his people. But nothing made them young. Not like this.

His visions of joining, of living forever with a single aspect, no longer seemed so far-fetched. But how could he get his hands on one of these marvelous, golden, youth-giving fruits? He was certain that for all their lack of guards that night, even these strange foreigners would protect the trees that gave this marvelous gift.

Itzanam slunk away from the window, full of wonder, as well as the beginnings of a plan.

"You cannot believe the noise they made! Worse than whole troops of monkeys at play. They're impossible!" Itzanam didn't allow himself to look at Feathered Serpent, his chosen audience for his outrage, but instead, kept striding back and forth in front of the other god. He had to make this act good.

"And their trickster! Asking for help. Not a proper god at all." Itzanam paused, then continued, allowing a thoughtful tone to creep through his anger. "Though he did seem to be renewed more fully than one of us when Yax Balam resurrected him." Itzanam breathed deeply while he raged, taking in as much of the incense that Feathered Serpent garnered as he could, letting it feed him, make him stronger, while pretending to be weak.

"Should have let him stay dead," Feathered Serpent said.

Itzanam kept his smile to himself. Just a few more gentle nudges and Feathered Serpent would volunteer for everything Itzanam had in mind. "You wouldn't believe how they live. Those awful wide-open places. No jungle. Draft, dark, smoky halls. The cold that they bring with them. They're closer to men than gods."

"They aren't worthy to live here. We should send them back to their little sliver of the universe."

"Yes. Exactly. Something needs to be done. But what?"

"Indeed, what?"

The flat tone in Feathered Serpent's response made Itzanam wonder if he'd pushed too hard. A quick glance showed that Feathered Serpent was merely deep in thought, brow furrowed, eyes focused on the distance.

"We can't just take their followers," Itzanam said.

"We can't?" Feathered Serpent asked.

"Not the ones here, no." Itzanam shuddered, remembering the foreign god that the land had taken. It hungered for more blood. He didn't know how it would respond if they took the humans without cause, if it would decide to take them with the same casualness.

Then Itzanam gasped, as if just considering something for the first time. "What happens when more of their followers arrive? And the foreign gods become stronger?"

Now he turned and faced Feathered Serpent, letting smoke take his leg and wither his aspect so he appeared less substantial than usual.

Feathered Serpent squirmed on his seat, like a boy who knew the answer to his tutor's question. "I can call the Chaob. They're still gathered in the realm of Ix, the Bacab. They'll force that ship down in water so deep that not even the foreign gods will be able to find their souls."

"Good. Good!" Itzanam said, before he returned to his pacing, hiding his smile. Feathered Serpent had volunteered for the first part of his plan—namely, sinking the ship that had brought the foreign men here. Now for the trickier portion of his plan: getting Feathered Serpent to create a distraction so Itzanam could steal one of the golden fruits.

Tyr rolled off his sleeping couch with a roar. The room spun, and Tyr worried momentarily that he was going to be sick. What was wrong with him? His feet had problems finding, and sticking, to the floor, as it seemed to swell and rock underneath him. Had he had too much mead? He *had* stayed late in his hall, drinking with Loki, plotting the tricking of the Itza, planning his own triumphant return to the position as head of the gods. He shook his head, then groaned at the pain. He hadn't had that much to drink. He'd made it to his own bed. He even remembered climbing under the furs. Had some foreign witch cursed him?

The room held too many shadows with just the banked fire. He yelled hoarsely, shouting for more, surprised that it took a few moments before all the torches blazed.

Even in the light, everything swayed.

He found it difficult to judge the size of his room anymore. The walls seemed to press in around him and loom, then stretch back out to their regular place. Strange currents wafted through the air, covering the tapestries and rugs with pale shades, draining them of their true colors, then blowing through the walls.

Something was wrong.

It took him a few more moments before he figured out what it was. The swirling in his room echoed the churning waves and wind that were swamping the *Golden Tree*. Every time he lost a man to the water, his room grew more ashen.

The storm wasn't natural. It blew from the world of men into the world of the gods, crossing the barriers between their two lands, bringing the scent of heated death and ancient painted bones.

Tyr despaired. If he tried to help, he would only condemn his men, no matter what Loki claimed about this new place. Yet it would be so easy for him. He could feel his power gathering in him, rolling through his joints, sparking like a ball of lightning. It wouldn't take much to turn the ship away from the dangerous rocks. If he did nothing, all his men were sure to die.

And he didn't know when, or even if, he could convince another ship full of his followers, and only his followers, to come to this new land.

He was damned if he was just going to disappear without a fight.

Ignoring the consequences, Tyr reached out his hand to guide the boat away from the reef . . .

. . . Only to find his efforts hurled back at him.

Angered, Tyr pulled light and shadow to him, weaving them into a bridge; then he stepped into the borderlands between the worlds, where his influence in the human world would be greatest. Punishing winds battered his body as he stretched with his power, trying to push the boat to safety. Magic flew from him in dark ragged lines, like a frayed net, wrapping around the solid oak of the ship and tugging at it.

For a moment, the *Golden Tree* obeyed his command. It swung away from the sharp, unseen rocks that stood between it and the shore, turning toward the open sea. Tyr pushed again, trying to free his men from the forces of this land, the will of the foreign gods. Twisting vines of power carried on the wind wrapped around Tyr's torso and up his arms, strangling him, constraining his force.

Tyr did not let them hinder him. He reached out again. Just one more push. He shoved, hard.

The *Golden Tree* smacked into hidden rocks standing between it and the wide whale road. Shudders and echoes slammed into Tyr, knocking him back, off his feet, out of the shadow worlds, back to his own rooms. The whirling winds sucked the remnants of his power into themselves, howling and furious.

From the floor, Tyr reached out again. He couldn't save the ship, but he caught four of the sailors before they were trapped by the grasping foreign Niflheim, and carried their souls to his hall.

The rest, along with their faith, were gone.

Stiffly, Tyr stood. The world looked normal again,

not drained of color or insubstantial. He walked back
to his hall, to the table always supplied with mead,
and filled his cup to the brim. After a silent toast, he
drained it, wondering if the ash he tasted was left over
from the battle, or if it was now just a part of his life.

He knew now, and his mind held no doubts, that
he must be resurrected, soon, if they were to survive
at all. He needed ties here, ties with the myths and
the earth and the followers who supported the gods.

After another cup of mead, he went back to his bed
and uneasy sleep.

Feathered Serpent hadn't seen the new land with
his own eyes before this. Cold air threaded through
the trees near the border and sent chills down his
spine. He longed to exile this foreign place, drive it
from his realm, but now that he had seen it, he had
to admit Itzanam was correct—he couldn't just banish
it. The lands intertwined with each other, roots,
branches, and bushes reaching for each other like
long-lost lovers. The sight made the serpents in his
headdress writhe.

A wide empty plain, bare like a courtyard of death,
greeted Feathered Serpent just past the jungle. He
forced himself to walk into the open as if he had no
concern, as if he were not exposing himself to all pred-
ators. How did these gods stand it? Echoing cries of
large white birds sounded above him. The bitter wind
carried scents of long winters and barren ice fields.

Why had he let Itzanam talk him into making this
challenge himself? Why hadn't he sent the monkey
scribes? He suspected that Itzanam had other reasons
why he wanted to engage the foreign gods.

Feathered Serpent crossed another broad, clear
river. Gray fish with spots and teeth chased each other
through the weeds. They looked wily and tough. Only
experienced fishermen could pit themselves against

fish such as these and win. Feathered Serpent was suddenly glad that he had come himself. The land would tell him more about his competition than Itzanam or the monkey scribes could.

The size of the wooden hall sitting on top of a slight incline didn't surprise him. No noise came from it, even though it was after noon. Large four-legged animals grazed in the enclosure. They had long faces, blunt teeth, and silky tails that twitched away insects. Feathered Serpent would bet that Itzanam hadn't seen these before either, or else he would have suggested them as prizes.

Two human guards stood outside the hall. Feathered Serpent allowed his stature to increase as he approached. Itzanam had warned him about the size of the foreigners. The foreign humans were taller than his people, and so their gods were proportionally larger as well.

The two humans greeted him formally and asked him to wait while they fetched the lord of the hall.

In just a moment, a large, barrel-chested god came out. Feathered Serpent wondered if he was some kind of sun god: his hair and beard flamed. He carried a large ax in his hand, the two-headed blade made out of the strange blood stone Itzanam had told him about.

Feathered Serpent had heard much of this hall from both Itzanam and the monkey scribes and so was looking forward to seeing it. However, the god's first booming words were, "Come. Walk with me."

Feathered Serpent turned and followed the god back toward the fence of the enclosure. The other god introduced himself as Thor as they walked. Sun sparkled on the short grass, wetting Feathered Serpent's bare toes and turning the leather of the other man's boots black. Thor took a slug from the horn he carried, then offered it to Feathered Serpent. Strong honeyed mead flowed over his tongue, sweet, yet as sharp as the wind blowing from the mountains behind them.

"See the brown filly? The one with the white hump? We're going to try and mate her next year," Thor said, pointing toward one of the animals.

"Ah," Feathered Serpent said, as if he knew exactly what the other was talking about. What did they use these animals for? For their coats? For their meat?

Thor stopped next to the fence, put one foot up on the lowest plank, and leaned his forearms on the top one. Feathered Serpent mimicked his position. They shared another moment of silence looking out over the open fields. Feathered Serpent didn't allow himself to shudder in the face of such emptiness.

"So what brings you here so early in the morning? I doubt this is a social call," Thor finally said.

Feathered Serpent cursed himself for not bringing up what he wanted first. But he did want the other god at ease. Itzanam had insisted that it was important, and Feathered Serpent agreed with him.

"Your Loki mentioned that sometimes you have games, though not like ours."

Thor snorted. "So, little man. You want to play *glima* with me?"

Feathered Serpent looked up at Thor. Though he'd increased his own height, the barrel-chested god still towered over him. He looked more carefully at the word "*glima*," teasing out that it involved some kind of wrestling your opponent to the ground. He didn't know if any of the Itza could compete physically like that with these new gods. Yet he didn't want to appear cowardly either.

"We could include this *glima*. As well as other contests. Like drinking," he said, nodding toward the horn filled with mead.

Thor nodded and grinned. "I'm good at drinking contests. That is, when there aren't any tricks."

Feathered Serpent had heard the tale thirdhand, about how Thor had drunk from a horn that had one end connected to the ocean. He hadn't been able to empty it, and so had lost the contest, but he had lowered the level of the ocean. Itzanam had told him to be sure to include that in his invitation, so the foreign gods wouldn't feel overwhelmed or threatened by the prospect. "And maybe spear-throwing contests. And riddles."

"That sounds like a good idea. Let our people come together. Make a week of it or more. Competitions and betting. I like it."

It was Feathered Serpent's turn to smile. This was all going to be too easy. He still didn't know Itzanam's real purpose behind these games, but he had his own. That was enough.

"And the prizes?" Thor asked Feathered Serpent as he turned to leave, after they'd set the time, date, and place.

"We'll set them as we go," he said with a casual wave of his hand.

The foreign gods didn't have to know the Itza were going to wager for the souls of the foreign gods' human followers. Not until it was too late.

Chapter 5

It had been a week since the Iselanders had gained their freedom, or at least, since the Itza had stopped treating them like slaves. They weren't free; Tyrthbrand and the others knew this. If they had decided to turn around and go back to Tzul where they'd landed, the Itza would have forcefully stopped them.

Tyrthbrand knew Cauac Sky wanted them to make the attempt. It was probably why he'd agreed to give the Iselanders their weapons. He watched them with greedy eyes, hungering for their deaths. The skeletal priest expressed little interest in them, what they had to trade, how they fought or lived. He didn't see to their welfare beyond the basics. Tyrthbrand knew the priest had a horrible fate planned for them once they reached their destination—a sacrifice bloodier than any he'd seen so far. Only Lady Two Bird stood between them and a painful, honorless death.

Of the twins, Tyrthbrand preferred to deal with Jeweled Skull. While it was obvious that the twin didn't like him, he liked to talk of weapons, battles, and fighting techniques when they spoke. Tyrthbrand felt he understood the older twin. Jeweled Skull had an extreme warrior's view of the world, everyone divided into friend and enemy, instead of seeing the questions and uncertainties, as a priest would. Waterlily Jaguar was more outwardly friendly, inviting Tyrthbrand to walk with him, asking questions about the iron they called the "blood stone" and their gods.

Tyrthbrand always wanted to wash his hands, and possibly the rest of his body, after talking with the darker twin.

Lady Two Bird watched over them, sometimes in obvious ways, sometimes more subtly. Tyrthbrand and his men acted as an honor guard for her and her attendants. He knew that the Itza would have been surprised at how thoroughly the Iselanders would have defended her. Tyrthbrand had made sure his men realized exactly how much their welfare depended on her. They always tried to have one or more of the Iselanders with her, whether she, or any of the Itza, knew it or not.

All of Tyrthbrand's remaining men began to learn the Itzas' language and stopped trying to teach their own; they were too outnumbered to make it worthwhile. Unsurprisingly, Vigfus picked it up the quickest, as he'd learned many different tongues while traveling with his father.

The Iselanders ate *atole*, peppers, strange long reddish black fruit, round green soft vegetables, and other things they still didn't have names for, drank as much watery mead they could get their hands on, stank, sweated, and groused good-naturedly. Tyrthbrand didn't understand how they could sweat so much. They wore the slave sandals instead of their boots because they were cooler. Illugi threatened more than once to cut his trousers off at the knees just to bring some relief from the heat. But the thick wool prevented the worst of the mosquitoes and other biting insects that attacked them at dawn and dusk.

At night, the Iselanders made their own camp within the camp of the Itza, circled together, weapons ready, ready to defend themselves or their lady. Vigfus always insisted on a fire, and though they didn't need the extra heat, no one would deny the boy his comfort. Snorri the smith spent his time drawing runes from his bag and muttering over the answers they gave him.

Ketil sharpened Wolf Feeder constantly and was quick to take offense at the tiniest infraction or crooked look. Tyrthbrand talked him down frequently. He knew that it was only a matter of time before the priest snapped and killed someone. Thorolf Mostur-beard and Illugi spent their time alternating between gambling with their guards—games involving compli-cated throws of strange tokens—and drinking. When neither Thorolf nor Illugi showed any signs of hang-over in the morning, Tyrthbrand knew he didn't have to worry about his men getting too intoxicated, that their loud singing of the night before had been an act.

During the day, the Iselanders tried to keep each other's spirits up by joking and storytelling. They re-counted tales of Thor and Tyr and came up with ken-nings for the jungle around them; heat choker and serpent-vine stand, baking emerald spray and prey hider.

The raised white road they traveled on went on for-ever; sometimes so narrow they could walk only two abreast, the trees encroaching on either side, while at other times it was so wide a war party of ten across could have marched down it. The group never saw anyone working on it. According to Lady Two Bird, it wasn't the right season. She'd looked resigned when she'd said it, and Tyrthbrand wondered if the road crews would have made their travel safer.

Thorolf joked that the road spread like milk squirted from the cow Audhumla, the one who had helped create the world before the time of man. Tyrth-brand tried to explain the concept of milk from a cow to Lady Two Bird. He shouldn't have blushed when he likened it to a nursing woman, but he did. The Itza didn't have any large land animals: no ox, horses, sheep, goats, or cows. They did have a piglike animal they hunted, the strange tapirs that lived in the water, and dogs they raised for meat. Tyrthbrand marveled at the size of the temples made from stones that had been quarried and dragged by only men and slaves. They didn't even have wheeled carts.

Awe over the wide road and the great mountainlike temples in the distance turned to trepidation as they approached the dead city. The Itza had abandoned it two generations beforehand, when no rains had fallen, then plague had blown through. Tyrthbrand didn't need Lady Two Bird to tell him it was a cursed place—everything about the city screamed its disuse and sent clammy fingers crawling across his skin: the way the trees disrupted the carefully placed rocks, the screeching animals above them, the oppressive silence that seemed to press in on them regardless of the other noises. However, the group had to stop. They needed water.

Tyrthbrand wasn't sure what made Cauac Sky decide to camp inside the city walls. None of the Itza seemed to want to do it. The soldiers grumbled to themselves as they entered, peered at their surroundings warily, hands clenched tightly around their spears and shields. The group headed straight for the main square, surrounded on all sides with huge crumbling temple pyramids. Warped rock and fallen statues marred the open area between the buildings. Sheets of stucco had slid from the walls and lay in crumbled heaps of color. Dust filled the air, choked the late-afternoon sunlight, and muffled the jungle sounds. It coated Tyrthbrand's tongue with the taste of great age and haunted places.

Streets led away from the center in all directions. Tyrthbrand noticed more than one person making warding symbols into the shadows in the murkier streets. Finally, Cauac Sky found the road he wanted and led them down it.

If Tyrthbrand had to speculate who had lived on this street before the city's demise, he would have guessed wealthy merchants. Stone platforms lined either side with a quarter of a boat's length worth of empty space between them. Space equaled money to Tyrthbrand—only extremely poor people lived on top of each other in the villages of his home. Lady Two Bird explained that plaster-covered wooden walls and woven roofs had at one time been built on the stone floors, but that they'd since rotted away. Some of the raised areas had had partial internal rock walls, as well as raised flat platforms for beds.

Small stone blocks lay in the center of the street, some nearly waist high. Lady Two Bird told Tyrthbrand that they'd been altars, each dedicated to a different god. When the people had left the city, they'd taken only a few of the statues with them, those of the living gods, while ceremonially burying the rest of them. The entire length of the road smelled sickly sweet, like rotting fruit and spoiled grain. The jungle seemed closer here: trees swelled up on either side of them and grew between the altars, through the centers of the platforms, and disrupted the fine stones of the white road. Tyrthbrand noticed his men drawing together and fingering their weapons, as if worried about an attack from the encroaching vegetation.

Monkeys scrambled above the group, leaping from tree to tree as if following them. Tyrthbrand asked Lady Two Bird about the animals, wondering if they'd been tame, or even domesticated, when people had lived there.

"People not feed them," Lady Two Bird replied.

Tyrthbrand understood that Lady Two Bird purposefully kept her language simple, but sometimes he resented it, feeling as though she treated him like a child who was not quite bright enough to pick up full sentences.

"Sometimes they steal," she continued. "People not angry. Not happy, but not angry."

Tolerated. Tyrthbrand started to ask for the actual word when a roar reverberated through the trees. The

creative cursing that followed told Tyrthbrand that it
was Thorolf Mosturbeard.

He tried not to laugh when he turned back around.
He really did. But he couldn't help it. Bright green
streaks ran through Thorolf's blond hair and dripped
down his forehead. The expression of disgust on his
face reminded Tyrthbrand of a two-year-old's upon
tasting turnips for the first time. The rest of the Isel-
ánders, as well as their Itza guards, laughed as well.

"That's a lovely hat—" Snorri started to say when
Thorolf interrupted him with a scream of rage. The
towering man raced to the nearest Itza warrior,
grabbed his spear, and hurled it into the trees.

"No!" shouted Tyrthbrand, but it was too late. Like
blind Hod's mistletoe dart, Thorolf's throw was too
true to miss. A dark figure came crashing down from
the trees. For a moment, the fallen form reminded
Tyrthbrand of a child burned to death in a village fire,
dark and curled on its side. Then the features resolved
into those of an animal with large lips, a pushed-out
snout, and weird, elongated fingers.

Tyrthbrand didn't remember drawing his sword, but
it had found its way to his hand. The Itza shouted
at Thorolf. Images of a human child superimposed
themselves again on the figure on the ground as Tyrthbrand drew closer. Lady Two Bird had told him stories
of the origins of monkeys. The Itza considered them
failed men who hadn't been able to worship the gods
properly and so had been turned into animals. There
were two other monkeys as well, scribes, who had
been the older brothers of the Hero Twins, changed
into animals by their brothers.

The yelling behind Tyrthbrand faded out. He prodded the creature cautiously with his sword. Just because it had fallen didn't mean it was dead, and a
wounded animal, no matter how manlike it looked,
was dangerous. But it was no longer breathing.

Goose quills pricked Tyrthbrand's spine. He turned away from the figure on the ground and saw that the Itza had their spears lowered and approached them on all sides. "Men!" Tyrthbrand shouted. As one, the rest of the Iselanders drew their swords, all kept sharp and ready since they'd been prisoners. They formed a loose circle, facing the outward threat, the animal in the center, as if it were a fallen companion and they were protecting its body.

Cauac Sky yelled something that sounded to Tyrthbrand like "Attack!"

At the same time, Waterlily Jaguar called out, "Stop!"

The two Itza stared at each other, anger radiating between the pair of them, spreading out so that even Tyrthbrand could feel its heat.

The guards stood with their spears poised, ready to rush the Iselanders.

Cauac Sky broke the silence, his voice oily, saying something that ended with "Tyrthbrand."

Tyrthbrand stiffened. So it was his turn to die.

Waterlily Jaguar shook his head, then started speaking in quick, measured tones, punctuating his words with sharp gestures, pointing to both Tyrthbrand and Thorolf.

Cauac Sky interrupted him with a harsh phrase, then gazed at the ground for a moment, arms wrapped tightly across his chest, as if he were holding himself back.

Waterlily Jaguar started again, using gentler tones, speaking more slowly.

After a moment, Vigfus spoke up. "He's retelling the story. How Thorolf was marked, then flew something at the something. That's the best I can do. Sorry." He shrugged.

No one lowered their weapons at the end of the recitation. The two Itza continued to stare at each other. Tyrthbrand readied himself for a fight. He didn't know why Waterlily Jaguar had chosen their side for this battle, if it actually had anything to do with them—or if there was some unknown power play going on between the two men, and the Iselanders were unwitting pawns.

Sweat rolled down Tyrthbrand's back. He shifted the grip of his sword in his hand. Would Tyr still take him into his hall, even though he'd turned his back on his god?

Finally, Cauac Sky nodded tersely to Waterlily Jaguar, then called for Lady Two Bird in a loud, demanding voice. Tyrthbrand knew that she'd protect them if she could, but he didn't relax his stance. He still might be greeting the gods in person that day. Thorolf had obviously broken a taboo by killing the monkey. Tyrthbrand didn't know what kind of *wergild* would appease the Itza, but he suspected it would involve blood.

After some hurried conversation, Lady Two Bird pushed her way through the forest of Itza swords and came up to Tyrthbrand.

"This again?" she asked with a smile, indicating the standoff.

Tyrthbrand had to laugh. This woman had bigger balls than Thor, Loki, and Tyr combined.

"Monkeys no kill?" he guessed.

She nodded gravely.

Cauac Sky pushed his way forward to stand next to Lady Two Bird. Waterlily Jaguar seemed content to stay behind, as if he'd gotten what he wished. The priest spoke harshly to her for a moment. When he finished, he turned a greedy eye to Thorolf. Tyrthbrand didn't like the bloodlust he saw, like a wolf eyeing a wounded deer.

Lady Two Bird shook her head, said no, but Tyrthbrand couldn't follow their conversation.

"Vigfus?" he called softly.

"Not sure," the younger merchant replied.

The Iselanders waited, tense, ready to die, until finally Lady Two Bird turned to Tyrthbrand again. Her wide eyes seemed to be pleading with him.

"Cauac Sky wants to know if Thorolf will be *ts'u'-uts'* under his arms."

Tyrthbrand glanced first at Waterlily Jaguar, but he now spoke quietly with his twin, as if he didn't care what happened anymore. Then Tyrthbrand turned his attention to Vigfus, who shrugged, indicating he didn't know.

"*Ts'u'uts'*?"

Cauac Sky replied. "Yes."

That didn't help. What did it mean? Bled? Killed? Tattooed? The priest's gaze had grown sharper, as if he could cut them with his eyes and was already tasting their blood.

"Like a mother. And a child. The child drinks the mother's *blood* milk." She put a strange emphasis behind her words.

Cauac Sky spoke to Lady Two Bird again, harshly. This time Tyrthbrand caught the name of Lady Two Bird's brother-in-law more than once. She hung her head, then, without raising her eyes to Tyrthbrand, repeated her original question, again using that one crucial word he didn't know. She seemed about to say more, but Cauac Sky cut her off with a sharp motion of his hand.

Tyrthbrand called over his shoulder to Thorolf. "I think he's asking if you agree to be suckled under your arms."

"By Hel's frozen tits, what does that mean?" Thorolf asked.

Tyrthbrand didn't know. "I would imagine it involves some kind of bleeding," he said.

Given Lady Two Bird's reactions, as well as the gloating priest, he suspected it meant death.

The Itza moved forward a step. The Iselanders fell back, making a tighter ring. Flies had already discovered the body at the center of the circle they made. Their buzzing swelled louder. The other monkeys had grown strangely quiet since their companion had fallen. Birds cawed imperiously, as if relaying the news and commenting on it.

"I'll stand in your stead," Tyrthbrand said in a low voice. Cauac Sky lusted after his blood, more so than his men's. Maybe he could bargain with the priest, for the lives of the others.

"Or you could both refuse," Snorri added.

Tyrthbrand nodded. They could all die, here and now, in battle, rather than be taken and killed one by one. Better a quick death than this slow bleeding away of hope.

The strident droning of the flies made Tyrthbrand's own spine vibrate. One of the Itza shifted. The loud snapping of a twig made both groups tense. The silence between them grew hard, brittle.

"Tyr will remember your sacrifice, and grant you lands in Heofon," Ketil the priest intoned.

"Or we can fight," Illugi said.

Tyrthbrand didn't say anything more. It was Thorolf's decision if they lived or died. If *he* lived or died.

"Might as well die doing something useful, even if it is saving *your* worthless hide, Illugi," Thorolf said finally, stepping forward. "Thor will protect me," he added, laying his sword down.

"May you be reborn with the *wyrd* of kings," Ketil said.

Tyrthbrand couldn't force any words out. Any wishes he might have had for Thorolf were far too late. He found that the hand clenching his sword was shaking. He fisted it tighter and tried to stop it, but he still pricked the fingers of his other hand while holding his sheath steady to put his weapon away. The beads of blood shone brighter than the strange flowers that choked the trees around them.

He didn't let any blood fall to the ground, but rather, put his fingers to his lips and licked them clean. He would not let even a drop leak out in this place, not until he had no other option.

He knew it was just a matter of time before all his blood would be spilled to feed this hungry land.

Lady Two Bird wanted to deny the large blond man's statement. She wanted him to step back, for the Iselanders to take a stand and fight. They would die like cornered dogs, but it would be quick. She had grown to respect them as they traveled together, their humanity growing more discernible. She wished she had had more time to explain their legends to Tyrthbrand, so that he would know what Cauac Sky was asking.

"To be suckled" was another way of saying "to be sacrificed." It was a trick phrase, something that the gods had used to fool their enemies into dying. And now Cauac Sky had duped the Iselanders.

She watched in sorrow as Itza soldiers stepped forward. She let Tyrthbrand see her sadness before plastering a pleasant smile on her face and turning toward Cauac Sky.

The hunger she saw in the priest's expression made her sick to her stomach. He looked more like a madman than a priest.

She quietly said to Tyrthbrand, in his language, "I'm sorry."

Cauac Sky yelled at her to be quiet, that she was a disgrace to her name, her family, her heritage, and her gods. She should never pollute herself by speaking the foreigners' language again.

Lady Two Bird ignored him, following the procession without looking at the Iselanders again.

Tyrthbrand trailed after the guards who led Thorolf to one side. None of his men followed him. Illugi split off from their group and stayed with Lady Two Bird. Tyrthbrand wanted to tell Illugi how much he appreciated him continuing this duty, that it had been Tyrthbrand's failure, not hers, that Thorolf now went with the priests, but Tyrthbrand could barely force air past the gravel in his throat. Words would be impossible.

The soldiers led Thorolf to a sunken pond on the edge of the city. Two of them hastily donned the blue robes of priests and cleaned the Iselander, spending extra time washing his head. Thorolf took out his comb and used it on his hair and beard until the long strands shone, to the fascination of the priests. He handed the comb to Tyrthbrand afterward and said, "Make sure it stays with me." Tyrthbrand nodded, prepared to burn it in sacrifice if he couldn't place it in Thorolf's grave.

More priests came and led them to a nearby clearing. Thorolf marched as if on his way to battle, proud and straight backed, ignoring his naked state, as if the twisted figures of Thor's goats tattooed down his shoulders and arms were more than enough covering. A stone platform rested in the center of the open area. The Itza made Thorolf stand on it, arms outstretched, while they applied blue paint. After a little while, Thorolf shook his head as if to clear it, then started singing a drinking song about Bretha's tits and how they'd keep him warm through the cold winter nights.

"Come on, you whoring mare's son. Sing with me," Thorolf roared out at one point. Tyrthbrand forced himself to join in the chorus. Tyrthbrand felt each stripe the priests made as if they painted them on his own skin, streaks of wet coolness covering his chest and arms, freezing his joints, wrapping him tightly until he felt as though he struggled for each breath.

Thorolf finished his song and bellowed with laughter. "You think your women are going to be safe now?" he asked, addressing the priests. "Ha! They're going to go into mourning when my sword's no longer

in play. You remember that whore in Skógar?"
Thorolf called out to Tyrthbrand, but didn't wait for
him to reply. "After three days I thought it really was
possible to die from too much sex. Ha!"

Thorolf squirmed and grimaced. "That's starting to
itch now. Don't think they're going to kill me by letting me scratch myself to death, do you?" Again he
continued before Tyrthbrand could say anything.
"You'll tell Tyr how I died, how *well* I died, right,
marked man?"

Tyrthbrand swallowed and nodded once. He would
tell Tyr again and again, if not in prayers, then in
curses. He'd never forget the sight of Thorolf covered
with obscene blue glyphs, standing in a jungle-
enclosed clearing under the pale shadows of a dead
city, singing, joking, and living more furiously than all
of them put together up until the moment he died.
Tyrthbrand knew the visions of it would fill both his
dreams and his nightmares for the rest of his life.

A new priest with leathery skin and large tattoos of
leaves on his cheeks came into the clearing followed
by a younger man carrying a lamp. Thorolf hadn't
seen him before and assumed he must be part of
Cauac Sky's entourage. The priest presented Thorolf
with what looked like a fat, short, brown stick. Thorolf
took it hesitantly.

"What do they want me to do with this? I ain't
going to bugger myself with it."

Tyrthbrand had seen these kinds of sticks at the first
sacrifice he'd attended. He made himself choke out a
laugh at Thorolf's comment. "No. They put it in their
mouths and inhale the smoke."

"Breathing smoke? Why in Hel's name would you
breathe smoke? Only poor idiots sit downwind of a
fire, hoping to catch its heat."

Tyrthbrand shrugged. "Just their way."

Thorolf grew silent for a moment. "Their way. My

way." The words sounded eerie and flat, as if Thorolf had just stepped closer the grave. Tyrthbrand shivered.

The priest pantomimed Thorolf putting the brown thing in his mouth, then sticking the other end in the flames of the lamp. Thorolf shook his head. Eventually, the tattooed priest lit the stick for the Iselander and offered it to him.

"Think I should do it?"

Tyrthbrand shrugged. "Only if you want to."

"Seems simple enough," Thorolf said. "Besides, you only live once, eh, marked man?"

Tyrthbrand closed his eyes at the barb and so missed Thorolf taking the stick and sucking smoke into his lungs. The fit of coughing and swearing made him open his eyes again. The priests and soldiers laughed with Thorolf. Tyrthbrand didn't. The priest took back the smoking stick and mimed just taking the smoke into his mouth.

"Tastes like honey-sweetened shit," Thorolf commented to Tyrthbrand as he tried again.

"And how would you know this?" Tyrthbrand made himself ask. If Thorolf could make such an effort to laugh while facing death, Tyrthbrand could as well, and just accept the occasional taunts as his due. Thorolf made a rude gesture in reply. Tyrthbrand forced another laugh.

After a few puffs, Thorolf started listing to one side. "By Thor's piece," he said. "Don't know what's in that smoke, but my head feels like I've just finished a barrel of mead."

Interesting. Tyrthbrand hadn't known that the smoke had that effect. Maybe he could bring the sticks back to Iseland. . . . He shook off his introspection. He would go back home if he could, but he wasn't going to dwell on that now, as tempting as it might be not to have to face what was going on before him. His daydreaming had already cost all his men enough.

However, if he ever did get back to Iseland, he was never going to leave it again.

Another priest came into the clearing, walking first up to Tyrthbrand and showing him a bowl of dried mushrooms. "Smoke and a meal?" Tyrthbrand asked as the priest approached Thorolf.

The Iselander chuckled. "What can I say? They like me. Smells like a well-fertilized field though," he added when the priest presented the bowl to him. He took one gingerly and put it in his mouth, then spit it back out immediately. "Tastes like dirt," he said, hacking and spitting again.

The priest didn't seem to be offended. The guards laughed, while the priest shouted over his shoulder for something. A young man came up, carrying a feathered headdress about half his own height. The priest yelled at him. He shrugged. The guards laughed more as they tried to put the headdress on Thorolf, who towered above them. Finally, the Iselander sank unsteadily to one knee so the guards could attach it. When Thorolf rose, they all continued laughing as they bowed their heads, acting awestruck since the Iselander was now twice as tall as any of them. Thorolf's booming voice rang out over them.

Another young man came into the clearing, carrying a flask of something. The priest poured it into the bowl with the mushrooms, then offered them to Thorolf again.

The Iselander sniffed suspiciously. "Honey," he told Tyrthbrand. He took one of the mushrooms in his fingers, the sticky liquid dripping back down into the bowl. "Not too bad. Still bitter though," he announced after eating one. The priest insisted that he have at least five, then handed the bowl to the youth. He relit the brown stick, indicating that Thorolf should smoke some more. The other priests now concentrated on painting Thorolf's back as he sucked in smoke and blew it out in a thick stream.

"Tyrthbrand?" Thorolf called out after a couple more puffs. "When did they build walls here?"

There were no walls. They stood on a square stone platform in the middle of a clearing. Even the wood that had once formed the building on the rock had rotted into nothing.

"What do you see?"

Thorolf didn't respond, just continued to gaze around the clearing, his eyes snagging on and examining things that Tyrthbrand couldn't perceive.

"What do you see?" Tyrthbrand asked again.

Thorolf shook his head, making his headpiece sway and bounce. "Murals," he breathed out. "Paintings. On all the walls. The ceiling. The doors. Pictures of war. Of planting. Heh." Thorolf took a few steps and put his hand up. Nobody stopped him. "Fucking. Birthing." He traced a path across, then up. "Dying. Ascending." He reached his hand up, fingers spread wide, and whispered, "Becoming stars."

The longing in Thorolf's voice made shock waves crash through Tyrthbrand's core, as quick and deadly as one of Thor's lightning bolts. How could Thorolf not want to go to Heimdall or one of the other heavens? Or even to be reborn with a better chance at life? The drugs had clearly taken his mind.

The priests exchanged words and seemed to agree that they'd finished their work on Thorolf. They picked up their paint pots and walked to Tyrthbrand, the priest with the leaf tattoo following.

They gestured with their brushes, clearly asking permission to mark Tyrthbrand as well. He acquiesced, and so they painted glyphs on Tyrthbrand's cheeks, neck, and hands, not blue, but crimson, green, and gold.

Tyrthbrand tried to ask about the significance of the colors; blue was obviously for sacrifice, and red seemed to be for warriors. He was uncertain about the others. But the older priest didn't have patience

for his stumbling words and kept interrupting with
questions of his own. The priest spoke so fast Tyrthbrand couldn't catch more than one word in ten,
something about "gods," "travel," and "talking."

The priest offered Tyrthbrand the smoking stick
when it appeared that neither would ever understand
the other. Tyrthbrand refused. Thorolf no longer
seemed to notice them; the new world he saw had
captured all his attention. Tyrthbrand didn't know if
it was the mushrooms or the smoke that had sliced
the veils between the worlds. He didn't want to see
for himself. He·didn't want to get any closer to his
gods. The priest didn't seem offended. He took two
tokes himself, then crushed the end of the stick,
snuffing out the embers.

By this time, Thorolf had wandered to a corner of
the platform. He sang in a quiet voice, watching his
hand as it traced paths across the invisible walls. Suddenly he spun around and shouted at Tyrthbrand,
"They're coming!" The headpiece leaned precariously
to one side until Thorolf impatiently shoved it back
into place.

"Who's coming? You great tree! You know you can
see farther than I can. Who's coming?" Tyrthbrand
used his most cajoling tone, the one he used with
drunken men.

"All the people. They're stepping out of the paintings. By Thor's beard! Did you see the tits on that
one?" Thorolf swung his head from side to side, as if
watching a grand procession.

The leathered priest asked Tyrthbrand in a low
voice, "Gods walk?"

Tyrthbrand relayed the question. "Are the gods
coming too?"

"Naw. Lazy bastards. Just sitting there. Watching."

What did it mean that the gods weren't coming?
Weren't walking? Did they ever come? Or were they

not coming because Tyrthbrand had turned his back
on them?

Before he could translate his questions into foreign
words, Thorolf's gaze darted beyond Tyrthbrand. He
put his hands behind his back, stood up straighter so
he loomed even more above them, and asked, "Time
for the show?"

Tyrthbrand turned to see a messenger coming into
the clearing. He walked up to the old priest and spoke
quickly for a moment. The priest started shouting orders. The guards swiftly arranged themselves in two
lines, placing Thorolf between them. Tyrthbrand
shook off the one trying to show him his place in the
procession. He would walk near his friend. Not in the
line of guards, but still close. The priest spoke to them
briefly and they let him stay.

Not that Thorolf would notice where Tyrthbrand
stood. His eyes were drawn by whatever was before
him. Tyrthbrand watched his gaze travel up the side
of something. A mountain? A temple?

After waiting, shuffling some of the guards around,
then waiting some more, the procession started, loud
drums and piercing whistles accompanying them. The
song Thorolf broke into as they marched surprised
Tyrthbrand. He'd thought the tall man knew only obscene drinking songs. This was a hymn though, one
that peasants sang when the sun came over the mountains and shone in their valley for the first time in the
spring. Sometimes people sang it for Baldur, but often,
farmers used it for thanks to the gods in general. This
was the version Thorolf sang now. It had a steady beat
and an odd tune that somehow matched the instru-
ments the Itza sounded.

Thorolf boomed with laughter at the end of his
chorus. "They *are* coming!" he called out. Though the
priests didn't understand his words, they seemed to
catch the gist of his meaning as they pulled themselves

up, flung their chests out, and banged their drums louder.

Hope rose unbidden in Tyrthbrand's chest. Maybe Tyr had forgiven him, forgiven his hubris, his wish to a foreign goddess, and would take Thorolf back into his bosom, shower him with his favor again. Thorolf started to babble fervently. Tyrthbrand listened hard, trying to decipher hidden meaning in the nonsense. He didn't notice the procession had reached its destination until he almost walked into a priest standing in front of him.

A large sinkhole loomed before him. Sand and bone-colored walls encircled the jade green water at the bottom. Tyrthbrand choked off his cry at the sight. Not death by drowning. Thorolf could swim. Tyrthbrand hoped fervently that between the smoke and the mushrooms that Thorolf had lost the ability.

It was still a horrible death for a warrior, though maybe Ran would be waiting with her net to take Thorolf to her hall, so he wouldn't be condemned to the Itzas' hell.

Tyrthbrand pushed forward, past the priests, so that he had a clear view of Thorolf's face from where he stood on the edge of the cliff. He was certain the shock he saw there matched his own.

"Bastards," Thorolf said. Hatred filled the word. His eyes were focused high up, watching the air. Tyrthbrand wondered if he meant the priests or the gods. He bit his tongue hard enough to taste blood to prevent himself from trying to stop the sacrifice, the drowning. If Thorolf asked him to, he would. He would die, here and now. But only if Thorolf asked.

"Do you see her?" Thorolf now called out to him, shouting above the intoning priests, gesturing across the open expanse.

"See who?" Freyja? Idun?

Thorolf didn't elaborate. He kept his eyes focused on a spindly, white-barked tree growing out of the side of the rock opposite them. Maybe a tree spirit had come to guide him. Maybe the gods would grant him some kind of peace.

Not another word passed Thorolf's lips—not when the Itza removed the headdress he wore, or when the priests held his arms and whipped red stripes across his back—not until he was about to be thrown to the waters. Then he laughed, loud and long, startling the ones who held him and halting the proceedings long enough for him to chant:

> *"Backs to me you give as your debt*
> *So in turning I turn from you*
> *My heart will pass through your net*
> *And stay trapped here, in branches and roots*
> *My soul no longer yours to recruit*
> *From this tree your heaven I shall view."*

Without waiting to be pushed, Thorolf flung himself from the cliff top, laughing as he plummeted straight as a white and blue spear, directly into the waters below.

He didn't resurface.

Tyrthbrand stared with gritted teeth and fisted hands for a long while after the bubbles had stopped rising and the ripples had died. When he finally looked up, he examined the spindly tree, which seemed to glow more brightly in the setting light. Had Thorolf been able to do what he'd just pledged? Was his soul still in the world of men, intertwined with the branches and roots of that tree? Tyrthbrand didn't know. He only hoped that Thorolf was happy, whether he'd gone to Thor's hall or stayed in Midgard.

He could guess why Thorolf had wanted to take his soul away from Thor. The gods had come to the ceremony. Thorolf had talked with them. They'd judged him unworthy and had turned away. So out of spite, he'd turned away from them.

Tyrthbrand told himself that the important thing was that Thorolf had died well, not as a prisoner, but as a warrior, sacrificing himself for his crewmates, the same way Tyr had sacrificed his hand for the safety of the gods. Tyrthbrand tried not to remember Thorolf's crazed eyes, glazed over with the light from the other world, tried not to speculate how he'd been judged as well, how all the Iselanders had been abandoned.

How without his god he couldn't save his men. Himself.

Cauac Sky came up while Tyrthbrand still stood on the edge of the sinkhole, Lady Two Bird at his side. They tried talking to him, Lady Two Bird asking simple questions about what Thorolf had said, what he'd done, why he'd laughed. Tyrthbrand didn't answer the blood-sucking priest. He noticed finally that his hands were clenched into fists. When he loosened them, he felt a weight in one.

He still held Thorolf's comb.

Tyrthbrand threw the comb far away from him into the water. He hoped that it would follow his companion. Maybe it would be sucked up from the water through the roots of the tree. The image almost made him laugh, but he had no laughter left in him.

He turned and started walking back to his men, ignoring the old priest and Lady Two Bird. Cauac Sky said many ugly things, obviously trying to provoke a response. Tyrthbrand could tell the priest drooled to sacrifice another of them. Lady Two Bird apologized with every other sentence. The priest even went as far as accusing Thorolf of some kind of cowardice. Tyrthbrand knew Thorolf hadn't been afraid. He'd been angry. He didn't want to explain what the gods had done, how they had judged the Iselanders. He didn't want to talk of his guilt, of how he'd condemned his men. He couldn't let the Itza see his own complicity. Lady Two Bird would just tell him it was the will of the gods.

Thorolf's leap off the cliff played through Tyrth-brand's mind repeatedly as he made his way back to the camp. Every step he took felt as though he walked on knives. His spine hurt from holding himself upright, as if it were a series of rocks balanced one on the other, grinding together, jarred by every movement. He held himself stiffly, as if he might break, as if it was he who'd been beaten and tortured, and not Thorolf.

The blade of Thorolf's sword had been plunged into the earth on the edge of the area where Tyrthbrand's men had stationed themselves, its hilt serving as both protection and warning for their camp. Tyrthbrand shivered as he passed it. Was it actually cooler inside the circle that delimited their temporary home? The air more hazy, more blue?

Illugi greeted Tyrthbrand and asked, "Is it done?"

"He'll live in Heimdall's lands forever," Tyrth-brand lied.

Ketil stayed silent, bowed next to Wolf Feeder, praying. Vigfus wouldn't look up from his contempla-tion of the fire they didn't need. Snorri sat on the other side, staring at his lap. He called Tyrthbrand to him without looking up. Reluctantly, Tyrthbrand joined him.

"Sit," the smith said.

Tyrthbrand sat carefully, with a grimace. He wanted to clean off the designs the Itza had painted on him. He wanted to curl up with some strong mead and drink himself into oblivion. He wanted to rage and curse Tyr, the Itza, all the gods. He felt like a sword that had been left in the forge for too long, the metal brittle and likely to crack under the smith's first blow.

Snorri thrust a well-worn leather bag out to Tyrth-brand. "Draw three."

Tyrthbrand hesitated, his hand heavy in his lap. He knew what he would draw. He knew there was no hope. He didn't want confirmation, for either himself or his men.

"Do it."

With a sigh, Tyrthbrand drew the first rune, using the hand that Tyr had marked with his brand.

Tyr. Of course, that would be the first rune he drew. It represented the past, where they had been.

The portion of the rune poem that accompanied this rune said *Tyr is the one-handed god; often must a smith blow.*

Tyr had led them here. Then Tyrthbrand had tried, and tried again, to gain honor for himself, his pride leading him away from the gods, blowing the fire hotter and hotter until it had burned him and his men.

"Again."

Maðr. The symbol for man. This rune told of the present.

Man is but augmented earth; mighty is the grip of the hawk.

From the earth they came, to the earth they would return. Is that what had happened to Thorolf? Had he chosen to go back to the ground? A hawk gripped most tightly as it killed. Were they all trapped in that death hold?

Tyrthbrand drew the third rune without prompting. *Sól*. The sun. He was almost surprised that hadn't been the second rune as it was always so hot in this land. Then he remembered the entire line from the rune poem.

The sun is the light of the land; I bow to holy doom.

Tyrthbrand couldn't run away from his god, no matter how hard he tried. Just because the gods had abandoned them all didn't mean the gods were through playing with them. He couldn't save himself or be a man without the gods. And all his men would die with him in this foreign place. There was no escape for any of them.

And the gods wouldn't take them. They were to be sacrificed without the promise of any of the halls of the gods. Death was coming to them. Death without

hope. Winter without a spring in this land hotter than
any summer.

Tyrthbrand sat, unmoving, after Snorri gathered the
runes back up and left, afraid that he might actually
shatter when he did try to stand.

Lady Two Bird greeted Illugi as soon as she finished
her morning ablutions, assured him that she was fine,
then sent him back to his own camp to pack up. They
would be leaving very soon to start their journey
again. For once he didn't argue, but turned and left.
Lady Two Bird was surprised, and wondered if he was
still in shock from his friend's sacrifice.

Lady Two Bird called Seven Waterlily to her. Seven
Waterlily arrived with the two other attendants in tow.

"Fetch more water," Lady Two Bird ordered the
attendants. They exchanged sullen looks, then grace-
lessly stood and went toward the center of camp
where the communal buckets were generally kept.

"Quickly," Lady Two Bird hissed as soon as they
were out of hearing range. Seven Waterlily followed
her out of the clearing.

Most cities were laid out following similar patterns,
with the same central temples and specific streets for
other gods and goddesses. Lady Two Bird headed
swiftly for the district she assumed once held the complex of her goddess Ix Chebel.

Cauac Sky had insisted that they rest another day
in the cursed city. Lady Two Bird wondered if he'd
hoped to cause another incident with the Iselanders—
she'd been shocked to hear from the guards how he
reveled in the blood of the sacrifice, and was even
more appalled when she'd witnessed it. She'd tried to
talk with Tyrthbrand twice since Thorolf's death; both
times, he'd barely responded, as if he were in shock.
She hadn't wanted to stay very long in the Iselander
camp. The air there seemed cooler, almost blue with
haze from their fire. The youngest member of their

group had stayed huddled beside it the entire time, as if seeking a warmth that was impossible to find.

She'd seen the sword hilt sticking out of the ground at the edge of their camp and had wondered what kind of protection it gave them. She wanted the sword for herself. She wanted to give it to the priests in the City of Wells, so they could discover the properties of the blood stone. She knew it wasn't appropriate to ask, certain that it had been the dead man's weapon. But she would get it, learn the recipe for the strange stone, sooner or later. It was her destiny to have her name written on the temple stairs, to give her permanence that not even children could bring. And it was Tyrthbrand's destiny to help her.

Lady Two Bird hadn't understood what Thorolf had said when he'd died. It had surprised Tyrthbrand, though, and hurt him deeply. At least, that's what she thought she'd read in his alien face before he'd lost all expression. Whatever it was that Thorolf had said, it hadn't been good.

It was only in the quiet of the dead city that she came to another realization: that she no longer thought of the Iselanders as a pack of dogs, loyal to one another, but as a group of men, as human as her own people, with bonds of duty and friendship between them.

According to the Red Hand guard who liked to keep Seven Waterlily company—a relationship Lady Two Bird encouraged purely for safety reasons, hoping to have at least one of the enemy on their side—Cauac Sky believed something had gone wrong with the sacrifice. The priest had spent the day sitting in a clearing by himself, trying first one, then another means of divination. But nothing showed his path. Were the gods angry over the death of the Iselander? Or were they supposed to sacrifice all the foreigners? Lady Two Bird suspected the former, not the latter, though she knew Cauac Sky had a different opinion.

After further meditation, she decided that she also needed guidance. Had the gods turned their backs on the Iselanders? She decided to ask Ix Chebel, to have the goddess direct her if she would.

Who would the Iselanders consult for guidance, she mused as she walked. From her talks with Tyrthbrand, she had learned much of their gods. In many ways, they were similar to hers: there was a god of war, a god of justice, a goddess of the hearth, among others. At different times of the year and in different circumstances, they prayed to Tyr, Thor, or even Loki. But each man was also dedicated to a single god, and asked for favor from that god alone. Was Tyr who Tyrthbrand would go to? Or was there another god, one who saw the future? She would have to remember to ask.

They passed more platforms, empty of gods. Lady Two Bird wondered what the Iselanders did with their empty cities. They didn't bury their old gods, like her people did. It sounded like they burned, then built anew, with their iron.

For the first time, Lady Two Bird let herself wonder if bringing the blood stone to her people was the right thing to do. It would change her people in more ways than she could ever know. The coming of the White Hands would change them as well, though. Lady Two Bird suspected that while more Iselanders weren't on their way, other foreigners were, and her people needed to be prepared. Only the blood stone would save them.

Lady Two Bird let her faith in her goddess buoy her spirits back up. If she did bring her people this gift, they would write her name on the temple stairs. She wouldn't have to fear the dark enclosed places. Something of her would live on, beyond her days. Sometimes, change could be good.

The statue to her goddess in the dead city was missing, of course, but stones still lay scattered on the

platform where it had stood. Lady Two Bird wondered
who else had prayed for protection from the madness
of the road, of no home, of months of travel.

She drew out the stone that she'd kept in a small
pouch, the one that she'd brought with her from the
white road they traveled on before they'd reached the
city. She didn't want to be without one, recalling the
last time she'd prayed. She was glad she had. She
didn't want to use anything from this cursed place.
And since she'd planned to ask about her future
course, it made sense to use something from where
she'd been.

Lady Two Bird warmed the stone between her
palms for a moment, closing her eyes and singing silent hymns to her lady, praising her sight in the darkness, her weaving of rainbows, and clearing of the way
after the storm.

It seemed darker when she opened her eyes again.
Lady Two Bird glanced toward the sky, but no clouds
had crept up on them. The air had grown thicker, and
it took more effort than it should have to push her
hand forward.

Before she could put the stone down on the pedestal, she heard Seven Waterlily suck in a deep breath
behind her. "Guards," she whispered.

"Hide," Lady Two Bird whispered back, palming
the rock. Though it was her right to pray as she wished
to her goddess, she'd purposefully left her Iselander
guard behind. She didn't think Cauac Sky would try
to sacrifice her yet, but she was related to royalty—
he would consider her blood precious and rare—and
his madness was growing. He'd already spoken to her
once about the dangers of traveling. She wasn't about
to put herself in the path of an "accident."

Seven Waterlily turned and started back down the
road, dodging between the trees that disrupted the *sak
beh*. Lady Two Bird followed her attendant, not rushing, but not moving sedately either. The jungle seemed

unbreachable next to them, but Seven Waterlily found an animal trail that they could walk along without too much trouble. Rotting leaves covered the path and muffled their footsteps. Lady Two Bird heard her pounding heart over the quiet. Verdant trunks with low branches surrounded them and snagged their skirts. She walked into a spiderweb spread across the path, the ghost threads momentarily robbing her of breath like a sticky, too tight mask. She clawed it from her face without slowing.

They heard nothing behind them. They paused, breathing hard. Neither spoke. Lady Two Bird told herself that avoiding the guards was just expedient. There was no reason for the fear she felt, yet bone-numbing terror still wound around her like a twisted vine.

After her breath had slowed to its normal pace, Lady Two Bird turned to lead them back. She scanned the jungle floor for the path they'd followed, but it seemed to have disappeared under their feet as they'd traveled along it.

"Mistress?" Seven Waterlily asked.

Lady Two Bird nodded and set a pleasant smile across her face, determined not to show her fear. "It's all right."

The pair of them turned around, searching the earth, seeking a way out, but the trail was no longer obvious. Monkeys screeched above them. Insects thrummed and sang.

They were *not* lost. Lady Two Bird refused to believe that just taking a few steps into the true jungle had confused them so thoroughly, though everyone knew the stories of the lost hunter, the lost twins, the lost jaguar. . . .

Lady Two Bird reached down and touched the ground next to her feet, to see if maybe the stones of the earth would talk to her, direct her. The dirt felt moist between her fingers, and smelled of decay as well as of rich growing things. From her lowered position, she saw a spot to the side where the vines weren't strung between the trees, and the bushes didn't strangle the ground. It wasn't a clear path, but it did appear to be some kind of trail.

It wasn't in the direction that she thought they'd come from, but she wondered if that mattered. There was a saying among her people: *every path in the jungle takes you where you need to go.*

She rose, brushed off her hands, and started to walk again, Seven Waterlily sticking close behind her. The trail hemmed them in on either side. It twisted like a meandering stream, forcing the two women to move slowly, stepping over trunks, branches and roots, as well as ducking under leaves and vines.

After some time, they heard something low and rhythmic just before them. They stopped, listening hard.

"Drum?" Seven Waterlily whispered.

Yes. A drum. Lady Two Bird nodded and walked forward cautiously. She didn't know what part of the camp they approached. They might have gone straight from the pot into the fire.

As they approached, she realized she'd been right. She recognized Cauac Sky's voice chanting above the sound of the drum. She'd never be able to explain their presence to him. He might instantly declare her insane, like Lord Six Sky. They needed to get out of there.

Then she heard him speak her name. She froze for a moment, then started forward again. Creeping more quietly than corn mice, they made their way through the brush.

The drum rattled to silence. Through the branches, Lady Two Bird saw Cauac Sky on his knees, praying. He spoke aloud another name, "Waterlily Jaguar," and thumped the drum a few more times. Then he put the drum to one side, drew out a handful of cacao beans from a pouch next to him, and threw them onto an elaborately painted cloth.

Lady Two Bird had seen charlatans in the marketplace do this kind of divination; only they used mere pebbles instead of expensive beans. She'd never known a true foretelling to come from such a casting.

Cauac Sky leaned forward, studying the ground carefully.

"What do you see?"

Lady Two Bird had to shift a little to the side to catch a glimpse of the other person in the clearing. She wasn't surprised to see that Jeweled Skull sat near the priest. But she'd been told that the priest had been casting alone. What had changed?

"I see barriers to our rightful ascension."

Ascension? Did Cauac Sky believe that he and his adopted boys could be declared as gods? That they could earn a place as stars in the heavens? He really was mad.

This was no true divination. This *was* a show.

"Lady Two Bird must die by the dawn of Etz'nab."

Lady Two Bird opened her mouth, but nothing came out, the proclamation of her death holding her as still as stone. Etz'nab—the Day of Flint. A day of chipping, a day of burning. A day for burying the dead or cutting new cloth. A day of stone, of course.

Five days hence. Five nameless, unlucky days.

"Either by death or by sacrifice."

Of course. He didn't care about anything but her blood.

"But what about the introductions?" Jeweled Skull asked.

"The foreigners provide us with all the invitations we need."

Lady Two Bird reluctantly agreed. The Iselanders were enough of a novelty that just with their presence alone the Red Hand troop might be able to get an audience. It would take not just bribery, but skill, to

get through all the ranks of guards and into Lord
Smoke Moon or Lord Kan Boar's presence.

Waterlily Jaguar could probably do it.

"All of them?"

Cauac Sky laughed, a joyful sound that didn't be-
long with all this talk of death.

"You can be just as insightful as your brother. No,
we need only one. The rest can—satisfy the gods.
Carry our messages. Strengthen our pleas."

All would die.

Of course. Cauac Sky could see only a single use
for the Iselanders—to prove the validity of his false
vision. The bloodthirstiness in his voice chilled her.
He didn't understand the importance of their knowledge, how the blood stone could save their people.
On the other hand, if anyone else bothered to learn
the foreigners' language, they'd quickly learn that the
Iselanders didn't think their ship had survived. Cauac
Sky insisted that the foreigners were the first of a great
horde. The Iselanders themselves didn't believe that
at all.

The priests in the City of Wells loved all knowledge.
They would work hard to understand the foreigners.
Cauac Sky's "proof" of his visions would also be the
means of proving its falseness.

"And my brother?"

"Your brother continues to help, not hinder."

Lady Two Bird grimaced. Only as long as he continued to be useful—he probably wouldn't live many
days beyond the introduction to the city leaders either.
It was obvious to anyone with eyes that Waterlily Jaguar didn't hold Cauac Sky in as high a regard as his
brother did. He was the smarter of the twins, and
probably saw the old priest's proclamations and visions for what they were: a play for power, not com-
munication dictated by the gods.

"How should we take Lady Two Bird?"

"Sacrifice, if we can. If we can get one of the lords

to read the letters from Evening Star. Accident, if we can't."

He would declare her mad. Like Lord Six Sky. And the attendants that Evening Star had sent with her would repeat all of his claims. The attendants didn't realize that he'd kill them as well. He'd sacrifice Seven Waterlily with Lady Two Bird, as a servant to help Lady Two Bird through her trials in Xibalba. All witnesses would disappear, and Cauac Sky would have the start of his ascension.

What could she do about it? She couldn't admit to eavesdropping. If she proclaimed foreknowledge, that would just prove his claim that she was too much influenced by her goddess. Besides, he could just deny anything she claimed. She had no proof.

Cauac Sky and Jeweled Skull continued to talk, to plot, to plan. Lady Two Bird stopped listening. There had to be a way out, a path that would save her from the darkness, past the day of her intended death.

Suddenly she remembered how the air had seemed so thick in the city, how she hadn't been able to pray to her goddess back at her statue. The jungle path really had taken her where she needed to go. Ix Chebel had guided her here, helped Lady Two Bird learn of this trap.

That meant that there was an escape. Lady Two Bird just had to find it. Her goddess couldn't do anything more for her, otherwise she already would have. Lady Two Bird didn't understand the rules that bound the gods, dictated their conversations with men, but knew that they existed, and that the gods must respect them.

It didn't take long for Lady Two Bird and Seven Waterlily to find a path out of the trees, emerging close to where they'd entered. They didn't say a word as they cleaned each other up, straightening hair and clothes, wiping off the remains from the jungle as best they could. Finally, Seven Waterlily walked to the edge of the cleared area and fell to her knees, staining her skirt, marking herself. "Oops," she said over her shoulder to Lady Two Bird. "I must have tripped over a root, which is how I got so dirty. You must have helped me up."

Smiling and shaking her head, Lady Two Bird did go over to help Seven Waterlily stand. Together they walked back to their area of camp, their alibi prepared, their escape, not.

"How are you this lovely morning?"

Lady Two Bird barely stopped herself from shuddering as Cauac Sky's voice oozed over her. Since their stop at the cursed city the day before, the priest had come up several times a day and been solicitous of her situation. It was as if, now that he'd named a day for her death, he could afford to be nice to her. Did he really believe he'd fooled her? Or that she wouldn't suspect anything after he'd been so insulting earlier?

"Our sleep was peaceful and dreamless." She raised her voice so that the others walking nearby might hear. Dreams came from her lady. Though Lady Two Bird didn't yet know how to escape the trap she saw closing around her as they drew closer to the City of Wells, she continued planting seeds of proof of her sanity in as many as she could. She knew that the guards closest to her were hand selected by the priest, and so predisposed not to believe her, but she still tried.

"And the foreigners?"

Cauac Sky's voice held no obvious tone of worry, but Lady Two Bird thought she detected one nonetheless. *Something* had happened during the sacrifice of the Iselander. Storms and strange clouds had chased them ever since they started again, out of season, unexpected, as if the gods themselves quarreled.

"Quiet," she said. Which was true. Withdrawn

would have been more true. Tyrthbrand had barely spoken with her, regardless of how she prodded. He held himself stiffly, like an old battered ceiba tree, as if he'd blow over and shatter in the next strong wind.

"Looking forward to the end of our journey? Being back at the city with your family?"

Lady Two Bird resisted the temptation to reply with a sarcastic remark about how happy her family would be to see her, especially with this ragtag group of renegade warriors. As for comments about her physical condition, well, even if she were tracking blood with every step she still wouldn't have told the priest.

"I'm sure my sister Lady Star Storm and I will have many things to talk about and share," Lady Two Bird replied, answering the priest's unspoken question about whether she would live up to her end of their bargain and still make introductions for him and his troop. She knew that only this promise, this hope of an advocate at the court, kept her heart in her chest for the next few days, until her time to die. It would be easier for the priest if she were still alive to make the introductions, bring him in with Lady Star Storm's good graces, but she had no doubt that she was easily disposed of, either before or after she reached her home in the City of Wells.

Home. Her sister. An idea suddenly came to her.

A guard called Cauac Sky away before the priest could ask more questions that Lady Two Bird didn't want to answer. As they approached the city the road split more often, and the group needed blessings more frequently as they passed through the crossroads. Lady Two Bird let Cauac Sky place the protection stones on the pedestals or cairns most of the time, though sometimes she also offered a small pebble, always giving thanks, never asking for more guidance.

Lady Two Bird already had the beginnings of a plan. She needed to escape with all the Iselanders. But to where? That was the problem. They couldn't

stay in the city—no matter how the introductions
went, Cauac Sky was too much of a threat. She
couldn't barricade herself in her temple, trying to
avoid the fate he'd selected for her.

Now she knew where they could go. When Lord
Smoke Moon had married her sister, he'd given her
sister a small estate. It was the least of his properties,
not because of its size, but because it was so close to
the City of Wells' city-state border. However, because
of its proximity to their rivals, it was enclosed behind
stone walls, like a small village, and easily defendable.
Lady Two Bird had been there once as part of the
purification ceremony Lady Storm Sky had conducted
after the birth of her second son. She remembered her
sister's bragging about how few men it would take to
make it a safe place to live. As well as how fertile the
nearby fields were.

And maybe, if the goddess had truly blessed Lady
Two Bird, the rocks in the hills close to the property
would be the right kind for making the blood stone.

It wouldn't be easy to escape with the Iselanders.
They were good fighters, though, and once they
reached the estate, they would be able to defend it. If
they left the day after they arrived at the city, they
would all still be used to traveling.

At the next crossroads, Lady Two Bird placed a
stone on the crossroad's cairn. She didn't allow herself
to imagine that it trembled under her fingers. She
knew that she'd chosen the right way.

Tyrthbrand walked dully along the road, alone with
his thoughts. He was grateful that the other Iselanders
had continued their duty, protecting Lady Two Bird,
because he wasn't certain he'd notice a wild boar attack until it was already upon them.

He didn't see a way out of their dilemma. He'd lost
the grace of his gods; he'd been abandoned, but not
forgotten. How could he and his men escape their

notice? Save themselves from Niflheim, or even Xibalba, the Itza version of the underworld? He reminded himself of his promise to teach Lady Two Bird how to make iron. It was the only thing that might save him.

When Lady Two Bird came up to talk with him, Tyrthbrand tried to make himself pay attention. He found it difficult to focus on what she was saying until he realized she was trying to teach him a new word, one with connotations that *did* mean something to him.

She was trying to teach him the word for "run."

Using a combination of his and her languages, Tyrthbrand asked, "After City of Wells? Run?"

The smile Lady Two Bird gave him told him he'd guessed correctly.

But just running—that wasn't enough. There was no guarantee that they'd escape. That they'd live to tell of it. That the gods would let them go. Lady Two Bird had already stressed to him, again and again, how dangerous the City of Wells would be for them.

Tyrthbrand already knew the word for "see," but he didn't know if "see" was related to "vision" in Lady Two Bird's language. He asked about it anyway.

"Have you *seen* it?"

Lady Two Bird hesitated, glancing around quickly at those who traveled near them. None of the Itza guards were in hearing distance—Tyrthbrand's men had made sure of that. He felt a quick rippling of pride at how well they did their duty, even in the face of certain death and dishonor.

"See?" Lady Two Bird asked. She nodded. "Yes."

For the first time in days, Tyrthbrand felt a brief glitter of hope flutter through him.

He couldn't rely on his gods to do anything but either play with or shun him and his men. Maybe, though, they could rely on his lady's goddess. Maybe they could escape the fate of torture and sacrifice.

Chapter 6

"Ekchuah! You greedy gullet! Open that big mouth of yours! Drink! Drink!"

Itzanam didn't join those shouting encouragement, but he couldn't help how his fingers curled tensely around the arms of the strange seat the foreign gods had provided him for viewing the games. The Itza merchant god was competing with the tall, red-haired god who carried a hammer—Thor, he thought the name had been—in a drinking contest. So far, there had been no tricks, and the two seemed evenly matched. Ekchuah *did* have a great appetite, though his aspect that day appeared thin and weathered. Thor stood larger in every way: height, girth, shoulders, and laughter. Itzanam recognized the emblem the foreign god carried for what it was: he was a fertility god, not a god of war. And drink would loosen the belts of men and the girdle of more than one woman.

The Hero Twins stood to one side, heads together, in quiet conversation with Loki. Itzanam wanted both to forcibly separate the three of them as well as agree to whatever it was they planned. They caused such havoc, and by such, created the opportunities the gods would need soon. Though the twins had stood beside him in front of Feathered Serpent, they followed their own crazed and looping path. He could not rely on them, or the changes they brought.

Itzanam stole another look at his counterpart, Tyr, also seated and silent. The other god had grown more

severe the longer he stayed in his chair, becoming
harsh and imposing. The weight of law bore down on
him, as well as flowed out from him. Itzanam understood what it was like to have power concentrated in
a single source from before the time when he'd been
split, before war and commerce had been stripped
from him, but it wasn't quite the same with Tyr. He
judged, but from a place of honesty and honor that
Itzanam both admired and ridiculed. He didn't know
the entire story behind how the god had lost his hand,
though he knew it had to do with promises Tyr had
kept, as well as ties he no longer had faith in.

"Come on, you great goat shagger! Or are you
going to shame us like you shame the lovely golden-
haired Sif?"

Tyr chuckled. It took Itzanam a moment to realize
that the latest insult had been hurled by the striking
woman who bore both a very long knife as well as the
implements of a household around her belt. Though
the foreign names were difficult for him to hold, he
remembered hers: Freyja. He wondered at her weapons, at all the women's weapons. Women didn't fight.
They were meant to raise children, weave, and sew,
brighten the long nights. He was curious what it would
be like to bed a woman unafraid to take his head, not
in madness, but in fair battle.

The cheering on both sides grew a little more
coarse, a bit more ragged. Tyr didn't join in, but now
Itzanam did, cursing Ekchuah for his bragging, for his
lack of manhood, for not being able to hold his drink,
for his wandering feet that had led him to forget
where he'd come from. None of it did any good. Thor
drained flagon after flagon of the honeyed wine that
the Itza had never tried before, his belly not increasing
in size, nor his swagger faltering. The merchant god
tried valiantly to keep up, but eventually landed on
the ground beside the table—Itzanam wasn't charita-
ble enough to call it sitting. The laughter of the foreign

gods floated high enough to bounce off the clouds.
They smacked their companion on the back and con-
gratulated him on a job well done, a couple of them
singing a few choruses of a drinking song that compared Thor's bottomless cup with his endless loving.
They even offered a hand to Ekchuah, helping him
up off the ground, treating him as a friend, not with
the disdain usually reserved for those who lost. The
entire tone of the end of the competition filled Itzanam with hope. These people fought hard, died well,
and yet laughed. He didn't understand it, but he
wanted to.

Though it didn't need to be said, Tyr's voice rang
out above the reveling. "Thor is the winner!"

Ekchuah, with a wide grin and unsteady hands, produced two handfuls of cigars from his great sack. The
foreign gods had never seen such things before.

With great ceremony, even though he still listed to
one side, Ekchuah lit the first one and presented it to
Thor after demonstrating how to smoke it. Of course,
the foreigner choked and coughed, his pink cheeks
turning redder. This was a constant joke among the
Itza, the virgin smoker. The Hero Twins laughed
harder than anyone else did. Ekchuah showed the tall
foreigner how to take the smoke into his mouth, savor
the taste, then blow it out before it turned bitter.

All the foreign gods had to try it. Tyr left his high
seat to join them. Itzanam refused, wanting to keep
his wits clear, to watch and observe.

This was the end of the fifth contest. The foreigners
had won three of them so far. Though the smoke
would confuse their senses in a way they'd never experienced before, they would win many more of the contests, Itzanam was sure of it. The Itza would be forced
to give away more sacrificial smoke, more honey,
probably even some of the sacred mushrooms.

Everything was going perfectly according to plan.

*   *   *

"Ha! Do you see that?" Tyr stood beside Itzanam's chair, pointing at Loki crossing the finish line well ahead of his Itza competitor. He didn't feel like sitting anymore. He wanted to cheer and pace and curse, and when he was in his high seat, those feelings were . . . lessened. Though he understood better why, he still fought against it.

And speaking of Loki—Tyr couldn't help but beam like a new father at the trickster god. Since his resurrection, Loki had been happier, stronger, yet pliant. It was as if the experience had reforged his will, bending it closer to the rest of the gods', reflecting rather than subverting. Tyr understood that Loki's chaos was as necessary as the seasons, but he still rejoiced in how Loki had softened.

The half god had just won the latest footrace with the strange Chaob, the Itza gods of wind. Tyr hadn't expected Loki to win, but the younger god had just winked and said, "What travels faster than a lie?" Tyr suspected that the way the course had been set, around trees and over boulders, had contributed to Loki's fleetness. While winds could blow around corners, it wasn't their natural state, while bending and changing courses was Loki's.

The god with the feathers down his back approached Tyr and Itzanam. Loki had warned Tyr about this one, how he was slyer than he seemed, but Tyr didn't see it. He'd sat in judgment long enough to know the way lies burrowed and hid in men's hearts. Tyr judged Feathered Serpent to be like the spear he always carried, straightforward and farseeing. In his opinion, Itzanam was the one not to be trusted.

Loki had told Tyr that the Itza gods had split recently—before the arrival of the Puuc, Feathered Serpent and Itzanam had been one. Tyr felt that just proved his point: if the honest part of Itzanam had

pulled away from him and enclosed itself in a warrior
aspect, then didn't it make sense to trust the mystic
less and the warrior more?

"Are you ready for the next contest?" Feathered
Serpent asked, his smile wide and friendly. He shifted
slightly as he stood, listing to one side. Tyr wondered
how much mead he'd had to drink. The Iseland version was much stronger than the one the Itza were
used to. Tyr pulled himself up straighter, pleased that
he'd managed to keep his senses about him. The
strange smoke the Itza had provided had gone to his
own head in different and interesting ways, giving the
world edges that he'd never experienced before, so
he'd stopped imbibing quickly.

He grinned back. "Of course, little man." Tyr
wasn't that much taller than the other god, but it never
hurt to remind an opponent of his defects.

Feathered Serpent seemed to have caught the spirit
of the Iseland gods and laughed. "Shorter I may be,
but my aim is still more true," he said, hefting his
spear in a lewd manner.

"More true than whose?" Tyr asked.

"Yours, of course."

"Mine?" Tyr asked, surprised. He and Itzanam
were the judges of the games. They weren't participating in any of the contests.

"Unless you're scared?"

"Of you?" Tyr put as much incredulity as he could
into his words. Justice was swift and precise, and flew
as far as the wind. He had faith in his spear-throwing
abilities. "And what would we be wagering for?"

"Souls," came the dry word from behind him.

"Souls?" Feathered Serpent asked, his surprise
matching Tyr's. "We don't want to lose the souls of
our people."

Tyr silently agreed. They had so few human followers here. He couldn't afford to lose even one until
more arrived. If any more arrived.

Feathered Serpent continued, hissing, as if by lowering his voice Tyr wouldn't be able to hear him even though he was standing beside them. "More souls would just strengthen *them*."

Ah. Tyr hadn't considered that aspect of it. Would foreign souls, even if they were already dead, fortify his hold on this world? More men for his hall, for fighting . . . it was worth considering.

But only if he was certain he could win.

Also, if he won he could continue raising the stakes until he reached his real goal: a resurrection similar to Loki's, re-creating him whole and two-handed again.

"An exchange of souls?" Feathered Serpent asked, turning to Tyr.

"Why would I agree to such poor odds?" Tyr asked. He had to keep them negotiating. "You have so many followers. I have so few."

Itzanam considered for a moment. "One of precious blood?" he suggested.

Tyr shook his head. "Though our lands have joined, we wouldn't benefit from the rarity of such a sacrifice."

Feathered Serpent spoke up. "How about ten of my elite? Guards and warriors all. For just one of yours."

"One hundred."

Even Itzanam look shocked. "No, that's too many."

Tyr shrugged, and turned his back on them to return to his seat. "We need them."

"Do it," Tyr heard Feathered Serpent urging Itzanam from behind him. He sat slowly, and for the first time, relished the sternness overtaking his features. Itzanam and Feathered Serpent would never be able to read his eyes while he sat in judgment. Besides, it was a fair trade. Anything less belittled the sacrifice he was making.

After more hurried whispering that Tyr ignored, Itzanam sighed and said, "Done."

Tyr nodded and called for his spear. Loki came with

it, not bothering to hide his concern. "What promises have you made this time?" he asked Tyr.

Promises? He hadn't promised anything. Just made a wager, one he was sure to win. Yet the trickster had tried before to get him to pledge not to make any promises. "Nothing that I regret," he said, cursing himself as the words slipped out. He couldn't help but tell the truth while on his high seat, something that he didn't seem to recall when he should.

"You needn't worry," Tyr added, pushing himself upright. And he wasn't worried. He would win. He had to.

Loki sighed and shook his head. "I make no proclamations," he said, "but I fear your oaths and your honor will be the death of us all."

Tyr couldn't contain a shudder at Loki's words. Of course, Loki was opposed to his law. That was his place, his purpose. And he wasn't foretelling anything with his statement—he'd even said so.

Still, Tyr felt nervous as they approached the line from which they would hurl their spears, especially when he saw the look that passed between Feathered Serpent and Itzanam. He wondered if maybe he should have listened closer to Loki's warnings about the colorful warrior god.

It was too late now.

Tyr took the first shot. His spear flew across the clearing where the gods had gathered, past the fields and to the foot of the first range of mountains. The Itza politely applauded and the Iselanders shouted when Feathered Serpent's spear nestled in next to it, head to toe, an even match. Tyr let his chest swell. His followers could use the extra hundred men. After he won this contest, it would be easy to continue to up the wager.

Tyr's second shot landed amongst the foothills, besting his first shot by a league. With seemingly no effort,

Feathered Serpent's sailed past it, passing Tyr's by a ship's length.

"Lucky throw," Feathered Serpent said, shrugging as he backed away from the line.

The sinking feeling in Tyr's gut told him otherwise. Feathered Serpent had grounded his spear exactly where he'd intended to. The disgust in Loki's eyes confirmed it.

Though Tyr's last spear skidded on the ice at the top of the mountain before it came to rest, Feathered Serpent's third flew as if caught by Njord and his winds, past the first ring of mountains, landing at the summit of the next. Tyr couldn't congratulate his opponent: his words stuck in his throat, pinned there by how they had tricked him. It was obvious that no matter how many spears they threw, Feathered Serpent's would go much, much farther than Tyr's would. War reached more places than justice did.

The Iseland gods couldn't afford to lose a single human follower in this iteration of Ásgard—but they had no choice. Tyr had promised. At least the Itza didn't make him choose Tyrthbrand. He picked instead the one who followed him with the least devotion: Thorolf.

Strength poured out of the towering blond warrior's spirit, then crystallized and glowed stronger as the gods focused their attention on him. It was easy to maneuver him into performing their will with so many gods lending their strength. And it was always the simplest of efforts to fate a man to die.

The twin monkey scribes shat on the chosen one, marking him more colorfully than the sacrificial paints that the human Itza would use later on, a mark that the gods could see, even after the physical attributes had been scrubbed off.

They also caught the spear he threw and ceremonially placed it at Tyr's feet. What good would a hu-

man's spear do him, a foreign human's at that? Tyr
picked up the spear with trepidation. No magic wriggled in its shaft, no vision was granted him upon
touching it. He wrapped his hand around it anyway
and squeezed, wishing that some of the towering humanity that had last touched the wood remained in it.
But it was just dead wood.

The gods arranged an area for watching the sacrifice. Tyr stayed on his high seat overlooking the platform. He judged himself harshly, called himself an
arrogant fool for letting the Itza trick him. He had no
one but himself to blame. He swore to himself that it
would not happen again.

He couldn't help but be fascinated by the sacrificial
process though. He hadn't seen other Itza sacrifices.
He'd stayed in his land, on their side of the border,
as he'd said he would. Loki had, and had reported it
in great detail, but there was always a difference
seeing it, tasting the priests' excitement and anticipation, smelling the swirls of incense, hearing the hearts
echoing the constant drums. This sacrifice seemed to
be following the same outlines as the ones that Loki
had told him about, so the cleansing, combing, and
painting didn't surprise him.

The effect of the mushrooms was startling. As they
took hold, Thorolf's skin started to shine with the
same cool blue-green luminescence as the mark the
twin monkey scribes had given him. Tyr had seen men
in the grip of a mortal wound bridge the worlds and
be able to peer through the veils, but Thorolf was in
no pain. The dried fungus let him step close to the
borders, as well as giving him sight through the spirals
of time, back to when the city still lived, not just the
most recent one, but the ones before that as well. The
Itza built one city on top of another, cocooning old
temples with new ones as prescribed by their books
and the stars.

People who had lived in the houses and fields, who

the scribes had captured in the murals on the city walls, came to life under Thorolf's gaze, under the gods' eyes. When the humans were ready to leave the clearing, the procession had swelled like a wave, completely filling the road to the deep sacrificial pond. Echoes of drums from the past and the present made the ground shake. Hazy ghosts marched on top of one another, eons of generations represented. Mad swirling colors rolled through the air like waves from the people to the gods and back.

Loki approached Tyr, took his hand, tried to pull him from his seat. "You gave his soul away. You must greet him."

The Itza gods already stood on the sidelines, watching the humans and their ghosts pass by. The Islanders held back, waiting for Tyr to lead them.

Tyr didn't want to leave his chair. He didn't want to release this proud, brave soul. Thorolf would have been happy in his hall, fighting, drinking, and casting deeds into song. But Tyr had given his word, and Loki had made no offer of help. Not that Tyr would have accepted even if the trickster had. He was more honorable than Odin. He wouldn't be known as an oath breaker.

With ill grace, the one-handed god shoved himself from his seat. The Iseland gods stepped up behind him. Thorolf began to babble as they approached, his eyes still catching on beings even Tyr didn't see. Older gods? Or other impressions of himself, from the other splinters of Ásgard? He dismissed the glamour around the stump of his sword arm and gestured with it toward the human: not a blessing—he couldn't do that; Thorolf's soul was destined for the Itza—but an acknowledgment of the human's honor, his bravery, his sacrifice.

None could understand Thorolf's words, but all knew his meaning. He asked after fallen companions, after his own fate. Tyr didn't answer. The man deserved better than what had befallen him. All Tyr could do was shake his head and turn away.

Thorolf fell silent for a while after that. Tyr had expected curses. With slow steps, each dragging through thick air, Tyr returned to his high seat and made himself watch.

The laugh the human gave just before the end of the sacrifice echoed through the realm of the gods, stirred the trees, and pierced the sky with strange colored eddies. Then he chanted his final verse, each word rolling with thunderous resonance, striking the mountains and bouncing back.

Tyr looked to Loki, to see if this were some hoax of his, but the puzzled expression on the smaller god's face told him that the trickster had no part of this. The Itza appeared to be just as confused.

Just under the water of the sacrificial pool lay Xibalba—a mass of vines, roots, and tortured souls screamed out for him to join them, the weight of their pleas sounding even in the heavens. Tyr assumed that if the human could see the gods, he could also see what awaited him, and so he understood why the human would want to escape. But he didn't know how a warrior could give his soul to a tree.

It appeared that the tree had heard the human's prayer, though. When Thorolf leaped, his spirit didn't fall with his body. A white and sea-green net caught it and wrapped around it, then pulled back, into the side of the cliff, just under the tree the human had spoken of. Instead of Thorolf's soul going to strengthen the Itza, it stayed in the land, strengthening it.

As the shimmering lights faded, Tyr's chest caved in as the power of the human's belief disappeared from the world. One more gone. He pulled himself up straighter in his chair and stared at Loki. They had to do something to boost their strength, to tie themselves more closely to this land, so they could be less dependent on their few human followers that remained.

Or the hungry jungle would subsume this sliver of Ásgard.

Itzanam struggled to keep his features humanesque, not to allow his iguana aspect to manifest. The other Itza seemed to be experiencing similar battles, many less successful than others. The two monkey scribes screeched and fled for the trees. The Bacabnob all bore identical expressions, as if they'd merged into one being, their characteristics only superficial. The ones who had joined the procession from the spirals of time sank into the ground where they stood, instead of flowing back into the paintings from which they'd come.

The Iselanders had all paled, some just in skin color, others more physically, as if they'd suddenly aged into ghosts like the elder gods. The loss of just one of their followers had weakened them more than he'd expected.

Without another word, all the gods turned and walked back to the grounds where they had been holding the games. The two groups stayed separate, though they walked as clumps rather than as individuals, wordlessly seeking comfort in each other. The Bacabnob came up to Itzanam.

"Just as with the strange foreign goddess," Muluk the eldest said quietly. "The one who was taken before our sacrifice was accepted. The land continues to strengthen itself."

Itzanam nodded. It wasn't the foreigners who were the threat, or at any rate, not these foreigners. He'd never seen this kind of greed before. The earth longed for blood, like plants for rain—the way Ix Chebel had said in her prophecy. He wondered if the elder gods had heard of a time like this, and wished, not for the first time, that he could force words through the spirals of history.

The gods went back to the tables still overloaded

with drink and food. All picked up full flagons, cups, or horns of alcohol. Ekchuah passed out more cigars, and most of the gods partook, wreathing the yard in smoke. Silence swaddled them. Even the strange winds that seemed to constantly battle for supremacy had died down.

Thor shook off the collective introspection first. "A singing contest! That's what we need!" Without waiting for anyone else, he stomped his feet and clapped his hands and started a bawdy verse about the frigidness of the earth and the warmth of his plow.

Though Ekchuah didn't know the words, he picked up the chorus quickly. Wrapping one arm around the waist of the giant redhead, he sang along. The thin trickster joined next, dragging the Hero Twins with him. One by one, others joined, some of the women now improvising the earth's part, swaying their hips and swinging their shoulders provocatively while complaining of the farmer's stamina, as well as the size of his equipment.

Even Tyr had joined in, not with the words, but the clapping and stomping from his seat. No one would judge this contest, except in retrospect, and then the only criteria would be whether it had successfully lifted the gods' spirits or not. It did seem to be working. All the Itza now bore only human aspects. The sallow complexion of the Iselanders had faded, and ruddy cheeks were again in evidence.

The insults grew cruder, and the sides divided not between Itz▮▮▮▮▮▮▮▮▮▮t among men and ▮▮▮▮▮▮▮▮▮▮▮▮▮▮▮▮ted insults at the ▮▮▮▮▮▮▮▮▮s. Itzanam had ▮▮▮▮▮▮▮▮▮times it lasted ▮▮▮▮▮▮▮▮ract themselves ▮▮▮▮▮lown occurred so infrequently.

Itzanam walked over to Tyr and said quietly, "The ▮▮s have not returned yet."

The laughter he got in return surprised him. "You think they should be recording the brilliance of these proceedings?" Itzanam had to smile at the formality in the other god's words, even though they'd been said in a teasing tone.

"No, though it will be a shame to lose such, ah, poetry."

Tyr lifted his mug in a toast, and Itzanam clinked his glass against it in return—a strange custom, but one that he found charming.

"They see more of the land, living as they do among the trees. I must find where they've fled to, to see if they perceive anything else."

Tyr nodded, serious again. "Of course. But you'll return here and we will speak more, yes?"

The heat and weight of Tyr's gaze baked away Itzanam's easy lie. He cursed himself for forgetting that this was a god of honor, of judgment. One who saw far himself.

"Yes. We have much to talk about." That much was true. Itzanam had not told the Iselanders about his vision of joining. If his aspect was to be dominant, they needed to be further weakened before they merged. He also wasn't sure if the time of joining had come, or if the gods had to unite against the land. A god without a land would be like a god without people—no home, no strength, and no hope.

"Your words are true. But there is more you do not say. We will speak again."

Itzanam pulled himself up to his full height, willing his smoke leg to stay physical. He still couldn't quite look the other god in the eye, not without stretching his aspect. The Iselanders were so damn tall.

"I said we would talk again. And we will."

Tyr merely shrugged and took another swig of his drink.

"We will," Itzanam forced himself to say, letting the ring of covenant sound through his words. If he couldn't lull this sharp-eyed god, all his plans would be for naught.

This drew a large smile from the other god. "Then we will," Tyr said, his words reinforcing the promise with something bright and sharp. The blood stone.

The ringing echoes sounded in Itzanam's core. He suddenly realized that this new material was essential for what he'd foreseen. And hadn't Ix Chebel mentioned it in her foretelling also?

Itzanam dipped his head, not quite a bow, not quite a nod, and slipped out of the clearing. He heard Tyr joining in the chorus as he entered the jungle. He paused for a moment, letting the deep scent cushion him, pad his lungs, brush feather-soft fingers across his cheeks.

He really did want to go find the monkey scribes, but not just to talk. They had a task ahead of them while the gods were sufficiently distracted.

The twin monkey scribes approached the garden of the Iseland gods with trepidation. Itzanam cooed behind them, assuring them of their safety, the simplicity of their task, the trivial nature of their deed.

They knew better. The trees swayed away from them in this foreign place instead of toward them. Grasses stuck to their legs, attaching strange burrs to their fur. Seeds, like stones, lay on the paths and hurt their feet. Towering pines brandished their needles and oozed sap, threatening eyes and staining palms.

Ominous creaks and groans sang out from the trees when the wind stroked them. The detritus of seasons past covered hollows that would swallow them whole if they strayed from the known trails. Streams spoke of recent ice and smelled of mountains and nets.

Finally, they came to the heart of the place, where ˌ fruit that must be sacrificed lived.

ʾe branches—"

ʾheir color?"

"Not the gray of age—"

"—nor the green of youth—"

"but the blood of a woman."

"Nonsense," Itzanam assured them. "They may be her children, and bear her likeness, but they're still just trees."

The twin monkey scribes looked at each other. Itzanam couldn't see all that grew. Couldn't taste the depth of the core of these trees, how month-long nights inspired myths of endless days. Didn't understand how spirits wrapped around roots, twisted vines, cracked bark. Couldn't feel the slippery forces that formed and reformed the branches above their heads, shifting continuously, the twigs holding on to midnight lights.

"They will know."

"Even if they don't catch us."

"So? By then it will be too late. We'll have eaten their fruit and will be young again. Now hurry."

With one last long look at each other, the monkey scribes reached out their hands in tandem, wrapped their long fingers around the trunks, and began to climb.

"What's wrong?" Freyja asked again. Idun swayed, pale, unseeing. Her robust figure, with its fertile curves, shrank and diminished. Idun took a step forward, tripped, and landed on her knees.

Freyja ran to her friend's side, put out her hands to help her up, then drew back. What if her illness was contagious? Or what if Idun was being taken, like Liðami?

It didn't matter. Freyja would fight regardless.

She fell to her knees and put her arm around the shaking young woman's waist, only to watch it *sink* into the other goddess.

Freyja found she couldn't pull away. She opened her mouth to call to the others, but no words came out, not even a whisper. She would have shaken with fear, but the stillness of the other goddess froze her, wrapping around her bones with cold hands. The taste of earth, solid and harsh, filled her mouth. An image of torn branches and falling fruit washed over her.

A keening wail filled the clearing. It took Freyja a moment to realize it had emanated not only from Idun but also from all the trees, the bushes—even the ground had taken up and echoed the call.

Tyr abandoned his high seat and came striding toward them. Loki was faster, leaving behind dignity and grace as he raced toward them. Dropping down, he put out his hands, then drew back as traces of anxiousness whipped across his face. Determination stiffened his jaw, and he pushed forward, wrapping his fingers around Idun and Freyja's shoulders.

Loki's presence didn't lessen the strange hold Idun had on Freyja. Rather, it seemed to push them closer together. She felt her breasts swell, her hips widen, and age fall from her, as if she were becoming more fertile, like Idun. A faint belt of the household appeared around Idun's waist, complete with ghost keys and saltcellar.

"What's happening?" Tyr asked.

They were merging. However, Idun's silence still wrapped itself around Freyja's tongue. She couldn't speak.

The strange cry from the forest echoed again, fainter this time. It faded quickly.

Loki seemed to be the only one who understood. "To the garden!" he called as he stood and ran. Thor shouldered his hammer and raced after the smaller god.

Freyja pushed herself slowly to her feet, dragging Idun up with her. She found she still couldn't remove her arm from around the younger goddess, but at least they could move again. Idun grew less pale as they drew deeper into the forest, closer to the heart and to her special trees.

Another call rang out, but this time, it was a roar of anger, followed by a crack of thunder. Freyja found she could remove her arm from around Idun's waist. She shifted her grip, supporting the young woman now as they walked.

Two brown streaks raced past them, swinging through the trees, leaping from branch to branch as easily as a bird flew from cloud to cloud. Idun gasped as they left, shuddering to a stop, bent over as if hit by a birth contraction. Determination and anger filled her face as she straightened up.

She grabbed Freyja's hand and marched forward, head held high, pushing past the men. Freyja followed easily, unsurprised to find Itzanam there, with dozens of golden apples plucked from the trees laying abandoned on the ground.

"Thief," came Idun's low voice from Tyr's side.

Tyr fought down the urge to tell Idun to step back. They *were* her apples after all, her gift to the gods. He would let her have her say. Then he would have his. His stern expression weighed down his face like armor, a good feeling, snug and protected, ready for battle.

"The single fruit you stole will do you no good," she warned.

Tyr was suddenly very glad he'd stayed quiet. He'd thought the monkey scribes had dropped all their misgotten booty.

"Are you so sure, young one?" Itzanam replied. The soft voice held so many overtones of Odin that Tyr wondered momentarily where the old man's eye patch was.

Freyja snorted. "You need to eat of them regularly. And why would we ever let you past our borders, let alone give you access to our garden, ever again?"

"Why indeed," Itzanam replied, looking directly at Tyr.

So *this* was what the Itza gods wanted—the youth of the Iselanders. Resurrection didn't make the Itza gods young; it just restored them to life, made their bodies whole again.

The time for negotiation had come. Tyr stared at Itzanam, trying to see past the tricks and mystic lies. He reminded himself again that Itzanam's face changed with the hour, not just his mood. They would not fool him again.

"We could sacrifice him, here and now," murmured Loki, standing next to Tyr.

The Itza rustled at that, like dried leaves in the wind, anxious, but not scared. Tyr wondered at their lack of fear, their faith in their leader's ability to be resurrected. Would he be though? If they sacrificed him here in Ásgard?

"We could. Kill him for theft. That's what we did to the giant Thiazi when he tried to steal Idun," Thor added.

"But then you wouldn't get what you wanted," Itzanam replied, still addressing Tyr while holding up his hand, stilling his own people. The action drew a silence over all the gods as they realized that more was at stake here.

"Don't," Loki warned as he walked up to Tyr.

Tyr glanced at Loki, wondering what Loki meant. Don't bargain with the old man? Don't trust him? Don't give away Idun's fruit?

It didn't matter. This was Tyr's opportunity to get what he wanted, what he'd really wanted all along, why he'd set the path he had for Tyrthbrand and the others. Not just to find a new land, empty and ripe for the taking, but to be whole again.

To be the head of the gods again. Not just here, but in all the reflections of their world.

"What is it that I want?" Tyr asked into the stifling

THE JAGUAR AND THE WOLF

quiet. He had to force Itzanam into being very clear
about his offering. Tyr didn't trust the other god, but
he did trust his own ability to sense when others told
the truth.

"Your spear hand."

Tyr didn't correct him that it was his sword hand—
the description was close enough. "You can give me
this?" Tyr asked into the shocked silence. Only Loki
knew of the advantages resurrection brought. All the
Iselanders had seen that the false one no longer bore
scars on his face, but they'd been encouraged to believe it was something he'd done on his own—through
trickery, of course.

"Coming back from the dead will make your body
whole."

The truth of Itzanam's words rang through Tyr's
body like the beat of a staff on a hollow tree. His
serious expression cracked under the pressure of the
joy rising through him.

He could have his sword hand again.

Freyja pushed herself forward. "So, like Frigga and
Baldur, you want to cheat death?" she accused Tyr,
her words blowing against him like an arctic wind
across a grassy plain, rippling the surface and sending
Tyr's thoughts scurrying. The cycles would continue if
he were whole, wouldn't they?

"It isn't cheating death," Itzanam replied. "It's
sacrifice."

Tyr heard the blood echoes, the strange resonances
the Itza words had, reverberations that he couldn't
dissect, resonating from ancient spirals of time. It answered Freyja's question, though. This type of resurrection was part of the circle of life and death.

"And in return?" Tyr asked, forging forward with
the bargain, still unsettled but eager.

Itzanam gestured at the fallen apples. "The fruit
that keeps you young." His aspect shifted. His features
grew gnarled. A staff appeared in his hands as one of

his legs turned to smoke. "My people age. Resurrection can't stop that. But with your powers, we will stay young."

Ekchuah stepped forward. "It's a simple bargain, really. We each share our greatest gifts. Our peoples draw closer together, each strengthening the other. It's a way of . . . living."

Tyr heard the unspoken undercurrents of the peace being offered, as opposed to war, a way to coexist without battle, each helping the other. And the merchant god was right. They would be exchanging their greatest gifts with each other, an artful balance that both sides would have to work at to keep fair.

Feathered Serpent cleared his throat, but before he could speak, Hun Ahaw separated from his twin and came forward, saying, "We have seen that together we will become a mighty force."

Tyr wondered exactly what the Itza had seen. He resolved to try to raise an aspect of Gullveig. Maybe she would foretell the future for him, as she had for Odin.

Hopefully she wouldn't just tell him of their own Ragnarok, here, in this foreign land.

Loki looked unimpressed. "So you would kill us all," he said dryly.

"Only to rise again, greater than before," Ix Chebel replied. She danced forward, swaying skeletal hips provocatively as she circled the trickster. The goddess disturbed Tyr like no other, her mingled aspects of soother and madwoman always making his spine tingle, as if just before a battle.

"How do we trust that you'll raise us?" Loki asked, cocking his head to one side, his lack of conviction apparent in his tone. He didn't seem bothered by the goddess, and Tyr had a sudden vision of the pair of them dancing together in a moonlit clearing, the youth laying down with the ancient crone and performing the oldest of rituals.

Thor hefted his hammer. "Why don't we see how effective this resurrection is? Just kill him now. Let him bring himself back." Blustering winds blew his hair back, and Tyr watched fingers of lightning outline his form.

Yax Balam tsked. "Patience. Ritual. Offerings. You know how it works." Why were the Itza tricksters united with Itzanam? Strange effervescent ropes seemed to tie the three of them together.

Ekchuah spoke up. "Besides, you could always stop delivering the fruit. As the young lady said earlier, if we stop eating the apples, their effects are lost."

"I think we should—" Idun started.

"Agree to their suggestion," Tyr interrupted. Yes, they were her fruit, but he was the one who ruled here. He stared at them, one by one. Of course, Freyja was the first to speak up.

"Would you bind us all to this god's word?" she asked. "The land—"

"Our lands are joined. Our fates as well," Ix Chebel sang out, then giggled as she spun in a tight circle.

All the gods paused. Tyr shuddered, Ix Chebel's tone sending sparks across his shoulders, as if he also bore the lightning.

"I can't believe you're actually thinking of granting our highest—" Feathered Serpent said, angrily shoving himself forward, into the fight, his aspect taking on Itzanam's features, as if they were still closely related.

"Believe," spoke Idun, her voice ghosting among them. "Your highest. Our highest."

"Don't," came the quiet word from Loki. Tyr refused to look at him, to pay any attention to him.

"Only me for now. Only my risk. I do not oblige the rest of you," Tyr said, letting his voice carry beyond them and through this entire version of Ásgard.

"For the fruit of *my* loins," Idun said, her tone still as wispy as the cloud trails left over from a dragon's flight.

Tyr turned to her. "Yes, as I direct it." He let his will bore into her. After staring for another long moment, the younger goddess bowed her head in obedience, giving of herself, as always, her bountiful nature still her primary aspect.

Before any other could speak, Tyr turned to Itzanam and chanted his oath.

> *"By my honor and my life,*
> *I give this to thee:*
> *My blood on the altar spilt,*
> *My heart for the land,*
> *In return for the youth*
> *That fair fruit gives."*

So it was done, his words carrying the weight of law carved in the stones of the mountains.

Itzanam smiled, the joy of victory warming his old, weathered skin. Such a foolish young god, to promise such a thing before making Itzanam speak his covenant. He let the silence shift and grow long before he replied, choosing his words carefully.

> *"And with your heart*
> *Forever living we both shall be.*
> *Your sacrifice shall not be wasted*
> *But will forge us together,*
> *With blood and land and tears."*

He spoke the truth, as the world stood at this point, and he knew that Tyr would hear it. He didn't promise, though, to raise the other. All Tyr had to do was to make this sacrifice. Then they would be joined. He was sure of it.

Winds gusted all around Itzanam. The trunks of the trees seemed to swell, the foreign species of bushes suddenly sprouting thin vines, twining through roots,

climbing branches, foliage flattening in the unexpected
heat. The gods grew indistinct until they became mere
lights, some stronger than others, all connected, and
knotted together in the brilliant spiral of time that he
now saw.

"This is the *k'atun* of joining."

He heard the words echoed inside, then outside, of
his head. Had he spoken them out loud? The mighty
river of his vision drenched him again, overwhelming
his senses, until it was all he saw, tasted, smelled.

> *"The ages come, surging like waves.*
> *Songs of courage, poems of the blood stone,*
> *The corn flees the fields*
> *But the gods live on."*

Brilliant colors exploded before his eyes, streaming
like feathers and flowers thrown off a cliff. He saw
the land, strong and proud, hard like a reef, shuddering under the constant waves breaking against it,
but not washing away.

Gentle fingers plucked at his arm. Ix Chebel had
drawn near. He recognized her touch though he
couldn't see her. It comforted him even through the
haze of sight.

> *"The people live,*
> *Praise us and feed us in all our forms,*
> *And the land bears us without change."*

Endless seasons stretched before him, leather tough,
scented with streams of burnt wooden figures and incense, sacred smoke enveloping the figures marching
across the land, the lime taste of death washed away
by sacrifice, blood, and worship.

The image stayed with him as the vision faded. All
the gods stood silent. Tyr nodded and shifted next to
Itzanam, as if agreeing with what had been seen. Ek-

chuah stood closer to the Iselanders than before, and
Itzanam knew that they'd soon proclaim him as one of
their own—the merchant god for a merchant people.

Interesting. The Hero Twins stood apart, still separated, while Loki, mouth agape, stood between them.
A threefold trickster god?

"I say that your vision is death, old man," Feathered Serpent said. He walked toward Itzanam with his
feet dragging strangely, as if he were held back by
some unseen force. When Itzanam looked down, he
saw that one of the younger god's legs was more
smoke than flesh—another indication that it was their
fate to merge again if his prophecy came true.

Feathered Serpent would fight it. But they had to
join to make Itzanam's vision bear fruit, to bring them
to this unchanging endless time. All of them must
twine together, the foreigners with the Itza, for them
to be strong enough to form the river he saw.

Itzanam found he still had no voice with which to
speak. He gazed down at his wife, her eyes whirling
with the madness that was never far away. Would the
changes calm her? She hadn't drawn closer to any of
the Itza or Iseland gods, but toward him instead.
Would he have to subsume her as well?

He leaned down and kissed her forehead, telling
himself that he'd never forget her, knowing that he
might have to.

Because what he gained would still be worth more
than the price he paid.

The turquoise-green light of sacrifice that burned in
Itzanam's eyes chilled Ix Chebel. He was willing to
give up everything for this vision. She had sworn that
she would do the same, do everything she could to
help him in this quest, to let him keep his hope, the
only hope she'd ever seen him have. Now she wondered if she too had made a fool's bargain.

The foreign trickster had said to Tyr, "I fear your oaths and your honor will be the death of us all." Ix Chebel was beyond fear—she lived now with certainty. What Itzanam foresaw meant death, for her, for their people. They would not recognize themselves after a single generation. Her ways and her followers would be lost, swamped by the overwhelming tide of the greater gods and goddesses, the ones who would survive.

For every loss, there *would* be a gain. That was the natural order of things. She knew the balance of the seasons, the flow of days, sanity into madness and back. Static scared her. If someone pushed you, sometimes you had to move your feet, or you would fall, no matter how well grounded you were. Stability wasn't the same as rigidity. She knew that, embodied it.

Itzanam did not. His vision might keep some of the gods alive, but at what price?

Ix Chebel dropped her head and started to dance again, letting her own inner light blind her. She'd sworn to watch over the Iseland humans. She knew the importance of the blood stone to Itzanam's vision—without it, there was no hope that their people would survive the coming of the White Hands. She'd helped her priestess repeatedly, showing her the soldiers from Cobá, letting her know of the plots against her life.

Now, well, if Ix Chebel were to get distracted? None would blame her. Her mad aspect did have its uses. She wouldn't turn her back on her followers, as Tyr had on that sacrificed human. However, she wouldn't talk through the stones again. Her priestess would just have to find her own way to acquiring the secrets of blood stone.

If she lived.

*　　*　　*

"You're all as mad as she is," Feathered Serpent said, pointing at Ix Chebel pulling away from them. "Don't you see what he's asking of you?"

Muluk, his black faced shining, replied, "Can you not see what we will win?"

"No!" Feathered Serpent shouted back. The fools. Their "leader" would send them off cliffs, into darkness, with no hope of ever reaching the stars.

"We know that these ones who have come aren't the White Hands. But that doesn't mean that they *aren't* coming. Joining with such as these won't stop them."

Feathered Serpent ignored the confusion on the Iselanders' faces. Their seers must not be very good if they hadn't heard of the White Hands. They would soon sweep over all the lands. Nothing would stem those storm waves. This, this, diminishing—of their own ranks by joining with these foreigners would be like throwing pebbles against the wind. It wouldn't stop the spirals from turning, or even slow them down.

"You want to know what I see?" Feathered Serpent asked, drawing into the center of them, shouting and angry. "I see abandoned temples overtaken by the jungle. I see our children forgetting our holy days. I see the end of the long count of *k'atuns*, the end of days. If we are strong, each of us, there will be a few who remember, who survive. If we lose ourselves before these dreadful days, we will only ensure our own destruction."

"What twilight are you predicting?" Thor asked, clenching his hammer. "Ragnarok will not touch this land. The Midgard serpent will not poison me here. And Fenris the wolf shall not eat the sun."

Feathered Serpent's lip lifted in a sneer. This was only a myth that belonged to these foreigner gods. It would die with them.

Itzanam stepped forward. "Enough!" he said, thundering over the younger god.

Feathered Serpent growled as the old man rounded on him, the Iguana god's walking stick lengthening and sharpening, manifesting as a spear, similar to Feather Serpent's Staff of War.

"We will talk on this more," Itzanam said, poking at Feathered Serpent with his newly grown weapon.

Feathered Serpent knocked it away with ease. "Bah. Talk. You've lost your balls already, old man, staring at the stars. You proclaim my vision false because it doesn't come from a seeing, doesn't use pretty words, or talk of a *k'atun*. I say it's true, because it comes from blood." Feathered Serpent wasn't a mystic—the veils didn't part for him, letting him see through the spirals of time. But his dreams had told him, again and again, of the coming of the White Hands.

"Your vision is still veiled, visiting you in your sleep—you cannot proclaim it to be true," Kan said, his yellow tattoos radiating an anger not apparent in his mild expression.

"You merely play at divination," Ix added angrily. "You should leave it to the those properly trained in the sight."

Feathered Serpent felt his face turning red with fury. "And you only have one brain between the four of you! You're supposed to be *my* servants. Remember who shares the smoke with you."

The four Bacab had the grace to look abashed and step back.

"What are you talking—" Thor started.

"Do not go where you are not wanted," Feathered Serpent interrupted. "Our battles are our own. You lost yours when you ran away from your lands and came here."

Without pausing, Feathered Serpent whirled and addressed Itzanam again. "Your visions will kill us all. Nothing can save us. Not this ruinous talk of joining the foreigners or even their magical fruit."

Before another could castigate him, Feathered Ser-

pent wrapped his cloak around him and took off,
shooting across the sky faster than his spear had flown,
letting the chill winds of the clouds cool his fury.

He landed high on the mountains near the center
of the world, well above the tree line so Itzanam's
damn monkey spies couldn't find him. There he paced
and fumed and shook his fists angrily and cursed at
the futility of it all.

No other god predicted the coming of the White
Hands as he did—no other shared his dreams, and
Feathered Serpent wasn't known for seeing the future.
Or for telling the truth.

That didn't make his recent nightmares falsehoods.
The White Hands were coming. He knew it. He
smelled it in every fight, heard it in every challenge,
foretold it in every spray of blood. Soon there would be
a last battle with men who didn't have the same laws
as their people, who didn't respect the seasons, who
wouldn't use war drums and whistles. Even the shiny
blood stone of the foreigners wouldn't help. A new god
was coming. He'd risen in the east and traveled across
the land, taking what he could from the other gods,
twisting their rituals into his own. His avatar—*Cortéz*—
would steal their sacrifices, their people, their World
Tree, and corrupt them into something unrecognizable.
Feathered Serpent would die in battle with his people,
instead of wasting away in smoke or being cocooned,
treasured, and cherished as he was put to sleep.

This new god had already made himself known to the
Iseland gods. It was part of the reason why they had
come so far across the watery land. They had a fear of
the World Tree, the cross it represented. He'd seen it.
This Tyr might want his spear hand back, as well as to
regain his place among his own gods, but only because
this new god gave him so much to be afraid of.

The world was changing, though not in the ways
Itzanam had seen. What little hope their people had
for surviving the coming years had vanished long ago.

Chapter 7

Tyrthbrand had assumed that the cursed city where they'd lost Thorolf had been the largest the Itza inhabited.

He'd been wrong. The City of Wells was much, much bigger.

A constant stream of merchants, pilgrims, and soldiers filled the white road, both entering and leaving the city. They carried all their goods on their backs, or on the backs of their slaves. Snorri talked of the cart business he could start, speculating how much money he could make with such a simple advance. Illugi pointed out that while carts might be an improvement, unless they had oxen or some other large animal to pull them, any wheeled vehicle had limited usefulness. Plus, heavy carts would disrupt the stones in the road.

The Iselanders ignored the pointed fingers, stares, and comments that came from everyone they passed. The farther they'd moved from the coast—where foreign traders were a more common sight—the more attention they'd attracted. Tyrthbrand noticed how all his men walked taller as the buzzing around them grew louder. They were freaks—white-faced giants trundling through a sea of small brown people—but they had nothing to be ashamed of. As people began to follow them on the road, Tyrthbrand, for the first time, was happy to have the Red Hand soldiers with them, surrounding them, keeping the crowds and the overly curious away.

Stone temples, painted in every color of the rainbow and as tall as hills, were visible above the city walls for miles when the road widened and the Iselanders had a clear view. The noise of so many people living together was a constant hum, similar to ocean waves at low tide. Fewer winds blew, making the air dank and heavy.

When they finally made that last turn and actually saw the walls and gates, a metallic taste filled Tyrthbrand's mouth—not fear, but something akin to it. Hordes of statues, flanked by sharp-eyed soldiers, lined the walls. Every warrior was equipped with a leather throwing strip. Every ship's length or so sat a bucket filled with throwing spears. The pace at which the group walked slowed to a crawl as people made their way through the small opening into the city.

A muted roar rippled through the crowd as they approached, echoing between the gate guardians. Everyone stared at them. Tyrthbrand swore even some of the statues turned their heads to watch.

How Lady Two Bird had planned to get them out of this citadel was beyond Tyrthbrand. There were too many soldiers, too many eyes on them. He told himself to trust her, to have faith in her visions and her goddess, but spikes of fear larger and longer than the spears carried by the soldiers jabbed through his gut.

He held himself tall as he walked through the gates, even as the knowledge that he would die within these walls settled through him.

Tyrthbrand didn't want to be separated from Lady Two Bird. However, her small residence wasn't large enough to hold them. He also had the impression that it wouldn't be considered proper to have so many men staying with a priestess. Instead, they were to stay in the courtyard of the temple of Ix Chebel. The walls were high enough that no one could casually look over them, even the Iselanders. Lady Two Bird appointed temple attendants to look after them and fetch them whatever they wanted. All the Iselanders seemed to breathe a little easier away from the staring eyes of the crowd that had followed them there.

It struck Tyrthbrand as curious that the attendants, even most of the temple priestesses, didn't find them such an oddity. For the first time, it felt as if they were treated with respect. The other men felt the same way. Tyrthbrand sent Vigfus, the Iselander who could speak the Itzas' language the best, to try to find out why.

It didn't take long for Vigfus's loud laughter to fill the courtyard.

Ix Chebel was the goddess responsible for madmen. The courtyard walls had purposefully been built high to prevent the people in the city from tormenting them. Because the Iselanders looked so strange, were under Lady Two Bird's protection, and barely spoke the Itzan language, the women in the temple had just assumed they were crazy.

The laughter of Tyrthbrand and his men echoed through the courtyard, bounced off the walls, and continued to spiral around them. And if any of them noticed how mad it sounded, none of them said anything.

Lady Two Bird shifted on her cushions, her body still protesting at the traveling she'd forced it to do, even though she'd rested most of the afternoon since their arrival at the City of Wells. At Lord Kan Boar's questioning look, she forced herself to smile and say, "These bones aren't as young as they used to be."

Lord Kan Boar gestured for his server to pour more of the frothy cocoa and honey drink for Lady Two Bird. "We are still pleased you suffered no harm at Lord Six Sky's madness."

Lady Two Bird merely nodded and held out her

cup, inwardly cursing Cauac Sky's delay at the cursed city. If they hadn't stopped, she would have been able to meet with Lady Star Storm and explain her situation in a more open fashion. However, her sister had left the day before for a purification ceremony and wouldn't return for another ten days. Lord Smoke Moon was in deep meditation, communicating with the gods, and none knew when he would return to the world of men. So she'd had to settle with speaking with Lord Kan Boar, the military leader of the City of Wells.

And if they hadn't delayed, maybe they would have arrived in the City of Wells before Evening Star's messengers. Lady Two Bird might have had her side listened to, without trying to combat lies already well seated.

No matter. She would be gone soon enough. Her aching knees didn't look forward to being on the road again, but she knew they couldn't stop for more than a single day here. Two days hence was Etz'nab. She intended to be out of the reach of the Red Hands priest before then.

The stillness of Lord Kan Boar's greeting hall surprised Lady Two Bird. She'd expected the room of the military leader of the City of Wells to have a warlike presence: bustling, chaotic, buzzing, and full of warriors and weapons. Instead, it was almost like a sacred well, quiet, with ripples of power echoing through the space. Lord Kan Boar saw her with a single attendant, not a full court. Though the murals on the walls showed scenes of battles and victories, the one directly behind the seat of power merely showed jungle and well-tended fields—no humans or animals in sight.

Lord Kan Boar noticed Lady Two Bird's attention. "I had to fight to get that painted as it is."

"Why did you want such an empty place behind you, my lord?" Lady Two Bird asked, as was obviously expected.

"We all return to the land. No matter what we fight for. That's where we'll always end up. Put our bones and our strength back into it."

"But—"

"The stars are for those greater than I."

Lady Two Bird bit her tongue, unsure if Lord Kan Boar was being humble or not. The scribes were sure to write his name on the temple walls, document his battles on the face of each stair. *He* had nothing to fear of the dark places under the earth.

Her claustrophobia suddenly closed in on her again. She took a deep breath and tried to imagine herself out in the fields she saw before her. It took her a moment to realize that Lord Kan Boar had asked her a question.

"I beg your pardon?" she asked, ashamed. She fought to keep her trembling inside, to not show her fear in the stiffening of her neck and back.

"I asked if you knew of some kind of poisoning inside our walls," he said.

"My lord?" Lady Two Bird asked again, startled. She realized then that she hadn't taken a drink from her newly filled cup. "I do not mean to refuse the hospitality of your hall. I am just tired. The journey was long." She forced herself to take a sip from her cup, wondering if she'd just killed herself by doing so. More than one king or relative had been assassinated over the years. And though she was only related through marriage to Lord Smoke Moon, her death could still be used to harm him.

"No, I don't mean the drink, though I am glad to see you enjoy it. I meant your servant. She was seen buying water gourds this evening in the market, as if preparing for another journey. I thought you'd meant to remain in the city for a while."

Lady Two Bird had instructed Seven Waterlily to be careful gathering the supplies they needed for their escape. Obviously, she hadn't been cautious enough.

"Are you sure, my Lord? Maybe my servant only purchased carriers, not the drink within. We will be using those types of vessels for the purification ceremony tomorrow."

"Ah, that must be it. My mistake," Lord Kan Boar said.

Lady Two Bird knew she hadn't fooled him. He would be watching them.

"Tell me of these men you traveled with," he said after a slight pause.

"The Iselanders are as fierce as they look, though they are human, and not beasts," Lady Two Bird started, having prepared herself for these questions. "They are brave—"

"No, not the foreign animals. The Red Hands. That priest."

Lady Two Bird blinked, then collected herself. The sweetness of the drink grew bitter in her mouth. "Cauac Sky is very . . . devoted to his cause. He is, um, enthusiastic about all sacrifices. The twins who follow him are clever and courageous. They—"

"Do you believe in this prophecy of theirs?"

Lady Two Bird found herself telling only half the truth. "They do." She did find that she believed in the White Hands. She wasn't sure if they were other Iselanders or people like them, but they were coming to destroy her people.

Lord Kan Boar grunted. "Yes, they do. I have men in their ranks. Cauac Sky is insisting on the most ridiculous things. A constant guard at the coast, always on the lookout for these invaders. More training. I've even heard mention of fighting during the growing season. Bah. Ridiculous, don't you think? Even with these 'white hand' foreigners they've now produced."

"I do not know if any of Tyrthbrand's people will return. But others will," Lady Two Bird said. She hadn't thought to try to convince Lord Kan Boar of the importance of the blood stone, how necessary it was to the future life of their people. She'd been so focused on speaking with Lord Smoke Moon about the visions her lady had sent her that it hadn't occurred to her to tell the military leader of it.

"If they come, we will fight. No prophecy or preparation can change that. Don't worry," he said softly.

Lady Two Bird quickly plastered a smile across her face. "Worry about what?" she asked.

"I will meet with your trained animals tomorrow."

Lady Two Bird wanted to object, but it wasn't the appropriate time to try to correct Lord Kan Boar's view of the Iselanders.

"I shall honor them with the courtesy of my hall. And you can introduce these Red Hands to me as well. I do not promise to do more than hear them once, but that is all you agreed to, yes?"

Lady Two Bird was suddenly grateful for Lord Kan Boar's spies. She and Seven Waterlily would have to be more careful, yes, but she no longer had to explain herself.

As she said her good-byes, she allowed herself to feel regret that Tyrthbrand and Lord Kan Boar weren't going to meet. The two warriors would have enjoyed each other's company, that is, if Lord Kan Boar could allow himself to see them as something other than beasts. It didn't matter, though. She and the Iselanders still had to leave the City of Wells. Even if Lord Kan Boar didn't agree with Cauac Sky, there were too many who did. She had to get the Iselanders away and produce enough of their blood stone weapons to make a difference, to prove her point.

To guarantee her name on the temple walls.

Vigfus was the most hopeful when he heard the news that they were leaving the city and going off on their own the next day. His face lit up, and he didn't start a campfire that night, as had been his habit, as

if he didn't need the extra brilliance. Tyrthbrand
didn't talk with him about it, afraid that his own darkness might seep into the boy.

Tyrthbrand worked at not showing his despair. He
had to believe that he could change his *wyrd*, and not
die in this city.

His very bones told him otherwise.

Illugi spent the evening sharpening his sword, his
dagger, then moved to the rest of their weapons. The
constant sound of the whetstone sliding across steel
was as soothing to Tyrthbrand as the whir of a spinning wheel.

Snorri took on the task of keeping them packed.
The Iselanders had to pretend to be settling, as if they
would be in this location for a while, not departing
the next day. They couldn't be obvious about leaving
all their things in their bags. Though they couldn't see
anyone watching them over the high walls, Tyrthbrand
was certain unfriendly eyes surrounded them. Plus,
they didn't want to alert the temple priestesses to anything. Snorri made a big deal of losing one of his
runes. He tore through all their bags searching for it,
tossing belongings everywhere. Illugi, as part of their
act, yelled at the smith and told him to put everything
back. So Snorri did, repacking everything, including
the things that normally would have been left out.

Morning arrived with angry clouds spread thickly
across the entire sky and hot air pressing down on
them. Everything Tyrthbrand looked at seemed out-
lined in thick black lines. His hand, his men, even the
priestesses moved slower than usual, as if through
water.

Even words were difficult to understand. He found
he couldn't focus on the simplest requests. It was as
if his body conspired with his belief that he would die
here, making him clumsy and awkward. He could
barely follow Lady Two Bird's orders to wash his face

in the water she'd brought, all of them preparing for a ritual as an excuse to leave the temple so early. Then he nearly walked into Illugi as they went through the gateway, and only Ketil grabbing his arm prevented them from both falling and making more noise than they wanted.

In the city itself, Lady Two Bird led them along poorer, smaller lanes, keeping to the shadows. It was early enough that not many people were out, and luckily, no crowd gathered to follow them this time. She sent Vigfus ahead of the group more than once, putting out lamps hanging on the walls so they could pass in darkness.

Tyrthbrand still marveled at the size of the city. The twisting streets seemed to go on and on, houses piled up on top of each other. The crowded lanes were more familiar to Tyrthbrand, more like the villages and towns he'd grown up with, yet at the same time alien, with buildings set at odd angles and strange gods in the courtyards. The air here pressed in on him not only with heat but with the constant scent of humanity, incense, and unrecognizable cooking spices. He had a sudden longing to be on the *Golden Tree*, with a distant horizon before him and clean winds whipping around him.

When Tyrthbrand saw the gate they were to use leaving the city, he felt his hope rise again. Maybe his premonition that he'd die in the city would prove to be false. The gate was much smaller than the formal gate they'd passed through the day before. In addition to the five statues standing guard on the walls were only two human sentinels. Lady Two Bird sent Seven Waterlily forward to distract them.

"Haven't been attacked in a while," was Illugi's quiet comment before Lady Two Bird shushed him.

Tyrthbrand had to agree. Seven Waterlily's flirtatious advances took in the guards too easily. Only real

war kept men sharp. Or better discipline. The Red
Hand guards who had watched them had been a lot
more attentive.

Lady Two Bird insisted on being the first one
through the gate. The Iselanders followed as quiet as
ghosts. The guards were in a side room built into the
edge of the gate. Loud laughter made them jump as
they crept stealthily forward, holding their swords so
they would make no sound.

The group paused just around the first bend after
they'd passed through the gate, waiting for Seven Waterlily to rejoin them. Tension wrapped all of them as
the time stretched out, though Tyrthbrand himself felt
only loose and numb. The clouds were breaking apart
across the sky, as well as in his head.

Maybe they would make it.

Illugi seemed to grow the most rigid as time slipped
by and Seven Waterlily didn't come. Tyrthbrand didn't
believe it was because the tall blond had formed an
attachment to the maid, but rather, because of his
sense of honor: you didn't leave one of your party
behind. Illugi had spent the most time guarding Lady
Two Bird, splitting the duty with Tyrthbrand while
they were on the road. Illugi hadn't spoken of it, but
Tyrthbrand understood that the Iselander now considered Lady Two Bird and Seven Waterlily as part of
their crew, members of the *Golden Tree*, even though
they'd never set foot on her deck.

Even Tyrthbrand had drawn his sword by the time
Seven Waterlily appeared, walking calmly down the
center of the road. They put away their weapons as
quietly as they could and started again, the predawn
light outside the city walls casting them quickly in
shadows.

Lady Two Bird seemed to be looking for something
as they walked. She scanned one side of the road,
while Seven Waterlily peered into the jungle on the
other side. Illugi offered to help, but Lady Two Bird

just shook her head, either wanting to avoid the noise
of talking, or not wanting to take the time. Eventually
she seemed to find what she was looking for—a small
animal trail off to the side. After verifying that no one
else on the road could see them, she insisted that they
go into the woods, even though it meant making a
racket.

Once they reached a small break in the trees, she
opened the large sacks she'd made Illugi and Snorri
carry, then pulled out Itza chest plates, loin cloths,
sandals, as well as pots of paint. The Itza didn't wear
any type of robes as part of their everyday outfits, so
there wasn't any way to completely cover the Iselanders and hide their white skin. In addition, there was
no way to disguise the foreigners' height. She still did
her best to dress them as her people dressed. It
wouldn't hide them, not exactly, but they might not
be as noticeable.

Putting on the strange garb wasn't as bad for Tyrthbrand as the acidic scent of the paints that filled the
clearing when Illugi opened them. He hadn't realized
how strongly they smelled, how much he associated
the scent with Thorolf's death. He tried to control how
he shuddered with every wet line drawn across his
skin. It felt like a soggy net trapping him, binding him
tighter and tighter.

Still, they were out of the city. He had changed his
wyrd. He would not die there.

Vines, branches, and roots all grabbed at Tyrthbrand, trying to trip him, slow him down, stop him
from escaping. As the sun rose, so did the heat. The
foreign clothing didn't protect their legs as their old
trousers did. Lady Two Bird insisted that they keep
to the animal trails that ran beside the road, however.
They stopped again and again as other parties passed
them, mostly traders going to the city, but sometimes
groups leaving as well. Tyrthbrand had wanted to ask
if walking next to the road instead of on it wouldn't

make people more suspicious if they were spotted, but couldn't bring himself to struggle with the words. Illugi spent most of the time in quiet conversation with Lady Two Bird, asking the names of strange plants, their properties, their value. The thickening jungle, along with the biting insects, drove them onto the road eventually. At least with the way clear they might be able to walk around the clouds of stinging gnats.

After a while, the road grew straight, and they could see that they were alone for a long stretch. Vigfus started singing. Though Illugi hushed the boy, he continued to hum under his breath. Tyrthbrand recognized the sea shanty, a hymn for Aegir, the god of the sea, thanking him for letting them leave the whale road in one piece, alive. How the sailors would weave their sea-steed around the country bones at the shore to reach the land, then stand among those bones and look back at the water and long to return.

They were still far from home, far from the safety of a hall, or even a ship. There was no reason to give praise for the end of a journey. Yet Tyrthbrand felt his spirits raise a touch more. Maybe he and his men would find a harbor. Maybe they could weather this storm, find a breach between the stones and the gods, a shore where they could live.

Finally, the cacao beans Cauac Sky cast showed him the future he wanted to see—that only by sacrificing one of the Iselanders now, today, could he show what a threat they were, how the White Hands would destroy everything. He wanted to crow when the beans aligned themselves perfectly. He even debated calling Jeweled Skull to show him as well, then decided not to. He justified his reluctance to himself by saying that he wanted to protect his boys. This was true. However . . .

The blood called to him, and he hungered to taste it alone.

He'd wanted to sacrifice the foreigners since he'd

first seen them. The sacrifice of the blond had done nothing to ease this hunger. He longed to see crimson strips of blood dripping across their white, polluted skin. He didn't understand this urge. He'd always had it, and assumed it came from the gods—that he enjoyed blood as much as they did. He always took pleasure in the torture of a victim before the sacrifice, more than he ever let anyone know. The cruelty in the smile that crept across his face at the memory of that dumb foreigner's blood-streaked back would have shocked his followers. He could almost feel the warm liquid pouring across his hands, staining his palms.

Cauac Sky couldn't just take one of the foreigners without a solid justification. Which he now had. He could tell the truth about how he'd seen the fate of the foreigners, how he'd cast the beans and gotten this configuration. Though he believed in the original prophecy, he needed more proof than just his own belief; hence this additional casting. He didn't have to speak of how many times he had had to throw the beans for them to be aligned just right.

It was still tricky. Officially, he didn't have the authority to conduct a sacrifice. Still, the rightness of the prophecy convinced him.

He called an honor guard to him, consciously picking brutish men who would follow him without question, who looked at everything foreign with disfavor, who would kill the Iselanders instantly if they resisted at all. They gathered weapons, quickly applied their signature red hand paints to their torsos, and headed out in the early-dawn light.

No guards stood outside the temple of Ix Chebel. Cauac Sky tsked under his breath. He'd noticed other faults in the protection of the city, deficiencies that a good military leader would never allow. He allowed himself to think only in terms of "that *he* would never allow" in his secret heart of hearts, and only by himself, late at night.

The priestesses kept their own guards, and they stopped him as soon as he passed through their gate.

"I'm here for the foreigners," he said, keeping his tone professional, bored. He was dressed as the priests dressed here in the City of Wells, in an attempt to fit in, though he still had a single red hand at the center of his chest.

"For the cleansing ritual? They're already gone," came the reply.

Cauac Sky glared at the young woman in front of him, but she didn't seem to notice. It was the appropriate time of day to perform such a ritual, and it was the first thing he would have insisted the foreigners do. Maybe someone in this city had some sense after all.

"Did Lady Two Bird take them?"

"Yes," the priestess answered and made as if to dismiss the priest and his men.

"Is it possible to see their belongings?" Cauac Sky asked quickly. Even if he couldn't get at the foreigners, maybe he could retrieve one of their strange long knives. Lady Two Bird had talked more than once of the importance of the blood stone, how they needed foreign weapons to fight the coming White Hands. The priest had pretended not to pay much attention to her, but he'd watched the foreigners handle their blades almost reverently. The material they were made of intrigued him. He also wanted to learn the recipe for this new type of stone. He didn't believe that the foreign weapons would be crucial in the coming days, but he wasn't going to throw away a potential part of his arsenal.

"They took them along to be purified."

Cauac Sky forced himself not to shake the girl, demand explanations. While the cleansing of bags and goods was sometimes done, it was rare. However, it still struck the priest as odd that such a complicated ceremony would be performed for everyday items, not just ones used for rituals.

After ascertaining which bath the foreigners had gone to, the priest left with his guards. It was all the way across the city, a private place, reserved for the royal family. It made sense that Lady Two Bird would take them there, away from crowds and curious eyes, to perform such rituals.

Yet misgiving gnawed at the priest's gut as he hurried through the twisting streets, still hungering for blood.

Lord Kan Boar didn't want to see the Red Hands priest. Particularly not without Lady Two Bird to provide a distraction, possibly soothe the confrontation. Plus, the news that the priest had brought was disturbing. Lord Kan Boar had sent his own men out to verify his claims, and, unfortunately, it appeared that Cauac Sky spoke the truth: Lady Two Bird, along with all the foreigners, was no longer in the city.

His men had double-checked the story the priestesses of the temple had told, then had gone to the private baths. No one there had seen the foreigners. Lord Kan Boar doubted the attendants were lying—the foreigners were impossible to mistake or miss.

Spies came to him soon after his men had returned empty-handed. They reported of poorer people pouring out offerings that morning to Feathered Serpent and the Bacabnob after seeing strange, giantlike beings walking through the streets just before dawn. Lord Kan Boar followed the reports, the general stream of where they came from, and eventually put together where Lady Two Bird had gone.

He himself went to the far gate to interrogate the guards there.

"Who has passed through this morning?" he demanded of the two men practically quivering with fear before him.

"M-m-merchants, my lord. And a few families going to market."

"Did you see the foreigners?" he asked. He knew he wouldn't have to elaborate. Even though the City of Wells held thousands of souls, everyone knew of the Iselanders.

"N-n-no, my lord."

"Have you been at your post all morning?"

The man hesitated before he responded. "Yes."

"You lie. Something happened this morning."

The other guard spoke up. "We were here the whole time. But—"

"But what?" Lord Kan Boar was starting to grow impatient. If they didn't tell him what had happened soon, he was going to hand them over to the priests for torture.

"A-a-a woman came to see us. She flirted and teased us, offering goods that we couldn't afford."

"I see." The perfect distraction for lonely men at the end of their shift.

"Go report to Five Jade."

The men paled even more, but went off to do their duty. Five Jade was responsible for the sacrifices for Feathered Serpent. Lord Kan Boar knew he could use more souls for the upcoming festival.

Lord Kan Boar stood quiet for a moment, watching the men leave. He hadn't realized that the guards had gotten so complacent in their duties. They had been at peace for only a handful of years. While he and those closest to him continued to train, obviously not all took their assignments so seriously.

The smirking Red Hands priest had insisted on accompanying him to the gate, and Lord Kan Boar hadn't found a good reason to leave the man behind. Besides, it was easier to keep an eye on him this way. The guards that accompanied Cauac Sky didn't impress Lord Kan Boar—a group of men obviously chosen for their brawn, not their brains. He wondered what had drawn the Red Hands priest out so early, seeking the foreigners. He'd listened to the man's fervent tales of how their sacrifice was ordained, but he didn't believe it.

"Pac Xul!" Lord Kan Boar called for his second in command.

"Sir." The old soldier came up and bowed, his movements precise and ordered.

"Find the foreigners. Bring them back, along with Lady Two Bird. Alive."

"Yes, sir." The guard executed another small bow, then turned and started shouting orders, gathering a small troop to him.

As the men were about to leave, Lord Kan Boar noticed that Cauac Sky and his men were planning to accompany them.

Lord Kan Boar called the priest to him. "We have much to talk about," he said, using his sweetest bribe to bring the man to him. He could, of course, order Cauac Sky and his entire Red Hands troop to stay within the confines of the city, but he preferred a willing victim.

Cauac Sky came toward him, visibly twitching with anxiety.

"Yes, we do."

The military leader nearly laughed at how hard the priest worked to control himself. He wanted to go after the foreigners himself. However, Lord Kan Boar doubted that many of the foreigners would come back alive if he allowed the Red Hands to go fetch them.

"Shall we?" Lord Kan Boar said, indicating that he and the priest should return through the city.

"My lord?" Cauac Sky asked, watching with greedy eyes as Lord Kan Boar's men marched at a fast pace through the gates.

"They'll return soon enough. I won't have the hospitality of my hall taken so lightly," Lord Kan Boar said, a slight warning tone creeping into his voice.

With a sigh, the priest turned and came with him. That the leader of the Red Hands had shown such restraint was promising as well as disturbing—it indicated a level of discipline that Lord Kan Boar had just forcibly had to acknowledge was missing in his own men.

He did owe the priest at least a short amount of his time for showing him that lack. But that was all.

And if the priest didn't continue to show restraint, there was always the Hall of Testing to help remind him of his place.

Though they made good time down the road, Lady Two Bird insisted that they keep going after they would normally stop, making them walk in the heat of the day. Tyrthbrand had believed that the strange Itza garb would help him feel cooler, but it had turned out to be a false hope. His sweat cut through the paint on his chest, making it a morass of streaked colors.

They did rest when they could, always in out-of-the-way alcoves off the road entirely. They walked quickly with their heads bowed whenever they went by other people. Too often though, Tyrthbrand heard the excited whispers that followed their passing. If anyone cared to follow them, it wouldn't be too difficult to find people who could report the direction they'd gone, the roads they'd taken. He hoped fervently that no one had noticed their absence yet, or if they had noticed, hadn't cared.

Worries nibbled at Tyrthbrand, as annoying as mice in the winter grain, and potentially just as deadly. A clear blue sky blazed down on them now, the haze of the morning and his thoughts overtaken with languid heat. Lady Two Bird couldn't tell him exactly how long it would take to reach their destination, but it would take more than a single day. The longer they were out on the road, the more exposed they were. Did they have enough water and food? Would they

be able to resupply themselves when they needed?
Should he and his men go hunting as soon as they'd
left the immediate province of the City of Wells, so
they would be provisioned? Or should they stop only
when they absolutely needed to? As they got farther
from the city, the curiosity of the people they met was
sure to grow, as they were less likely to have seen any
kind of foreigner before. What if they gathered a
crowd around them again? How could they warn
them off?

Tyrthbrand had Illugi stay at the back of their
group, watching for potential enemies coming up from
behind them, while he walked with Lady Two Bird at
the front, keeping a sharp eye out for any threat.
When they rested, the men worked out their own
shifts, standing guard at the edge of the group, a little
apart, so as to hear anyone approaching.

Late afternoon arrived before trouble came. They
heard the troops before they saw them—the sound
was impossible to mistake. Quickly, Tyrthbrand found
a route off the *sak beh* into the jungle. They stood in
a space between the trees, breathing hard, weapons
drawn, as the marchers drew near to where they stood,
then passed them. The jungle was too thick for them
to leave the ease of the road and go cross-country.
They would lose too much time hacking a path for
themselves, as well as possibly attracting too much
attention with the noise.

One by one, they crept back onto the road. Tyrthbrand stretched his senses until he thought they would
snap. He heard nothing, saw nothing, smelled nothing
but rotting jungle, sweat, and acidic paints. They
started walking again, moving more slowly now. Vigfus joined point with Tyrthbrand, while Illugi and
Snorri kept to the rear. Ketil walked with Wolf Feeder
out, just in front of the two women, head swinging
from side to side like a nervous hound.

A short while later they came upon a small trail

leading off the main road to a resting area. Statues
filled the clearing, and Lady Two Bird declared that
they would stop there for the evening. Tyrthbrand
looked askance at the World Tree that stood near the
center. He'd asked about the significance of the symbol, and had been reassured when he'd learned what
the different parts represented. Still, it made him, as
well as his men, nervous. Though the standing piece
was the tree of the world, and the crosspiece represented the milky way, it looked too similar to the cross
the damn monks from Eire worshipped for any of the
Iselanders to be comfortable with it.

They quickly established their perimeter, set up a
rough camp, and handed out dried fruit and pieces of
flat bread made from cornmeal. Vigfus didn't try to
start a fire, for which Tyrthbrand was grateful. He
didn't want to fight the boy, even over something as
trivial as that.

Illugi took first watch, standing off to one side, leaning into the jungle, listening hard. Tyrthbrand went up
to the tall blond as soon as he discerned that everything that passed his lips tasted strangely lifeless, as if
it were made of sand.

"What do you hear?" Tyrthbrand asked quietly.

Illugi shook his head. "I'm not worried about what
I hear. It's what I don't hear. Where's the cicada
chorus?"

Tyrthbrand opened his mouth to say he didn't understand when suddenly, he did. Insects sang around
them all the time, both before and behind them, but
not in their immediate vicinity.

To the side where Illugi listened, the bugs had gone
strangely quiet.

"Men—" Tyrthbrand started to say, drawing his
weapon, when soldiers poured out of the brush all
around them.

Tyrthbrand quickly determined that the Itza were
holding off—they weren't looking to kill the Iseland-

ers, but to recapture them. This made him fight harder, blocking the spear haft whirring in his direction, leaping over the leg kicked out to trip him.

Ketil's shouted curses drowned out the other sounds of battle. The priest had finally found an outlet for his simmering rage. Wolf Feeder glistened strangely in the afternoon sunlight. He roared and snarled as he fought, like a vicious dog, teeth bared and harsh blows splitting the Itza shields.

A lucky hit sliced open Ketil's chest, from sternum to belly, but he continued to fight, as if unaware he'd been mortally wounded. Tyrthbrand didn't see Ketil fall—he was too busy fighting his own battle. The other survivors told him later that the only way the Itza had been able to stop the crazed priest was to knock him down and kick the sword away from his hand.

Tyrthbrand did see Snorri die. The smith fought with curses, jokes, and strong blows using sword and fists. He was the most squat of them though, and he didn't make a leap all the way over a spear sweeping the ground looking to trip him. He landed on one leg, and in an effort to right himself, threw himself too far in the other direction, only to impale himself on the knife of the soldier standing there. Snorri cursed and shouted, "That wasn't supposed to happen!" He fell heavily to his knees, then dropped slowly to his side.

The sword in Tyrthbrand's hand rang as he fought harder now, backing up toward the others, automatically forming a circle with them, back to back, defending each other as they always did.

Tyrthbrand didn't see the blow that struck his wrist and made him drop his sword. A familiar pain rang through his arm, memories of that first time, when Tyr had marked him, echoing and overlaying the skirmish before him. He threw a punch in the direction of the closest soldier and had the satisfaction of feeling warm wetness spilling over his knuckles before a sharp *thwack* to the back of his neck dropped him to the ground.

Illugi fell next, his sprawled form creating an obstacle for friend and foe alike. Vigfus fought on, trying vainly to protect the tall man's prone form. Lady Two Bird wasn't screaming, but she was shouting, and soon only her cries were heard over the harsh panting of the battling men as the spear storm died.

The soldiers didn't bring out the white and black paints or ropes to bind the Iselanders. They didn't strip the clothes off them. It appeared that the guards were supposed to escort them back to the City of Wells. Though the sun hadn't set yet, all the light washed out of their surroundings as Tyrthbrand realized what was happening.

They were being brought back alive—not as prisoners but as warriors—to be sacrificed.

Illugi turned out not to be dead. He rose complaining of a great headache, but the rest of his wounds were superficial. Tyrthbrand helped rig a gurney to carry the bodies of Snorri and Ketil.

He didn't try to fight the judgment laid down on him, didn't complain of how his wrist hurt when he tried to use it, didn't respond when Lady Two Bird tried to talk with him.

With Snorri dead, Tyrthbrand knew he couldn't fulfill his vow to teach Lady Two Bird the recipe for iron. What little honor he had left to him had been struck down, knifed in the gut in the clearing, dying under the cross of the foreign World Tree. Now his life was forfeit. He had created this *wyrd* for himself when he'd made his oath to his lady. His impression had been right—he was to die in the city.

And as far as he knew, the gods approved.

Though dusk gathered, they started back, the soldiers providing torches that set the white rocks in the road gleaming. All Tyrthbrand saw was the brightness beneath his feet leading into darkness.

* * *

"You can't just sacrifice him," Lady Two Bird said, still kneeling at Lord Smoke Moon's feet, her head lowered not just to show respect, but to help her fight the closed-in feeling his hall always brought her. There were never enough lights in her brother-in-law's rooms. He preferred the dark, and talked often of mingling the mysterious with the mundane. However, the shadows he reveled in seemed to close in tightly around Lady Two Bird. The few murals she could make out contained scenes of death and sacrifice, the flickering lamps blending the colors together until it seemed only bloodlike red coated the walls.

"My dear, it really is out of my hands," came the mild reply.

Even as his voice had matured, it had never lost its gentleness. Lady Two Bird had always loved listening to him conduct ceremonies, wonder and excitement tingeing the often-repeated words.

"Lord Kan Boar has decided to take offense to how the foreigners left. He's declared that their leader must pay the penalty. He wants his heart. There isn't anything I can do to stop him."

She knew he was glossing over her part in their leaving, everyone politely ignoring her responsibility because of her position. "Please, my lord," Lady Two Bird said, looking up.

Kind brown eyes gazed down at her. She suspected the expression wasn't completely an act, though she could never be certain. She chose to believe, though, that her brother-in-law did sympathize with her position. However, he could do only so much. She wasn't being sacrificed—just the Iselanders, who both he and Lord Kan Boar didn't consider completely human. "You must believe me when I say that all the foreigners are important to our people, to—"

"Why? Do you believe in this White Hands prophecy?"

"I—" Lady Two Bird interrupted herself. She'd promised herself that she would tell Lord Smoke Moon of her visions. If anyone would believe her, it would be him. She still found herself oddly hesitant.

"Speak."

Lady Two Bird bowed her head and bit her lip. She feared it was too late for her to say anything about Ix Chebel speaking to her. She didn't know what he believed of Lord Six Sky's death, what poison Cauac Sky, and probably Evening Star, had already spread about her.

"I command you to tell me what you've seen."

How did he know her lady had gifted her? She glanced up, startled. "How did you—"

A low chuckle greeted her. "I didn't know, my dear. But I do now. Please. Tell me what you've been shown."

Lady Two Bird remembered the young man who had first greeted her sister—calm, intelligent, caring. Years in the employ of the service of Itzanam, solving the riddles of the smoke and deciphering the shifting aspects of the god had added a gentle trickster to the personas he represented. She never remembered how much he wore his own face like a mask until too late.

She bowed her head again and surrendered to the inevitable. The dark closeness of his hall made it easier to speak of visions and the gods—the way her words hushed themselves after she uttered them making it seem as if they were part of a ceremony. It didn't take long to tell of the few times the stones had trembled under her fingers, the first images of the blood stone and change, how they had warned her about the attack against the group, then caused her to run into the jungle, only to learn of Cauac Sky's greater treachery. She didn't name the day he'd assigned to her demise, but she told Lord Smoke Moon that the priest planned to kill her soon.

Lord Smoke Moon didn't interrupt her speech, but

let her words trail off. They sat in silence for a moment. While the lord seemed deep in thought, Lady Two Bird continued to tamp down on her rising panic, clutching her hands by her side, willing the pain of her nails biting into her palms to distract her. If Cauac Sky claimed that she was too influenced by her lady now, Lord Smoke Moon certainly had enough evidence, in her own words, to convict her of such charges and arrange for her sacrifice in less than a day.

But if he believed her . . .

After what seemed like days, Lord Smoke Moon rose from his chair and stalked to the end of his hall, shouting for his attendants to bring them refreshments. Lady Two Bird didn't know if this meant he believed her, or if they were to have a nice drink together before he took her heart.

She told herself to trust in Ix Chebel, though she knew the goddess wouldn't save her if it was her fate to die.

Tyrthbrand tried to sleep when they arrived back at the temple after their aborted escape attempt, but every time he closed his eyes, all he saw were his men falling. First Ankel dropping into the ocean after being poisoned by the darts of the *skraelings*, then Thorolf throwing himself into the glassy green pool, and finally Snorri floundering like a feather in a stiff wind.

Illugi didn't try to sleep. Instead, he requested, and then drank, a large amount of honeyed mead. He didn't sing, didn't shout, didn't curse, just silently drank, not offering to share. He spent most of his time sitting in a dark corner, staring at the wall, lifting his cup every once in a while in a silent salute.

Vigfus fell asleep immediately after they arrived back at the temple until just after dawn. The first thing he did when he awoke was start a fire. The priestesses were curious, but no one asked him about it or tried to stop him. He collected a very small pile of wood with which to feed it. When the sticks were gone, the boy sat staring at the dimming coals, not even leaning out of the way when a sudden gust of wind blessed him with smoke. He didn't move until after the fire was completely gutted and all the embers were black. Then he doused the area with a little water, walked over to one of the watching priestesses, and started practicing the Itza language in earnest.

After morning came and Vigfus had had his fire, Illugi joined the boy and they conducted conversations, pushing each other to remember more and more Itza words. Soon they were laughing with the priestesses, making mistakes, and exaggerating their successes.

Tyrthbrand ignored their calls to him, staying instead on the side, in the shade, wrestling with his thoughts, seeking a way out of the *wyrd* laid before him, always coming back to the same realization. He needed to sever his path from that of Illugi and Vigfus. It need be only his fate to die inside these walls. His men had to profit from his death somehow.

The midday heat arose and both Vigfus and Illugi succumbed to a nap after lunch. Tyrthbrand still couldn't sleep. Numbness wrapped around him like a second skin. Everything he'd done since leaving Iseland had been wrong. He'd ended up killing not only himself, but also everyone on the *Golden Tree*. No amount of *wergild* could make up for the lives he'd wasted with his stupid pride.

A soft voice at his side made him open his eyes. A priestess stood next to him, saying something, and gesturing toward the doorway.

Cauac Sky stood there with a handful of guards, all brightly decorated in sacrificial blue.

Tyrthbrand rose and started walking toward the priest. What did he want? As Tyrthbrand drew closer, he saw the bloodlust in the priest's eyes.

Cauac Sky had come to collect the Iselander for sacrifice.

Tyrthbrand slowed for a moment, thinking furiously. Lady Two Bird had told him that Cauac Sky couldn't sacrifice him here, in the city. If he'd understood her correctly, the priest didn't have the authority.

Yet there was no mistaking the priest's intent. Tyrthbrand didn't allow himself to shiver, but met the gaze of his executioner. A plan for how he could use his death began to unfold. He started walking again, tall and proud, and came to a complete stop only when he reached the threshold. He stared for a moment at the priest.

If Tyrthbrand allowed Cauac Sky to kill him, would that protect his men? Would the Itza punish the Red Hands leader? Could that delay the death of his men long enough for them to try another escape?

It was his only hope.

He nodded slowly, hoping that Cauac Sky realized that Tyrthbrand knew what was being asked of him. Then Tyrthbrand said, "Me, go. Them," he said, indicating his sleeping men, "here."

The priest considered his request for a moment, before he replied, "Today."

Grimly, Tyrthbrand nodded, hoping that one day would grow into a week, a season, a year—that his sacrifice would have some purpose, unlike the deaths of the rest of his men.

Lady Two Bird tried to stifle her yawn while Lord Smoke Moon poured them yet another cup of honey-sweetened cocoa. The skill with which her brother-in-law interrogated her about what she'd seen amazed her. In some ways, he reminded her of her father, and the logic games they'd played. Lord Smoke Moon kept circling back, drawing out every nuance of meaning and then adding shades of interpretation to her visions that she'd never considered. His thoroughness exhausted her, though, and the heat of the afternoon had seeped into the hall, making the incense-laced air difficult to breathe.

She still didn't know if he believed her. He believed that she'd seen something. But had it been a sending from Ix Chebel? That seemed to be the crux of his questioning now.

"Tired?" Lord Smoke Moon asked as he handed her the cool liquid.

Lady Two Bird nodded, chagrined.

"We're almost finished here, my dear. Drink up."

Lord Smoke Moon thoughtfully waited until Lady Two Bird had taken a few sips before he started again.

"What about—"

A servant came hurrying in and interrupted him before he completed his question. After a moment of whispered conversation, Lord Smoke Moon nodded.

Lady Two Bird rose and opened her mouth to ask if she should leave.

"Stay," Lord Smoke Moon said. He took another sip of his drink and said nothing else, frowning at the bottom of his cup, swirling the liquid now and again as if it were telling him a future he didn't care for. Servants entered the hall with more torches, driving away the intimate darkness.

Then Lord Kan Boar came striding into the hall. He walked straight up to Lord Smoke Moon to greet him, direct as a thrown spear, seeming to ignore everything else. Again, the man's incongruous demeanor struck Lady Two Bird; how large he was, bristling with weapons, yet he carried a quiet around him that eddied and flowed like currents in a sacred pond.

The welcoming words between the two men were scripted, courteous, and short. After accepting a low bench from a servant, as well as some of the honeyed cocoa, Lord Kan Boar turned to where Lady Two

Bird had reseated herself and said, "I suppose you've come here to beg for the lives of the foreigners."

Lord Smoke Moon answered for her. "Yes, she has. And she has an interesting theory as to why they're important. I suggest you tell Lord Kan Boar what you've been shown."

Lady Two Bird tried to maintain a pleasant smile on her face, hoping to hide how her brother-in-law's order scared her. She suspected that Lord Kan Boar could sense her fear anyway. She didn't want to expose herself, her visions, this way. Torches now lit the hall like a bright noonday. Talk of communications with the gods should be revealed through ceremony and ritual, written down, then read aloud. To just speak them like this, in front of such a rough man, seemed crude.

"Everything," Lord Smoke Moon said after Lady Two Bird paused again.

Without adding any of the speculation that she and Lord Smoke Moon had indulged in earlier, she gave the bare bones of her visions. When prompted again by Lord Smoke Moon, she also told of Cauac Sky's threats.

Lord Kan Boar listened politely, without interruption. When she finished, he drained his cup in one gulp, put it down beside him with an audible click, and said, "Prove it."

Even Lord Smoke Moon seemed startled by the proclamation. "And how would you go about testing her?" he asked, his gentle voice challenging.

"She says the rocks talk to her. Let them save her."

"Ah," Lord Smoke Moon said. He leaned back with his fingers laced together, thumbs rubbing against each other. "No other guide?"

Lord Kan Boar shook his head.

"What are you proposing, my lords?" Lady Two Bird asked.

The two men exchanged a glance, then Lord Smoke

Moon answered her. "Below this temple is the Hall of Testing. It's often used for . . . establishing the truth of one's faith. It's a relatively easy test, as tests go. You merely have to walk from the start to the World Tree. And survive."

Lady Two Bird raised her chin, hiding the fear she felt. She knew they weren't telling her everything. A purely physical test didn't seem appropriate for a follower of Itzanam to propose.

"Come," Lord Smoke Moon said, standing. "I will show you the hall. Then you will have until tomorrow to decide if you want to take the test or not."

"And if I choose not to?" Lady Two Bird asked, rising as well.

The two men looked again at each other. "Your life won't be forfeit," Lord Smoke Moon said, though it seemed to be more of a question than a statement.

Lord Kan Boar nodded. "But *all* the Iselanders' lives will be."

Although Lord Smoke Moon wouldn't sacrifice Lady Two Bird if she refused this test, she would lose what little standing she had. Her brother-in-law might no longer agree to see her or allow her access to his court. Lord Kan Boar certainly wouldn't. She didn't want to die alone, old, and powerless, without even a child to brighten her days. But she might not have much choice in the matter.

Lord Smoke Moon led the way out of his hall to a blanketed opening. The men went through first, down a short passage, to a tiny, steep, crooked staircase. A person couldn't go through it arms akimbo without having her elbows scrape both sides. The men didn't have to duck their heads. The walls sweated with the afternoon heat. Orange light from the single lamp Lord Smoke Moon carried drew grotesque faces out of the shadows. Lady Two Bird trembled and closed her eyes, letting her fingers lead her down the stairs, grimacing at the slime oozing down the walls, but

knowing that it was the only way she would survive
being in such a closed-in space. She gulped air as quietly as she could, afraid that it would all run out before she reached the end of the staircase.

Three passages led from the bottom of the stairs.
Lady Two Bird had gotten too turned around to know
if the one they went down led west, the direction of
Xibalba. She suspected it did. She didn't allow herself
to look at the ceiling, to speculate about how many
tons of rock now pressed down on her. Murals of sacrifices covered the walls, along with gory depictions of
battles. Red and blue swirls coated the floor as well.
Lady Two Bird felt dizzy from the lack of air. When
she looked down, it seemed as though the designs
under her feet moved in lazy waves, sweeping her
along.

They stopped in front of another blanketed door.
Lord Smoke Moon pulled the covering to one side.
Stale air, like from a deep, unused well, floated out.

Lady Two Bird came forward, then squinted, to see
better. Another, wider set of crooked stairs led down
into a long corridor.

Shadows danced all along the passage. A few flickering torches burned in brackets near the entrance,
but the far end was hidden in inky darkness. Large
boulders standing in the center of the hall made it
impossible to walk a straight line from one end to
the other.

Lord Smoke Moon held his lamp out and cast the
light it shed toward the floor, illuminating the huge pit
that was at the bottom of the stair, black and endless.

"You must walk with blind faith, with only the rocks
to speak to you, from here to the World Tree in the
next chamber and back."

Lady Two Bird swallowed around the sudden boulders blocking her throat. It was her worst nightmare,
manifested in the physical world. Lord Smoke Moon
and Lord Kan Boar would blindfold her, possibly dis-

tort her other senses as well with smoke and drugs;
then she would have to make her way with the huge
stones in the hall as her only guide. She was certain
that other candidates, when tested, would have the
riddles from the *Chilam Balam* to guide them around
the pits. However, she'd claimed the rocks had spoken
to her, saved her. This would indeed test whether or
not they would continue to direct her, or if she was
destined to fall to her death, buried deep within the
earth, with no chance of climbing out of Xibalba. She
shuddered, seeing in her mind's eye hands reaching
out of the pits, grabbing at her, pulling her down.

She didn't ask how many had survived this test without the riddles. Few probably had.

And she certainly wouldn't. Had Cauac Sky been
right when he'd said she'd die by Etz'nab? The day
Lord Smoke Moon wanted her to walk this hall?

With many words of courtesy, she bowed her way
out of the hall, fleeing up the stairs, out of the dark,
dank passages, back into the sunlight and fresh air.

She stopped in the center of the plaza outside Lord
Smoke Moon's hall and looked back. Even in the
bright sunlight, a gloom clung to the temple walls. She
never wanted to return.

And when she refused the test, she would never be
allowed to.

She couldn't save Tyrthbrand and his men. They
were fated to be sacrificed, sooner rather than later.
Maybe she could wrest the blood stone recipe from
Tyrthbrand now, before he died, so his death wouldn't
be a waste. Because she couldn't go through the trial
as proposed by Lord Smoke Moon and Lord Kan
Boar. She would rather be sacrificed on the temple
stairs.

Noisy vendors from the marketplace called to her
as she stepped outside the walls enclosing Itzanam's
temple plaza. Though she'd had little to eat that day,
the aroma of spicy braised peppers only turned her

stomach. With reluctance, she turned toward the temple of Ix Chebel. She needed to find Tyrthbrand. She doubted that his language skills were adequate for her to explain the test, how she wasn't willing to give her life for his or the other foreigners, of her fear that the stones that had saved her would now be her death, how he needed to tell her the recipe, and at least help her save her people.

Illugi was shouting at the priestesses at the entrance to the courtyard. When Lady Two Bird drew closer, she realized one of the words Illugi was yelling was "Tyrthbrand."

The tall blond calmed down when he saw her, and said in almost accentless Itza, "Tyrthbrand has gone."

"A priest collected him, my lady," spoke up an attendant.

Lady Two Bird didn't understand how the air in the open plaza suddenly became as closed in as when she'd descended the staircase in Lord Smoke Moon's hall, but it did. She found herself panting.

"Who?" she asked, though she already knew.

A different attendant stepped up. "We don't know him. He was dressed like a priest. An older man, tall, skinny, with a bald head."

"Did he have a red hand painted on his chest?" Lady Two Bird asked.

The two attendants seemed puzzled. "How did you know?"

It appeared that Illugi knew the words for "red hand." "Cauac Sky," he said, his tone eerily flat and focused.

"Stay here," Lady Two Bird said as she turned and left.

Tyrthbrand told himself that the reason it felt as though his skin was crawling with ants was because of the paint the priests were applying to his body, that it wasn't because of the gleam in Cauac Sky's cruel

eyes. He tried to control the shiver that overtook him
when the Red Hands leader came close enough to cast
his hot breath on Tyrthbrand's skin. Tyrthbrand closed
his eyes against the madness in Cauac Sky's gaze,
wishing he could close his ears as well to the urging
tone in the priest's voice, knowing that he was trying
to speed up his death.

When the priests offered him the dried mushrooms
that smelled like shit, he took one from the bowl and
raised it in a silent toast to Thorolf before he ate it.
Then he ate more, as many as the priests urged him
to. He wanted to see the gods, face Tyr one last time,
and spit in his eye. He was going to turn his back on
his god, one last time, even if it meant diving into the
Itza Xibalba.

After finishing the mushrooms, Tyrthbrand cleared
his throat and tried to sing like Thorolf had. Cauac
Sky came up close to him again, tilted his head to one
side, and tried to hum along with him. Tyrthbrand
swore the priest's eyes were whirling holes, sucking
him in. He stopped singing quickly, refusing to pour
more of himself out.

Too soon, the priests put away their pots. It was
time. He tried to stiffen his spine, but he wasn't quite
sure where it was anymore. Weird colors swirled
through the air. He tried to chase them with his eyes,
follow where they went, but they slipped through the
walls or the floor before he could. He started when
he looked at Cauac Sky. Knives seemed to float all
around him. No wonder he was mad and hungry for
blood—they pricked and bled him all the time.

The priests took Tyrthbrand's arms and led him
around the chamber three times. He tried not to look
at them, or the guards in the room. They all seemed
more animal than beast, with pushed-out snouts and
salivating fangs.

He shivered again as they approached the stone slab

altar. It looked as barren as ashes or salted earth.
Gingerly he lay down on it, the cold seeping into his
limbs, freezing him, making him like stone. Suddenly,
there didn't seem to be enough air. He breathed as
deeply as he could, unable to control his trembling as
the priests grabbed his arms and legs.

Tyrthbrand refused to let himself regret his death.
He was giving his men more time, maybe enough so
that they could escape. But he wished he could have
said good-bye to Lady Two Bird.

Could she save Tyrthbrand on her own? Without
alerting Lord Smoke Moon or Lord Kan Boar? What
Cauac Sky was probably doing—sacrificing one of the
foreigners without telling anyone—wouldn't be
condoned.

Lady Two Bird didn't have time to get back to Lord
Smoke Moon's hall. Tyrthbrand might already be
dead. She walked quickly back to the crowded streets,
then up to the first guard she saw.

"Here," she said, pulling the flowered turquoise earplugs from her earlobes and thrusting them into his
hand. Lord Smoke Moon had given them to her a
very long time ago.

He stared at it, then at her, as if she were crazy.

"I am Lady Two Bird. Take those to Lord Smoke
Moon and tell him to meet me with more guards, at
the Cycle-Star Temple. You hear me?"

The soldier nodded slowly. When he just stood
there, Lady Two Bird yelled at him. "Now!"

Still nodding, the man backed away for a few steps
before turning and marching swiftly toward Itzanam's
temple. Lady Two Bird walked in the other direction,
toward the gates of the city, where she was certain
the priest was holding the sacrifice.

Most human sacrifices took place outside, with
crowds of people all benefiting from the death. How-

ever, the City of Wells also contained two caves that the priests had blessed for use in a human sacrifice ritual.

Lady Two Bird was certain she would find Tyrthbrand at the smaller of the two. Cauac Sky didn't want others to know of his deed until he'd finished it. Or to share in it. Besides, he was enough of a stickler for the absolute form of ritual and protocol that he could be using only that space.

It seemed that all the lanes of the city swelled with people as the late-afternoon heat dropped off. Lady Two Bird went as quickly as she could through the crowds to the temple cave, silently cursing every time she had to pause for a burdened merchant, a family, or even a priest.

Two of the Red Hand guards stood outside the entrance to the cave. Lady Two Bird ignored them, going down the path toward the opening of the cave. It took a moment for the guards to catch up with her.

"You can't go in there." One of them reached out a hand toward her arm.

Lady Two Bird froze him with a look. He stopped before his fingers actually made contact with her. Using the most formal phrases she knew, Lady Two Bird, in a tone dripping with ice, said, "You will not dare to touch someone from the royal house. You will not deny someone from the royal house. You will go back to your post and see that no one *undeserving* disturbs us. Have I made myself quite clear?"

With nods and quiet shuffling, the men backed up and away, leaving the way open for Lady Two Bird.

Holding her head high, Lady Two Bird walked toward the cave opening as if in a procession. She hated the way her breath seemed to catch as she approached the dark opening. But she couldn't allow those guards to guess how frightened she was, how much it took for her to force herself to walk back into a tight, shadowed place, underground.

Brightly burning lamps hung on all the walls of the chamber. Tyrthbrand lay on his back, naked, on the grand slab at the front of the hall. Soldiers held his widespread feet and hands. Cauac Sky stood at his side, sacred blade in one hand, his other hand still moving above it. Lady Two Bird recognized the cleansing prayer the priest said.

"Stop!" she called, disturbing him before he could finish. He wouldn't be able to sacrifice Tyrthbrand with an improperly prepared knife. Maybe making him redo that part of the ceremony would be enough of a delay for Lord Smoke Moon's guards to arrive.

Murderous rage filled the look that Cauac Sky shot her. Lady Two Bird didn't step back, though it felt like what little air remained in the chamber had just been burned away.

"You," he hissed. He took one step toward her, the blade clenched tightly in his hand, before he seemed to remember himself. "Grab her," he directed his guards.

Only then did Lady Two Bird notice the other men in the ritual space, lurking in the shadows against the walls. The two holding Tyrthbrand didn't move. The others did.

She tried to drive them back with the fierceness of her scowl, but they refused to be quelled. They gripped her arms tightly and brought her forward.

Cauac Sky's smile seemed to drip with the blood he longed to spill. "You've polluted this sacred space with your womanhood," he stated simply.

"I—what—you—" Lady Two Bird couldn't think of a single thing to say. Certain temple spaces were sometimes dedicated to men or women, as were specific rituals. This ceremony couldn't be so specialized. Sacrifices were for all the people.

The priest started to nod, as if Lady Two Bird and he were conducting a conversation. "The only way to cleanse this space is with your blood."

Lady Two Bird wanted to laugh and remind him that he wasn't supposed to kill her until the next day. But she couldn't. He was serious, and the guards tightened their hold on her until her arms ached.

How could Cauac Sky believe that he'd get away with killing someone of her stature? He couldn't just do it here, now, no matter how much he claimed that her goddess influenced her.

He truly had gone insane. From the fanatical look on his face, he didn't care if he got away with it or not, just as long as he tasted her blood.

She was struggling to pull away from the guards when she heard a warning growl. She froze and looked toward the altar. Had Tyrthbrand decided to fight for her? No, his eyes were more glazed than the priest's. The guards who held her, as well as Cauac Sky, all glanced around the chamber, trying to find out where the noise had come from.

It came again. Louder.

Then the ground began to shake.

"We all return to the earth."

Lord Kan Boar's words echoed in Lady Two Bird's head as a large crack opened beneath her feet. She pulled free of the men holding her and tried to run toward the cave entrance. Anything but be taken like this.

She managed two shaky steps before a hole beneath her opened and she fell. The entire world roared, louder than anything she'd ever heard before. She held herself up with one arm, and only her shaky grip prevented her from sinking into the pit beneath her. The ground before her eyes undulated like a wave coming into shore. Bile filled her mouth as she clenched her aching muscles and tried to pull herself up. Small pebbles and pieces of earth rained down on her like hail.

For a moment everything stopped. The sound of her

panting breath filled her ears. She heard Tyrthbrand's voice, from somewhere close behind her, call out. "Lady Two Bird!"

In response, the ground bucked again, harder.

Lady Two Bird woke to darkness and pain. She tried to take a deep breath, but dirt filled her mouth. Dust choked her lungs. She spat, coughed, and tried to sit up.

That was when she found the earth encased her.

Panic held her tighter than the dirt. This was ten thousand times worse than the Hall of Testing. There was nothing but blackness, whether her eyes were open or shut. She lay on her side, sifting the dirt holding her in place. When she flailed her arms, her cocoon expanded a little, then more loose rocks fell on her.

She tried to breathe normally, but there was no air. She didn't know how long she'd been there, if Lord Smoke Moon's men were still coming, or if they'd been killed in the earthquake as well. She strained, listening, trying to hear anything that indicated that there was someone other than herself alive, but the roaring from the quake still echoed in her head.

Fine then. She would just have to save herself. She clawed at the earth, willing her hands upward, out toward the blessed air. She would *not* be stuck here, in this simulated birth canal. She would force her way back to the living.

First one palm found open air, then the other. Rocks bound her in place now. She struggled to shove them from her. She had to rest sometimes. Once when the boulder that pinned her legs refused to budge, she nearly screamed, but her fear lent her strength and she finally managed to force it to one side.

Even once she found her way up, so that nothing enclosed her but air, it was still as if the world had just been born—no stars or fires to guide her, nothing to light her way. She swayed on her feet. If she could only find her way out of the cave, back to the world of men.

The rocks wouldn't guide her. Her goddess was no longer paying any attention to her. She would have to find her way on her own.

Lady Two Bird dropped back to her knees and began to crawl. Every path in the jungle took you where you needed to be. She prayed that the way she found amongst the rocks would be the same.

Her hand landed in something slippery after a short while. Lady Two Bird gingerly reached out. The round shape her fingers found was cool to the touch. It took her a moment to realize it was Cauac Sky's head. She found his nostrils. No breath was coming out of them. He was dead.

She bit down on her lips hard. She was not going to scream. But had she already died? Did she only believe herself alive, wandering forever in some sort of charnel house, specially created for her by the Lords of the Underworld?

With shaking fingers, she made herself touch her chest. Her heart still beat there. Chances were, she hadn't died.

Yet.

She forced herself to keep crawling, away from the body, dreading finding any more, but knowing that she might. She discovered that the ringing in her ears had faded when she placed her hand on something sharp and she yelped in pain.

Finally, she felt a slight breeze stroking her right cheek. When she looked that way, she nearly sobbed with relief. There was an opening. A crack of light through the barrier of rock. She would get out. She would save herself.

But what of her people?

Lady Two Bird stopped abruptly. Lord Kan Boar had been right. They all went back to the land. As would her people someday. She couldn't stop that. She couldn't save them from the White Hands and the coming plague. Their fate was now beyond her, if it had ever been in her hands. She could save only herself.

And maybe, one other with her, if he still lived.

The recipe for the blood stone no longer mattered. She no longer needed to see her name on the temple walls. She had her life. That was what mattered. Tyrthbrand's life was important as well. He, too, shouldn't die here. It should not be his fate. He deserved one more chance to die as a man.

So she turned away from the light and began to call his name, hoping that he would hear her in the darkness and be able to come to her, birth himself from the ground as she had.

Tyrthbrand heard someone calling for him, but the sound was filtered, as if he clung to the bottom of the *Golden Tree* and water clogged all his senses. Midnight blackness greeted him when he opened his eyes, along with grit. His head still swam from the drugged mushrooms he'd eaten. When he tried to move his arms, he realized that though the soldiers no longer held him down, rocks and loose earth did.

Only then did he remember the earthquake—the tremulous, treacherous land, its vibrations picking him up and throwing him from the altar on which he'd voluntarily placed himself, giving his life so that his men might live.

Was he dead? Did being dead mean that he should hurt as much as he did? He didn't know. He could imagine a torment like this, buried forever, aching, unable to find his men, his family, or his gods.

Who was calling to him in this closed-in place? Was that Tyr?

Tyrthbrand turned away from the noise, turned his back on the voice. He would not go back to his god.

He would rather die. He had to die. Wasn't it his time? Hadn't the priest said so? Hadn't he known so, from the beginning?

With a grimace, he shook his head, as much as he could, encased as he was. His lungs yearned for clear air. His traitorous heart continued to beat. He still existed in the world of men. A shameful yearning to live shot through him.

The call came again. Tyrthbrand realized it was a woman's voice.

Lady Two Bird. Come to save him. Cauac Sky had been about to sacrifice her as well.

Anger poured through Tyrthbrand as he came surging out of the ground, flinging away the stones that held him, toward the only light he'd ever beheld in this land of gods and darkness, toward his lady.

Lady Two Bird didn't bother to change her clothes or clean her face on her way back to Lord Smoke Moon's chambers. Fury radiated from her. No one stood in her way or tried to stop her as she marched directly into his greeting hall.

"Why did your soldiers take Tyrthbrand? Why must he still be sacrificed?" she asked as she strode in, not bothering with the niceties of properly greeting her brother-in-law.

Lord Kan Boar, still seated beside Lord Smoke Moon, answered her. "Just because you saved him from one sacrifice does not mean my honor has been repaid. They all must die. I've sworn that I will hold this foreign leader's heart in my hands."

Lady Two Bird gasped as if the words were physical blows. She'd saved Tyrthbrand, only to have him sacrificed anyway?

No.

"I will take your test. Now."

Both lords looked surprised.

"My dear, are you sure you don't want to think

about it? Or at least get cleaned up? Take some
refreshment?"

Lady Two Bird laughed at her brother-in-law's sug-
gestions. The cawing sound that came out did nothing
to settle the constant itching of her spine, urging her
toward action. "Do you think the gods will care how
I look when they take me?"

An attendant appeared at her side with a cup of
lightly sweetened mead. Lady Two Bird swallowed the
contents in a single gulp. She imagined the honey filling her body with a golden light as it coursed through
her system, mingling with her blood, making it rich
and fine, tempting for the gods.

She'd escaped, twice, from the earth that had buried
her. Once for herself, then the second time, with
Tyrthbrand. She doubted she'd make it a third time,
but she had no choice. She could only try.

"Shall we?" she asked, impatient for her fate to be
known to her.

Both men nodded. They rose as one and left the
hall, going through the same blanket-covered opening
they'd used before. Descending the stairs, Lady Two
Bird didn't feel the air enclosing her like the earth
had. She suspected she never would again.

She was no longer afraid to die.

They paused before the doorway to the Hall of
Testing. Lord Kan Boar bound her eyes with a leather
strip, harsh and stiff against her skin. Lord Smoke
Moon told her, "I will be waiting for you beneath the
glory of the World Tree. You will be able to rest there
for a short time and see the wonder yourself, before
you return."

Lady Two Bird nodded. Now that darkness had
folded its wings around her again, her fear returned,
not that all the air would disappear, but that she
would fall into one of the very real pits in the hall.
The stones, she knew, would be silent. She would have
to make her way by her other senses, her own wit and

cunning, even though she was exhausted, filthy, her hands not shaking only because of her will.

She listened to Lord Smoke Moon's soft steps fade away, down the stairs, through the hall, before she descended. Behind her blindfold, she kept her eyes closed and breathed deeply. She knew there was a pit at the bottom of the stairs that she had to swerve to the right to avoid. She began angling that way, unsure how many steps there were. After steps that she was too nervous to count, she felt a dip underneath the sole of her sandal. The next step was a bit steeper, and then the stairs were finished. She'd reached the bottom, was standing on solid ground, with the pit to her left.

With slow, shuffling steps, arms extended awkwardly before her, she made her way to the first boulder. How many were there? How many pits did she have to go around? How could she get from one to the next?

As much as she wanted to, she knew she couldn't crawl. This was a test of human, not animal, strength and intelligence.

Lord Smoke Moon had made it clear that he expected her to run her fingers along the boulders, to see if they would talk to her. The rock beneath her palm didn't tremble, no visions stole over her own blackness. However, a circle with grooves shooting out from it ran along the top of the first one. They had to be artificial, placed there as a clue by the priests for the initiates. It was a representation of the sun, but what did it mean?

She found a second set of grooves carved just below the rays, perfectly spaced so her fingers found their slots without trouble. It took her a moment to remember the start of the current age, the world of men, with the fingers of dawn streaked across the sky.

If the hallway faced west, then she needed to head east, toward the rising sun. She turned and walked that way, palms brushing against open air now, feeling an emptiness beside her. She believed she'd just passed another pit. She reached the wall, and let it guide her.

The next one was obvious. Four bumps on the top of the boulder. Obviously, the four pillars of the earth. She needed to go straight, down the center, avoid what were sure to be traps on either side.

Lady Two Bird gained confidence as she passed from one stone to the wall to the next large rock. The dark, which had for so long been a threat, now cushioned her. Most of her will was expended moving one leg in front of the other as exhaustion, not fear, plucked at her. She forced herself to focus, to pay attention to every clue her trembling fingers found on the rocks.

She was startled when two hands enclosed her outstretched fingers and drew her forward. A warm cup was pressed between them; then someone removed her blindfold.

The brilliance stung her eyes. Through a teary prism, she finally saw what Lord Smoke Moon had meant by the World Tree: a cave column that grew like a holy ceiba tree. The top branches held up the roof of the gallery. Stalactites dripped from the ceiling, like vines with nubbly leaves. Tiny oil lamps dangled on thin black threads attached to wooden posts driven into the tree. Long rock segments divided the trunk, growing down into planklike roots. A great mound surged up around the base of the tree, festooned with offerings: pots with horrible grinning faces colored in sacrificial blue and red; ear upon ear of corn; *matate* and *mano*—boards and rollers—used by women to grind corn into flour so it could be eaten; wood-covered books, filled with pages of secret knowledge; as well as cool, carved jade, shaped into pendants, spear points, knives, and rings.

Lady Two Bird caught her breath and turned to

Lord Smoke Moon. He smiled, a nice, boyish smile, probably the truest smile she'd ever seen him wear.

"Magnificent, isn't it?" he whispered, his voice sounding as solemn and sacred as if he were conducting a ritual.

Wordlessly, Lady Two Bird nodded. She glanced at him for approval before she walked a little to the side, around the path circling the tree. Faces of shadow and flickering light emerged in the asymmetrical trunk, coming out of hiding then disappearing again as she continued along the trail.

As she finished her cocoa Lady Two Bird made her way back to Lord Smoke Moon, who had stayed at the entrance and stared up at the frozen tree, captivated.

"Every time I come in here I wonder about our ancestors. The ones who found this place. Did the gods lead them here? Were they seeking a door to Xibalba? Or just explorers, curious about what was here?"

Lady Two Bird stayed silent as Lord Smoke Moon rebound her eyes. Just as she was about to step back into the Hall of Testing did she reply. "The Iselanders. They're explorers, you know."

"What do you mean Tyrthbrand is still to be sacrificed?" Lady Two Bird couldn't believe what she'd just heard.

"The other Iselanders are to be spared," Lord Smoke Moon said, trying to calm her.

"No. I did your test. His life is mine."

"His life belongs to the gods. I want only his heart," Lord Kan Boar said.

"Please," Lord Smoke Moon said. "Lady Two Bird did survive the Hall of Training. Isn't there some other way for your honor to be satisfied?"

Lord Kan Boar crossed his arms over his chest and didn't reply.

Lady Two Bird felt herself on the verge of tears.

Her skin crawled with dirt and sweat. Returning through the Hall of Training had been more difficult, her limbs weighted by even the air. She'd remembered the sequence and walked the same path she'd originally followed, but it had seemed twice as long.

"I swore I would hold his heart in my hands. Would you make me an oath breaker?"

Lady Two Bird turned to Lord Smoke Moon. She would plead if she had to. He held up his hand before she could say another word.

"Must it be his actual heart? Or just a symbolic one? One that would mean he'd given over his life to us?" On the last words, he stared at Lady Two Bird.

"He *has* already pledged himself to me," she responded quietly.

Lord Kan Boar looked amused, but didn't say anything.

"Then a ceremony formalizing this act is appropriate. Wouldn't you say?" Lord Smoke Moon said, switching his gaze to Lord Kan Boar.

Lord Kan Boar wrinkled his brow in thought.

Chapter 8

Ix Chebel and the rest of the gods followed Itzanam up the steps of the temple to the platform at the top. The young aspect she found herself wearing wanted to skip and jump and she had to make herself slow down more than once. The jungle shimmered under a rainbow haze, as if the drops from a recent rain still covered the leaves. The birds grew quiet as the gods rose, the singers of prophecies waiting to see the outcome of this ceremony.

At the top of the platform, Itzanam raised a strange, plateau-like altar. It was crude, unadorned with murals or glyphs—a simple square of power. Itzanam fashioned a knife from the tears of the mountain, put the golden fruit from the foreign gods down on the center, then hesitated.

An excited thrill ran through Ix Chebel. This was *new*. It was the first time the gods were to perform this ceremony. They were creating a ritual that couldn't be found through the spirals of time. The words that needed to be said, the prayers and gestures, how their acts would echo out into the human realm and be manifest, all would be determined in these next few moments by her husband, Itzanam. Pride buoyed up Ix Chebel's spirits, shrinking her worry.

"Timeless we are, timeless we remain," he intoned with the first cut, halving the apple. Then he lifted the knife, turned it, and cut again. "All the parts to make us whole."

Ix Chebel shivered at that refrain. She knew that Itzanam foresaw a time of joining. She didn't want to be subsumed, to lose her own aspects and days.

Now she understood how Feathered Serpent felt when he faced her husband, this other aspect of himself. Is that how she would spend her days, mad with jealousy as she faded and grew gray?

"We alter as the river flows, the water always moving, but never changing."

Ix Chebel didn't fight the rictus grin that widened her mouth, or the death's head mask that took over her features. Maybe this was what she was to become, merely an insane goddess, one to be appeased, not respected or worshipped. She had enough sanity to recognize that fear had brought on this madness, as much as anything Itzanam said.

Then she cared no more.

Protocol no longer bound her as she saw more and more of the years that had not come, the weight of that knowledge splintering her consciousness. With a cackling yell she leaped from where she stood and twirled, spinning as fast as the river flowed in Itzanam's spiral of time. She wove a ribbon around those who stood there, marking the chosen from the not. Pushing and pulling, yelling and singing, she moved the other gods and goddesses around, directing them to stand in the places she saw, where they fit in the twining ropes that Itzanam spun. Itzanam sliced the foreigner's golden sun into smaller pieces until its light started diminishing. Ix Chebel couldn't warn him not to remove the heart of the myth—the lines between the fruit and the people she'd placed closest to the table strangled her. But he seemed to realize it on his own.

There weren't enough pieces for all the gods to have a slice. Ix Chebel hadn't known that—her vision wasn't that complete, and in her madness, she couldn't be that articulate. She'd only known that these, the gods and goddesses she'd pushed to the front, were the most important, the strongest of the net to which the rest of them would cling to when the flood came. These were the ones who had to survive, if any of them did.

"These unchanging few," she said, cackling as Itzanam began to pass between them. Ix Chebel laughed out loud when sticky fingers of time clung to Itzanam's sleeve as he passed through them. He would bind them all into one, if he could.

A few others saw the ropes, though they didn't understand the significance of them. Itzanam didn't see why the gods must join together, how that was the only way that they might save themselves from the White Hands. No one besides Ix Chebel tasted the land's fear of their failure braided into the long strands.

Before Itzanam could hand out the last two slices, a whirring rainbow landed in the middle of the platform. With two long strides, Feathered Serpent walked up and snapped up the remaining apple slices, tossing them into the maw of his mouth.

"Two hearts as one," Ix Chebel called out. She put the piece of fruit that Itzanam had given her into her mouth and bit down.

The fruit was as sweet and crunchy as she'd expected. Tangy like citrus. A darker aftertaste lingered near the roof of her mouth, the back of her tongue.

It was like a cool spring in the hot jungle, refreshing.

And all too quickly, polluted and gone.

Ix Chebel giggled and spun after she finished, licking her fingers. The ones around her, who had also taken the fruit, also glowed.

As for the ones who hadn't had any of the fruit— she could already see through the spirals of time how their names would turn to dust. They wouldn't be remembered, no matter what, no matter which spiral came true. But why was she seeing both so clearly?

Did another influence what she saw? Who else fore-told these dark times?

A thread of sanity tugged her toward Feathered Serpent. He saw only the one possibility though: her people overrun by foreigners, abandoned in the jungle.

The other star in her sky called to her, offered her sanctuary, and she turned toward Itzanam.

What she saw made her weep.

He wore a smile—a true smile—the only one she'd ever seen. He stood frozen by the *geis* of his own foreseeing, blindly staring out at a world with static gods and unchanging seasons. His vision was so pure, so poisonous.

The discordant currents yanked at her, threatening to split her in two. She had no choice but to let her world fracture more. She released all the pieces that held her in place and became unreachable by prayer, sacrifice, or even the call of the gods. The fate of the world could no longer be her responsibility, and she would not let herself be tempted to duty. She could not choose between the dueling visions, both possibili-ties that existed beyond this sphere of the now, each frighteningly possible, if the blood stone survived.

However, it would have to endure on its own. She must stand clear of all of it.

It was up to the humans now.

Itzanam watched his wife leap down the temple stairs, the weight of the world no longer binding her to the earth. He didn't follow her aspects or days, but he suspected that it was more than the usual changes that had caused her to lose herself so completely in madness. He couldn't ask her—she was too far gone. He would try, though, when she came back.

But even her insanity didn't dim the light the day held.

The rest of the gods followed suit, slipping over the edge of the platform in groups of twos and threes. Itzanam watched them flow in and out of the river of his vision, older images superimposed upon the now.

Finally, only Itzanam and Feathered Serpent remained. The warrior stood with his spear held tightly in his hand, staring at the altar Itzanam had raised. A single stroke of thunder bounded across the sky. Itzanam just laughed. Poor boy, wanting a fight where there was none to be had. Itzanam hadn't been angered at Feathered Serpent's antics: it just meant that as this ceremony became formalized, more of the fruit would be allotted to him after the pair of them merged.

"Don't you see?" Feathered Serpent hissed at Itzanam.

"Don't *you* see?" Itzanam asked back, keeping his voice mild. The edges of everything—the altar, the temple steps, the leaves of the jungle trees surrounding them—still sparkled, like precious stones spotted with dew.

Feathered Serpent reached out and gripped Itzanam's forearm. "You don't understand the consequences of your vision," he said, despair tingeing his voice.

A flicker of darkness, like a thin veil, cast itself over Itzanam's sight. Before the blackness could build, Itzanam grabbed Feathered Serpent's arm in return. "Yours is the more deadly future," Itzanam said, willing that the younger god taste Itzanam's vision.

Itzanam ignored the reciprocal effect, how he began seeing Feathered Serpent's . . . nightmare. Itzanam wouldn't deem it a true vision. It was a horrible hallucination, a misguided dream, with foreigners rolling over the land and breaking it, enslaving their people, destroying their culture, warping their rituals.

With a shake, Itzanam freed himself from both foretellings and willed his eyes to see only the day, the temple platform, the altar he'd raised, that already had faint designs gathering on its edges. Feathered Serpent still seemed trapped, his eyes glazed and unfocused. The arm not firmly gripped by Itzanam hung loosely at his side. With a startling clank, the spear Feathered Serpent had been clutching fell to the ground and he took a shuffling step toward his enemy.

Unthinking, Itzanam also moved forward, closer. The other god's eyes stared at him, dark and liquid, unblinking. Hot breath grazed his cheek. Itzanam tried to release his hold on the younger god, but instead, found his other hand moving up to wrap his fingers around Feathered Serpent's shoulder.

And sinking in.

Glee filled Itzanam's heart. He felt like laughing, but found the sound was trapped in his throat.

They were merging. As he had seen through the spirals of time.

He roughly pulled the other to him, unable to wrap his arms around him, but still wanting to subsume him, draw him into his chest, and swallow him whole. Feathered Serpent's rough heart beat in time with his own. The younger god now stood noticeably shorter than he had, and Itzanam could rest his chin on the top of the warrior's head.

Birds screamed from the trees surrounding them. Thunder rolled across the sky once more. The air thickened and pressed up against them, forcing them closer to each other. Scents of incense and sweet burned blood drifted down on them, blessing their skin.

Itzanam floated on the river of his vision, the constant nature of the gods soothing his trembling. He let his inner sight take him where it would. For a while, he found himself traveling down a road with the foreign humans, dressed in his people's garb. Contentment drifted with him, the warm air relaxing his guard.

When the soldiers attacked the party and cut down

the foreign smith, Itzanam felt the knife against his
own skin, stealing his lifeblood, separating him from
Feathered Serpent. The pain ate through his body and
into his bones, shattering the river, emptying it and
blowing it away, as if it had never existed. The dream
of the blood stone had vanished as if it had never
been.

As he became aware of his surroundings, he realized
that blood dripped through his fingers from a wound
on his side. Feathered Serpent had a matching injury.
Anger now filled the younger god's face.

"You idiot!" Feathered Serpent hissed. He drew his
hand away from his cut and looked at it.

"The land," Itzanam said, his voice grating like
boulders harshly scraping together.

They both looked down. The drops of their blood
didn't mark the dirt—they didn't rest there long
enough. They flowed directly into the earth, as if being
sucked down by a hungry mouth.

"You will pay for this," Feathered Serpent warned
as he wrapped his rainbow around himself and
streaked into the sky.

Itzanam stood alone on the platform, the altar he'd
raised crumbling before him. All his hope was gone.
Only now did he see the importance of his vision.
Combined, the gods would have survived. Separated,
now, all the gods would turn to ash. Itzanam felt the
tears on his cheeks solidify, turn to dust, and blow
away.

The wind started gusting harshly, picking up the dirt
and ash and swirling it around. Itzanam hacked and
coughed as the air at the top of the platform filled
with dust. Blood continued to leak out of his wound,
only to be absorbed by the thirsty earth. He went
down the back stairs of the temple, cursing Feathered
Serpent. The younger god didn't understand what he,
what their people, could have gained. They might have

been able to withstand the foreign tide. Feathered Serpent knew only what he had almost lost.

And now, the god of war's vision would turn out be the real one as the spirals of time wound down. All because he had fought with Itzanam—fought, and won.

With a steady hand, Tyr threw the last of the dried seaweed into the cauldron at his feet. "Come forth and tell your tale," he intoned. Then he bent over and looked into the water.

Nothing. Not a glimmer.

Damn it. How had Odin raised Gullveig? There was an old story of how the Father of Magic had drawn her head out of a barrel and forced her to speak. Other tales had him traveling to her grave in Niflheim. But Tyr didn't have time to go to Hel's domain. He had no magical horse, no Sleipnir, to ride. He needed answers now, before the Itza collected him for the sacrifice. He had to know what Ragnarok they were facing, what was going on in the battle between the feathered one and the old iguana god. Before Tyr let them take his heart, with only promises of returning it, and him, better than new. Though he would keep his word, he wanted to know if they would keep theirs.

In anger, he threw the rest of the herbs he had at hand—salt dried in a silver bowl by the light of the full moon, juniper berries picked from only the northern sides of the slopes, bark from a slippery elm—into the pot. The water stirred as the offerings dipped below the surface.

A sickly green light arose.

Tyr felt his heart quicken at the sight. He wasn't scared, but something was responding to his magic, something he'd never seen before. He wondered what gave the light an eel's glow. It hovered for a moment before going slowly toward the door. Then it paused there.

Tyr knew it was waiting for him. It appeared he was going to have to make a journey after all.

As he passed by the honor guard standing at the entrance he said, "I will return." Echoes of his words bounced between the doors—a prophecy and a promise combined. This wasn't the last of his travels. He also heard reverberations of how close the end possibly was.

The light paled in the bright open fields, growing stronger under the cover of the trees. It circled thrice sunwise, east to west, around the strange tree that had sprung up in the hole left by Liðami. Tyr did likewise, following it. The planklike roots of the tree grew as tall as Tyr, even contained by the sand surrounding it. He'd never seen a tree so tall, with such smooth bark. Its upper branches mingled with clouds resting low in the sky. Faces appeared in its shadows, staring at him when he looked away. He listened to the wind name the tree, *ceiba*, but he didn't understand the meaning of the word.

They passed through the sacred grove quickly, the golden fruit shining like miniature suns. The light stayed low, almost knee height through the rest of the trees, as if lighting an unseen trail. Tyr strode after it, his long strides easily covering the ground. Though he went quickly, he tried to follow the exact path the light had taken. So far the trip had been easy, though that didn't lessen the band that Tyr felt tightening across his chest.

Soon they had cleared the trees and traveled beside one of the streams that came from the mountains. The light skipped over the water, almost as if dancing on it, floating close to the surface, then shooting up again. Tyr wondered at its antics. The gods had burned Gullveig three times, attempting to kill her and her knowledge, but she'd always escaped, risen again. Did she love the water as a result?

Or was this someone else's light he followed?

Tyr paused, but found he couldn't stop. His steps had taken on the weight of prophecy, dragging him forward toward his destiny. Though this was new to him, what was happening had obviously been foretold somewhere, by someone, in the spirals of time. Someone whom he was going to meet.

Without pause, the light left the stream and headed up into the hills, then beyond, where the bones of the earth lay strewn. Tyr relished the thinning air, how it burned clean in his lungs. He hadn't come from the mountains—his home before coming to Ásgard had been the sea—yet he still appreciated them. He and the light passed waist-high trees, bent and twisted by the wind, clear pools reflecting the impossibly blue sky, knife-sharp ridges where pockets of snow still gathered, secret and fading. Above the tree line more snow awaited them, packed into dense clumps. Birds graced the air, appearing to be swimming more than flying through the stiff winds. Insects thrived in between and under the rocks, scurrying away from the death that flew above them.

In the distance, high on the pass, Tyr saw his destination—a place storms had wiped clean of snow or greenery, leaving the stones naked and pale in the brittle sunlight. A few branches, like mock bridges, connected the boulders together. The elements had stripped the bark away, and the weathered remains held the iron-gray look of driftwood. A torn piece of muslin fluttered like a field marker in the constant wind.

The seeress awaited Tyr between the two main boulders. A single wide branch rested across the tops, making a kind of doorway. Her appearance wavered, as if Tyr viewed her under a strong current of water. She was vaguely transparent: he could see the sharp edges of the black rock door behind her, cut into the mountain, leading straight to Hel's domain. Her dress was ash gray, aged and rent, the bottom edge of it caked with mud. The blouse she wore had at one point been rich, with gold plackets around the cuffs and collar, but now just a few curled threads remained. Her hair had dulled to the color of dried wheat wintering in the fields, and dirt and twigs streaked through it. Pale green light filled her eyes, sickly and wane, akin to the light that had led him there.

She called out to him in a voice surprisingly strong and hale, deep like a man's, but not stone bound like a god's.

"First you called me, then you gave offerings three,
From a shared past we spring, roots beneath the World
*   Tree,*
You would have me foretell, a future that's clear to see
Would you know more?"

"I would," Tyr said, stepping forward. The smell of limestone graves, drowned animals, and rotten grain long buried strengthened as he drew closer. Though the wind still swirled around him and tugged at his shirt, it didn't stir her gown.

"I know of the sun, how the iguana swallows its tail,
Fresh-born you would be, yet tied to their tree,
Two hearts, one vision, a mighty river that flows,
Unchanging through the seasons, yet able to bear the
*   tide,*
Would you know more?"

"Aye," Tyr replied, seeing the river in his mind's eye, how it connected him to Itzanam. This was the foreign god's vision. Those strange golden ropes that had tied all the gods to each other, Itza and Iselander alike.

"The land knows change, sunrise to sunfall,
The hunted sees the blood of kin, the seat of ruin,

The wolf stops running and turns to fight the sea,
The fates step beyond swirling time, new cycles to
*   foretell,*
Would you know more?"

Tyr rocked back and forth in time with the measured words. He didn't understand all that the seeress
told him. What he did understand was that change
was coming, change that came with nonchange, whatever that meant. "Aye," he responded.

"Netted together by myth, forged by linked iron,
The gods join—"

Gullveig interrupted herself with a hoarse scream.
Tyr felt the sound deep in his gut, as if mountains
collided inside of him, scraping against his bones, hurt-
ing him greatly. The cry boomed out from the peak
they stood on, down into the valley, causing mini land-
slides. The wound in his belly grew, the pain forcing
Tyr to bend over. He wrapped one arm around his
middle, and without thinking, put the other on one of
the rocks the seeress stood between to support
himself.
    Visions stole his sight.
    He saw the world crumbling to pieces. The great
temples of the Itza fell as foreigners from lands east
of his own arrived, with their bloodied cross and stolen
holy days. He gaped as they poured over the land,
searching for gold that the Itza had never possessed.
    It was only after he tore his hand away and filled
his lungs with the putrefied air of the seeress did he
see the cause.
    Two more of his followers had fallen, and with
them, the secret knowledge of iron that might have
turned the tide, kept the other foreigners at bay.
    Gullveig's screams turned to insane laughter. Tyr
turned his vision outward again. Wind now howled

around her, whipping her skirt and flinging rocks and stones. Darkness ate at her legs, as if the mountain itself consumed her.

"It is the other eye that sees now, the one not left
      behind,
The vision now is clear.
The White Hands come.
You will be taken, eaten as the golden fruit,
But your heart will not revive.
I shall say no more."

With another bone-melting screech, the seeress raised her hands above her head. The blackness around her knees surged up her body, covered her torso, then quickly enclosed her face. For an instant, she looked as if she were a statue, carved of obsidian. Then she shattered with a loud crack, like a dried-out tree breaking in two. Fist-sized chunks of her fell into the hungry earth beneath her feet, absorbed faster than a thirsty field drank in the rain.

Tyr looked out from where he stood and saw a lighter shade of darkness veil all the land. He thrust it away, concentrating instead on the sunlight, the chilling winds, and the clean snow. These were real. Not this witch's words. His vision began to clear and he heard the hopeful call of a hawk, far above him.

Behind him, all the branches had fallen, as had the two standing stones the seeress had used for a doorway. A dull slab of gray slate now stood where the gate to Helheim had been. The muslin cloth that had marked the grave had torn free. Tyr watched the winds push it around the peak, then send it sailing through the blue sky. Soon it was a white speck, smaller than a dove.

It didn't head for the sea, but rather, for the jungle, where it was lost among the trees.

*   *   *

Tyr set the fire in the center of his hall blazing, but cold fears still pricked his skin. Shadows lurked in the corners, between the torches on the walls, at the high point of the ceiling. Tyr doubted he could banish them, even if he broadened the windows wide enough to let the sunbeams pour in. The gold and crimson inlaid snakes moved through the stone floor sluggishly, sounding like distant waves. He sat at the foot of the platform of his high seat, the flagon of mead in his hand untasted. Every once in a while a flicker of lightning swirled across his chest as his mood changed from melancholy to anger, but then it faded and the darkness gathered closer.

Though Tyr had left instructions that no one was to be allowed in to see him, it didn't surprise him when Loki came barging in.

"What did the seeress say?" he demanded as he strode toward Tyr.

Tyr let out a bleak, echoing laugh. He shook his head and finally took a sip from his cup. It tasted like ash, as he'd known it would. Memories of the night the *Golden Tree* had sunk swirled up his tongue.

"That bad?" Loki said. Tyr looked up at the gentle tone. Loki still had a solid appearance. Tyr knew it wouldn't last. They would all soon be dust. None would remember them, though they might still celebrate their high days, falsely worshipping this newest god.

He stood and walked over to the table by the side of the hall, filled another flagon, and brought it back to Loki. "To sacrifice," he said harshly as he lifted his cup in salute. The sweetness of the honeyed drink tickled the sides of his tongue, tugging at the bitterness. It wasn't enough to cover it, and never would be, but it helped a little.

Loki stood, frozen, the cup halfway to his mouth. "You're kidding, right? You're not going through with it. You can't."

Tyr filled his cup again. Maybe if he was drunk he wouldn't notice how gray everything looked, tasted, smelled. He picked up the pitcher and walked back to the stairs. Loki followed him, but he didn't sit down; instead, he stood with one foot raised on the platform and contemplated the bottom of his flagon.

"Cycles. Spirals. Always the same, eh?" Tyr asked. He held up the stump that had once held his sword hand. He'd sacrificed his rightful place, his flesh, to save the gods, to delay the inevitable end, at least for a little while. What was he gaining with this latest offering?

Anger flared through Tyr again. Flickers of blue light extended past the end of his arm, forming the faint outline of a hand. He'd had so much hope. This land. These people. To rule again . . . but it had all been false. Itzanam would have taken his place, as surely as Odin had. Even if he'd been part of that river, that golden net would have bound him so tightly he'd never have been able to move.

He remembered the first time he'd thrown lightning, when Loki had come and calmed him, leeching away his anger as surely as the ground would absorb his blood. The trickster had tried to get him to make a promise then, an oath to not make any more promises.

How much had the half-god known, before all of this? Could Tyr have avoided this end by binding himself to the trickster? Or was his *wyrd* as inevitable as the changing seasons? As Odin losing his eye, as the twilight of the gods?

Tyr spat as memories and the light faded, leaving him with an aching stump and feeling more empty of life than a snow plain in a mountain pass. He took another swig of the mead, almost relishing the imagined grit in his mouth.

"Why?" Loki said. The single word didn't sound so much like a question as a demand. Loki stood straight now, his back stiff with ice.

Tyr didn't know if he could explain. Not to one

such as Loki. "It's all I have left," he said. "My word." He'd bound himself to Itzanam, to this sacrifice. It was the only thing he could do.

"You mean your pride," Loki said, unbending enough to pour himself another cup of mead.

Tyr shook his head. "No. I took an oath."

"And you will not be an oath breaker. That's pride in your accomplishments. Not merely holding to your word."

"No!" Tyr surged up and began pacing. "It isn't. It isn't pride." He walked away, then came back. He didn't want to say the words. No one else should have to know this pain, carry this burden. He didn't want to remove all hope from the other god, though he suspected Loki probably already knew. "Pride occurs only when there is someone to witness the act."

Loki grunted in acknowledgment. Tyr wondered at his wooden expression, what the trickster was hiding.

"You still don't have to do this."

Tyr didn't answer, but merely drained his cup and held it out for more. Loki opened his mouth to respond, but nothing came out. He filled Tyr's cup instead.

As the sky blazed orange and purple with the setting sun, the two remained silent, drinking, letting the twilight gather in the hall, neither trying to dispel it anymore.

Feathered Serpent growled and cursed as he paced across the mountain platform, above the tree line, away from the jungle and any spying eyes. He'd hoped that the cold, clean air might clear his head, but his thoughts continued to spiral in on themselves, much as the wind swirled around him.

Their people were doomed. And though it wasn't all Itzanam's fault, if he just hadn't weakened them both with that damn stupid merging, maybe they would have had more of a chance. . . .

The wound on his side no longer leaked his precious life fluid, but Feathered Serpent still felt the blood loss. The land knew what was coming—a time when there would be no gods to oversee or help it—and it was taking care of itself, strengthening itself so it would survive the coming days.

If only the gods could do the same.

Feathered Serpent knew it wasn't possible. The White Hands would come and destroy everything, exchange their World Tree for their bare cross, take his people's rituals of baptism and confession and sacrifice and corrupt them. The foreigners would ruin everything, but rule it all the same.

He paused for a moment and looked out over the land. The strange mountains in the east caught his eye—the ones the foreign gods had brought with them. They shimmered across the distance, as if they were insubstantial. Would this new land stay, after the last of the foreigners were dead? Or would it, too, be absorbed by his own land, strengthened by it?

And why couldn't he, as well as the other gods, be strengthened by the foreigners? Why couldn't he take their lives, use them to build himself up?

Hadn't Tyr promised his heart in sacrifice?

Feathered Serpent quickly found a path down out of the mountains, into the trees, trusting it to take him where he needed to go. The winds didn't follow him down. The cool air deserted him, and the heat of the jungle collapsed around him. The birds sang of his passing, giving music to prophecy and myth. A chorus of insects buzzed in the joy of his being.

It didn't surprise him when after only a few turns he found himself at a small stone temple, the steps covered with iguanas sunning themselves in the bright afternoon sunlight.

"We must perform the ceremony, sacrifice the foreign god Tyr," Feathered Serpent announced after seating himself carefully on the throne that had been brought for him.

"I agree," Itzanam said.

"We—" Feathered Serpent interrupted himself. He hadn't expected Itzanam to concede so quickly. To tell the truth, he found it impossible to read Itzanam's iguana-like expression: his eyes were black on black, solid; his mouth had pushed out, like a snout; and his nose had flattened against it, the nostrils mere slits now. When Itzanam drank, Feathered Serpent could see his pointed teeth. Every once in a while his tongue flicked out. He bobbed his head, sometimes faster, sometimes slower, as if listening to drums Feathered Serpent couldn't hear.

Feathered Serpent took a sip from his cup, paused, and thought for a moment before he continued. "It should be performed at dusk today."

"The sooner the better." Itzanam's voice held strange reverberations, as if it were being produced by more than one throat, though the tone remained flat.

Feathered Serpent merely raised his eyebrows. He was certain that Itzanam's reasons for wanting to do the ceremony quickly weren't the same as his own, but it didn't matter. "After I cut out the heart, you shall perform the dedication ceremony."

"No."

" 'No'?"

"I shall cut out the heart, drive my dagger into his flesh, and wrench that precious organ from its cage. I shall also dedicate the lifeblood to the gods, let his wound heal ours," Itzanam said, staring into the depths of his hall, unblinking. A rasp had broken into his voice, carving the words into separate stones. After another moment, Itzanam continued, as if he'd only just remembered there was another sitting with him. "You can do the resurrection."

Rage simmered in Feathered Serpent. He slammed his cup down beside him on the throne and stood up, yelling. "No! You selfish bastard. You've already weakened us—not just me, but all of the gods. You will not be the only one to gain strength from this. I know your tricks."

Itzanam regarded him without replying—without even blinking. Feathered Serpent stormed down the stairs of the dais and paced in front of the older god. It no longer mattered to him if his head was in a lower, less powerful position. He couldn't stay still. The torches in the hall flickered as he passed, though the diffuse golden light filling the chamber didn't diminish.

"I will perform the ceremony. It will be my knife that cuts open the foreign god's flesh, lays bare his beating heart," Feathered Serpent said.

"And what makes you think you've skill enough?"

Though Itzanam's expression didn't change, Feathered Serpent still heard the scorn shading the words.

"The foreigners are different than us. You've never dealt with them. I have, through the echoes of time."

Feathered Serpent chuckled. "Any knife will score their skin. Their hearts are located in the same place as ours. The ceremony won't be so different. And I have many of the memories you do. As well as my own, from the west." He chuckled again. "I will not cheat us of this strength."

Itzanam merely stared at the other god, his head bobbing faster.

After going back up the steps and draining his cup, Feathered Serpent added, "If you insist on this, I will make the gesture meaningless. How much strength do you think you'll gain if Tyr has no followers left?" He gazed down into endless black eyes. The iguana god flicked his tongue into the air a few times, as if tasting the truth of the younger god's statement.

"Why would you weaken us all like this?" The flat tone had returned to Itzanam's voice, making his emotions unreadable.

Feathered Serpent shrugged. "Neither of us knows if the sacrifice will matter past this circle of time. The White Hands are coming."

The bobbing slowed as Itzanam considered his words. "You wouldn't do it," he proclaimed after more silence had passed between them.

Anger boiled through Feathered Serpent. Itzanam had made too many proclamations, decided too much for the fate of their people. Feathered Serpent's will was just as strong.

"Kabrakan!" he yelled as he marched back down the stairs of the dais. He called again for the demon that shook the mountains and brought earthquakes, stealing souls for its own benefit. "Take the City of Wells! Take it now!"

A ripple buckled through the air, turning it hot, then cold, as the veils between the worlds were shredded. Continuous rumbling sounded in the distance, as if a thunderstorm had spilled out of the mountains and into the valley, the loud booming echoing between the peaks. The floor tilted and shuddered, as if the pounding of Kabrakan's hammer had started beneath them.

"No!" screamed Itzanam. "Call him back!"

"And the ceremony?"

"You will perform the cutting! I shall do the dedication!"

"Agreed." Feathered Serpent didn't take time to celebrate his victory, but opened his arms wide and called for the demon.

"Kabrakan! Return to your cave under the hills. It's time to sleep once more."

An echoing growl answered him.

"Kabrakan!" Feathered Serpent shouted, banging his war staff against the floor, causing the hall to shake. "You will go back to the depths of the mountains and hide in the heart there, or I will steal back all the souls you've taken!"

The earth shrugged once, twice; then the rumbling stopped and the air cleared.

Itzanam stood and walked down the steps of his dais, over to one of the larger murals. The existing figures there dissolved into the limbs of the World Tree. A brown haze grew, then resolved into the City of Wells, its buildings not too damaged. In another section of the painting, Tyrthbrand lay under the ground, loosely ensconced by the earth. He would get out. Blue-green trails of life led both to him and away from him.

And lines of blue-black death wrapped around their other followers.

Feathered Serpent watched as the priests led Tyr's main follower away, then he turned to Itzanam. "We need to perform this ceremony today."

"Yes. Let it all be over soon."

The twin monkey scribes came scrambling into the hall. Feathered Serpent didn't know if they'd come because of the earthquake or because of some summons that Itzanam had just silently given.

"Go to the one-handed god. Let him know that tonight is his time for sacrifice. Bring him to the temple here."

Without a word, they barreled out of the hall.

Feathered Serpent didn't like the way Itzanam continued to stare at the mural, as if the strings of life and death could weave a coherent pattern, or a new truth. Draining his cup, he decided it didn't matter. If nothing else, he would gain a little strength from this.

Not enough though. Nothing could be enough. And he would have to be content with that. They all would.

Loki tried to speak, more than once, but he found Tyr's silence and the gathering gloom had hold of his tongue. Instead, a rambling discourse took place inside his head. He didn't beg or plead—he wasn't drunk enough to do that—but he did find a long run of mocking monologue toward his taciturn companion. "Going to leave the rest of us to die without you? Wonderful. No, it's not a problem. You're too scared to stick around, to see the end of days. That's not our problem. Go and die by your word, with your heart beating in your enemy's hands."

The sun hadn't quite touched the horizon when a quavering voice called to them, announcing visitors.

Tyr brightened the hall automatically. The fire leaped up in the center hearth, the walls grew taller, the torches multiplied. Still, it didn't seem enough. A thin shroud of gray touched everything, draining the colors out of the day. The twin snakes entwined in the floor continued their endless shifting, neither speeding up nor slowing down, as steady as an afternoon's rain on needy fields, their movement the only sound in the hall.

The two monkey scribes came in, hunched and quiet. Loki had never seen them up close before. He barely held back a shudder: they were too similar to men for his liking.

"We bring you greetings," said the one standing.

"O one-handed one," added the one who had sat and was now getting out his folded book.

Loki sighed heavily and rolled his eyes as they proceeded to remind Tyr of his obligations, then invited him to be killed by their own gods.

There had to be a way out of it, out of the promise Tyr had made. Maybe he could claim he'd meant heart in a figurative fashion, and give up his sword or something. Then he'd only have to bleed a little on their altar . . .

When the monkey scribes paused for Tyr's response, Loki surged forward.

"No. He won't go. He promised me—"

"Silence!" Tyr shouted. The single word roared through the space, making the fire flicker and dance as if a great wind had blown by.

"I will do this," Tyr said, rising from his high seat and stalking toward Loki. "I have bound myself to this with my honor and my life. As Itzanam is so bound."

"You don't have to." Loki knew he was repeating himself. He didn't care. Given time, he could wriggle out of any trap. He didn't lose. And Tyr didn't have to. Not like this.

Tyr stared down at Loki, his eyes lost in the shadows of his face.

"Yes, I do."

And that was all he would hear of the matter.

The trail through the jungle was short, almost as if the land itself was eagerly anticipating the ritual. It made Loki hurry his words, trying to get as many jabs in as possible.

"Think Tyr's appropriately dressed for a ceremony? I mean, look at him! Bare chested. Those bright blue pants. We're just going to have an orgy, right?"

Thor threatened him again with his hammer. "I will pound you into the ground so far not even the dwarves will be able to dig you out if you keep on like this!"

"What else would you have me do?" Loki asked, trying to keep his tone reasonable. "Mourn as silently as a stupid mountain?"

"I would have you show respect," Thor grumbled. Before Loki could respond, the redheaded god reached out and grabbed Loki by the throat.

It didn't matter that Thor wouldn't—couldn't—kill Loki. The way his fingers dug into the smaller god's windpipe, choking off his air, made him struggle to get away.

"It is Tyr's wish to go through with this. He does not want to escape this doom."

Loki tried to nod, but found his movements cut off by Thor's hand. He clutched at the massive fingers, trying to claw at them. Thor only laughed.

"I shall put you down. But keep your twisted words to yourself."

Though Loki still couldn't move, Thor seemed to sense his acquiescence and put him back on the ground. Loki glared at the larger god and rubbed his sore throat, but he didn't say anything else the rest of the way through the jungle.

The trail opened up onto a wide clearing. A stone temple rose on the far side, trees closing in again on the back of it. Massive stone snakes lined the stairs rising toward the platform at the top. Murals of bloody battles were interspersed with scenes of everyday life: fishing, hunting, and farming. The limbs of great trees were painted between them, linking the pictures together. The roots of the trees appeared to go below the base of the temple. A sunset and sunrise near the top flanked a scene of the black night sky and the ribbon of the Milky Way.

Drums and whistles greeted them as the gods stepped out of the jungle. Loki wanted to ask where the other people were—hadn't that human, Thorolf, amassed a huge following as he walked to his death? He opened his mouth to say something when a heavy hand landed on his shoulder. He closed his mouth again without speaking.

Tyr deserved better.

Four brothers—Loki didn't know their names, and so could only distinguish them by their colors—came up to Tyr. They removed the open gray vest he'd worn, then the red one swirled blue paint across Tyr's chest, down his arms. After chanting for a bit, they encircled him, each of the brothers at a cardinal point with Tyr in the middle, and began marching up the temple stairs. The rest of the gods followed, first the Itza, then the gods from Ásgard. Loki placed himself near the front, ignoring the glares from the others.

He'd warned Tyr. He'd known that the god's oaths, as well as his stubborn pride, would get them all into trouble. And Loki had tried, he'd really tried, to get Tyr to stop, not to go to this ceremony, to turn this defeat, this sacrifice—this suicide—into something else.

Tyr hadn't listened to him. Then again, none of the gods ever did.

A gray tinge seemed to roll over the brilliant murals as Loki climbed the steps. He wasn't certain if it was his grief and anger that stole the colors out of the world, or just the approaching end of days. Painted glyphs marked the front of every step. It wasn't difficult for Loki to imagine them bleaching, falling, and turning to dust.

Though he hadn't spoken to a seeress, and though Tyr hadn't said anything, Loki knew with a certainty planted deep in his chest that theirs was not the only Ragnarok approaching, that the gods in this land had seen their own end as well.

The music reached a raucous crescendo as the last of the gods stepped onto the platform and wound around the altar there. Then it abruptly halted. An eerie silence encircled them for a moment before the songs of the jungle rang out again. It didn't reassure Loki that this cursed land would survive the passing of the gods, the coming of the cross.

Loki rocked back and forth on his heels, arms wrapped across his chest, while Feathered Serpent chanted and the brothers placed Tyr flat on his back on the altar. Ix Chebel hadn't come back from her madness. She gibbered and danced at one corner of the platform. Loki would have liked to encourage her—maybe she could disrupt the ceremony, ruin it so they would have to start again, give them all more time—but she stayed where she was, alternating between mouthing nonsense words, cackling with laughter, and silently shaking.

The Hero Twins stood opposite Ix Chebel on the

far side of the platform, shoulders touching, apart from the rest of the gods. They seemed almost as sad as Loki's companions, and leaned heavily upon each other. He wondered what they'd foreseen, what dire fate would befall them.

Feathered Serpent's chanting seemed to go on forever. Loki didn't try to stop from yawning widely. Tension went through him in waves when he remembered why they were there, then boredom would creep back in and he'd wish it were over already.

Finally, Feathered Serpent brought out a carved jade knife. Its blue-green edge glittered dangerously in the evening light. After a short, one-handed blessing of the blade, Feathered Serpent approached where Tyr lay. He raised his arm over his head, then plunged it down, into Tyr's chest. A collective gasp came from Loki and his fellow gods as the blood spilled over Tyr's ribs, onto the altar, then dripped to the ground.

Loki couldn't hear a lapping noise, though it seemed like he should have been able to when he saw how the thirsty earth drank up the spilled droplets. Columns of smoke from incense rose up from all four sides of the altar, mingling with the metallic smell of the blood, churning Loki's stomach.

He wrapped his arms tighter around himself as he watched Feathered Serpent make three more cuts. He bit down on his tongue, tasting his own blood, to prevent himself from calling out, trying to halt the proceedings. Dread coursed through him, chilling his skin. The end was so near.

Tyr had jerked slightly at the first incision, but hadn't moved again after that, even as Feathered Serpent reached in with his other hand and extracted Tyr's still steaming heart.

A rustling sound went through the Itza, like a flock of ravens settling in to a feast. The dread that encased Loki tightened its grip around him, making it difficult to breathe. All the color drained out of the world, making everything gray and ghostlike. Or was he now the ghost? He laughed without making a sound.

With great ceremony, Feathered Serpent crossed the platform to Itzanam, waiting at the altar of the dawn, handing the heart over to him. Loki felt a moment of fear. The old god wore an animal aspect on his face, with black eyes, an elongated snout, and sharp, pointed teeth. Would he eat Tyr's heart? If he did, then how would his friend be reborn? Loki was certain that wasn't how it had happened for him, how the Hero Twins had resurrected him.

He willed himself not to say anything though. This was what Tyr had wanted. The doom he had wished upon himself.

Itzanam accepted Tyr's heart from Feathered Serpent, raised it above his head, then threw it to the ground. All the gods cried out, louder than gulls on the shore. Then the iguana god spat on it and stepped on it, spoiling the sacrifice and the purity of its blood.

Loki felt his own heart twinge in sympathy.

It had never been foretold that Tyr would be resurrected. Itzanam had never promised that.

Itzanam ignored the rest of the gods, walking to a basin behind him, rinsing his hands clean of the blood, then spitting in the water before he spilled it on the ground, spoiling it as well.

Loki finally broke free of the shock that had held him frozen, even though he'd guessed that this was going to happen. He pushed toward the front of the crowd that surrounded Itzanam, shouting questions. While the other gods held back, Loki walked straight up to Itzanam, grabbed his arm, and shook it.

"Why?" he demanded. Itzanam's fathomless eyes turned to him, regarded him without blinking, maybe without recognizable thoughts. The air felt thin around Loki and he tried to swallow, his suddenly dry throat making it difficult. "Why ruin this for everyone?"

"Nothing lives forever."

The quiet words silenced them all. Itzanam had spoken a truth beyond visions and foretelling. Though the gods might curse and wail at the coming twilight, their cycle had to end, so that another might begin.

Ix Chebel sang out into the quiet, with a broken, childlike voice, "The White Hands are com-ing, the White Hands are com-ing."

Loki wanted to argue. He wanted to fight against their collective doom, though he knew it was as useless as trying to fight the tide.

He still would have made a different choice than Tyr, still would have fought.

So Loki marched down the stairs beside Thor, determined to dance and drink even while the walls of his hall crumbled, vowing to keep his eyes open until the very end, to watch the vines creep across the border of their lands, see the jungles cover their fields and the earthquakes tear down their mountains.

Chapter 9

Darkness and trails of incense wrapped around Lady Two Bird as she carefully walked down the crooked stairs. Descending into the closed-in chamber beneath her no longer filled her with fear. Her hands stayed relaxed by her sides, and she didn't feel the need to gulp or chase the air. She found she could even smile solemnly as she circled around the edges of the chamber, taking her place beside the two priests in front of the altar, facing the stairway.

Too many knew that a foreigner had been taken into custody by Lord Kan Boar's priests for them to maintain any semblance of order while performing the ritual outside. Lady Two Bird couldn't believe that she'd agreed, or even possibly preferred, the tiny chamber Lord Smoke Moon had suggested. So much had changed for her. The smaller size also meant she could stay close to Tyrthbrand, help him if he needed it.

Tyrthbrand already stood naked in the center, the priests just finishing painting swirling blue glyphs on his back. Thin tendrils of blue had been added to the knotted snake tattoos circling his arms. A headdress made of owl feathers and corn husks greatly increased his height. He swayed slightly, but he still took another honey-coated dried mushroom from the bowl the priest offered him, followed by another drag on the ceremonial cigar. Lady Two Bird had seen how glassy-eyed Thorolf had been after only a few puffs, and that had been outside, in the fresh air. No wonder Tyrthbrand was having difficulty staying upright.

A few more people filed in after Lady Two Bird; then the circle was complete. The sacrificial ceremony they were performing that day was only symbolic. Lady Two Bird didn't know what she'd do if Lord Kan Boar, or even Lord Smoke Moon, drew a blade or appeared to want to do a real sacrifice. She would find a way to stop them—that she knew.

After encouraging Tyrthbrand to take one more mushroom, the priests stepped back. Tyrthbrand seemed not to see them any longer. He peered around the chamber with great interest, as if just realizing where he stood.

One of the priests called Lady Two Bird forward, then said, "Please ask him what he sees."

"Snakes," was Tyrthbrand's reply to her question.

The priests nodded and chatted quietly with each other, making much of his response. Lady Two Bird wasn't certain how to interpret it. Did it mean that Feathered Serpent had accepted him? Was he really a chosen of the warrior god, and not Ekchuah, the merchant god?

"Ask him if the gods have come."

When Lady Two Bird did, Tyrthbrand firmly shut his eyes.

A flutter of worried sounds circled the room. Low muttering conversations sprung up everywhere. Tyrthbrand kept his eyes closed, swaying more now, nearly toppling over. Shivers racked his body, as if unseen fingers ghosted over his skin. He pressed his lips together tightly, his jaw turning white with the strain.

After a while, Lord Smoke Moon spoke up. "It isn't necessary for the gods to witness a symbolic ceremony such as this."

Lady Two Bird breathed a sigh of relief, along with most of the other people in the room. She moved a little closer to Tyrthbrand and translated Lord Smoke

Moon's words, then added, "Please open your eyes again. I don't believe they will come."

Slowly, Tyrthbrand opened one eye, then the other, then announced in a loud voice that boomed through the chamber, "No gods."

Lady Two Bird felt her skin prickle at the announcement, as if a cold wind had suddenly caressed her. She knew that Tyrthbrand was just describing what he saw in the chamber, not that the gods had ceased to exist. Her stomach twisted uneasily for a moment. Just because Ix Chebel had stopped talking to her through the stones didn't mean the goddess was unreachable, or no longer accepted their prayers.

After another moment, the priests stepped forward and led Tyrthbrand on a promenade around the hall, thrice sunwise, before leading him to the altar. They carefully stripped off his towering headpiece and lay him on his back, his arms stretched out at his sides. Three priests held him down, one at his feet, one at either arm.

Everyone in the chamber turned to face the altar. Lord Smoke Moon stood in the position of high priest, while Lord Kan Boar stood to the side. Lord Smoke Moon welcomed the gods into their presence, opened the heart of the altar, then picked up a large basket and raised it over his head. All the priests in the room began chanting a cleansing prayer. Lady Two Bird joined in silently with her own prayers, adding entreaties to her lady between verses, asking for her to keep Tyrthbrand safe, weather him through the continuing storms.

Lord Smoke Moon lowered the basket. Lady Two Bird found her shoulders tensing until she saw him draw out an ear of corn, not a ceremonial dagger. The cob was partly exposed, partly sheathed. Fine hair dangled down the side, shimmering in the light of the chamber. Lord Smoke Moon held the ear as he would a blade, doing a one-handed blessing above it, then used the cob to mark Tyrthbrand's chest, drawing four lines, a box around his heart.

After declaring the sacrifice purified and prepared, Lord Smoke Moon placed the corn flat against Tyrthbrand's chest, over his heart, holding it steady with one hand. Tyrthbrand flinched when it touched him, as if it burned. The priests tightened their grip. Lord Smoke Moon caught Lady Two Bird's eye, and she reviewed the foreign words in her head that she'd need for calming Tyrthbrand.

But the large foreigner didn't move again. Lord Smoke Moon intoned the words of the sacrifice, begging the gods to accept the sacrificial heart, describing how it symbolized mankind's relationship with the gods, how it would feed the gods as they fed the world.

Lord Smoke Moon lifted the corncob off Tyrthbrand's chest, symbolically removing his heart. He turned and gave it to Lord Kan Boar. The lord nodded, his pride appeased: he now held the foreigner's heart in his hands.

After Lord Kan Boar handed the corn back, Lord Smoke Moon immediately began the words of the ritual of resurrection. It was an older prayer, used by farmers at the start of spring, bringing the soil back to life, growing new corn plants from the dried ears. Words of baptism were used, birthing Tyrthbrand into his new life. Lord Smoke Moon placed the corn back on Tyrthbrand's chest, giving him a new heart, one that made him native, not foreign, and welcomed him to his new home.

Lady Two Bird couldn't stop the shiver that racked her when the cob lay on Tyrthbrand's chest a second time. She told herself that she was just imagining things. The torches hadn't all just flickered. The world hadn't just been drained of color.

The mark on Tyrthbrand's wrist—the one that came from his god—hadn't just wriggled like a worm and fallen to the floor.

No, everything was the same.

After the ceremony, Lord Smoke Moon presented Lord Kan Boar with the ear of corn. It was to be his to keep, both the old and the new hearts.

The two lords held a whispered conversation while the priests helped Tyrthbrand stand. He had closed his eyes again, so they led him, blind, from the altar and across the chamber toward the stairs. Lady Two Bird had turned to follow when Lord Kan Boar called her.

"We want you to be in charge of this," he said, presenting the ear of corn to her, using both hands.

Lord Smoke Moon came up and nodded. "He is your responsibility now, much as a child would be."

Lady Two Bird knew there was enough air in the chamber for her to breathe. She still found herself gasping. She would never have any children of her flesh. Tyrthbrand was too old for her to mold into a proper Itza warrior, even if she wanted to.

It still filled her with delight that he was to stay with her.

"But I will be checking. Some year I, or my successor, will have his beating heart," Lord Kan Boar added.

Lady Two Bird smiled and agreed. When Tyrthbrand was old, his joints were in pain, and life no longer brought him joy, she would grant him this honor. But not until then.

With many thanks and words of praise for both of them, Lady Two Bird left the chamber and climbed back up into the clear night air, plans for Tyrthbrand, the others, already forming.

She had saved him. And though her name would never be written on the temple walls, it would have to be enough.

*   *   *

Cold paint tickled Tyrthbrand's back. Colors swam around the room, like seaweed floating on a strong tide, washing over some of the priests, splitting into long trails and going around others. A bitter earthy taste, not masked by the honey, filled his mouth. Thin trails of smoke from the incense stretched lazy fingers toward the ceiling.

Goose bumps ran across his skin as the priests stepped back and Lady Two Bird came forward. So deadly. So beautiful. Her filed, pointed teeth, elongated skull, and tattooed face all meant more to him than home did now. She held his life in her sculpted hands, as surely as the gods ever had.

He wasn't to die, though. Not today.

She asked him what he saw. He knew the words in her language for all the colors, but their beauty wasn't as important as the way they moved and linked people together, like a living net. As he watched, a crimson thread butted between two of the priests, wiggling as if it were alive.

He looked back at his lady, how she held herself, and he thought of the totem she represented.

"Snakes," he said, because it was true. The colors, all the foreigners, the ceremony, the way they'd marched down here, it was all serpentine.

The priests seemed satisfied with his answer, but then Lady Two Bird asked him about the gods.

Tyrthbrand knew he was committing a sacrilege by participating in this ceremony. That thought had stayed with him, even as the smoke and the mushrooms had kidnapped all his others. This was a defiant act against his god, not something light like wishing on a stone.

But if he couldn't see the gods, perhaps they couldn't see him. So like the two-year-old son he'd never have, he closed his eyes and refused to look.

The colors still danced behind his eyelids, sliding

against one another with a sound like snow softly sifting down from a gray sky. A crimson and gold pair of snakes looped around each other continuously in a pattern he almost recognized, but refused to name. He pressed his lips together tightly, holding on to himself, refusing to let the configuration draw him in.

Finally, Lady Two Bird called to him, told him that gods were not coming.

Tyrthbrand let himself believe her. When he looked for himself, the colors had dimmed. While there might have been more priests now than there had been, they all appeared human.

The priests led him around the room. He let them guide his feet while he swam in the brilliant stream. The colors shimmered and blew coolly on his skin. He wanted to joke, to tell them that he no longer felt overheated, probably for only the second time since they'd arrived there. But only Thorolf Mosturbeard would have laughed with him, and the tall blond wasn't there.

Tyrthbrand's skin itched from the paint, but he didn't allow himself to scratch at it. Besides, when he looked at the swirling design on his arm, the bright blue lines intermingled with his faded black tattoos. He was afraid that if he touched his finger to the slowly crawling trail, it would be stuck there somehow, carried along with the undercurrent.

He sighed with relief when the priests made him lie down on the cool rock altar. It felt unbelievably hard against his spine, more solid than earth. He willingly spread out his arms, amused by how the threads of paint crept off his wrists and onto his captors', how it bound them together, how startling his white hands looked clasped around brown arms.

It was a sight he would have the rest of his life to get used to.

The darkness near the top of the ceiling hid the colors swaying there. Tyrthbrand watched Lord Smoke

Moon lift a box scrawled with luminous orange circles, then pray, his words forming a steady stream of blue-green smoke, wrapping around the box, slipping in between the designs. Then he drew something from the box—a knife? No, a cob of corn. It was small, barely longer than the priest's palm. The kernels sucked the light to them and glowed with the darkness of a fire's coals.

After Lord Smoke Moon drew a square over Tyrthbrand's heart, the Iselander watched the black lines grow thicker, spread and multiply, until it appeared a gaping hole had been made. He couldn't help but start when he felt the corn fall into his chest. Rustling noises spread and mingled with the vines of color, like snakes slithering through the grass.

Suddenly, the altar Tyrthbrand lay on was outside. The sun was just setting. Lord Smoke Moon seemed to grow squat, while his nose grew larger. A headdress of colored feathers spread over his head. Next to him stood something that was half man, half iguana. Four huge priests held him down, not three, and glowing tattoos covered their bodies.

This new priest reached his hand through Tyrthbrand's chest and lifted his heart straight out, the blood flowing through his fingers.

Tyrthbrand felt his eyes close of their own volition as breath and life left his body. He could still feel the cool fingers of the priest clutched around his heart, how they sucked at his strength, weakening the still living organ. The grip loosened for a moment, and Tyrthbrand felt relief. It was going to be all right. He would live. Then the iguana-person grasped his heart and squeezed it too tightly, making Tyrthbrand wish he had air enough to gasp in pain. Grit from the iguana's fingers abraded the sensitive organ, and his claws dug in slightly. Tyrthbrand wished he could laugh, or at least tell the thing to go rinse his hands in water, but he couldn't.

The room began to darken. Tyrthbrand saw one image of his heart thrown to the ground, stepped and spit upon.

But another iguana image reverently placed his heart back in his chest.

Tyrthbrand heard the rustling again, though now in time with the beating of his heart. Twisting vines grew out from the corn newly planted in his chest, wrapped around his bones, pushed out seeds into his blood.

When the ceremony ended, Tyrthbrand tried to fight his exhaustion, but he found he had to close his eyes again. In his mind's eye, he was at the strange other temple again, outside. He heard screaming birds and felt the jungle's heat enclose him. He recognized Thor now, and Loki, and even the lovely Freyja walking down the platform stairs, leaving him lying on the altar.

The solid stone beneath him started to shift, then crumble. The beautiful murals faded and turned to dust, and the trees crept over him, binding him to this place, caging him with their roots.

Tyrthbrand woke to the sound of laughter pounding into his skull. He struggled to sit up, his head feeling three times bigger than it normally did. The last time this had happened had been when he and Thorolf had just come into port and had spent the night whoring and drinking. He looked down at himself blearily.

Then the constant city noises slammed into him and he remembered what had happened. Had Lord Smoke Moon really removed his heart? Dropped it on the ground, then defiled it? He put a shaky hand to his chest and was relieved to feel its steady beat under his fingers. Images of the sacrifice came back, as well as the dreams that had gone with it. He listened to his heart for another moment, searching for the sounds of rustling that his corn heart had made. Maybe he heard something underneath the slow thumping, but maybe it was just the slight breeze shuffling the leaves together.

With a loud groan, Tyrthbrand forced himself to stand. He was back in the garden of Lady Two Bird's goddess, Ix Chebel. The laughter he'd heard had belonged to Vigfus. Squinting against the too-bright daylight, Tyrthbrand peered into the corners of the yard until he found both the boy and Illugi standing in the shade of a doorway talking with one of the priestesses. Already they spoke the Itza tongue too quickly for Tyrthbrand to follow. Though the movement hurt his skull, he smiled.

His men were still safe.

"Sir?" came a quiet voice from his side. Tyrthbrand spun toward the speaker, then nearly fell over. Why was he so dizzy?

The temple attendant led him to a low bench, pressed a warm cup into his hand, and mimed drinking it. He hesitated for a moment before bringing it to his lips. Someone had tried to mask the drink's vinegary taste with honey, but it wasn't too bad. Actually, once he started drinking it he found he couldn't put it down. When he finished he found that the attendant had already brought him a second. He also noticed that the drums in his head seemed to be muted now, as if more cloth covered the skins, muffling the sound.

After eating a corn gruel sweetened with some kind of fruit, Tyrthbrand felt mostly human, and his head had shrunk back to normal proportions. He wanted to go talk with Vigfus and Illugi, but the attendants had other ideas. He was taken to a small depression lined with bricks and filled with water, where it was made clear to him that they expected him to wash off the blue glyphs still adhering to his skin. Then they dressed him simply, in Itza clothing. Tyrthbrand willed himself to stand up straight, his head towering over the others. He told himself that there was no reason for him to feel more vulnerable dressed in this fashion.

His old clothing wouldn't have saved him from a sword or a knife.

The attendants didn't lead him back to the garden of the temple, but to a side room, just inside the main gate. The priestesses seemed to be waiting for something, or someone, so Tyrthbrand passed the time trying to talk with them, to learn something new in their language. They were going through the different articles of clothing when a messenger arrived.

Tyrthbrand followed the man out of the safety of the temple and into the crowded street. He again felt exposed with his chest and legs mostly bare, and only his tattoos covering his arms. People stared at him. The skin across his back sweated and prickled under the heat. He still held his head high. It didn't matter if they stared.

They went to a part of the city Tyrthbrand hadn't been in before. The buildings looked very different, with many more masks on the walls and very few serpents. He heard a crowd shouting as they passed by a small, slanted structure—it sounded like some kind of sporting contest was going on.

Finally, they arrived at their destination: a long, low rectangular building. Statues stood guard at the door, but only murals decorated the outer walls.

It was the first building he'd entered where he didn't have to bow his head to pass through the door.

The messenger brought him to an inner chamber with no windows, lit only with torches. Lady Two Bird stood to one side, near the far wall. Tyrthbrand couldn't help the smile she brought to his face. Lord Smoke Moon stood on the other side, flanked by two others, priests, Tyrthbrand guessed. The acidic scent of paint swirled up to him as he walked closer. He'd wondered why the priestesses hadn't painted new glyphs on him after bathing.

Lady Two Bird greeted him in her language. Tyrthbrand returned the greeting, letting the words flow without thought. He must have done well, for this time she did grant him a smile.

He exchanged welcoming words with Lord Smoke Moon, who asked him to be part of a ceremony. As Lady Two Bird didn't seem worried or frightened, Tyrthbrand agreed. Lord Smoke Moon gestured for the priests to begin their work. Tyrthbrand looked around the room while his skin was painted. Many battle scenes decorated this place. He wondered if the artist had used real blood for some of the pictures. A strange calm filled him.

Tyrthbrand hummed under his breath while the priests finished, wishing he could sing out loud as Thorolf had. He also wondered if the priests had some unknown way of measuring how much his skin itched and only stopped when it had reached a certain point.

He found his eyes kept seeking Lady Two Bird's. Though she seemed deep in conversation with Lord Smoke Moon, he found her looking back at him sometimes. And more than once, she smiled. At one point, she seemed to glow, but that appeared to be in response to something Lord Smoke Moon had said.

After the priests left the room, Lord Smoke Moon came over and led Tyrthbrand to a large rock that had been placed in the doorway. Through a few spoken words and some charades, Tyrthbrand determined that Lord Smoke Moon wanted him to place his palms on the lintel of the door. He stepped on the rock and touched the smooth stone slab. Lord Smoke Moon had him change the position of his hands a couple of times until he finally seemed satisfied. "Remember," Lady Two Bird then told him.

Tyrthbrand looked carefully at the placement of his hands and nodded. He memorized where and how he'd placed them. "Why?" he asked as he climbed down, but neither Lady Two Bird nor Lord Smoke Moon seemed inclined to answer him.

A small boy came into the chamber, bearing bril-

liant red paint. He solemnly looked up at Tyrthbrand
and took his hands, then painted his palms. Now
Tyrthbrand understood. As soon as the boy was finished he stepped back up on the rock and planted his
hands, exactly how they'd been.

Both Lady Two Bird and Lord Smoke Moon
seemed pleased with how he'd done, and after the boy
brought water for him to rinse his palms, he was offered a frothy, honey-sweetened drink.

"Why?" Tyrthbrand asked again, sipping his bever-
age and waving toward the door.

"Protection," Lady Two Bird replied.

Tyrthbrand didn't quite understand. Was Lord
Smoke Moon now aligned with the Red Hands? Or
was he just hedging his bets?

As soon as he finished his drink, they began the
next part of the ceremony, the naming. The priests
had only rebirthed him the day before. He hadn't accepted his name as a man needed to.

While Tyrthbrand thought about what his new name
should be, a scribe came in. He squatted at Lord
Smoke Moon's feet and carefully arranged his folding
book, his pens and ink. When he was ready, Lady
Two Bird very seriously asked Tyrthbrand for his foreign name, his full name and lineage. It took them a
while to work out the glyphs that would represent the
foreign sounds, but eventually, the scribe duly recorded it.

Then they asked him for his new name. Tyrthbrand
pronounced it carefully, certain that they would
understand.

Two Corn Heart.

Both Lord Smoke Moon and Lady Two Bird approved, with large smiles and pleased looks. The
scribe recorded his new name as well. It seemed that
now he was related somehow to Lady Two Bird,
though he didn't understand all the connotations.

There was nothing else to do. Two Corn Heart followed Lady Two Bird out of the temple, back into the City of Wells, then after a few more days, to her walled farm.

It seemed that he'd never fully escaped his *wyrd*, and that he was to be a farmer after all.

Lady Two Bird walked through the city without seeing where she was going. Somehow, all that she'd ever wanted had come true. She'd been happy as a priestess, dedicating her life to her goddess. But now she had a son to look after her for the rest of her days, a companion that she'd never expected, or even deserved, to find.

And her name had been written on the walls. Only inside the Akba house, next to Two Corn Heart's foreign name, a kind of protection against the coming days, but it was enough. Her destiny had been fulfilled. She could retire now, leave her goddess' service with grace.

"Do you see that bird?" Illugi asked, pointing in the distance to a small white creature sitting in the trees. He didn't know if his companions could make it out—he still had the best eyesight of all of them. It was why he generally walked ahead of the merchant's traveling caravan, sometimes even in front of the slaves cutting new paths through the foliage.

Waterlily Jaguar replied, "The priest in the last village told me a story about a quetzal without color that lived in the jungle."

"And?" Illugi asked, already knowing what the warrior was about to say, his gut tightening with anticipation and anxiety.

"If you can follow it to its nest, which is hidden on the slopes of the lost gorges, you will find your heart's desire."

"Or your death," Jeweled Skull added.

"Of course," Vigfus said.

Illugi nodded. Of course. That was how all the Itza legends went.

They'd followed rumors at first—stones that shed blood tears when it rained, pools of water that had a red tint and tasted funny—but they'd never found the right kind of ore with which to make iron. They'd discovered many other treasures that proved to be valuable trade items: precious herbs, unknown birds with magnificent plumage, hidden villages with amazing carving skills.

Though they were all now rich enough to retire, they still searched, following legends and myths of treasure, stories told and retold by elders and priests.

Illugi knew the answer to his question before he asked. They were all dedicated to one thing, to finding the materials to make iron, the blood stone. The Itza twins still believed in Cauac Sky's visions, of their people being destroyed by white-handed foreigners. Vigfus journeyed with them because he knew how valuable metal would be to the Itza, and like his father, would go anywhere for a good trade. Illugi wondered about the Itza prophecy of the White Hands, wondered if the damn priests from Eire with their one god would eventually reach this land, if they were this foretold doom. So he searched as well.

"Do we go after it?"

As one, the other three nodded.

And the elusive chase was on again.

The priests didn't arrive until late spring that year. Lady Two Bird wasn't worried about their coming, no matter what Seven Waterlily thought. They wouldn't take Two Corn Heart from her, not yet. Though it had been many years since he'd given her his heart, it would be many more before it would leave his body for good.

She greeted the priests and brought them into the main part of the house, inside cool shaded walls. She served them frothy cocoa and inquired after their trip, asking for news of the City of Wells.

They told her that Illugi, Vigfus, and the twins had been to the city earlier that season, with wild tales and many exotic trade goods, though they still hadn't found the right ingredients for the blood stone. Lord Smoke Moon's eldest son had been accepted by Itzanam and would make a fine priest. Lord Kan Boar had been injured in one of the latest border skirmishes, and rumor had it that he would retire soon.

Eventually, the priests turned their conversation to their formal request. It varied little from year to year.

Lady Two Bird's response was always the same, that she would have to speak with the stones.

That afternoon Lady Two Bird went out into the fields. She watched from a distance. Two Corn Heart was still easily distinguished from the others, even discounting his height and girth: his skin was more red than brown, even after all these years. The tattooed snakes ascending his arms had faded, but they still marked him as well.

He didn't always work in the fields he oversaw; however, he was never afraid to lend a hand when it was needed. Though he spoke her language well now, he was still silent much of the time, particularly in the evenings as they sat together, resting from their day. He shared her lands as a son would, looked after her welfare like a father, laughed with her like a friend, but never shared her bed as a lover.

She didn't know why he'd stayed with her instead of wandering with his men, but she was always grateful that he had. After a day in the fields, his eyes sometimes shone with a peace that she envied. It was his proper place, a niche that she had only ever partly found.

After watching him for a while, she went to the garden at the back of their enclosed estate, to the statue of Ix Chebel she carefully maintained there.

Small stones littered the base of the figure, surrounding her feet. Lady Two Bird pulled out a stone she'd gathered earlier, pure white, from the *sak beh* leading up to her home. She warmed it in her palms, thinking of Two Corn Heart's strong brown back, how his laughter still boomed, the way he wore his now graying hair in long braids. With steady fingers, she placed the rock on the statue's base, and waited.

The stone never trembled under her touch, never flooded her eyes with visions, so the next morning, as always, she went to the priests and told them that the time hadn't come yet, that there were useful as well as useless sacrifices, and that Two Corn Heart's heart should remain in his chest.

The priests left, saying that they would be back the following year.

And the rains came, and the corn continued to grow, as if the gods were pleased.

Selected Bibliography

This is not a complete bibliography of all the sources I used for this novel. It is a good starting point for those interested in either Mayan or Norse history or mythology.

Nonfiction

Bergþósson, Páll. *The Wineline Millennium: Saga and Evidence.* Reykjavík: Mál og mennig, 2000.

Björnsson, Árni. *High Days and Holidays in Iceland.* Reykjavik: Mál og menning, 1995.

Coe, Michael. *The Maya.* New York: Thames and Hudson, 2000.

De Landa, Friar Diego, author, and Gates, William, ed. *Yucatan Before and After the Conquest.* New York: Dover Publications, 1978.

Jones, Prudence, and Nigel Pennick. *A History of Pagan Europe.* New York: Routledge, 1995.

Prechtel, Martin. *Secrets of the Talking Jaguar: Memoirs from the Living Heart of a Mayan Village.* New York: Jeremy P. Tarcher/Putnam, 1999.

Sabloff, Jeremy, and E. Wyllys Andrews eds. *Late Lowland Maya Civilization: Classic to Postclassic.* Albuquerque: School of American Research, University of New Mexico Press, 1985.

Schele, Linda, and David Freidel. *The Untold Story of the Ancient Maya*. New York: William Morrow and Company, 1990.

Schele, Linda, David Freidel, and Joy Parker. *Maya Cosmos: Three Thousand Years on the Shaman's Path*. New York: Quill, William Morrow, 1993.

Tedlock, Dennis. *Popol Vuh: The Mayan Book of the Dawn of Life*. New York: Touchstone, 1996.

Thompson, Eric S. *Maya History & Religion*. Norman: University of Oklahoma Press, 1970.

Wahlgren, Erik. *The Vikings and America*. London: Thames and Hudson, 1985.

Wawn, Andrew, and Þórunn Sigurðardóttir. *Approaches to Vínland*. Reykjavík: Sigurður Nordal Institute, 2001.

Webster, David. *The Fall of the Ancient Maya*. London: Thames & Hudson, 2002.

Whitlock, Ralph. *Everyday Life of the Maya*. New York: Dorset Press, 1976.

Fiction

Sands, Marella. *Sky Knife*. New York: Tor, 1997.

Tiptree, Jr., James. *Tales of the Quintana Roo*. Sauk City, WI: Arkham House, 1986.

Poetry

Magnusson, Magnus, and Pálsson Hermann, trans. *The Vinland Sagas*. London: Penguin Books, 1965.

Sawyer-Lauçanno, Christopher, trans. *The Destruction of the Jaguar: Poems of the Chilam Balam*. San Francisco: City Lights Book, 1987.

Sturluson, Snorri. *Edda*. London: Everyman, 1987.

————. *The Poetic Edda.* New York: Oxford University Press, 1996.

Myth

De Spain, Pleasant, ed., and Lamo-Jiménez, Mario, trans. *The Emerald Lizard.* Little Rock: August House, 1999.

Montejo, Victor, ed., and Kaufman, Wallace, trans. *The Bird Who Cleans the World and other Mayan Fables.* Willimantic, CT: Curbstone Press, 1991.

Web Sources

Web sites disappear into the jungle faster than a ruined city. However, the last time I verified these (November 2004), all these sites were available.

General

Good general sources for myth:
www.pantheon.org/mythica.html
www.myths.com/pub/myths/myth.html
www.mythsearch.com/index.html

Food time line:
www.gti.net/mocolib1/kid/food.html

Native American technologies:
www.nativetech.org/

Iron working:
www.regia.org/ironwork.htm

Medieval science:
http://members.aol.com/mcnelis/medsci_index.html

Mayan

General all around Mayan information:
www.jaguar-sun.com/maya.html

Mayan astronomy:
www.michielb.nl/maya/astronom.html

Mayan stories:
www.kstrom.net/isk/maya/mayastor.html

Pictures from a Mayan trip:
www.smm.org/sln/ma/teacher.html#top

Green iguana society:
www.greenigsociety.org/body.htm

Ceiba tree of the Mayans:
www.utopiasprings.com/ceiba.htm

General Mayan information:
mayaruins.com/yucmap.html

Norse

Translations of Eddas:
www.squirrel.com/squirrel/asatru/free.html

Germanic myths and legends:
www.pitt.edu/~dash/mythlinks.html

Gullveig's Confession:
www.nycpagan.com/gullveig.html

Northvegr, the Northern Way:
www.northvegr.org/main.php

Poetic Edda:
www.sacred-texts.com/neu/poe/poe03.htm

Prose Edda:
www.blackmask.com/books29c/proseeddadex.htm
www.blackmask.com/
books29c/proseeddacon.htm

Introduction to runes:
www.futhark.com/intro.html

Viking archaeology:
http://bubl.ac.uk/link/v/vikingarchaeology.htm

Viking sword:
www.vikingsword.com/